D0011868

Bill Wadman

Dexter Palmer holds a Ph.D. in English literature from Princeton University. He lives in Princeton, New Jersey.

www.dexterpalmer.com

THE
DREAM
OF
PERPETUAL
MOTION

Dexter Palmer

Picador

St. Martin's Press
New York

THE DREAM OF PERPETUAL MOTION. Copyright © 2010 by Dexter Palmer. All rights reserved. Printed in the United States of America. For information, address Picador, 175 Fifth Avenue, New York, N.Y. 10010.

www.picadorusa.com

Picador® is a U.S. registered trademark and is used by St. Martin's Press under license from Pan Books Limited.

For information on Picador Reading Group Guides, please contact Picador.
E-mail: readinggroupguides@picadorusa.com

Book design by Rich Arnold

The Library of Congress has cataloged the St. Martin's Press edition as follows:

Palmer, Dexter Clarence, 1974–
    The dream of perpetual motion / Dexter Palmer.—1st ed.
    p. cm.
    ISBN 978-0-312-55815-4
    1. Prisoners—Fiction.   I. Title.
    PS3616.A33885D74 2010
    813'.6—dc22

                                        2009040231

Picador ISBN 978-0-312-68053-4

First published in the United States by St. Martin's Press

First Picador Edition: February 2011

10 9 8 7 6 5 4 3 2 1

CONTENTS

PROSPERO. —Dost thou hear?
MIRANDA.   Your tale, sir, would cure deafness.
                                         —William Shakespeare,
                                                The Tempest

Here opened another totally new education, which promised by far to be the most hazardous of all. The knife edge along which he must crawl, like Sir Lancelot in the twelfth century, divided two kingdoms of force which had nothing in common but attraction. They were as different as a magnet is from gravitation, supposing one knew what a magnet was, or gravitation, or love.

                                         —Henry Adams,
                                The Education of Henry Adams

THE

DREAM

OF

PERPETUAL
MOTION

PROLOGUE

aboard the good ship chrysalis

sssss
    sp
    spiraling
    spiraling down
    Into. The. Sea?
    spiraling slowly down and crashing into the open sea?
    Morning, and the voice has already begun. It was speaking even before I awoke. It has never stopped.

If my reckoning of time is still accurate, the day on which I begin to write this journal marks the one-year anniversary of my incarceration aboard the good ship *Chrysalis*, a high-altitude zeppelin designed by that most prodigious and talented of twentieth-century inventors, Prospero Taligent. It has also been a year since I last opened my mouth to speak. To anyone. Especially my captor. I refuse to speak to my captor precisely because it is the one thing that she desires, and my silence is the only form of protest that remains to me.

Writing, however, is a different thing altogether from speaking. The written word has different properties, and different powers. If I learned anything in the world before my imprisonment here, it was certainly that.

The only person aboard this ship besides myself is Prospero Taligent's adopted daughter, Miranda. For this past year I have been unable to escape from the sound of Miranda's voice. It follows me relentlessly through the corridors of this zeppelin's immense gondola as I continue to seek out her hiding place, where I hope to confront her, face-to-face. Her voice never stops: even when I sleep, it is a shining silver thread running through most of my dreams and all my nightmares, whispering, beseeching, threatening: *One word from you is all I want. Just speak one word, and we'll begin. Name, rank, and serial number, perhaps the misquoted lyrics from a popular song: anything will do. From there we'll move with slow cautious steps to gentle verbal sparring, twice-told tales, descriptions of the scarred and darkest places of our old and worn-out souls. I'll love you back; I'll tell you secrets—*

Miranda's father was kind to me when he built the place that would become my prison. This craft is what one might call a miracle of engineering, fully staffed by a crew of mechanical men who wordlessly go about the hundreds of tasks necessary to keep the *Chrysalis* in the sky: tending to the small garden whose fruits keep me alive; interpreting the readouts of the dozens of instruments that continue to claim that this ship will never crash, despite my growing fears that they're wrong; repairing each other, sometimes even harvesting their own limbs to replace the malfunctioning arms and legs of their metal colleagues. And somehow through Prospero's craftsmanship the sounds of all the machines in the ship have been muffled to silence, a sharp contrast to the world beneath me where mechanical noises fill the air, day and night, never ceasing. So the only sounds that I have heard for the past year are the echoes of my footsteps as I drift down the gondola's walkways, and the bell-clear voice of Miranda emanating from what may well be thousands of speakers scattered throughout the ship, inset in the floors, hidden behind paintings and secret panels, swinging on wires hanging from the ceilings, so that not one place here goes untouched by her endless lunatic stream of words: *Soon our culture's oldest dreams will be made real. Even the thought of sending a kind of flying craft to the moon is no longer nothing more than a child's fantasy. At this moment in the cities below us, the first mechanical men are being constructed that will have the capability to pilot the ship on its maiden voyage. But no one has asked if this dream we've had for so long will lose its value once it is realized. What will happen when those mechanical men step out of their ship and onto the surface of this moon, which has served humanity for thousands of years as our principal icon of love and madness? When they touch their hands to the ground and perform their relentless analyses and find no measurable miracles, but a dead gray world of rocks and dust? When they discover that it was the strength of millions of boyhood daydreams that kept the moon aloft, and that without them that murdered world will fall, spiraling slowly down and crashing into the open sea?*

She begs me to speak, but I won't. We live in our own little universe, she and I, and she is mad, and I am sane. This is the one thing that I know for sure. Prospero Taligent drove her mad: thirty years of being his daughter broke her mind, but I won't let the same thing happen to me. She is mad, and I am sane. To speak to her, even the first word, would be an acknowledgment and an acceptance of her madness, and from there I would have no choice but to follow her down the hole until both of us would be here alone in this ship among the clouds, endlessly circling the earth, our needs carefully ministered to by mechanical men, howling ourselves hoarse and counting off the ticks of the clock before the moon falls out of the sky.

I am going to try to tell a story now, and though I've made a life out of writing words, this is the first time I have told a story. There are no new stories in the world anymore, and no more storytellers. There is nothing left but the fragments of phrases that signaled their telling: *once upon a time; why; and then; the end.* But these phrases have lost their meanings through endless repetition, like everything else in this modern, mechanical age. And this machine age has no room for stories. These days we seek our pleasures out in single moments cast in amber, as if we have no desire to connect the future to the past. Stories? We have no time for them; we have no patience.

Sometimes I have a little trouble holding things together. It seems strange and inaccurate, when writing of what oneself once was, to speak of oneself as "I," especially when I find it difficult to own up to some of the actions performed by the people I once was: the ten-year-old boy who played innocent games on Miranda's magic island; the twenty-year-old who returned to that island when he had no business there; the thirty-year-old who committed the crime for which I have been imprisoned aboard this ship, with the madwoman. In this last year I've spent time with all of my past incarnations (oh, yes, they have their voices, too, they have just as much to say to me as Miranda), and we have decided that the only way to make sense of our existences is to set the stories of our lives down on paper, to try to make one tale that shows how the twentieth century turned Harold Winslow into Harold Winslow into Harold Winslow into me.

Any story told in this machine age must be a story of fragments, for fragments are all the world has left: interrupted threads of talk at crowded cocktail parties; snatches of poems heard as a radio dial spins through its arc; incomplete commandments reclaimed from shattered stones.

Every story needs a voice to tell it though, or it goes unheard. So I have to try. I still have enough faith left in language to believe that if I place enough words next to each other on the page, they will start to speak with sounds of their own.

ONE

nightfall in the

greeting-card

works

ONE

Hello? Hello.

Hello. My name is Harold Winslow. Yes. I need help.

Yes, I've used your services before.

Don't tell me everything's going to be fine. It's not. You can guess I know better than that.

I need help. This is one of my bad mornings. Some of the dreams I have are worse than others. This one isn't the worst, but it's bad enough for me to need your services.

I need to be taken to the Xeroville Greeting-card Works. I have to get to work.

No—no I still don't have insurance. I'll pay cash.

No—no I don't have a voice of my own.

But if you need a voice I can give one to you. It's the thing that I do best.

TWO

Some of the dreams I have are worse than others, and though the one I had last night wasn't one of those especially vivid ones that keep me riveted to the bed and soaked in sweat for a half hour after I've woken from it, it was bad enough to warrant placing the call for a shrinkcab. It is there waiting for me by the time I hang up the phone, dress for work, and descend to the lobby of my apartment building—except for the light on its roof, white instead of the usual yellow, it is indistinguishable from the hundreds of other cabs that clog the city's downtown streets each rush hour. The drivers of shrinkcabs usually make a gesture toward dressing a bit better than the usual cabbie, and as I slide into the backseat, I see that this one is wearing a starched shirt with silver cuff links—unfortunately, the intended effect is spoiled by a sleeve sporting scattered stains of ketchup and scrambled egg, the remnants of a breakfast sandwich whose foil wrapper lies discarded in the passenger seat.

Without a word the shrinkcabbie starts the meter and pulls off. Then, unconscionably, he turns on the radio, as if he intends to listen to me with one ear and the news of the world with the other. This is not the grade of service I expect. Periodic static interrupts a parade of voices as he twiddles the dial.

—fffffsssssfffff—

"—after fifteen years of marriage you can see her disgust whenever she looks at you. You know her heart's a block of ice."

—fffffsssssfffff—

"—full fadom five thy father lies, of his bones are coral made—"

—fffffsssssfffff—

"Hello out there! I just want you to know that I'm just like you, and, just like you, sometimes I have a little trouble holding things together."

—fffffsssssfffff—

"—but then you give her the greeting card. And she opens it, and she reads it, and the color comes back into her cheeks. And the smile spreads across her face that you haven't seen since both of you were young. And she bakes the casserole that you like. And she enters your bedroom and kneels before you.

"The Xeroville Greeting-card Works. When you need a reliable immediate intense targeted emotional response—"

—ffffssssfffff—

"—those are pearls that were his eyes: nothing of him that doth fade—"

—ffffssssfffff—

"—and I'm just like you. And between a seventy-hour workweek and a romance that's crumbling before my eyes, who can spare an hour to go to a therapist to get the help we all desperately need, every once in a while, to help us hold things together? To stave off the oncoming specter of insanity? Not me, I tell you! Not me. That's why, every once in a while, only when I need it, I pick up the phone and call a Shrinkcab. Shrinkcab's fleet of drivers are all rigorously trained in clinical psychiatry and licensed to dispense prescriptions, and will happily help you combine your necessary psychological therapy with your morning or evening commute for the maximum in twentieth-century convenience. Our cabs are handsomely upholstered in soothing colors and completely soundproofed for the ultimate in comfort. You just sit back, open up your head, and—"

—ffffssssfffff—

"—our proprietary emotional-provocation technologies. Xeroville Greeting-card Works. The key to the human heart. The best in the business."

—ffffssssfffff—

"—sea nymphs hourly ring his knell. Hark: now I hear them. Ding-dong bell."

—ffffssssfffff—

"—relax. We'll help you hold things together."

I lean forward and tell him to turn off the radio in a tone meant to be peremptory, but the intended note of command in my voice has too much squeak and quiver. Nonetheless, after looking at me for a moment in his rearview mirror, he reluctantly shuts off the radio, leaving us in soundproof silence.

Then I begin.

THREE

This is costing me a lot, isn't it. By the time we make it into downtown Xeroville I will have spent two days' pay in cab fare. So I guess I'd better start talking, and get my money's worth.

My name is Harold Winslow. I'm in the sentiment-development division of the Xeroville Greeting-card Works. Right now we're working on Christmas cards. That's right—even though it's the middle of July, we're working on the Christmas cards for next season. Time is always out of joint in the greeting-card works. Outside the works heat-shimmers rise from concrete; inside the works it's ice-cold, that special kind of ozone-flavored cold that machines make, and we've got Styrofoam snow strewn across the floors and red and green tinsel hanging from the walls. For inspiration. You'd be surprised: it's hard to summon the Christmas spirit in the middle of July. We hired a group of dwarves to dress up in elf outfits and run up and down the hallways, carrying lovingly handcrafted wooden toys and singing high-pitched, cloying songs of holiday cheer.

I've become disillusioned with my job: that's part of my problem, I think. I am a failed writer. I went to a university, hoping to become a successful writer, but I failed. Miranda, back then, tried to tell me that terrible things were in store for me, for all of us. But even though she was wise beyond her years, she was still young, and so was I, and all of our words were drowned out by the noise of our beating hearts, screaming at us that we were, after all, creatures of flesh and blood. So instead of taking our only chance of escape, we went back to her magic island when we had no business there. In a life full of failures, that was yet another.

I'm a failed writer with no voice of my own. What I do at the greeting-card works is this: I try to guess what kind of voice a voiceless person would choose if he could have any voice he wanted, and then I try to speak with that voice. I speak the words of love and affection that people would speak for themselves if they could. If they weren't paralyzed. If their lips didn't lock every time they even thought of expressing their own love for themselves. You have seen them, drifting up and down drug-store aisles like ghosts, their hands shaking, their teeth grinding, their jaws locked as they try to find the words that say the thing they mean to say. They are blind and dumb. I don't know what they'd do if they were confronted with greeting cards that were blank on the inside. Paralyzed. Blind and dumb.

My special talent is greeting cards that are designed to be given by boys between the ages of nine and sixteen, when they are too old for naïve sentiments that tumble clumsily off the tongue, and too young for cookie-cutter blank verses about love that perseveres through ravaging Time. My masterpiece is a greeting card I wrote for the Father's Day season three years ago, a large two-dollar affair that opened out into three panels, illuminated on both sides in brilliant pastels. As far as greet-ing cards go, it was an epic. The text was in iambic pentameter. The son, the implied speaker and the person presenting the card, details a fantasy in which his father is a monster, and the son is a smaller version of his father, a monster as well. And the father and son do monstrous things together, like throwing around automobiles and knocking down build-ings and breathing fire and biting the heads off innocent bystanders. Then on the climactic final panel, the son thanks his father for being a "monster of a dad!" and for making him a "monster of a son!" It was a big seller. It went into several printings.

I know what little boys like. Little boys like monsters.

I have a recurring dream that goes something like this. I am lying naked on my back in the midst of an endless field of poppies, staring up at a blue sky. It is dead quiet, the way it is never quiet in the world any-more, now that machines are everywhere. Even when you think a room is quiet, there's always some damned machine in it, making some kind of noise: plumbing; an air conditioner; a fluorescent lamp. But in this endless field of poppies it's dead quiet, as it must have been when the world was still young.

Then the virgin queen comes. I can tell she's coming because, al-though I still have my gaze fixed on the sky, I have also shifted it to look at the queen as she leisurely walks across the poppy field with her retinue trailing behind her, in that way in dreams that you can look at two things at once and see them both with crystal clarity. The queen is wearing a crystal crown that glitters in the sunlight, and an intricately embroidered dress shot through with threads of gold and silver. She is accompanied by several small boys. Some are naked; some are clothed. Some are dressed like girls, with long dresses and two pigtails tied with red ribbons. Some have human torsos, but haunches and horns and hooves, like creatures out of myths.

Then the queen stops walking and sits in the midst of the poppies and crosses her legs and smiles and laughs, and the boys assemble in front of her and begin to enact some complex kind of dance, taking slow steps, moving in interlaced circles, swaying their bodies to a rhythm that only they can hear. Then the queen turns to look at me, and it's just before I see her face that I wake up.

Waking up from the dream is the worst part. It always takes a few seconds. It's like . . . suppose you were underwater and naked and running out of air, deep down where all the light's gone, and you *have* to come up for air. And you spend every last precious ounce of your life's energy in the effort to rise to the surface and take that badly needed breath, and just as your head breaks from the water you remember, too late, to your horror, that you are a fish.

Why don't you just let me off here. I'll walk the rest of the way.

FOUR

In the morning, when the sun is rising, the building that houses the Xeroville Greeting-card Works is eclipsed by the long, yawning shadow of the Taligent Tower. The Tower is the uncontested dominant piece of architecture in the city, the defining element of its skyline, and it is owned by Prospero Taligent, reclusive genius, the richest person in the known world, the inventor of the mechanical man.

Prospero Taligent's tale is one of the last real entrepreneurial legends of the twentieth century. Not many people that anyone knows have actually been inside the Tower, a forbidding monolithic place with obsidian walls rising straight up to the sky, but it is said that Prospero endlessly walks the darkened corridors inside, that he never sleeps, that he has knowledge and talents that border on wizardry, and that miracles are commonplace within the Tower's walls. That there are manufacturing devices with tolerances so small that they can be used to make gears and pulleys and cranks that are nearly invisible to the naked eye. That Prospero's mechanical servants are so intricately and ingeniously constructed that they can play chess competently with masters of the game. That, at this moment, on the top floor of the Tower, a team of engineers and mechanical men under Prospero's direction are at work on the largest zeppelin ever made, a fantastic flying craft that will have a motor the size of a child's fist, and that this motor will be powered by the world's first and only perpetual motion machine.

And, of course, everyone knows about Prospero and his beautiful daughter, Miranda. How one of Prospero's servants found the toddler crawling about naked and grime-covered in a street in the red-light district and, moved to tears, brought her back to sanctuary in the Tower to sue for Prospero's help. How the never-married, childless Prospero fell in love with the girl on sight, used his considerable legal muscle to rescue her from her biological father, an abusive alcoholic semipsychotic schizophrenic gruel salesman, and adopted her to raise just as surely as if she were his own flesh and blood. How Miranda's playroom takes up an entire floor of the Tower, and that it contains creatures for her playmates of all kinds, both human and animal, both living and automatic, including, as the playroom's centerpiece, a breathing, warm, real, magnificent white unicorn.

I could confirm some of these myths if someone asked me to. When I was a child, I saw that unicorn and rode on its back. But now I am no longer a child, and that unicorn is dead and rotted away.

FIVE

Ophelia Flavin was six and a half feet tall, and beautiful. "For the first time in years," she said, "I feel *young*."

Ophelia and Marlon Giddings and I were sitting in the writers' lounge of the greeting-card works. Outside, in the city, it was stifling hot, the immense mirrors of skyscraper walls beaming down the sun's scorching rays on asphalt streets. Inside the greeting-card works Christmas morning hung suspended in glass.

Marlon slouched in a corner next to a watercooler, wearing a poorly tailored brown suit, the top button of his shirt undone, the knot of his faded tie loosened, lighting a new cigarette off the tip of the one he'd just smoked down to the butt. "I'm gonna suck some neck tonight, Harry," he said, "you mark my words. I *will* be sucking neck before dawn tomorrow."

Sugary Christmas music dripped from tinny overhead speakers. Reclining in her chair, Ophelia reached up with a long arm and absently plucked a long, glittering strand of red tinsel from the festooned Christmas tree behind her, pulling it down and winding it around her neck as if it were a feather boa. Ophelia's specialty was birthdays, especially the arbitrary lines that we've invented to separate youth from old age: thirty, forty, fifty, sixty. Jibes about the loss of eyesight; mean-spirited jokes about gravity's hands clawing at the bodies of once-beautiful women, stretching them like putty, twisting them out of shape, painting stomachs with marbled scars. "I feel young again, for the first time in years," she said sleepily. "This morning I had a dream of what it must have been like before the machines. There was a song that you sang when you were young. But only under specific circumstances. The rules were these: if you spotted a male and female alone in each other's company, frequently and willingly, you were to sing the song, immediately, without hesitation. I cannot exactly remember the lyrics, but the song itself was part accusation, part admonishment, part threat. It began with an insinuation, that the youths had been indulging in certain moderately erotic physical contacts in the false security of arboreal camouflage—"

"I want you to smell my neck," Marlon Giddings said to me. I was lying on a couch, staring at the ceiling with my gaze unfocused, trying not to think about the machine noises: the refrigeration unit in the watercooler; the hum of the air-conditioning units behind the walls that were doing their damnedest to simulate winter in the dog days of July; the hissing white noise submerged beneath the high strings and horns of Christmas music. "Smell my neck!" Marlon said. Suddenly I found that he was huddling over me as if he were about to embrace me, and the tip of my nose was pressed against the underside of his chin. I blinked.

"Do you smell that?" Marlon said, standing up and taking a drag off his cigarette with a flourish of his hand. "That, my friend, is Love. *That* is why I'll be sucking neck tonight. A woman said I looked loveless, and she gave me Love in a bottle.

"This is what happened," Marlon said. "Listen. I was walking through a department store, and this woman behind a perfume counter, with too much makeup and the plumage of a peacock ready to mate, pointed her finger at me and said, 'You look loveless.' I spend a lot of time in department stores because they're good places to meet women. Women are very open to suggestion when they're shopping. Their defenses are down. I have a collection of name tags that I stole off the shirts of different workers in department stores. How I steal them is: I just walk up to a clerk all confused-looking like I need help finding something and the guy says, 'Can I help you?' and then I say, 'I'll take *that*!" and I rip the tag right off his shirt before he can even blink. And he just looks at me thinking, what the hell, that guy just stole my name tag and now he's running away, what would he want with that, my shirt is ruined, that was a remarkably irrational act, and I am troubled. Meanwhile I'm ollie ollie oxen free.

"I have a collection of name tags, one for each department store in the city, and I cover up the name that used to be on the tag and put my own name on it. Then I walk into a department store wearing the right tag and just hang out for a while in an aisle, maybe straightening merchandise on the shelves or something, and soon enough some babe comes up to me all panicked, saying, 'Please help me! I don't know where I can find henleys! Please help me find henleys!' And I kind of casually slip an arm around her shoulder and stroke it and say, 'There, there. There, there. No need to fret, honey. I'll help you find all the henleys you need.' Then I point to my name tag. 'My name is Marlon. I can help. Please let me help. I'm going to help you.' That's the secret: to get to them when they need help. That's when they're vulnerable. That's when they're weak. Next thing you know you're *sucking that neck*. Actually, that little gambit doesn't work all the time. Actually it hasn't worked yet, but it's bound to soon. Actually, anyway.

"Anyway this woman selling the perfume says to me, 'You look love-less.' And I go over to this counter that she's standing behind, where there's a bunch of perfumes in this glass case in a bunch of different-colored glass bottles, and I say, 'Listen lady, you said a mouthful. Let me tell you.' And then she reaches out with an index finger and puts it to my lips: hush. And I hush.

"Then she reaches under the counter and pulls out the tiniest glass bottle in the case, which is filled with this golden liquid, and a piece of paper that's about a foot square, and a big glass jar that's got *wasps* in it. There's a bunch of yellow jackets in this jar buzzing around, knocking their heads against the inside over and over again. She puts all this stuff on the counter and then she sprays a little bit of the golden stuff in the bottle on the piece of paper. 'A concoction distilled from the crushed and liquefied glands of animals from sixteen different species,' she says. The stuff smells sickly sweet, like honeysuckle, and my eyes start to water. 'Some are still alive,' she says. 'Some were wiped out decades ago.' Then she puts the piece of paper down on the counter, and she picks up the glass jar and shakes hell out of it, like she's mixing a martini. Then she unscrews the lid of the jar and lets out the wasps.

"So now I am thinking: you foolish woman, you have just released a horde of angry yellow jackets in a crowded department store, and this will not be good for business. But get this: the wasps fly out of the jar and straight as an arrow they make for the piece of paper. Soon the whole paper's almost covered up and still there's more coming, and not one of them flying off on its own to sting somebody, all of them just flying to-ward the smell of the perfume, crawling all over the paper and I guess probably trying to hump it. And the lady behind the counter, she's gazing down at this with her eyes all glazed over and she says, 'Beautiful, isn't it. Soon the smell will drive them mad and they'll start to sting each other to death.' Then she looks at me and smiles. 'We have different fragrances for men and women.' And I say, 'I have *got* to get me some of *that*.' Hey, Ophelia—smell my neck! Smell that? Does that drive you nuts or what?"

Ophelia looked at Marlon, and her bright blue eyes widened and she smiled with the sudden recollection of something long forgotten. "Marlon and Ophelia, sitting in a tree," she sang with a gentle tremolo. "K, I, S, S, I, N, G. First comes love, then comes marriage. Then comes a baby . . . in a *baby carriage*!"

"What? Oh, hey, wait a second," said Marlon, backing off from her as she rose from the chair and started to approach him, grinning and seductively fingering the Christmas tinsel around her neck (and I could look into Ophelia's twinkling eyes and see that Marlon had paid good money for snake oil). "I'm just joshing—you know you're too tall for me. I mean, I'm too short for you, is what I meant to say—"

"I'm going to eat you alive," Ophelia purred, sauntering toward Marlon as she looked down at him, backing him into a corner, spreading out her arms to catch him, should he run. "Mmmm, yes. Yes indeedy." She licked her lips then, and I couldn't figure out why Marlon couldn't see that she was about to burst out laughing. "You look *scrumptious*," she said. "Oh, I believe I can *barely control myself*. I feel so *young*."

"Aw—come on," Marlon said, his voice going high and breaking. "I was just joshing. Stop, Ophelia. Don't touch me." Then I couldn't see him anymore.

SIX

After two more hours of staring at a blank page, I threw down my pen, said a cursory good-bye to my coworkers, punched the clock, and hit the street in the middle of the afternoon. I hadn't written a thing, but if I wasn't inspired, sitting at a desk was a waste of my time and the company's money. There's another thing at which I was a failure: being able to write without being "inspired" by some sort of Muse. Belief in a Muse isn't conducive to optimal performance in a place like the greeting-card works. I figured my days there were numbered; at any rate, I thought the best thing for my mood that weekday afternoon would be a few mind-numbing hours of radio in my apartment, followed by a slowly sipped absinthe drip in a recliner, with a mask over my eyes and plugs in my ears. Then sleep.

Since I'd spent so much on cab fare that morning, I was forced to take the overground shuttle out of the heart of the city, and the only people who rode the decrepit, outmoded shuttles in the middle of a weekday afternoon were either elderly, mechanical, or crazy. So I wasn't surprised when a man who was both elderly and crazy sat down next to me, wearing a suit whose cut was several seasons out-of-date. He leaned close to me and whispered, "You look awfully *lax*, my friend. And I wouldn't be so *lax* with so many *mechanical men* wandering about. Taligent controls all of them. They're his spies. He controls *all of them*. One day you'll see."

Four tin men were scattered through the shuttle's passenger car, carrying courier parcels and bags of groceries, staring straight ahead, silent.

"Has he given you your heart's desire," the man said.

At that I turned to look at him. "What do you mean?"

"You know what I mean," the madman said. "I was at the party twenty years ago. So were you. I sat next to you in the banquet hall. I know your name, and I know your work, and I know you. You write greeting cards." He pointed at himself. "My name is *William*. And if there is one thing in life that I *looooove*, it's morphine." The tender flesh on the inside of his arm was covered with needle tracks. He wasn't nearly as old as I first thought. He must have been my age. "Morphine makes me feel so *good*. Tell me—has he given you your heart's desire."

"No," I said, looking away from him. "No, he didn't. But that was just talk. Fairy stories for children, to keep us entertained. He didn't mean a thing he said."

William hawked loudly and spat a clouded gob of phlegm on the car's floor. "Oh, that's what we *all* thought, once we became adults. We don't *believe* in that kind of thing anymore. We think that things like unicorns and heart's desires are *clichés*, in spite of what we saw with our own eyes. The ones who got it when they were children were the luckiest. They just got *pets*, or *toys*, and they were happy, because they were children and they didn't know any better. But he waited for some of us to grow up. He's patient, and he has the resources to bide his time. And he's been watching *all* of us, just like he said he would. He has agents, throughout the city, watching. And I watch him watch. And I watch what he watches, when I can." He grabbed my shoulder. "He ruined my life. I get morphine for *free*, once a day, delivered to my doorstep in a pretty little carved crystal bottle. Not enough in it to kill me; just enough to make me content. I use up what's in the bottle by noon and then pawn the bottle in the afternoon to get the money I need for whatever drugs I can get that'll get me to the next morning and the next bottle. It's all I think about. Listen—he's committed crimes. Six of the hundred boys and girls that entered the Tower twenty years ago have *died* because of these *gifts* of his. Have you received your heart's desire. Because if you have, then it's over. I think you're the only one left."

"No," I said. "Or maybe I have. I don't know."

"Oh, you'll *know* when it comes," the madman said. "I guarantee you that. You'll be dead certain—"

SEVEN

Maybe Ophelia talks to herself when she's alone. Perhaps she sits in front of her bedroom mirror nude, having shed her working clothes and undergarments like second and third skins, thrown in wicker hampers, hanging over chairs. She is six and a half feet tall and beautiful, and in a just world some kind of master artisan would be here to paint her at this moment. But that can never be: part of the beauty of this image results from Ophelia's knowing that no one is here to capture it and preserve it against time. She sits in the chair in a completely relaxed and unpaintable pose, reveling in the pleasures of inhabiting such a body, silently sounding out the length and the strength of what she is, and she knows that these hundreds of seconds after a day spent toiling in the greeting-card works are hers alone. She has sold them some of her time for the money she needs to live, but hoarded these moments for herself, and each one is precious, to be wasted as she wishes. Ophelia has an obsession with time. Besides, no one paints anything anymore anyway.

Now she leans closer to the mirror to examine her face in greater detail. She tries various poses: propping her chin on her hand and resting her elbow on the mirror's dresser, looking half-asleep and slightly bored as if she's on a bad date; then surprise, her eyebrows arched and her mouth forming a ridiculous *O*; then a flirtatious pout with a coyly tilted head and fluttering lashes; then bug-eyed comic fright. She has removed all of her makeup, and she can see all the tiny little blemishes and nicks and scars that her face has gathered as it's aged. Dark spots sit under her eyes, which are an almost luminescent blue. Her mouth moves soundlessly, and this is what it silently says: "Where does all the time go? Other lives wind themselves into your own and then leave for distant places or wink out like extinguished lamps, and then all the evidence you have that there was ever any time is a few scribbled words and a few blurred pictures. Then those burn in fire or blow away in wind and you have nothing. So many millions of seconds I've misspent. So many people that robbed me of my time and ran away. I tried once to keep a diary to preserve all the seconds of my life likes flies in amber against the future, but the record read: 'Dear Diary. Today I spent 86,400 seconds writing in a diary. Today I spent 86,400 seconds writing in a diary. Today I spent—,' and in the time I spent reading the diary I lost more precious time. I had to give it up as a hopeless enterprise. The only reliable record I have to tell the years is my own face, where the spiders etch their careful marks at the corners of my eyes and remind me that I am still human. Still human."

EIGHT

Now I'm home.

It's the magic hour, and the setting sun's rays shine through the yellow-green liquid in the drip glass. I hold the glass up to the window, carefully pouring a small measure of water into the receptacle in the top. The water begins to fall drop by drop into the absinthe in the bottom of the glass, making ripples and swirls, slowly changing its color from a translucent deep-water green to an opaque and opalescent white.

NINE

Nervously flicking his gaze into his rearview mirror again and again, the shrinkcabbie sits in the middle of dozens of gridlocked cars, stuck on the main drag out of the city. He's edgy because he likes to be out of Xeroville when the sun sets.

His glove compartment is stuffed to the point of bursting with hundred-dollar bills, each with a story stuck to it. The shrinkcabbie has not spoken a single meaningful word today: he has only listened. The years of diligent, rigorous training that shrinkcabbies get, that you hear about in the radio commercials: that's a hoax. Shrinkcabbie training takes all of a week, a crash course in which they're taught the fine art of paying attention: how to throw reassuring glances in the rearview mirror while driving, to catch the eyes of the fare; how to punctuate the fare's discourse with encouraging phrases such as "Go on" and "Yes, of course," and how to modulate the pitch of these occasional utterances so that one sounds engrossed, not bored. Nothing that anyone with a little common sense can't pick up.

In his soundproof cab, the shrinkcabbie is isolated from the cacophony of car horns and curses outside. In the automobile next to him he can see another driver beating his clenched fists against the steering wheel, grimacing, the muscles tight in his neck, the veins standing out in sharp relief. The angry driver looks through his window at the shrinkcabbie, sees him looking back, screams something he can't make out, and makes an obscene gesture with his hand. The shrinkcabbie indulges himself in the pleasure of imagining the man's jugular vein bursting, spraying the inside of the windshield glass with his blood, drenching the upholstery of the seats. Then he turns away.

The job is starting to get to him. For ten hours today the shrinkcabbie has driven around the streets of the city, listening to stories from strangers who had tales to tell and no one to tell them to. Not one had a happy ending. Most didn't have endings at all and couldn't rightfully be called stories because they were just ramblings, results of futile attempts to make narratives out of a causeless, disconnected series of events that refused to be narrated. . . . Right now the shrinkcabbie would give one of his hundred-dollar bills to hear a simple story with a happy ending, concluding with an edifying moral in the form of a rhymed couplet. He wants to hear a story in which good things happen in threes to women who are poor but beautiful, who have the bodies of adults but the hearts of little girls.

He glances into the rearview mirror again, looking into his own eyes and fingering the grips of the steering wheel. He looks good. Not great, but good; as well as can be expected. He can do again tomorrow what he's done today. He will usher the city's tarnished spirits into his chamber, romance them with attentive silence, be their magic mirror, and spit them back out on the streets with their souls washed snow white.

It is reassuring to the shrinkcabbie to know that the troubles of his fares aren't leaving marks on his face. The attrition rate for his profession is considerable. Seventy percent give it up after a year. There is always the threat that someday you might be alone in the car, escaping from the city at night, and that you'll look into the rearview mirror and see a face that's not your own. That it will have changed into someone else's without even the courtesy of serving you notice. And that will be enough to break you.

The gridlock is breaking now, and the cars around him are slowly starting to move. The cabbie tears his gaze away from the mirror and back to the road in front of him. The sun is descending behind the forest of towers that make up the city skyline. Night is falling.

TEN

I have a night-mask over my eyes now, and rubber plugs jammed in my ears to shut out the sounds of machines. I am shuddering in the reclining chair. The glass of absinthe has slipped out of my hand and fallen to the floor, where it has come to rest after rolling in a circle, describing an arc of liquid behind its rim. The sun has set.

It is not until the room has rotated almost ninety degrees that I realize it is tipping over. By then I'm powerless to do anything about it, and I soundly bang my head as I fall out of the chair and collide with the ceiling. I rip off my mask and look around me, at the flickering lightbulb falling up on the end of its chain, swinging regularly back and forth like a metronome, and at the little boy, dressed in servant's livery and sporting a satyrlike pair of hooves, casually walking on the ceiling as if it were a floor.

A small cloud of gnats orbits the lightbulb. One alights on its shining surface and burns.

I am lying supine on the ceiling, spread-eagled and afraid to move, and the satyr-child stands over me, sneering, showing stained and crooked teeth. "You oughta watch what you drink, friend," he says. "That stuff'll make you see all kinds of *crazy* shit." He reaches into his vest and, with a flourish, pulls out a gilt-edged envelope with a wax seal and drops it on my stomach.

"An invitation," the satyr-child says, and chuckles. "To a dance with the virgin queen."

ELEVEN

And nightfall has come to the greeting-card works.

The building is nearly silent. Most of the machines are resting, with only an occasional, isolated whir or hum in the darkened corridors. Christmas tinsel rustles in the dark from stray drafts of ice-cold, air-conditioned wind. The building's struts and columns contract with quiet creaks and pops in the coldness of night.

And now the mechanical men concealed in hatches and secret doorways come out by the hundreds, creeping on cat feet like burglars or mischievous sprites, carrying huge burlap sacks on their backs. Quietly, they remove the red and green and silver and gold decorations from the walls and ceilings, stuffing them into their bags, replacing them with red cardboard hearts with arrows drawn on them, and long twisting billowing strands of pink crepe.

And in a stuffy room in the basement of the greeting-card works, a dwarf standing in front of a half-length mirror removes his elf costume, squeezes into a bright red pair of tights, and straps a pair of cardboard cherub's wings around his naked hairless chest with a belt. A quiver full of arrows completes the outfit. Christmas is over. Tomorrow is Valentine's Day.

INTERLUDE

aboard the good ship *chrysalis*

—and forever and forever and forever you and I, turning in circles in the midnight sky. Speak to me and we will trade stories, one for one. Don't think I don't know about your sweet little secret diary. Don't you know it would be so much more meaningful to hand your thoughts over to me than to record them in some worthless book that no one will ever read besides yourself? Speak the first word to me and we're married; speak a sentence and that marriage will be consummated, and in a short conversation about the weather you and I will grow old together, as we circle the earth in our little sealed-off world forever and forever and forever—

But it cannot be forever, no matter what Miranda says, or how strongly she believes it, or how often she repeats it. Her father's last and greatest experiment, the perpetual motion machine that keeps the zeppelin aloft, is a failure. The ship will crash. It must. It is only a matter of time.

At the moment I have no proof of this. I did once. In the cockpit at the belly of the ship I once saw the altimeter's counter spinning slowly backward, ticking off our descent foot by foot. But now the altimeter holds steady (even though I still believe that this ship is slowly descending as it circles the earth, falling a certain small distance with each successive circumnavigation), and my evidence is gone.

I am writing this at a desk in the airship's observation room made from a single obsidian slab, and through a plate-glass window that makes up most of the front wall, I can see clouds massed beneath the zeppelin, as if they are the turbulent surface of a dreamed sea. Against the rear wall of the room, standing upright, is the absolute-zero chamber where Prospero Taligent lies in state. I can see him through a pane of glass in the chamber's door: frosty fingers have combed through his hair and bleached it from silver to white, dangled tiny icicles from his eyelashes like Christmas ornaments, and drawn a mischievous beard and mustache on his naked face to make him look like Old Man Winter. The internment in the cryogenic chamber was his last request. He spoke his last words and asked his last question with bubbles of blood sputtering from his lips, and then he gave up the ghost, as they say. It seemed the decent thing to do to fulfill his last request, since, after all, I murdered him.

How did I come to be imprisoned aboard this ship, here with my warden's frozen corpse?

All in good time.

—and forever and forever and forever and forever and sometimes . . . sometimes I think it might be good to be young again. Do you remember those timeless days we spent together in the playroom? And when I played the virgin queen for you, and when you and I tried to be we that one last time . . . no. No. I would not trade all the days from those to this to lose what I have now become. I have undergone a transformation. From caterpillar to beautiful brilliant butterfly. Even as I spat blasphemies in my father's face, cursing him as he worked his magic on me, he said he forgave me, for I knew not what I did. Now I know. And now I believe in him.

What I remember: looking into the glass-walled womb hanging beneath the gondola of the ship, a mechanical man at the controls, I saw the altimeter's counter spinning backward to zero, seconds passing before the eye could register the movement, but still going back to zero, one digit at a time. Only a matter of time. The tin man saw me looking down into the pilot's pit, saw me looking at the dial, and somehow, I don't know how, it *knew.*

The next time I peeked into the control chamber it had ripped open the display panel and was tearing out the nest of wires that lay behind it. Two hours later it had replaced the panel, and the altimeter's dial held steady. I'm sure the tin man broke it, to eliminate the evidence. I don't know how it knew, but it knew.

What Miranda said to me afterward:

My father built a perpetual motion machine, and it works, and he believed in its perfection. He designed the mechanical men that pilot this ship, and they believe in the perfection of the perpetual motion machine because he designed them to believe in it. And I believe in the perpetual motion machine because, for all my curses, in the end I must always be my father's daughter. And you alone say that this little world of ours is destined to end, thinking that you have proof in something you call the "laws" of "physics." And you have the rank temerity to believe that you, instead of I, have not gone mad?

I have a recurring dream that goes something like this. There is a tower in the midst of a pastoral field of poppies, its smooth obsidian walls reaching to touch the underside of heaven. On the edge of the tower's roof a woman dances, wearing a glittering crystalline crown. She is light on her feet and flirting with jumping.

I am in a crowd of onlookers at the tower's base, all of us jammed shoulder to shoulder. The crowd is made up of young boys, some dressed as girls, some with horns and horses' hooves . . . they are beckoning the woman to jump. In fact, although I am not aware of it (and I am never aware of it, no matter how many times I have the dream) her suicide is a foregone conclusion. It is this way in dreams: when decisions are being made, they have already been made. One of the boys in the crowd is wearing a dingy, ragged white shirt with block letters painted on it: I SAW THE VIRGIN QUEEN DANCE WITH DEATH AND I SURVIVED.

Now the wizard appears, a cartoon wizard with a long white beard, wearing a pointy, deep purple hat dusted with glitter and decorated with golden five-pointed stars and stylized comets, with a robe to match. In his hand he holds a wilting stalk of celery. "She's going to die," he says. "And even though you have seen this death in uncounted previous dreams, it will still be the most horrific thing you have ever witnessed in your life, and it will be the stuff of nightmares for years to come. You will have to watch as she hits the ground headfirst, and her skull splits open, and her brains and her blood spatter on the faces of the crowd, and the watching young boys lick their lips and taste the blood on their faces and run to the mangled corpse to dabble at the flesh with their fingers and tear at it with their teeth. She will die unless you speak the word that stops her. This is a magical stalk of celery," he says, shoving it into my hand. "I have *enchanted* it so that it will amplify your words and carry them to her ears. Now it all depends on you."

So I look up to the sky where the virgin queen is giggling and twirling in pirouettes on the tower's edge, and I hold the stalk of celery to my mouth and start to speak. The right word will make the miracle come. The woman is toying with the crowd, pulling up her skirts and stretching her bare left foot over the edge, then the right. The cheers of the crowd go louder with each of the queen's taunts, and so when I speak to the enchanted celery, I can barely hear my own voice, and I am reduced to having faith in the wizard's magic, hoping that my words are somehow being lifted to the virgin queen's ears.

I try hundreds of words, but nothing works. I try several of the words that we use on a regular basis in the greeting-card works, like *heart* and *happiness* and *love*. Especially *love*. Isn't that the fabled magic word that fixes everything? Isn't that the only word that can't be worn out by its repetition on the covers on a billion greeting cards? In the distant past I remember believing something like that, but when I fill my lungs and shout the word into the head of the celery stalk it sounds so weak and overused and thin, as if I were opening my mouth and saying nothing at all, or reading a tax return or a train timetable. The woman is close to the edge and I am running out of time. First her left foot shoots out, then her right, as if she is testing the temperature of the water in a tranquil swimming pool. But there's too much noise and all the children are screaming their heads off and nothing I say works. In desperation I start from the beginning: "Aardvark. Aardwolf. Aba. Abaca. Aback. Abacus." But it's too late, she gently hops off the edge and down she goes, tumbling end over end and I know what happens next, I've seen it before, even when I'd dreamed the dream the first time I'd seen it before, and everyone else in the dream has seen it, too, because they're uncorking spewing bottles of champagne and pouring overflowing glasses and making toasts with the ease of familiar custom, and as the virgin queen falls from the sky she looks me in the eye and her gaze is full of blame and it says: "Why did you let me die? Why did you not speak the word I needed to hear to comfort me? And why, instead of speaking to me, when I needed you, when you *knew* I needed you, why in the hell were you talking to a stalk of celery?"

Miranda. In her hysterically babbling voice I can no longer hear the quiet, gentle girl she once was, who sometimes seemed as if she might never learn to speak at all. She has changed so much since we were young, when I was Harry and she was Miri, before we stretched to fit the names our elders gave us. There was the playroom, and the birthday party, and the unicorn. There were hints and intimations of the shape of things to come.

Now shapes appear in the fog. Now fragments piece themselves together.

Now it's time for a story of coming of age. Who can resist a tale of coming of age?

Harry and Miri. Sitting in a tree. K. I. S. S. I. N. G.

First comes love.

Then comes—

TWO

lovesongs for

a virgin queen

ONE

"Miranda.

"Miranda. Miri. Darling.

"Wake up, Miri."

". . . mmmf. Hm. Father."

"There is a very important day coming soon. Do you know what it is?"

The girl turned over on her back, rubbed her eyes, and snuggled beneath the quilts and silken sheets to shut out the cold. It is so cold in the bowels of the Tower, even when Ferdinand, the master of the boiler room, works his crew the hardest. . . . "Soon. My birthday."

"Yes," Prospero said, and stroked his adopted daughter's forehead. "Soon you will be ten years old, and in recognition of this I will give you two things. A birthday party, with smiles and songs. And your heart's desire."

TWO

"When I was your age," Harry Winslow's father says, "miracles were commonplace. To me my childhood and adolescence seem as if they happened just a little time ago, just on the other side of the line dividing centuries. But you, who cannot remember a world that was not filled with machines, will never be able to imagine the drastic differences between your youth and mine. When I was a child people could fly without the need of jerry-rigged contraptions that were just as likely to explode as not. When I was young angels and demons walked the city streets. And they were *fearless*."

The surface of the aged, scarred oaken desk in the back room of the apartment where Allan Winslow works is dominated by a metal tray composed of dozens of compartments, each containing a number of miniature facsimiles of body parts, made from tin. The arms and legs are the size of Allan's smallest finger. These days Allan assembles mechanical dolls to earn a living wage, at eight cents each for a fully assembled and painted work. It isn't much, but in these lean years of a twentieth century whose newness has not yet worn off, this is the best that the Winslows can do. Harry is too young to be put to work by anyone who has a conscience; and his older sister, Astrid, has such atrocious social skills that she can't hold a job for more than a week and a half. So it's Allan who is left to work whatever magic is necessary to put food in all their mouths, to provide the rare sugary thing or cinema ticket for Harold, or pencils and parchment for Astrid.

The twentieth century is still new, and the idea has not yet come to the minds of the city's lawyers that people have the rights to their own visages as works of art. The dolls that Allan is assembling are supposed to look like Miranda Taligent and are meant to be on shelves within days, for sale as mementos of her upcoming tenth birthday. They are sold by the Happy Family Toy Company, whose employees speak a language that Allan doesn't understand, and who write in a script that seems to him more like a series of small pictures than words. Each week one of their employees drops off a box full of body parts and some instructions for assembly in front of the door to the Winslow apartment, then a few days later the employee comes back to pick up the completed dolls, representations of whatever young woman has caught the eye of the city's populace that month.

To be truthful, the dolls that Allan is making do not look anything like Miranda Taligent, by any stretch of the imagination. The first problem is that Allan can't accurately decipher the printed directions for assembly that are supplied by the Happy Family Toy Company. There are line drawings of what the finished products are supposed to look like from various angles, and cutaway schematics with arrows pointing into the innards of the doll, meant to indicate the proper placement of springs and coils. But all of the illustrations are annotated by the foreign picture-script of the toy company employees, and Allan cannot read this, except for the occasional numeral, or an exclamation point that seems to denote a warning. Allan gets the feeling that he is missing something. While he thinks that the ideal mechanical Miranda is supposed to walk forward across the table, tottering back and forth on its spindly tin legs with its arms outstretched to balance its center of gravity as the windup key turns in its back, Allan's dolls tend to stumble forward a step or two and then fall over, their ramrod-straight arms breaking their collapse. They lie there frozen then, as if they are in the midst of an overly strenuous push-up.

The second problem is that the design for the Miranda Taligent dolls is aesthetically inept, even if (Allan imagines) technically competent. Part of the blame for this goes to Allan himself, who is a terrible painter, and renders Miranda's blue eyes with two large white circles in the middle of her face, with two small smeared blue dots for their irises. Miranda's mouth is a straight red line, drawn with a single quick stroke of the paintbrush. But other problems can't be blamed on Allan's artistic ability: the hair of the dolls, for instance, which is made of curled metal shavings, dipped in red and yellow lacquer and welded straight to the skull. The real Miranda's hair is not curly, but falls down her back, between her shoulder blades, with just the slightest bit of a wave in it, and even though Harold has never seen an image of the girl that wasn't in shades of gray, enough journalist's ink has been spilled over her hair's reddish golden hue for him to know that the Happy Family Toy Company's attempt at metal approximation isn't even close.

But in the end none of this matters, and the Happy Family Toy Company knows this, which is why Allan continues to get paid eight cents a completed doll despite his shoddy workmanship. As long as the finished products look recognizably human and aren't missing legs or sprouting extra heads, the Toy Company will put them in boxes, slap the name of Miranda Taligent on them, and watch them fly off store shelves into the hands of eager customers. This is the magic that the girl's name has, in this city, in this season.

"Fearless," Allan says. "You could be strolling down a sidewalk one morning, minding your own business, chewing on a still-steaming hot cross bun and planning your day's youthful exploits, and then suddenly an angel would fly out of nowhere and stand in your path and just *stare* at you. Winking and leering, doing a little dance and flapping its wings, chuckling to itself, as if to say: *Go ahead and try it, child. I dare you to disbelieve in me.*"

THREE

"On your birthday you can have your heart's desire," Prospero said, kneeling at his daughter's bedside. "On your birthday you can stop time or bring back the dead. All you have to do is tell me what you wish."

"I have read things in books," Miranda said, "that say that the best birthday presents are surprises."

"*I've. I've* read things in books."

"*I've*," Miranda said, wrinkling her brow and pursing her lips. "Read things in books."

"Yes, that's right."

"I want . . ."

"Yes?" He leaned closer.

"A unicorn."

Prospero smiled and sniffed in mock derision. "Is that all?"

"And I know what you are thinking now. I do not want a life-sized doll, with legs of pistons, and eyes of camera lenses, and guts filled with wires and clockwork."

"*Don't.* Don't want."

"I want a *real* unicorn for my birthday. Flesh and blood. Not a machine. I can keep it in the playroom. I can teach it to lay its head in my lap and carry me on its back."

Prospero sighed. "I'm disappointed," he said, rising and frowning, "and I think you lack ambition. A daughter of mine ought to wish for even more that that: she ought to wish to stretch out her hand and pull the Moon down to earth. She should wish to talk of the intrigues of lunar politics over afternoon tea with its King; she should want to dine on tarts filled with the strange fruit of its gardens. But as far as miracles go, a unicorn is easy enough, and I suppose I shouldn't complain."

"You said I could have what I wanted," Miranda said, her eyes closed, already starting to fall asleep again. "I do not want much."

Before he left, Prospero stayed in the darkened bedroom for a minute or so, staring down at the sleeping girl. "Miracles don't come cheap these days; they don't grow on trees," he said, sighing. "But I suppose now is as good a time for you to learn that as any."

FOUR

Allan Winslow looks up from his desk and squints at Harold through the jeweler's loupe clenched in his eye socket, his eyebrows asymmetrically arched. "But words are not enough to make you know what angels truly were," he says. "Words are not enough to give a shape to miracles— there's nothing left that's miraculous anymore, and that's your loss for being born too late. Of course, this fellow Prospero Taligent, who's always on the radio shilling some new device or other—many of the things that his company sells are *called* miraculous, like the high-speed egg-hatching machines and the mechanical men. But that's nothing more than advertising."

It is nearly night, and Allan is done with work. He plucks the loupe from his eye and puts his tools and brushes back into their case, each one in its correct compartment—even if he has little skill with them, he can at least organize them properly. Astrid is beginning to cook in the kitchen, and the odor of her peculiar improvised recipe for stew is beginning to fill the apartment, pungent and slightly rancid. There are sounds of clanging spoons and pots. Harold winces and wrinkles his nose. It is hard to imagine how someone could screw up cooking stew, but it seems like Astrid can—it seems that all of the talents of his fourteen-year-old sister are ones that no one with good sense would want.

"In case someone should ever ask you," Allan says, pushing back his chair and rising from his desk, "the difference between a miracle and an invention is that inventions have initiates, and miracles do not. Take our radio, for instance. I really have no idea how it works, and if I did not know better, I might think it miraculous that I could turn its dials and hear the voice of a man in another country, or a piece of chamber music performed many years in the past, almost as clearly as I can hear my own voice as I speak to you now. But there is *someone*, Harry, perhaps your teacher in school—"

"My teacher doesn't know anything," Harold says. "The books know everything for her."

"Well, then, the men who wrote those books. Someone knows how to attach a bundle of wires and vacuum tubes together and place them in a box to make this radio, yes? And what is a mystery to me is not a mystery to them. And even if I do not understand the working of this thing myself, the knowledge that someone else *does* somehow makes it less entrancing, less enchanting than it could be, if I didn't know any better.

"Now, when I was young, in those days when angels walked the streets, the world was full of mysteries whose solutions were available to no one, and never would be. Once I saw a toothless man who couldn't count to five restore a blind child's eyesight, merely by kissing a silver coin and placing it on her forehead. It was worthless to ask him how the coin *worked*—he would simply say that God had told him in a dream that love and silver could cure the blind, and foolish in these circumstances to look into the mouths of gift horses, prying into the how and why of things even as the film was fading from the surface of the girl's eyes.

"But here is a paradox: that mysteries such as these provided not disquiet for us, but comfort. Because they granted us permission, and in fact made it *necessary*, to believe in a God to Whom all mysteries had solutions. With belief in God comes the certainty that the world that He masters has an order. That every single thing in it at least makes sense to Someone."

Harold follows his father into the living room, not understanding what he's going on about, but realizing that he is performing a service, that of playing the part of the patient listener. He can see that this makes his father happy, and seeing this makes him happy in turn. "When the machines came, and when they drove away the angels from the world, they ruined everything," Allan says. "Each time I hear of one of these new, so-called miraculous inventions, it weakens my faith in the underlying order and beauty of this world. Because what worth are miracles if ordinary men such as myself can make them and understand them, even if I cannot? What need do we have of a God if man-made miracles are two-a-penny? And without a God to comprehend this world in its entirety, what surety do I have that at its heart it is not chaotic, and"—gently tapping Harold's button nose now with his index finger—"therefore meaningless? Now *there*!" Having made whatever point he was making, Allan triumphantly seats himself in a rocking chair in the middle of the room, facing the radio that towers in one corner. The evening edition of the paper awaits on a three-legged table beside him, untouched. It still has the faintly inky smell of the press: that's nice. For Allan, reading a newspaper that comes to him secondhand is like eating cold leftover food off someone else's dinner plate. With pages that are wrinkled and stained with spilled coffee and spots of grease, and ink that's smudged by someone else's dirty oily fingers, it isn't the same. It is even somewhat disgusting. News that is touched by too many hands becomes nasty and false.

"Dad?" Astrid says, banging the soup spoon against the inside of the pot as she stirs the stew. Pools of clear oil glimmer on the liquid's surface.

A large bubble rises to the top and bursts, releasing a gas that smells like the breath of something sick.

"Astrid?" Allan says. What's she mad about?

"Dad," says Astrid, "you're *full* of it. Quiet. *Please.* Let's *eat.*"

FIVE

Now the three of them are seated at the square table in the kitchen, each with a bowl of Astrid's questionable concoction in front of them. They eat in silence, but the silence that hangs in the room has its own sound, and it's undeniably unpleasant. Harold's father tries to listen to it, attempting to determine why it is the way it is, wondering if there is any appropriately fatherly thing he can say to repair it, to make it into the kind of silence that exists between people so comfortable with each other that they do not need to speak. But fatherly speeches aren't Allan's bailiwick. He can be a good provider; he can deliver esoteric monologues on machines and miracles; but the minds of his children are ciphers.

"I just put in it what was *around*," Astrid says in a harsh, whiny voice, daring the others to criticize her culinary skills. "That's all I did!" Then there is silence again. Harold pokes at his stew with his spoon and a piece of animal flesh rises to the top, pale and rubbery, with one of Astrid's long dark hairs wrapped around it like a ribbon tied around a gift.

Harold has no desire to soothe Astrid's feelings; he has nothing to say to her whatsoever. He has decided that, after what happened between them on the boardwalk today, he is not speaking to Astrid ever again. They will both grow old and die and he will never speak to her again.

SIX

It is clear enough to Allan Winslow that, for whatever reason, Astrid hadn't wanted to take her little brother along with her to the Nickel Empire; it is clearer still that if he hadn't made her take him, then he'd have never heard the end of it. For weeks beforehand Harold had gone dead quiet whenever the advertisement for the Empire's new mechanical entertainment had come on the radio, the announcer shouting superlatives over children's screams and sounds of heavy weather. *The Tornado. The largest, longest, fastest, scariest, thrillingest thrill ride in all the known world. Experience an unprecedented view of the entire city of Xeroville as you climb the Tornado's enormous ramp, then get ready for seventy-five seconds of sheer terror that will climax in the biggest loop-de-loop ever constructed. The Tornado. Only at the Nickel Empire. The Tornado. The Tornado! The Tornaaaaa-DOOOO!* ("Tornadoooo!" the child would echo, his arms stretched out like a pair of wings as he spun himself dizzy in the middle of the living-room floor.)

That was why Harold found himself in the midst of a throng of similarly minded thrillseekers slowly filing through the row of turnstiles admitting them to Xeroville's premier amusement park, his unwilling sister's hand held in one of his while the other clutched a dingy cloth bag held shut with a drawstring and containing three dozen five-cent pieces. To him it seemed that thirty-six nickels wouldn't be nearly enough to see all the myriad wonders advertised on the garishly colored posters plastered on the walls by the Empire's entry gates—the Human Pincushion; the Baby Incubator; the Taligent Industries Camera Obscura; the What-Is-It—but they'd be enough to let him fill his belly with amusement-park confections, see a few freaks shambling around half-clothed and dour-faced behind iron bars, and end the day by scaring the life out of himself in the loop-de-loop. To his ten-year-old mind one had little right to ask for more.

As they made their way past the turnstiles and down the crowded tunnel that led into the park itself, Astrid bent and placed her lips to Harold's ear to overcome the echoing din from the entertainments just ahead: "I have *adult* stuff to take care of here! *Adult* stuff, not stuff for little kids. So sometimes I'm going to have to leave you by yourself while I take care of things. And you'd better not cry about it. If you're a little man, if you think you're man enough to ride this Tornado without crapping in your didies, then you're man enough to take care of yourself when I go off to do adult things. And you're man enough not to go running to tell Dad that I let you go *all* over the park *all by yourself*, doing *whatever you wanted*. If you tell Dad? If you do *that*? Oh, you'll get pinched and pinched. In the middle of the night, just when sleep is gonna steal upon you: *pinch*. So if you know what's good for you you'd better not do it. And if you see me talking to other *adults*, not snot-nosed didie-wearing little *kids* like you, then you'd better get scarce, and quick. Remember I didn't want you along with me anyway—"

They emerged from the darkened tunnel into sunlight, the noise and the colors and the choices for pleasures overwhelming Harold's senses. Loudly decorated booths and tents and pavilions full of games and rides and oddities stretched in all directions, and even the constant susurration of the crowd of thousands was overpowered by the rhythmic pitches of dozens of carnival barkers, their voices amplified by microphones attached to arrays of speakers mounted on tall, stout wooden poles. In staccato singsongs they begged and threatened and pleaded and commanded customers to try their wares, and much of what they said came halfway close to poetry.

Earlier thoughts of moderation and contentment were driven from Harold's mind by the sudden blast of sound, and he looked back on the person that he had been twenty seconds before and found him to be embarrassingly naïve. The five-cent pieces in his sack became weighted down with all the possibilities for what they might buy him, and he briefly thought them to be so precious that he might not be able to bring himself to spend them at all. In the Nickel Empire every good and service that could be bought and sold cost a single nickel, no less, no more: change was never made, and dimes were dead currency. For a nickel you could purchase a cupful of caramel custard, its surface gleaming, its taste seemingly sweeter than that of sugar itself; for a nickel each you and your sweetheart could ascend to a wooden platform, embrace each other, and strut through a fox-trot accompanied by a trio of mechanical men banging away on three slightly out-of-tune spinet pianos; for a nickel you could watch a woman toss her head back, open her mouth, and slide an eighteen-inch steel blade straight down her throat; for a nickel you could try your luck against Montgomery the Mechanical Three-Card Monte Player, a tin man seated behind a folding table whose metal-sheathed skeletal hands moved faster than the eye could follow as it tried to hide the ace of spades. ("Three-card monte," cried Montgomery's human "assistant" into a microphone. "Monte, monte, three-card monte. Risk a nickel, get back plenty. Their games are dirty, but this one's clean. A man will steal, but trust a machine. Monte, monte, three-card monte.") Best, perhaps, to keep one's nickels forever in one's pockets, to savor delicious possibility over mundane experience—

"Get moving!" said Astrid, yanking at Harold's hand, bringing him out of his daze. "I gotta get to the Tunnel of Love. I am meeting adults there at eleven o'clock." She pulled at his arm again and they stumbled forward through the crowd.

SEVEN

They had to wait at the entrance of the Tunnel of Love for a whole half hour before Astrid's friends showed up, and Harold spent the time watching passersby and nursing a caramel custard that he'd convinced Astrid to let him pick up on the way there, eating each spoonful as slowly as he could (for with each bite he tasted not just the irresistible sweetness of the dessert, but the deliciously agonizing negative flavor of all the imagined foodstuffs that he could have bought with that nickel instead—a turkey leg the size of his forearm, or a milkshake with a pair of deep red strawberries floating on its surface. The single relinquished nickel sat in the custard seller's till, its gold transmuted back to lead). He watched people entering and leaving the Tunnel of Love—a man and a woman would present the attendant with a pair of nickels and slide into a car that would then jerk into motion and roll into the tunnel's entrance, which was decorated like the enormous gaping mouth of a clown with twice as many teeth as a normal human's. Above the tunnel's entrance the clown's nostrils flared and its black eyes stretched wide, as if it were suffering digestive difficulties from spending its day swallowing lovers. No matter how the men and women behaved toward each other when they entered the clown's mouth, even if they sat apart from each other with arms folded in silence or were in the middle of an argument, when they came out of the other end of the Tunnel and alighted from the car, they were always holding hands and wearing sly smiles, reluctant to let each other go. It looked to Harold like some kind of assembly line, though he could not imagine what fantastic machines might be laboring away in the tunnel's darkness, repeatedly welding part to part or sliding tabs into slots.

"Are you going into the Tunnel of Love?" said Harold.

"Shut up," said Astrid.

"Tell me what's in there if you go in," said Harold.

"Shut *up* I said," said Astrid.

"I'll guess your weight," a nearby huckster shouted. "I'll guess your weight; I'll guess your age. Bring your sweeties to me, men; I guarantee I won't offend. I'll guess your weight; I'll guess your age."

Eventually the adults whom Astrid was waiting for showed up—college kids, three men and two women. The women were each arm in arm with an escort, a matched pair of long-legged gazelles in swishy pleated skirts, daintily biting at paper sticks supporting pink clouds of cotton candy and being careful not to get stray fibers stuck to their faces. Their boyfriends were a barrel-chested twosome with square heads set atop thick necks and sweaters decorated with large bold letter *X*'s, orange against a field of black; they must have been from the university.

The third man, the one by himself, completely lacked the rugged if incompetently hewn looks of his companions—despite his pear-shaped fatness, his face was sunken and sallow, and an excess of pomade did nothing to tame the spikes of hair springing from his head in all directions. All about his face was crookedness—a nose that seemed as if it had been broken and improperly reset; a mouth whose corner rode up in a permanent involuntary smirk; skewed eyes that jittered behind eyeglass lenses with the thickness of the bottoms of pop bottles, seeming to speak of the crookedness of the mind that lay behind them. This was the man who approached Astrid, took her hand, dipped awkwardly, and pecked at it with pale, fleshy lips.

"Oh, *no*, Jerry," said one of the women, "tell me this isn't the—"

"Hush, hon," said the grinning man on whose arm she hung.

"But she's not a *day* over—"

"*Hush*, hon," her boyfriend said to her, and then to his seeming twin, "See? I *said* this was gonna be good."

"Hey, Astrid," said Jerry, rising. "Hey. It's. It's nice to meet you finally." He smiled, and to Harold it seemed as if his mouth had too many teeth, like the clown at the entrance to the Tunnel of Love. "Hey. I want you to meet these friends of mine. These are my friends. This is Hortense, and this is Clyde," he said, gesturing at the woman who'd spoken just a moment before and her boyfriend, "and this is Frank. And this is Julia. But you already know Clyde. I forgot that. You already met Clyde."

"Hey, Astrid," said Julia, curtsying and cutting her gaze back to Hortense.

"Hey—hey Astrid!" yelped Hortense, and then she inexplicably turned her back to the girl, her hand placed to her mouth and her shoulders quivering.

"This is messed up," said Frank to Clyde, laughing. "Don't get me wrong: I came here *expecting* something messed up. But this is messed up."

"Hush," said Clyde. "I got a sawbuck riding on this so you just *shut your mouth*. And you know what the deal was. Fair is fair." To Harold the conversations of adults seemed so cryptic sometimes, as if they only bothered to say a third of the words they needed to.

The cotton candy fell out of Hortense's hand to the ground.

"Now Jerry," Clyde said. "Now Jerry I got to explain something, and I am *sure* that Hortense will agree with me from personal experience— sometimes, see, when the ladies come they come with an unannounced *little man* in tow, who gets it in his little head to throw a monkey wrench in your well-laid plans. Now I gotta show you what to do to little men, when they try to step up to bat.

"When little men step up to bat, Jerry," Clyde said, standing over Harold and looking down at him, "what you gotta *do* is—"

Clyde's hand shot out and clamped itself around Harold's face, so large that his little finger and thumb stretched from one ear to the other.

"—you gotta take 'em—"

Harold looked through the cage of Clyde's fingers at Jerry, who just looked confused and a little dim, and at Astrid in her loosely fitting boy's trousers and button-down chambray shirt, stepping backward from Julia in her skirt and heels, who towered over her by a full six inches.

She isn't doing anything. Astrid isn't doing anything—

"—and you gotta make 'em *shove off*," Clyde said, pushing Harold backward. He took two, three steps; he stumbled and nearly fell; he kept his footing, barely.

"Hey?" said Jerry. "Stop it?" His voice was barely a whisper.

"Caricatures, caricatures," yelled a carny, dressed in a flattop straw hat and a white suit with red stripes that made him look like a walking candy cane. "Caricatures, caricatures. Sit before our mechanical portrait-maker *if. You. Dare*. With its magic-camera eye and lightning-quick hands it will sketch your face in comic style in sixty seconds flat. Reveal your shameful secret self; see the ones you love made ugly. Caricatures, caricatures."

"Come on," Clyde said, and Frank began to whisper in Jerry's ear while glancing now and again at Astrid. "We've got to go. We've got to make hay while the sun shines. I got to get my *sawbuck*."

As Harold recovered himself, Astrid bent over and placed her arm around his shoulders as a gesture that must have been intended to reassure. "Now you have to get scarce," she said. "I will meet you back here in *two hours*. You can go on the Tornado over and over again. And you had better not breathe a word of *any of this* to Dad. If you do, you will get pinched, and you will get *diseases*. You will get shingles and lumbago."

"Good-bye, Astrid," said Harold.

They left him there. As the six of them walked away down the boardwalk, Clyde turned to shout behind him, "She's got to go on a *date*, little man! She is going into the Tunnel of *Looooove*! She is going into the *mouth*!"

EIGHT

Did young Harold consciously sense that his sister might be in some sort of danger? Unlikely: he was only ten years old, and did not have an adult's instinctive facility for reading the menace that could lie beneath words seemingly spoken in jest, or the way in which hands and glances might communicate intentions thought too vulgar to speak aloud. He didn't like that Clyde guy, he knew that much—he seemed a bit too large to engage in schoolyard horseplay. Or Jerry, either—to be blunt about it, Jerry seemed to have more in common than one would like with the gibbering wild men and tattooed pinheads depicted on the posters just outside the Nickel Empire's freak shows. But Harold had no real reason to believe that Clyde would treat Astrid the way he'd treated him—she was bigger, after all, and being a girl, certain codes of honor applied. Harold could not guess what things went on inside the Tunnel of Love; he did not think to wonder where his sister had met these older, stranger people.

But still, there was a pit in his stomach, entirely distinct from the anticipation of the gleeful terror of the Tornado's loop-de-loop, or the nervousness of being left to his own devices in such a place as this. His desires yanked him in different directions—he wanted to run off toward the latticed wooden ramp in the distance with a train of cars laboriously climbing it; he wanted to return to the security of home to stand before his father's desk and watch him make his windup dolls; he wanted, some-how, to be near Astrid, if not quite to watch over her (for it was she who ought to do the watching, you would think); he wanted not to be pinched at night, or not to contract lumbago, which sounded like something that riddled one's face and body with purplish buboes and oozing sores and turned your mind to porridge.

Most of all he wanted to get away from the endless, ever-shifting noise of the park, which was starting to get to him. All the myriad re-peating pitches of the carnies, and the mindless looping melodies of the tin men banging on pianos, and the cheers of the audiences who sat on bleachers beneath tents, watching amateur actors perform classic scenes from Shakespeare's romances or cheering along prizefighters as they shuffled through their forty-seventh round—all of these things brought back to him that acutely uncomfortable and yet irresistibly exquisite sense of indecision that he'd felt ever since he'd entered the gates of the Nickel Empire.

In short, the boy's guts were tangled in knots. Even more than wanting to ride the Tornado, he just wanted somewhere that he could sit in silence for a while, somewhere that he could think for a few moments.

It was then that he saw a sign in the midst of all the others, advertising a most peculiar attraction. While all the others had their dedicated pitchmen shouting into microphones, this one had just the single sign to advertise itself; that and the unusual nature of the building in which the attraction was housed. The sign sat next to a spiral staircase made out of metal and mesh, its entrance protected by an automatic turnstile; the staircase turned and turned around a metal pole that rose to the sky, until it reached the base of an odd, cylindrical hut that sat atop it, like a man-made nest designed for the gigantic, predatory birds of creature features.

The sign next to the staircase read:

SEE THE TALIGENT INDUSTRIES CAMERA OBSCURA
A DEVICE INVENTED BY PROSPERO TALIGENT HIMSELF
HIS WONDROUS ARRANGEMENTS OF OPTICS WILL ALLOW
YOU TO SEE THE ENTIRE CITY IN ASTONISHING DETAIL

EXTRAORDINARY
MIRACULOUS
SOUNDPROOF.

NINE

There was no one standing at the turnstile, no one ascending the staircase, no one coming down—without a carnival barker to pitch the attraction, the ears of the throng were drawn elsewhere. Harold extracted another precious nickel from his drawstring bag and dropped it into the slot cut into a box next to the turnstile. He heard a click from inside the box, and he pushed through and began to climb the staircase.

As he rose and became not part of the crowd but one who looked down on it from above, his perception of the park changed—from here it seemed not so relentlessly oppressive, not quite so hard to tolerate. The unending mumble of the thousands of people in the park and the incessant advertisements of the barkers were not so loud and insistent up here (though even from here he could tell that one of the barkers was, yes, actually barking into his microphone like a dog, as if he'd come to realize that what mattered was not what he had to sell or how he chose to describe it, but merely the act of selling, in and of itself). And since Harold had committed to a course of action, however temporarily, the charms of all the pitchmen were lost on him, at least until he entered the hut perched atop the pole around which the staircase turned and saw whatever inevitably disappointing wonder lay inside.

The sky above him was still clear, though it was beginning to darken in the east. Looking in that direction he could see the Nickel Empire's boardwalk with families and couples strolling up and down it; beyond that lay the bay that separated Xeroville's middle- and lower-class residential areas from the business districts of its downtown. A few boats dotted the bay's surface: a couple of smallish yachts drifting slowly on the calm water, and a racing pontoon driven by a crew of four mechanical men, their arms bending back and forth in an inhuman double-jointed fashion as they worked the oars in perfect synchrony, propelling the blade of the boat's prow through the water. Beyond the bay rose the city's skyscrapers; in the midst of them, taller than the rest, was the obsidian pinnacle of the Taligent Tower, its upper floors shrouded in a wreath of fog.

The spiral staircase terminated in a tiny platform with a protective railing, hundreds of feet above the ground. From here a ladder rose up the pole to a hatch set into the floor of the hut. Harold saw that affixed to one of the rungs of the ladder, just at his eye level, was a small metal plate inset with a red button and inscribed with two words in gold: RING BELL.

Beneath Harold, a child released a bundle of helium-filled multicolored balloons, which rose to the sky and separated, carried away by the wind blowing from over the bay. The rain would be here in a couple of hours at most.

He stretched out a finger and rang the bell, and immediately the door above the hatch swung downward, as if whoever was on the other side had been lying there in wait. The man who poked his head through the hatch was gaunt and sported an asymmetrically receding hairline and a beak for a nose, his gigantic pale green eyes set in a long, oddly elfin face. He looked at Harold, laughed, and called to someone else outside Harold's view: "I think we found one."

"Bollocks," a gruff voice bellowed from the hut's interior. "You always say *we found one, we found one*, and he never is one, and he never has the nerve to take the whistle when it's offered to him. Get back here, Gideon. Leave him there."

"No, I can look at his face and tell that we've found one," the elfin man said, lowering his arm through the hatch and beckoning Harold to climb the ladder. "We have found one of the saddest, loneliest boys."

TEN

With Gideon's assistance, Harold climbed the ladder, poked his head through the hatch, and clambered into the interior of the camera obscura.

Here, at last, was something that was like nothing he'd ever seen. The interior of the hut was occupied by a complex array of brightly polished mirrors and lenses attached to slender brass rods that dangled from its ceiling or sprouted from its floor, that could swing on fulcrums or spin in place or glide along rails, reflecting and refracting light in innumerable carefully controlled directions. Harold had the distinct impression that he was looking at a device that was more complicated than it needed to be, needlessly baroque just for show.

A narrow passageway cut through the tangle of machinery, with enough clearance above it for Harold to stand without bumping his head against the lenses suspended above him, though Gideon had to stoop slightly. The passageway ran from one side of the cylindrical hut to the other, with the entrance hatch at its middle. At either end of the passageway was a console studded with dozens of levers and switches and dials, which Harold assumed controlled the orientations and positions of the optics; over each console hung a large canvas, with an image projected on it. One of the images showed the base of the staircase that Harold had just ascended; the other showed the view across the bay that Harold had seen as he climbed the staircase.

Each console had a chair in front of it; the one in front of the console whose image showed a view of the downtown district across the bay was empty. The other chair held a man who was as stocky and muscular as Gideon was wiry and thin; his neck was even wider than his brick-shaped head. He squinted at Harold with small, dark eyes and said, "Mistaken, Gideon. You have made another mistake. This is not one of the saddest, loneliest boys. Look at his face, for one thing. I had half a dozen frown lines by his age. Between my eyebrows. Running from my nose to my mouth."

"I think you're wrong. I think that when we make him the offer, that he'll take the offer," Gideon said. "That's Martin who's being so pessimistic, by the way. Martin, and Gideon. That's us. Welcome to the Camera Obscura—

"Listen to that," said Gideon, cutting himself off. "Listen."

Harold heard nothing. "What am I—"

"No talking—did I say *talk*? No. Listen!"

"I don't hear anything," Harold said.

"That's *right*," said Gideon. "Nothing is *exactly* what you hear: this place is soundproof, and once its hatch is shut, all the noise from the park below falls dead against this building's walls. Up here we are deaf to all those endless salesmen's pitches. We sit here in *peace* and *quiet*. We sit and we *think* on *wonderful things*—"

"—and we play cards," said Martin. "We play gin mostly, and Gideon loses most of the time because he's no good—"

"—and we meditate and hover over the people of this park like *gods*."

"Gideon has some kind of a *complex*," said Martin.

"Hey, I paid a nickel to get in here," said Harold. "Now you guys have gotta show me something. What do I get to look at with this camera for five cents."

"Impatient," Martin said, shaking his head. "Impatient. Ending his questions with periods and everything."

"Impatience might be good," Gideon said sideways to Martin, and then to Harold, "Usually, we let the people who come up here—"

"But no one ever comes up here," said Martin. "No one ever does."

"—select two things to view: one thing that is *nearby*"—Gideon gestured toward the console where Martin sat—"and one that is *far away*." He pointed at the other. "But in your case, if you don't mind, we'd like to make an exception. You can pick whatever person or thing you want to look at in the park itself. But—and trust us on this, please—leave it to us to demonstrate the strength of this device's distant vision, and we will show you something—perhaps even *someone*—you thought you'd never see yourself."

So those were the two decisions to make—near, and far. Near was easy, and even just saying this eased some of the tension in the boy's stomach: "I want to see my sister."

"Unimaginative," said Martin. "First you are impatient; then you are unimaginative. You can see your sister anytime you want, yes? Better with your own eyes than you can with this machine. So you should pick something else. Choose to see the sleight-of-hand tricks that the carnies use behind their backs to cheat their marks. Or say you want to see a dancing girl, kicking her legs up and showing glimpses of her garters. Ask to see something like that."

"I want to see my *sister*," Harold said. "I paid five cents."

"Fine," Martin said, and shrugged. "Where is she?"

"Somewhere around here. I don't know. She's with adults."

"Well why don't you go ahead and make it hard for me," Martin said. "Why don't you make me have to search. Well what's she look like at least."

"She's taller than me, and she's got pigtails, and she's with a bunch of adults—"

"Strangers?"

Harold nodded. "And she's with adults and her face is like my face except there's always a look on her face like this—" He squinted and pinched his lips shut and frowned, as if he were sucking on a lemon.

"Good enough," said Martin. "I'll find her. But it'll take time. But no one can ever be bothered to come up here anyway, so it doesn't really matter."

"And while he's looking," Gideon said, placing his hand on Harold's back and leading him toward the other console, "I will show you the Taligent Tower. And on the Tower, near its top, a balcony. And *perhaps*, if you are lucky: on the balcony, a girl, waiting."

ELEVEN

Gideon seated himself in the empty chair while Martin turned his back to him and Harold, focused on the image of light projected on the canvas that hung in front of him. As if notified to begin by some unseen conductor, they simultaneously started to operate the banks of switches and levers in front of them; in response the conglomeration of optics with which the hut was packed came to life, the rods to which the lenses were fastened telescoping and retracting and gliding along their rails. Things spun and danced and clicked, and Harold felt a slight jolt in his feet as the entire hut began to turn on the pole that kept it suspended above the park. The skyline of Xeroville's downtown began to crawl past one of the hut's windows from left to right; a slightly different image of that same skyline moved on Gideon's canvas in the opposite direction, right to left.

"You have to stop it somewhere," Martin said. "Stop it."

A second jolt came from beneath Harold's feet, and he steadied himself against a wall.

"Stopped," said Gideon.

"Good," said Martin. "Now go ahead. Give your little speech."

"Look there!" said Gideon to Harold, pointing not out the window, where Harold could see the Taligent Tower plain as day, but at the canvas directly in front of him, on which was a somewhat blurred image of that same Tower, diluted by its trip through the camera obscura's lenses. "Look: look at this magnificent Tower!"

"He tries to put a little drama in it, you know," Martin said to Harold. "So pay attention, and remember to look excited—else he'll be disappointed, and later on he won't lose hands of gin to me with his usual good cheer. Try, you know, dropping your jaw, or making your eyes all wide."

"That Tower was erected by the same man who conceived of this camera obscura," Gideon said, gesturing expansively at the optics that stuffed the hut's interior. "Now think of this. You, child, live in the future."

"No I don't," Harold said. "You're saying something silly now."

"But listen," Gideon said. "Right now, you yourself are in the future of the person whom you were just five seconds ago, when you began to speak that ill-considered sentence about how silly I was. And the person who you were five years ago—could he have conceived of a world in which this Tower exists, or this camera obscura, or the mechanical men who inhabit the park beneath us, so common that they are reduced to five-cent entertainments that fail to merit a second glance?"

"When I was little," Harold said, "I used to draw pictures with crayons of people who had gears inside them instead of the stuff that's inside normal people. So, yeah."

"Wait a moment," said Gideon, as if this interruption to his well-rehearsed monologue had thrown him off track.

"He gets it already," Martin grunted. "The future's always ordinary, by the time you get there. Too young to have figured that out. A shame, really." He went back to fiddling with dials, the image of the canvas above him showing the faces of women wandering through the park, one after another.

"Everybody who's a kid thinks about stuff like this, like when they're *six* years old, if they're boys," said Harold. "If you're a boy you think about this stuff when you're five and a half. I used to draw pictures of flying cars, and for the first time a couple of months ago I saw a flying car, a real one. And I thought, it's like the pictures I used to draw. Except that my flying cars had tommy guns stuck on the sides—*rat-a-tat-a-tat*."

"Wait a moment," said Gideon.

"What I say is," said Harold, "if you're gonna go to all that trouble to build a flying car, why not go the distance and put some guns on it, too. Flying cars with no gangster typewriters on 'em get the *raspberry*. They get the *raspberry*. Pffffbbbt."

"But the difference!" said Gideon. "The difference between you and Mister Taligent is that while you can do little more than draw pictures in crayons of a future that you wish for, Prospero Taligent is the richest and smartest man in the known world. So he need not guess, or dream, or pretend to foretell—he raises his hand, and the future that he wishes for the world comes to be."

"Okay," said Harold. "That's fair enough."

Martin snorted.

"Day and night he labors, manufacturing the futures of all the people who live in this city," Gideon said, turning back to the console. "Think of him as something like those rare benevolent kings of prior, more miraculous centuries, before corporations took the place of nation-states— always concerned with the greater good instead of his own ambitions. He understands the secrets that light carries as it moves through glass, and of flying machines that are heavier than air, but one thing escapes him—"

"Is it love?" Harold said excitedly. "I bet it's love. It always is with these smart types."

"That's what it always is, isn't it," Martin grumbled. "Oh, would you look at *this* one." He stared at the canvas hanging above him. "Bouncy bazooms and a face that belongs on a coin. And all the kid wants to see is his sister. Ain't that a shame."

"The last secret of human love escapes him," Gideon sighed.

"Look at her," Martin said wistfully. "She'd say nice things to you. She'd make you breakfast."

"And so," said Gideon, "one of his greatest experiments. Look here, child—don't get dizzy."

Gideon pulled a giant lever on the side of his console, and the regular grinding of the gears that powered the optical array became a high-pitched whirring; then, on the canvas above Gideon, the image of the Taligent Tower began to fly *toward* Harold, as if a camera were strapped to the back of a giant bird unerringly winging its way from the camera obscura across the bay to the city's downtown. He had never seen anything like it before, not even in motion pictures. It made him feel a little queasy.

"His adopted daughter, Miranda," said Gideon, "the light of his life. But often when he tries to speak to her his tongue turns back on itself; raised in a Tower that holds twenty times as many machines as men, she's little better. Their dinners together take place in silence, or they're accompanied by fugues made from the flanging noises of engines—the lullaby that sends the girl to sleep is the sound of steel scraping against steel."

The walls of the Tower filled the entire canvas now—Harold could see many small round windows, like the portholes of a ship, set into them at irregular intervals. Gideon turned a dial and the viewpoint of the image began to rise, the Tower's windows scrolling downward. Finally, the image settled on a single balcony, presumably somewhere near the Tower's roof. The balcony seemed empty at first, but once Gideon pressed a button and it suddenly shot still closer, Harold could just make out the head of a girl peering over it, braids of golden red hair coiled about it in a wreath. Her face itself was hard to discern.

"She is, without doubt, a very strange girl," Gideon said, twiddling knobs in an attempt to focus the image; resolving it in sufficient detail seemed to be beyond the camera obscura's capabilities. "The only one in the Tower who will dare to speak to her is her own father—"

"Right enough," said Martin. "I've seen the girl once, and once was enough. She gives me the creeps. She looks at you like she knows the name of the man who'll dig your grave."

"—and so the basic rudiments of the spoken word escape her, never mind the subtleties," Gideon continued. "If she chooses to talk to you, then by turns she seems impolite, or crass, or simpleminded. Bereft of companions she is failing to master the crucial art of conversation."

"You're saying that she doesn't have any friends," Harold said. "You didn't have to say all that to say that she doesn't have any friends."

"One does not make friends with Prospero Taligent's daughter," said Martin. "It seems unwise."

"No—no friends," said Gideon to Harold. "No friends; no one to talk to; no one to teach her how to talk. Prospero is approaching the rearing of his daughter in the same way that he'd tackle any other experiment, you see—cold and methodical. He has a certain hypothesis. . . . He believes that the best thing for her would be to have a birthday party for her. With children her own age. But not the sons and daughters of his company's employees—that'd be a self-selecting group, well-off, with their minds dulled by privilege. He wants to throw her in the midst of strangers from across the city who speak in different voices. He said to us—he said to me: 'Go out into the city; bring me sickly girls with bad manners who only own one good Sunday dress; bring me the saddest, loneliest boys. Bring me children who—how do you say it?—*cuss*. I want her to hear some *cussing*.' And here we have been, searching for them, and we think that one of them is you. I can look at your face and see it."

"I don't cuss *that* much," said Harold.

Martin turned in his chair to face Harold. "He's going to make you an offer now, and you're not going to have the nerve to take it. That's okay. I wouldn't have the nerve either, knowing what I know about the girl and her father. I'd be scared to death."

TWELVE

"So I'm having trouble finding this sister of yours," said Martin. "These adults—what do they look like?"

"Some of 'em had big letter *X*'s on their sweaters," Harold said. "Big orange letter *X*'s."

"Ohhh," said Martin. "College kids? I thought you meant *adults*." But concern was in his voice when he turned back to his console. "At the Tunnel of Love, either going in or coming out. I'd bet money on it."

Gideon turned in his chair to look Harold in the eye, and Harold was surprised to find that the once genial smile on Gideon's face now had a twist in it that made it seem somewhat cruel. "Here we are, at the Nickel Empire, and everything costs a nickel. Did you get to see everything you wanted to see?"

"Gee, I haven't even gotten *started* yet," said Harold. "I could be here all day and feel like I hadn't even gotten *started*. There's a bunch of different things I wanna try—I wanna find some cotton candy and get some of that. And I wanna play a couple of games. And I wanna ride the Tornado—that's why I came here in the first place. Maybe twice. Maybe three times."

"Well, you sad and lonely boy," said Gideon, his grin full of toothy menace now, "I am afraid that there will be no cotton candy for you this day. There will be no treats but the ones already turning to acid in your belly; no games but the one you are about to lose; no frights but the ones in your nightmares tonight. That is, if you want *this*."

Gideon flourished with both hands—nothing up his sleeves—and reached behind his back. When his hand came into view again, a whistle lay on its open palm. It seemed an ordinary whistle, made of metal. It did not glow with an inner light, and no spotlight shone down on it from above. It did not emit the hum of a siren's voice just inside the range of human hearing. It was rusty.

"You are not the owner of this whistle," Gideon said. "But if you were, and *if*, at midnight tonight, you were to lean out your window and blow into it with all your breath, *once*, then the sound that it made would carry all the way to the Tower, and it would be a message that Prospero Taligent himself would receive. Then he would know that, yes, you accepted the invitation that we are extending to you, to the party held to celebrate the tenth birthday of his daughter, Miranda."

Harold reached out a hand to take the whistle, but Gideon's own hand quickly closed into a fist. "But there is, of course, a price," he said. "How much money do you have on you?"

"I've got a bag full of nickels, which is all I've got," Harold said. "I had all the dimes I had changed into nickels. But this is the Nickel Empire and everything here is a nickel so five cents is what I'll pay for it."

Gideon's fist extended a finger and shook itself at Harold—no, no; naughty, naughty. "That would be true if we were still *in* the Nickel Empire. But we're not—we are *above* it, and the rules of life are different for those in high places."

"Now he gets all legal," said Martin. "He should have been a lawyer. I think I see her, unless I miss my guess. Give me a moment."

"This whistle," Gideon said, "will cost you all the nickels that you hold. I will have *every last one.*"

Tears welled up in Harold's eyes at the enormity of this proposition, its unmitigated gall. "That isn't *fair,*" he shouted (and the whistle lay there and he wanted it, based on nothing more than the memory of a blurry image of a girl standing on a balcony; even that might have been some kind of parlor trick). "That's *unfair—*"

"It is unfair," sneered Gideon. "It's downright dishonest. And let me be clear, just so you're certain just how unfair this is—I don't give a flip about your money. As highly ranked employees of Taligent Industries, Martin and I are quite well paid—I might stick my finger down my throat and vomit forty thousand nickels if I wished. After you hand me the money and leave, I may forget about it, or fling it out the window for my amusement."

"Yes," said Martin to himself. "This must be her. These boys look like they'd think of themselves as men."

"It's the principle of the thing," said Gideon. "It's the simple act of depriving you of your money that matters, for two reasons. First: Prospero told us to bring him sad boys, and we would be remiss if we did not do our best to ensure your sadness. Second: I know you were thinking of all the things you might do today with those coins, but a man who *makes* the future will not allow a little boy who can only *dream* of a future to dictate the terms of a bargain. As an act of goodwill you must sacrifice all the futures you might have for the one that he designs for you. Now. The whistle. Yes or no."

THIRTEEN

"Maybe you're being a little rough on him," Martin said, staring up at the canvas above him. "Maybe, you know, you should take it easy." Had Harold been able to see what Martin was looking at, he might have understood why a certain unaccustomed note of sympathy had crept into Martin's voice.

But Harold had his eye on that most ordinary whistle, held out to him on Gideon's palm. Dear imaginary reader, you must have guessed by now that young Harold traded his bag of coins for that whistle, and that this barter set in motion the long and intricate chain of events that took place over twenty years and led to my imprisonment aboard the zeppelin *Chrysalis*, writing of this person whom I once was. But here is a sad thing. You have probably also guessed that it hurt Harold to make the trade, that that first burst of tears was not just a simple sign of shock, but a true indicator of his feelings. You must think that his mind operated like a child's mind does, and that he believed that each of those nickels offered him a chance to tumble the locks of heaven's gates. And though this is true, it isn't all of the truth.

What is sad is that he half suspected a scam and that the whistle could not do what Gideon claimed, but even if there had been a ruse in the works, he would not have cared. He had had a rough day at the park, all things considered—the sharp-tongued sister and the shove in the face had been bad enough, but on top of that the park itself with all its noise had just been too much. The constant clamor of the booths and barkers served as an endless exhausting reminder that he had to choose a fate, and that no matter which fate he chose he could be certain that it would not be the best, that in other timelines rendered inaccessible with each spent coin, other versions of himself would be having more fun, or winning golden ribbons, or becoming taller. The thought was unbearable.

But here, in the rusted whistle, lay the chance to have a man of no little means and reputed wisdom choose his fate for him. And for a boy too weak and cowardly to choose, what price could be placed on the freedom not to *have* to choose, the chance to blame someone else for the outcome of his life by proxy? If he lay alone in his bed at night and found the whistle useless, at least as he fell asleep he'd have the pleasure of telling himself that he'd been taken in, and that there was nothing to be done for it.

Most important, what the whistle and the loss of nickels were buying him was the freedom not to have to listen. The camera obscura was soundproof, and the only noises within it came from the people and the machines that were inside; after he gave up his money to Gideon and descended once again to the park below, purified, his mind would be soundproof as well, for a little while. Instead of having to choose one or another of the barkers to pay heed to, he would be able to listen to none of them at all, because he had no choice. In the midst of chaos he would be at peace.

Besides, he figured he could wheedle a last five cents from Astrid for the roller coaster—he wasn't stupid. He'd blackmail her if worst came to worst—seriously, how bad could a midnight pinch or shingles be?

So he wiped his eyes dry, swapped his bag of nickels for the rusty whistle, and called it fair and square. Only then did Martin beckon him to the other viewer, to see his sister.

FOURTEEN

She was with Clyde and Hortense and Frank and Julia and Jerry at the entrance to the Tunnel of Love; the six of them were stepping into one of the cars, which had three seats. Clyde and Hortense took the front seat; Julia and Frank sat in the rear; Astrid and Jerry slid in between them, in the middle.

"I don't like the way she's being touched," Martin said. "I don't like it." While Frank was nowhere near Julia's personal space, and Clyde had his arm draped around Hortense's shoulders with a casual ease connoting that they both believed it belonged there, Jerry's manner with Astrid was alternatively furtive and possessive—he'd reach out and clamp her shoulder with his hand, then draw it away as if she were aflame or contagious. Then he'd do something weird like stick his nose in her ear and rub it all around. Their backs were to the view of the camera obscura, so Harold couldn't see Astrid's face, but he imagined that she couldn't be enjoying what Jerry was doing—still, though, her body language was passive, with no sign of struggle or displeasure.

The car jolted into motion, throwing its passengers backward, and it began to slip into the Tunnel's open mouth. Clyde and Hortense vanished into the darkness first, the last sign of them a glint from a silver flask that Clyde held to his lips with his head tilted back.

Just before Astrid disappeared behind them with Jerry, she turned to look behind her, as if she somehow knew that she was being watched. In that moment the image of her face on the canvas came into the sharpest focus. She stared right at Harold, and she looked, without a doubt, dead frightened.

Then there was nothing but a circle of black.

FIFTEEN

Martin accompanied Harold on his trip back down the spiral staircase. The weather had drastically changed in the time that Harold had spent inside the camera obscura—the once-blue sky was now overcast with thick, heavy clouds, and lightning flashed in the distance behind the downtown buildings, the muted thunder from the strikes reaching Harold's ears a half minute later. A wall of rain was coming toward them, and the ripples from the raindrops were already stippling the surface of the bay. The few pleasure boats that dotted the water were returning to their docks; the tin men in the racing pontoon rowed on with strong strokes despite the weather, oblivious and stainless.

"I wouldn't have had the nerve," said Martin as the two of them descended. "To admit that I was coward enough to want the whistle. That was what made you take it, right? Not bravery, nor a boy's desire for adventure? It was cowardice, yes?"

"I don't know," said Harold. But he knew. He reached into his pocket that had once hung heavy with coins and clutched the whistle, insubstantial by comparison.

"I'm not criticizing you for cowardice," said Martin. "I'm a coward, too. Whenever he waves the whistle under a little boy's nose, I want to shove the boy out of the way and take it for myself. But I don't have the nerve. And Gideon tries to lord it over everyone because he hands the whistles out, but if you could switch places, so that you were the man and he was the little boy, he'd want one, too. He'd want the sweet relief of having one—you bet."

They reached the turnstile at the bottom of the staircase. "Hey," said Martin with a tentative touch to Harold's forehead, a sort of benediction. "Look after your sister. She's bigger and older than you, but still— look after her. And I don't mean standing between her and men who are larger than the both of you put together—that'd be foolish. Just be present, when you're needed."

Martin stepped back, turning to climb the staircase again. "Don't worry about being a coward," he said. "All of us are cowards." Then he rose, and was gone.

SIXTEEN

When Harold made his way through the park back to the Tunnel of Love and found Astrid, she was waiting there, by herself. She wore her lemon-sucking face. Her eyes were red, and a small cut on her lower lip bled; as Harold approached, she reached up and rubbed it, looked at the red on the tips of her fingers, rubbed them together until it disappeared, and clasped her arms about herself, as if she were cold despite the sticky, humid weather.

"Hey, Astrid," said Harold, somewhat shyly.

She said nothing; she merely rubbed her lip again, looking out across the park.

"Perpetual motion," hollered a shiller. "Perpetual motion. Witness this little wooden pyramid, handcrafted by the tribesmen of the darkest forests at the edge of the known world. Merely place it within ten feet of the engine of your choosing and watch that engine transform into a perpetual motion machine—that's right: more energy going out than coming in. Is it magic, or science beyond our ken: who knows. Perpetual motion. Just five cents."

The adults whom Astrid had come here to meet were nowhere to be found, not even Jerry. Harold surmised that whatever devices lay inside the Tunnel of Love and riveted soul to soul had failed when they'd come up against Astrid's intractability. Perhaps somewhere else in the park, Jerry had the same red eyes and the same bloodied lip.

Harold had thought that after he returned to earth, he'd be at peace with the din around him, but this wasn't the case—the noise of the park still pounded at him, and the absence of the bag of nickels weighing his pocket down was like an amputee's memory of a phantom limb. Somehow it seemed important that in the midst of all this sound he should guess the proper thing to say to Astrid, that he ought to take that last admonition to heart that Martin had given him as he'd turned to climb the stairs. But his sister's face was a sign that he saw but could not read, and in his ears above all, for just this moment, was the noise of the Tornado, of the screams of its passengers as they saw the world upside down for the first time.

So forget the look on her face, then. Forget it.

But he could not decide which tack to take with her, and so he blurted bits and pieces of excuses, all half-expressed: "Astrid I didn't go on the Tornado and I wanted to go on it. I wanted to wait until you were done with your friends so we could go together. Because it's special. Because I'm scared. I don't have any nickels. I spent them all and I was dumb. I was robbed. I thought you wouldn't mind just five cents. If you don't do it I'll tell Dad. Come on let's you and I go on the Tornado before we go back home. Come on let's go."

"I want to get out of here," said Astrid, hugging herself.

"I'll tell Dad," Harold said. That seemed to be the thing to say that'd be most likely to work.

When Astrid looked down at him, there was a new expression on her face that Harold could not interpret, because he'd never seen it there before: a certain squinting, cutting stare. Her lips were pinched in a thin line across her face, like the mouth on the dolls of Miranda Taligent that his father made.

"You want to go on the Tornado?" she said.

"Yeah!" said Harold.

"Then I'll take you on the damned Tornado," said Astrid.

SEVENTEEN

By what seemed like good fortune at the time, Harold and Astrid ended up in the front seat of what would be the final car to ascend the Tornado's ramp that day. The rainstorm was only a few minutes away, and it would effectively shut the Nickel Empire down when it arrived—already, a fine cold mist hung in the air. Before Harold, the tracks of the Tornado's coaster converged to a vanishing point in the sky; beside him, across the bay, skyscrapers grew forward and upward out of a slanted earth. Beneath him the barkers ceased their endless entreaties and shut down their speakers; the windup keys in the backs of the tin men spun down, the springs that coiled around their spines going slack; shutters descended to cover the fronts of booths; customers began to leave the park or look for cover.

"Damn it," said Astrid. "Oh damn it all *damn* it." She rubbed her lip; she rubbed her fingers together. "If Dad hadn't made me take *you* along this would have turned out all different. But you came along and look what happened. You look what happened." She rubbed her lip; she rubbed her fingers together.

The wheels of the car trundled as it rose. In the seat behind Harold and Astrid, a woman let loose with a single high-pitched barking guffaw, like whistling in the dark.

"Stupid," said Astrid. "Stupid me, and I have to go home now to stupid Dad, and I don't have any stupid friends, and the worst of it all is that I have to sit at the dinner table across from stupid *you*. Stupid."

Harold's eyes were on the track in front of him, and his heart was full of anticipation of what was coming. And so he did not think to look at Astrid's face when next she spoke. Had he done so, he might have seen that same cutting squint there that he'd never seen before today; he might have been smart enough this time to take it as a warning sign; he might have covered his ears or steeled himself before it was too late.

"Hey, I have something to tell you," said Astrid, her voice suddenly melodious and chatty. "Do you ever wonder why it is that there are only three people at our dinner table in the evenings, and not four? I mean, it ought to be that there's me and you and a dad and a mom, right? But there isn't a mom. Did you ever think about that?"

Harold said nothing, but he clutched the safety bar in front of him a little tighter. The coaster's car neared the top of the ramp.

"Because normally," Astrid said in that same bouncy conversational tone, "when a mom and dad decide to have a kid they plan it out in advance—beforehand, they think about it, and they talk about it, and they fill out forms and do things with slide rules. That's how people end up getting born most of the time. That's how I was born.

"But that's not how *you* were born."

The car began to slow and level out. Behind Harold, a squeal slipped from between someone's lips.

"I'm sorry to tell this to you," Astrid said, "but you weren't planned out like I was. You were a *child of passion*, is what it's called. You were an *accident*. Mom just woke up one day after being passionate and she was *pregnant*, and it scared her so much, because not only did she not *want* another baby because one was already *enough*, but when a kid is an accident you never know *how* it's going to turn out. When a kid is born because of a *plan*, like *me*, then she turns out okay. But kids who are accidents might need glasses, or they might have four legs and no arms, or their insides might be where their outsides are supposed to be, and they have to walk around carrying their stomachs in their hands."

The car stopped, locked at the summit of the ramp. Before them lay the dip, the turn, the spin, the loop. The storm was here. Fat raindrops spattered against the boy's face.

"So when Mom went to the hospital to have you she was *so scared*: I can't even tell you how scared she was. And when you were finally born, and the doctor said *here is your new baby boy, Mrs. Winslow, I'm so sorry,* and you were all ugly and crying like an ugly damn monkey, *waaah, wahhhh, I'm an accident, hey watch I'm gonna pee all over myself, how do you like that,* then Mom got so sick that she *died right then and there.* Yeah, that's right. First she died. Then she *melted.* Then she *exploded.* And now I have to take you to the amusement park and have things *ruined* by you, and now we have to live with *stupid you,*" Astrid shrieked. "Because you were an accident, accident, acci—"

The rest was a blur—the ground before him, the sky behind him, his sister bawling herself hoarse in the seat beside him, her cries a ragged counterpoint to the giddy screams of the other passengers; the threat of vomit rising in his throat as his organs tossed themselves around inside him; pellets of rain stinging as they smacked against his face; the whistle pressing against his thigh through his pocket. And in the distance, finally, the Taligent Tower, pointing downward like the dark finger of a God indicating those whom He wishes to torment. And inside it, perhaps, the girl, waiting.

Get scarce. Get moving. Shut up. Shove off. Little man. Coward.

Look after your sister.

Damn it all damn it.

Accident. Accident. Accident.

EIGHTEEN

Sitting at the dinner table, Allan knows none of this. Astrid and Harold both finish their meal, saying nothing, and Allan eventually guesses from observing Astrid's petulance and Harold's attempt at a firmly set jaw that one of them has committed some unimaginable and merciless cruelty on the other, the sort that could only arise out of mutual unconditional love between brother and sister. It is, perhaps, within his power to smooth things over, but one of them will have to crack first. He decides to work on Astrid—she seems shaken, so she'll be the easier of the two to break. He guesses that she's the offender, and her brother the offended—it's probably more complicated than that, but isn't it always.

Harold chokes down his stew first and asks to listen to his radio in his bedroom—unusual, since he prefers the vacuum-tube-driven radio in the living room to the smaller crystal radio that's by his bed, with its finicky tuning, its sounds fading in and out of the ether, its songs and poems overlaid with static. But Allan wants to be alone with Astrid anyway for a little while this evening, so that's fine. The newspaper that Allan had planned on spending time with tonight will probably have to go unread—already he senses the information within it aging like quickly spoiling meat.

"Radio till nine o'clock," he says. "Then noises off, and lights out. I want you wide awake tomorrow, for those teachers to cram those books of theirs into your head."

It is the usual joke that father and son make on Sunday evenings during the school year, and Harold dutifully delivers the proper response, covering both his ears and rolling his eyes back in his head to make fun of the teaching machine that he hates. Tonight his performance seems half-hearted, though—when he's at his most amusing he usually makes a little line of drool fall from his lip. There's definitely something on his mind.

NINETEEN

When alone in his bedroom, he prefers to listen to the radio in darkness. His father built it for him as a birthday present three years ago, and after Harold dons its headphones and slides the tuner across the coil of copper to pick up the channel he wants, he shuts out the lights and slides under the covers. But though he knows he must stay awake until midnight tonight, his fatigue outweighs his resolve, and in minutes he falls into a twilight sleep. In his semiconsciousness, the words of the radio announcers who cry out the news of the world and the conversation that he hears through his bedroom door merge together into a single dialogue, so that he cannot identify which is which—sometimes the world's news seems as if it's being screamed from the living room; sometimes it's relayed through the radio in his father's voice, grown uncharacteristically nasty and harsh.

Astrid. Tell me something.

"—and our team of meal-replacement engineers have concocted some of the absolute *best* distillation formulas you'll find in the city."

A female voice in a sultry contralto: "All of the pleasure of eating with none of the effort, right?"

"That's right—you can enter our restaurant confident that you'll still fit into your little black dress when you leave for the theater. Here—try this one."

"He's . . . okay. He's handing me a vial, a test tube full of a clear, deep red liquid. It looks like blood. Is this blood?"

"No-ho-ho! This isn't blood at all."

"Do I sip it, or just drink the whole thing? Just toss it back?"

"Just drink it! All at once!"

Astrid. What happened at the Nickel Empire today? I can't help but notice your silence during dinner. Are you hiding something?

"Okay, here goes . . . I'm a little nervous about this . . . here we go . . . it tastes . . . oh my goodness. It tastes . . . wait . . . it tastes *exactly like steak!* A nice, juicy strip steak: oh, steak and potatoes and *bourbon*—"

"That's right! And it *is* strip steak! In fact, it's better—it's *essence* of strip steak! That vial had all the vitamins and nutrients that you'd get in a complete meal, and—"

"Yes, you're right! My stomach feels positively *stuffed*, just like—oh. Wait—the feeling is getting beyond stuffed now. Oh—oh God what have you *done* to me—"

It doesn't matter much whether you want *to tell me what happened, Astrid. I believe you'd better, whether you want to or not.*

"And now from scientific advancements at the *dinner table*, we're moving to advancements in the *air*. We're going now *live* to Taligent Park, where none other than the man himself, the great Prospero Taligent—"

Did you just talk back to me? Astrid. You come back here.

"—hhsssfffsssnnn . . . nnfff . . . hnnnn . . . hnnnfff—excuse us we're having a little trouble with the transmission—"

What? I can't hear you. Speak up.

"—ssssssso then. Mr. Taligent, you're going to test . . . what is this? A mass-transit flying machine."

"Yes: it'll hold up to twenty passengers. Not quite capable of trans-oceanic flight yet, but we're thinking that, once sizable production runs of this engine become viable and we can start building whole fleets of these ships, we'll erect a kind of inflatable port at several strategic places at sea, where the crafts can land and refuel—"

"An air-port."

"Yes. Yes exactly."

"Listeners, this sounds like yet another miracle from the Miracle Man, Prospero Taligent. Would you like to describe what we're looking at, here, this truly magnificent machine?"

"Well, the pyramidal shape of the craft is one that we've tested on miniature models in our laboratories. On the models we get really good lift, as opposed to other shapes we've tried in the past, such as spheres and cubes—"

"I'm sure all that science is very interesting. Let me just say that everyone that's *anyone* is here for this fantastic night launch of a mass-transit flying machine: the stars in this audience rival the stars in the sky. We've got the Mayor of Xeroville, arm in arm with the former Miss Xeroville 19—, who will both be present on the maiden voyage, and let's try to catch a few words from the esteemed mayor on his way to board the craft. Hey! Hey Mister Mayor—"

"—goddamned contraptions I am so sick of these maiden voyages damn contraptions breaking down—"

"—hey there thanks Mister Mayor—"

Astrid, I am having trouble believing what you just told me. Let me get this straight. You were approached by a man, a college boy, who of-fered you three trifling *dollars if you would kiss his hideous virgin friend on the lips. And you are only fourteen years old: you are a fourteen-year-old girl. And you said yes to this.*

"—and now the air-craft is getting ready to ascend. The pilot—hey there!—the pilot is *waving* at us from a glass window in the side of the pyramid, and through the window we can *also* see the Mayor, and Miss Xeroville 19—! And Prospero Taligent is waving right back from the ground! Say there, Prospero, how's young Miranda doing?"

"Quite well, these days. She's a beautiful young girl. Full of life. Her tenth birthday is next week. And I'm throwing a party for her—I've invited a hundred boys and girls from across the city. Most of the invitations have already gone out."

Because this man bet one of his other *friends* ten *dollars that within two weeks he could find a woman who would kiss his unimaginably hideous virgin friend. And this is referred to as friendship. What kind of friendship is this?*

"There'll be lots of cake, and ice cream of a thousand different flavors, and candies that come from all around the known world. And all the surprises that they can handle."

"That's wonderful, Mr. Taligent. That's absolutely wonderful. Isn't Mr. Taligent wonderful, folks? Mr. Taligent is wonderful."

Astrid, you might have demeaned yourself a little less if you'd held out for half of the take. If I've failed to instill any sort of moral values in you, I'd have thought that at least you'd picked up some basic financial sense. But that doesn't explain why Harold's so upset.

Go on: tell me the rest and then you can cry all you like. Soonest begun is soonest done.

"The air-craft! Ladies and gentlemen the air-craft is actually *lifting from the ground*! It's impossible to convey the beauty of this machine over the airwaves to you, listeners. The gigantic pyramid is rising into the sky, illuminated by dozens of panning spotlights, lifted by the hundreds of rotor blades all turning on their axles . . . five feet off the ground! Six feet . . . ten!"

Accident.

Accident!

"What's—what's wrong with it? The pyramid's body is shaking. It's shaking. Is it supposed to do that, Mr. Taligent?"

"I—no—I don't know—"

Astrid, I ought to wring your neck! The nerve!

Accident!

"My God—my God—the craft is breaking apart—oh my God *the great ship is bursting into flames*—"

You stay right there, Astrid, and don't you move a muscle. I'm not through with you.

"—oh God ladies and gentlemen the worst tragedy I've ever had the misfortune to see in all my years of reporting fireballs of flame ballooning to the sky bodies hitting the earth already charred to carbon Miss Xeroville 19— is a walking wailing column of flame oh God oh God oh God please strike me blind—"

The boy is blinded by the light from the bedroom door, startled by his father's bursting in. Allan runs toward him and takes him up in a clumsy embrace and begins to rock him back and forth: "You're not an accident, son. You're not. You're not an accident. None of us are accidents, and don't you dare believe you are. You're not. You're not an accident. You're not." The net effect of all this on Harold is fright rather than comfort—still bleary-eyed, he can't figure out what all the commotion is about. Larynx-tearing screams are coming from the radio's speaker as his father clasps him and repeats himself. What is this?

Allan looks his son in the eye, and Harold sees a tear running down his cheek. What *is* this? First Astrid on the coaster getting all weepy-eyed, and now him, too! Crud!

"You didn't kill your mother," Allan says, choking back a sob. "You're not an accident, and you didn't kill your mother. That's a silly thing to think, son. Isn't that silly."

"I didn't?" This is all so confusing and uncomfortable, and Harold wishes that he could skip the next ten minutes of time.

"Your mother was a miracle," says Allan. "She was a miracle. But the thing is, we just don't have miracles in the world anymore. All the miracles are gone."

TWENTY

Later, at midnight, when the rest of the apartment is asleep, the arguments ended and the tears gone dry, Harold climbs out of his bed, rummages through the pockets of his trousers until he finds the whistle, goes to his open window, sticks his head out, and blows it for all he's worth—

exactly once, as Gideon instructed. It makes no sound that he can hear; when he shakes it afterward, he hears no pea rattling inside.

He falls asleep believing he's been robbed, not knowing that the summoning of demons is almost always unwitting.

TWENTY-ONE

And within the Taligent Tower, it is dreamtime.

Miranda is a little girl, and her dreams are little-girl dreams, pure fantasies unfettered by the adult desire for symbols and secret meanings. There is an endless, tempestuous sea, blue as a perfect shining sapphire, and across this adult-sized sea moves a child-sized boat, its hull made from toothpicks and matchsticks, its riggings from twine. Little boys and little girls in tailored sailors' outfits run frantically up and down the deck. Rain lashes across sails of stitched-together silken handkerchiefs. Spheres of ball lightning erupt in the sky, illuminating the children's cherubic faces. They scream to each other in high-pitched squeals, hands cupped to their mouths: "Heigh, my hearts! Cheerly, cheerly, my hearts! yare, yare!" The ship rocks metronome-like in the storm. The apple-cheeked children pull industriously on the riggings, the skin of their tender hands rising in welts when the string runs uncontrolled through their fingers. "Take in the topsail!" "Tend to the master's whistle!" "Blow till thou burst thy wind, if room enough!" The sea is still a perfect blue, despite the tempest. "Boatswain!" "Here, master, what cheer?" "Fall to't, yarely, or we run ourselves aground!"

TWENTY-TWO

In Harold's dream he is, at last, entering the Tunnel of Love, though it is not a tunnel, but a long, vast cavern so wide that darkness shrouds the walls on either side. Beneath him is not a track, but a river; the boat he is in holds six, and it glides along the river of its own volition, pilotless. A rhythmic booming sound emanates from somewhere up ahead, and the noise heralds troubled water.

He is holding hands with Astrid, and this seems good, but also incorrect. Her palm is hot and has the raspy feel of sandpaper. In the seat in front of him are that Clyde fellow with what seems like a woman wearing a large, lacy Sunday bonnet, but when the woman lifts her head off Clyde's shoulder and turns to look at Harold, Harold sees that she is, in fact, Jerry. Jerry is not wearing his pop-bottle glasses, and he has the eyes of a Kewpie doll—they take up half his face, and they have thick, inch-long black lashes and pupils that look like a pair of black pies with a slice removed from each.

"You gotta make 'em *shove off*," Jerry says to Harold in a thin falsetto. He puts the tips of his fingers to his lipstick-smeared mouth and titters as he flutters his lashes. Then he goes back to cuddling with Clyde.

Boom, boom, boom goes the noise up ahead, and a few moments later the boat rocks slightly.

Behind Harold and Astrid is seated Prospero Taligent—he is not with his daughter, but with a phony mechanical replica of Miranda, one of Allan Winslow's windup dolls enlarged to life size. The tin Miranda stares straight ahead with its painted eyes, and though Astrid seems herself and human, she also looks ahead of the boat with the same unblinking, glass-eyed expression.

When Prospero opens his mouth he speaks in Martin's voice. "Look after your sister," he says. "Just be present, when you're needed."

Boom, boom, boom: the boat shakes.

"We're all cowards," Prospero says. "Now *here it comes—*"

And suddenly Harold is in the air and rising—a pair of mechanical hands have plucked him into the air by his shirt collar. Up here at the roof of the tunnel there are dozens, no, hundreds of mechanical hands and arms, all tangled together and interlocked and writhing, communicating to each other in sign-language gestures that Harold can't interpret. Twenty kid-gloved tin palms support the boy and stop him from falling into the river, and twenty more strip off his clothes, tearing them to scraps that flutter down to the water. The hands carry him over to Astrid, who is hanging up here as well—he can see that she is naked, too, but her body from the neck down is a blur, as if he's viewing a censored film.

It is then that he sees how people are joined to each other inside the Tunnel of Love: the process is so simple that it's a wonder that he didn't think of it himself. But that doesn't mean that it isn't painful, and as one mechanical hand approaches him and Astrid with a hammer, along with another that's holding several twenty-penny nails, he screams and screams until he wakes himself up and the only thing left of the dream is the *boom, boom, boom* of whatever undefined but surely terrifying thing it was that lay at the tunnel's end.

Wait—that isn't part of the dream. That noise is *real*. It's muffled now, but it's shaking his bedroom door.

He rolls out of bed and stumbles out of his bedroom and down the hall, to see Astrid still in her dressing gown, standing in the middle of the living-room floor, staring wide-eyed at the door to the apartment: it's shaking on its hinges as whatever's on the other side bangs against it. Whatever it is must have a fist the size of a canned ham. *Bam. Bam. Bam.*

Now Allan shuffles out of his bedroom and stands next to Astrid and Harold, the three of them staring at the door. From the floor below they hear the curses of neighbors, muffled to unintelligibility. It's still not yet dawn—the noise is inexcusable.

"I blew the whistle," Harold says.

"What on earth are you *talking about*?" says Astrid.

"I blew the whistle!" Harold cries gaily, and before his father can stop him, he runs to the front door, stands on his tiptoes, shoots its bolt, and yanks it open.

On the other side of the door stands a mechanical demon, eight feet tall, its skin a red burnished metal, with shoulder blades that extend into large, delicate, batlike wings. A pair of curled horns jut from either side of its skull. Its eyes glow and roll madly in its head. Streams of steam jet forth from its flaring nostrils.

In its oversized, clawed right hand, it holds an envelope.

The demon lurches into the room on its hinged legs, its insides making all manner of noises, *twangs* and *clicks* and *snaps* and *boings*. A delicately filigreed windup key slowly rotates in the center of its back. When the demon reaches the center of the room, it halts (and all the noise inside it ceases, except for the quiet grinding of the key) and it raises its right hand straight out, proffering the elegantly decorated envelope to empty air.

Though Allan and Astrid are completely baffled, Harold knows what this is, and now that he knows it's really going to happen, he doesn't know if he should be ecstatic or scared to death.

Cautiously, Allan approaches the demon, reaching up and taking the envelope from its hand. The demon remains there, absolutely still, its arm outstretched.

Allan looks at the envelope, runs his finger over the gilded edges, turns it over, squints at it, picks with his finger at a wax seal embossed with the logo of Taligent Industries, turns it over again.

"Harry," he says, "I don't know why, but—"

"It's for me," Harold says, because he knows. He takes the envelope from him. "It's mine because I blew the whistle."

With his father watching intently, Harold Winslow carefully removes the wax seal from the envelope with his index finger and opens it, revealing a card inside. He slowly extracts the card, opens it, and reads the message printed neatly within:

> *Girls are angels of goodness and light.*
> *Boys are demons with malice and spite.*
> *Come to my party and you will see*
> *What fun fun fun a party can be!*

> *Saturday morning, at the Taligent Tower, at sunrise.*
> *This demon will conduct you there.*
> *It will have to stay in your home until the day of the party.*

I hope that you do not mind.
Please take good care of it and wind it twice a day.

Your new friend,
Miranda Taligent

The mechanical demon stands statue-still in the center of the room, tendrils of smoke drifting from its ears, its arm outstretched, beckoning.

TWENTY-THREE

Dawn is coming, and the dreamship floating across the sea of Miranda's mind is taking on water and splitting apart. Little girls, caught by surprise in their petticoats, clamber to the deck as the ship begins to tilt. In their arms the girls cradle cunningly wrought porcelain dolls, with real human hair shorn from the heads of virgin princesses, that can roll their painted glass eyes, belch, defecate, and stretch out their arms to beg for a bottle or a desperate embrace. . . . The little boys are below, doing their futile best to bail out the ship, saying their last high-pitched hysteric good-byes to the earthly world: "Farewell, wife and children! Farewell, brother!"

"We split," the child captain says, standing on the bridge in his little captain's uniform with its smart cut and shiny golden buttons. He stares up at the sky, resolute as the ship goes down beneath him, the matchsticks of its hull scattering across the ice-blue sea. The sky clears to reveal a packed and twinkling starfield. A single bright clear child's tear courses down the captain's face. "We split," he says, and hangs his head in sorrow. "We split."

TWENTY-FOUR

The tin demon stands in the middle of the living-room floor of the Winslows' apartment for a solid week, its head nearly touching the ceiling. As if he is taking care of a pet, Harold is careful to wind it twice a day, as Miranda's invitation instructed. He does this once in the morning before he goes to school and once again when he gets back, after he shakes off the effects of the teaching machine and he can think clearly without involuntarily reciting villanelle or bursting into tears.

As far as Harold can see, the demon never moves, though Allan claims it does when Harold is away at school—when the sun hits the living-room window around one o'clock, the demon's eyes light up as it swings its arms and rotates its head on its neck like an athlete preparing for a strenuous round of calisthenics. Then it clomps over to the window to sun itself, and a few hours later it clanks back to its original place on the floor to stand at attention, stone still. Since he spends his day making windup dolls, Allan feels that he's somewhat mechanically inclined, but he can't sort out how the kinetic energy supplied by a single windup key that a child can turn can power a device that seems devilishly complicated and must weigh at least a quarter ton. "Perhaps the sunlight has something to do with it," he hypothesizes one evening, during dinner. "Perhaps it can somehow take advantage of the same energy that makes plants grow, in a limited way."

"Maybe it just likes the sun," Astrid says. "Maybe, you know, it's thinking, if I didn't have to stand here all the time waiting for whatever, I'd be outside, picking daisies and such."

"It's *mechanical*," Allan says. "It doesn't think. It doesn't prefer overcast skies to clear ones, or thunderstorms to droughts. Or daisies to nasturtiums, for that matter."

"You don't know it doesn't think," says Astrid. "It's not like it's *said* it doesn't think."

"If it said it couldn't think, then it'd be thinking," says Harold, speaking through a mouthful of mashed potatoes. "Wouldn't it."

"Yeah *thanks for proving my point*," says Astrid lamely.

"Astrid," says Allan, "let's not be silly. I won't have you *personifying* that—"

"Shut up Dad it'll *hear* you," Astrid says.

The mechanical demon, of course, says nothing.

TWENTY-FIVE

"Prospero," Allan says once during another dinner conversation, stretching out the syllables. "Prossssspero."

"Prospero *Taligent*," says Harold, drumming out the waltz meter of the magnate's name on the table with his fork and knife.

"Do you think his mother named him that?" says Allan. "Think about it—Mrs. Taligent née McGillicuddy holds her newborn baby boy in her arms and looks into his eyes and says to herself, *this one will grow up to be a maker of magic. He needs a name that suits him.*"

"Nah, he probably named himself that," says Astrid. "Like he was probably a teenager looking through a book of Shakespeare plays or something, doing a homework assignment, and he pointed his finger at a page and said, *There. That's the name I want. And that's the person I'm going to pretend to be.* And then he ran away from his home in the sticks, and when he showed up in the big city he pretended to be that new person so well that he actually turned *into* him. But every night, the last thing he thinks about before he goes to sleep is what a fake he is."

"Shut up, Astrid," says Harold.

"His real name is probably Brad," says Astrid. "Brad Jones."

"Shut *up*, Astrid!"

"Fred Smith," says Astrid, with one of her rare faint smiles.

TWENTY-SIX

In separate sessions during the week, Harold tells his father and Astrid the story of the whistle that summoned the demon. When he tells his father, he leaves out the part where Martin calls him a coward, because it's embarrassing, and he leaves out the part where Clyde nearly knocks him down, because he senses that Astrid is in bad enough trouble as it is.

His father is struck dumb for a little while, at first. Then he comes close to him and says: "Now Harry. Listen to me. When you go to this party, I want you to be on your *best behavior*. You are a *very lucky boy*, and Prospero Taligent is a *very important man*. If you gain his favor, he may make you privy to his secrets. So be on your best behavior. Remember everything you see. When you come back, write it down. I'll buy you some pens and some clean new paper, and you can sit at my desk and write down everything you remember. You'll want to have it written down to look back on later, when your mind sands all the sharp edges off your memory and makes it into a dream that it will have you believe is true.

"You should try to gain the favor of the girl. I'll give you this doll that I made, and if you get a chance, you can give it to her for a birthday present. If she decides that she likes you, you may be allowed to return. Perhaps—ha ha, perhaps the father will make a marriage match! Don't make that face, son. I'm not advising golddigging, but perhaps you'll be the heir to an empire. Then after he dies, you will take his place and ascend to the top of the obsidian tower and live with your beautiful wife among the clouds. And wouldn't that be nice. Isn't that the way that fairy stories end.

"Be on your best behavior. Say *please* and *thank you* to Mr. Taligent; end your sentences in *sir*."

TWENTY-SEVEN

When Astrid hears the same tale, minus Martin's admonition to Harry to look after his sister and minus the look that Harold saw on Astrid's face in the camera obscura, she says: "Okay. Okay listen. You are probably going to have to talk to the girl at some point. So don't screw up. Don't worry about airs and graces. Remember: she's not a monster, and she's not untouchable. No matter where she lives or who her daddy is or what expensive fabrics she's been swaddled in she's just a little girl, and her head is full of little-girl stuff like lollipops and lace—not the kind of stuff that runs around in circles in my head and it repeats and it repeats and it never shuts up. No matter what happens, when you see her, you just talk to her. You just say: *Hello, Miranda*. Like that. No need to take a breath first; no need to get up your nerve. Easy-peasy. Got it?

"*Hello, Miranda*. That's it. That's all you need to say to start."

TWENTY-EIGHT

In the week before the birthday party, every night for Harold is like a night before a Christmas morning, torturous and sleepless. As Saturday approaches Harold drifts drowsily through his days, and yet he spends his nights just as wide awake as if he'd eaten a giant-sized chocolate bar just before bedtime. He is waiting for the demon in the living room to do something, but he doesn't know when it'll make its move, or how. The few days left between his ordinary present and the future that Prospero Taligent has in store for him are like pages in a book that he'd like to skip but can't. Seconds feel like minutes.

There is one night, Thursday night, when he hears the noise of someone rustling around in the living room, and thinking that he will get his chance to see the demon move, doing whatever thing it does when it isn't being watched, he untangles himself from the sheets in which he's been tossing and turning for four hours, slips to the floor, pushes open his bedroom door slowly enough for the hinges not to squeak, and pads into the hallway that leads to the kitchen and the living room. He sidles along the hallway's wall like a sneak thief until he can just see the demon standing in the middle of the floor. It isn't moving. But Astrid is there in her dressing gown, speaking to it while pacing back and forth with her hands clasped behind her. Harold is concealed from her view for the moment, and so she continues talking as if he weren't there at all.

"And do you know what Father said?" says Astrid to the demon. "He said that the worst thing that a person can be is a liar, and that I was a liar because the kiss I gave that guy was a lie. But how can a kiss be a lie? A lie needs words to make it a lie, doesn't it? Doesn't a lie need sound? Don't you need to *speak* a lie?

"I guess you could say that a kiss means something, some one thing, and then if you kissed someone and it meant something else, then that'd be a lie. But that's not even true, because it wouldn't be the kiss that was the lie: it'd be the thing you said the kiss was that was the lie. The kiss would just be a lip touching another lip and that would be it. A kiss can't mean anything just by itself unless you say what it means. It can't be a lie, or truth, or anything at all but what it is.

"It's not like before I kissed that guy I looked at him and said, 'This means I love you,' or 'This means that the sun is shining,' or anything at all. I just kissed him, and that was it—well, that would have been it, except that inside the Tunnel of Love things got a little crazy. It doesn't matter that I got three dollars at all.

"And so what if you think a kiss *does* mean something? You can't expect everybody to write a whole *contract* every time they kiss somebody—like this means A, and B, and sometimes C but never D. And everybody probably has an idea in their head about what it means when someone kisses you, and everybody probably has a *different* idea and no one has the *same* idea, and everybody thinks that their idea is the exact right one. So if it mattered that a kiss meant something in your head, and everybody had a different idea of what a kiss meant and no one had the same idea, then every time any two people kissed each other they'd be lying to each other. And it is hard to believe that people who have been, like, married to each other for sixty years or something have told lies to each other all that time. So a kiss must not mean anything at all. Right? Right. It would mean just as much if I kissed you as it would that I kissed Jerry, or someone I was in love with. Not that I'm ever going to be in love with anybody. The things that are running around in my head won't let me be in love.

"Can you hear anything I'm saying to you? When I say something to you, do gears turn around in your head to help you make sense of it, the way an adding machine makes four out of two and two? Dad thinks you can't think, but I think you can. If you can think, are you going to say something?

"I'll tell you what—I like you, whether you can think or not.

"I am going to kiss you, I think."

As Harold watches from his hiding place, Astrid drags a chair over from the kitchen and stands on it, so that her eyes are level with the demon's. "I'll tell you what," she says. "Either you can't think, or you can think and you're just hiding it because you don't want people to be onto your little game. But either way you're getting a kiss. If you *can* think about what a kiss means, then this means that I like you. Not that I love you. I *like* you. I think you're nice, and I appreciate your attention.

"If you *can't* think—well, it'll be like kissing a rock, and it doesn't matter, does it. But it'll make me happy even if it doesn't matter to you one way or the other. So it's not so bad."

Then she leans forward, nearly losing her footing on the chair, and plants a firm smooch on the demon's steel lips. It does nothing in response.

She stares into its eyes for a few moments, looking for a reaction that will probably never come, sighs, and climbs down off the chair.

By the time Astrid replaces the chair in the kitchen and enters the hallway on the way to her own bedroom, Harold is gone—he's scooted back to his bed and ensconced himself under the sheets, covered from head to toe. For some reason that he will never quite understand, even years afterward as he sits aboard the zeppelin writing this story down, he is shaking, literally shaking, with rage.

TWENTY-NINE

Finally Friday night turns to Saturday morning, and before dawn, Harold's father rousts him out of bed. "It's doing something," says Allan, once the cobwebs have cleared from Harold's head. "I think you'd better get ready to go."

Harold turns on a lamp and puts on the outfit that Allan purchased for him for the party—a crisply ironed button-down white shirt, short pants, black dress shoes and matching black socks, a muted blue tie, and a sharp new hat, dark gray with a blue sash tied around it to match the tie, which will promptly fall from his head within the next ten minutes and which he will never recover. He grabs the windup Miranda that his father has left on his nightstand and puts it in his pocket.

When he comes into the living room, the demon seems to have partly awoken from some kind of trance—twin tendrils of steam are drifting lazily from its ears, and it blinks occasionally. Its arms are once again outstretched, as if it desires a comforting embrace.

Astrid comes into the living room, rubbing her eyes. "What's it doing?"

"I don't know," says Harold. He is trying not to be scared, but he is.

The demon's arms suddenly jerk up and down, as if it's attempting and failing to dance.

"I think we have to figure this out rather quickly," says Allan.

"It wants a hug," says Astrid. "Harry. Put your arms around it."

"Astrid," says Allan, "don't be—"

"But it's obvious," says Astrid. "Go on. Give it a hug."

And so, as he'd seen Astrid do, Harold gets a chair from the kitchen, places it in front of the demon, and stands on it. He can feel heat coming off the demon, as if it has a pile of hot coals lying in its stomach.

He slips his arms around the demon's torso as tightly as he can—he can only manage to get them a little more than halfway around it. He looks up at the demon, which is still staring straight ahead, blinking every few seconds. He says to Astrid, "I don't think this is—"

As if Harold has tripped a snare, the demon's arms spring shut, pinning Harold against its chest. "Agh!" he cries in surprise—its embrace is also slightly painful, and try as he might, he can't do more than move his arms or wiggle his feet. He's stuck.

Two jets of steam shoot horizontally with a hiss out the demon's ears, and it turns toward the apartment's front door.

"Open the door before it breaks it down," shouts Allan, and as the demon marches toward it, Astrid gets there just ahead of it and throws it open.

The demon lurches through the hallway, and Allan and Astrid stand at the door, saying their good-byes. Harold can't say much in response for fear of biting his tongue—his head is bouncing around on his neck due to the demon's jarring, loping gait as it descends the stairs, and this evening when Harold returns, he'll be feeling aches and pains from head to toe. He screams again as the demon bashes straight through the front door of the apartment building, leaving splinters behind.

Now that the demon is outside, it begins to run straight down the empty street, the wings on its back twitching as if they are about to spread. Here and there, squinting, frowning tenants in bathrobes and gowns are poking their heads out of the windows of the apartments that overlook the street, wondering what the commotion is.

The demon begins to run faster and faster, and Harold is starting to wonder if the demon is planning on running *all the way* to the Taligent Tower—even at this rate, it would take hours to get there, and Harold would be jostled to pieces in the process. For that matter, he'd never thought to ask how the demon got to his apartment in the first place.

This is when the demon's black wings spring out to their full span, and as Harold bawls and his brand-new hat falls off, it leans forward so far as it's running that it seems it's about to trip and fall, and it takes to the sky.

THIRTY

Dear imaginary reader: unless you are from a future so far distanced from my present that I cannot guess at the fantastic nature of its engines, and you have some means of travel that lies beyond my comprehension, the idea of machine-powered flight must be commonplace for you. Even for the young Harold Winslow flight was not unheard of, though the drawing boards of Prospero Taligent's engineers had yet to produce reliable mass-transit airborne devices that wouldn't tip over and fall to the ground in flames. There were flying cars, for instance, though not the fleets of them that choked the skyways of some cities in my final days on earth. You might have gone weeks without sighting one, but they were there.

So when I say that there was nothing to which young Harold's flight to the Tower compared, and that there are few events in my life for which I could say this, then you may be reluctant to take me at my word. But believe me—when Harold was hundreds of feet in the air over the bay that lay between his family's apartment and the city's downtown, the wind rushing by him and filling his ears, his only support the demon whose arms gripped him so tightly that he would later find two bands of dark purple bruises across his back—well, the only thing he could think was that life must have been something like this during the age of miracles that his father sometimes talked about. Not exactly like this, but something like this, something close.

This feeling doesn't last for him for long, though. For one thing, he's somewhat uncomfortable; also, because of the position in which he's pinned, he can't see as much as he'd like—he can look over the demon's shoulder to see the sky above him, and when the demon banks for one of its occasional swooping turns, he can look out the corner of his eye to see the water of the bay beneath him. Eventually he gets used to this awkward situation, and he nods off in the demon's arms for a little while, in the way that young children can fall asleep in the most unlikely of places—

he hasn't been sleeping well this past week, and something about being up this high in the air makes him light-headed, forcing him to drowse against his better judgment.

When he wakes again he sees an angel just above him, flying on the same course as the demon that holds him. The rising sun gleams off its face, which is an expressionless mask of silver with full lips and a nose with wide, flared nostrils; its eyes are blank and have no pupils. A yellow neon halo is fastened above its head, and it blinks on and off at regular intervals like a sign hanging in front of a diner. Its wingspan is wider than that of the demon that carries Harold, and each feather of its wings is long, white, and distinctly detailed—Harold thinks that the feathers might even be real, plucked from birds of a species with which he's not familiar. In the angel's arms is a girl in a sleeveless white dress who looks down at Harold. Her dark curling tresses toss in the wind and obscure her face from him.

"Crazy!" the girl screams at Harold, as best she can. "Crazy!" She yells some more things to him that are unintelligible, and Harold says nothing, not knowing how to respond.

The angel suddenly rises upward, pulling the girl away from him, and Harold can see that it is one of a triangle-shaped phalanx of ten that's flying in formation, each one holding a little girl that is smiling, or weeping, or passed out from terror. He turns his head as much as he can and figures out that the demon carrying him has joined a similar configuration, and that the other nine demons nearby are ferrying little boys like himself. One of them is letting forth loud, exuberant yells: "Yaaaaaa*hoo.* Yeeeeeehah."

The demon carrying Harold banks sharply, and after recovering from the sudden jolt he can see that he is above Xeroville's downtown, with the people on the streets below reduced to the size of ants; in fact, he and all the other mechanical angels and demons who hold their party guests have formed a single line and are now circling the Taligent Tower, climbing higher and higher in a spiral that has the Tower in its center. He can see inside the windows of the Tower as he flies by, though he doesn't get more than a couple of seconds to look through each—he sees secretaries seated at long rows of desks, banging away at typewriters; he sees men in wire-rimmed spectacles and lab coats, operating devices with mysterious purposes that seem unimaginably complex; he sees a man sitting at a grand piano and playing it while a researcher has his head poked beneath its propped-up lid, carefully observing the movements of its hammers and strings.

The demon that holds Harold reaches the roof of the Tower and flies through a wide, high loop above it, bringing back discomforting memories for Harold of the Nickel Empire's Tornado. It orients itself so that its feet are pointing downward and lands on the roof of the Tower, breaking into a rapid run once again as soon as it makes contact. It manages to bring itself to a stop before running off the roof's edge and its arms fly open, unceremoniously dropping Harold on his bottom without warning as he scratches up the palms of his hands in an attempt to break his fall.

Harold comes awkwardly to his feet and sees other boys and girls with dazed expressions scattered across the roof; they are being tended to by Prospero's servants, who are leading them to an elevator that will presumably take them down into the Tower itself. The tin demons and angels that brought them here are standing near them and still as statues, their single purpose for existing served. In the distance Harold can see another late-arriving squadron of mechanical demons that carry ten more boys, lit from behind by the rising sun.

He feels a hand on his shoulder and turns to look up at Gideon, the man who'd sold him the whistle inside the camera obscura. Gideon has a smile on his face, but there is no hint of menace in it, nor salesman's guile—he's genuinely happy.

"I knew you'd make it," says Gideon. "I knew you'd make it." He begins to steer Harold toward the entrance to the elevator. "Come with me. We'll get you cleaned up and refreshed after your trip. Then we'll take you all to the banquet hall, and the birthday party will begin.

"We have so many wonderful things planned for you," says Gideon. "I've seen what's in store for you with my own eyes, and I can't even make my mind accept it. You can't imagine. You cannot even imagine."

THIRTY-ONE

Prospero Taligent does not know what to do. He isn't very good with children (in fact, the only child he's ever had any real experience with is Miranda), so for him the crowd of boys and girls milling around the banquet hall (red-faced and screaming, kicking and pulling hair, already discovering innovative ways of messing up their brand-new outfits) is something out of nightmares.

(Actually, not *everybody* is kicking and screaming and generally being rambunctious. The girls are all standing in a row against a wall, resplendent in their fine dresses of linen and lace and silk, waiting politely with their hands clasped behind them for the festivities to begin. They are glad they are girls and not boys, they think to themselves as they look on with girlish curiosity at the forty-nine-boy brawl on the other side of the hall, fists yanking at ties, teeth biting arms, a mass of prepubescent children in a disorganized pile in which some work their way to the top while others are buried, the boys giggling gleefully as they hurt each other.

(Wait: forty-nine. Who's missing? One little boy is standing by himself in corner shadows, shy and timid, watching the goings-on. That would be our hero, Harold Winslow. Watching the pile of children tussling in the middle of the banquet hall, an amorphous writhing mass of arms and legs and fists and faces, he is coming to the realization that a boy's life, by definition, involves ass-kicking, and that he will most likely be on the receiving end for much of it.

(Wait: everything's not quite in order among the girls, either. A little freckled redhead has procured a clod of mud from somewhere—resourceful child, isn't she!—and is vigorously rubbing it into the golden curly locks of the girl standing next to her. The blonde, whose locks are rapidly losing their golden sheen, is clearly displeased. "Waaah," she says. "Nnngaaaah! Stop . . . stop . . . *stop it*!" Now she's scratching at the redhead's face, raising little welts across her freckled cheeks. Prospero, watching all this, does not know what to do—)

Prospero does not know what to do. He had the banquet hall redecorated for the occasion, painted in simple triangular tessellations of primary colors. There are festive balloons, and crepe streams hanging in parabolas from the high ceiling. Two dozen clowns with makeup caked on their faces stand at the ready, primed to entertain at a moment's notice. Mechanical women with buxom, gold-plated bodies (the mechanical women, like many of Prospero's other inventions, are something that he feels he must keep to himself, something he feels the world at large will not yet accept: the idea of a man made out of wires and gears is one thing, but a mechanical *woman* is quite another) stand next to wheeled tables that hold towering, elaborately frosted cakes, and sumptuous pies filled with sweet fruits grown under the hot sun of a distant land. A team of chefs is in the Tower's kitchens, their flying shining cleavers blurred to the eye as they slice with precision into the finest cuts of meat, cooking dishes that children are guaranteed to like (a consideration that severely restricts their palettes, or palates, as the case may be. No salads, no broccoli, no brussels sprouts, no eggplant, no ostrich, no dolphin, nothing with bones or strange shapes: the list of restrictions goes on without end. The chefs raise their eyes to heaven and curse in foreign languages, incensed that they must sacrifice such succulent specimens of chicken, so plump and tender, to make "nuggets"). A single table with a hundred and two places runs the length of the hall, with two chairs the size of thrones at either end, one for Prospero, the other for Miranda. Everything is planned to the best of his ability, and he really does want this to come off well for his daughter, because he loves her. But the children are causing chaos.

"Children?" Prospero says. (He is trying his best to look nonthreatening, to play the part of the kind and wealthy uncle, given to pulling silver dollars out of ears. He's selected a flattering outfit in consultation with his public-image consultant, a smart, deep blue pin-striped suit with a matching silk tie and a deep purple shirt, also silk, beneath. Still, children might find something about his appearance off-putting. He is not tall, but everything about his build is long and thin: his arms; his legs; his fingers; his long, narrow, bony skull with its prominent cheekbones; his long, thin, middle-aged mouth, frozen in a moue that gives a hint of the gaunt, sunken character his face will have in his declining old age, after he goes mad. His dark brown hair, pomaded and swept back, is starting to thin, and it's already gray at the temples. Long, thin eyebrows arch devilishly over his narrow eyes, which are so brown as to almost seem black. Poor guy: no matter how colorful and stylish his clothing, he will still cut a spectral figure. But he is trying his best.) "Children?" he says, a little louder. One of the boys in the midst of the fracas lifts his head long enough to make eye contact with Prospero, but then the boy is socked in the nose, and with an incomplete set of baby teeth latched into his finger, he is pulled back into the pile and out of sight.

"*Children!*" Prospero snaps. This isn't the impression he's going for, but he gets their attention. The pile of forty-nine mauling, tearing, and biting boys stops its mauling and tearing and biting and disseminates as the roughed-up kids, faces bruised and clothes torn, go to join Harold, who is uncomfortably standing alone against the wall, facing all the girls. Being in the Taligent Tower seemed like it would be fun at first, but now that he's actually here, and considering what he had to go through to *get* here, he's nervous and sweaty and has a funny feeling in his stomach.

"Sorry," one boy says.

"We was just fightin' some," says another.

"We're sorry Mr. Taligent," says a third.

"Oh, you don't have to call me Mr. Taligent," Prospero says, looking around nervously, steepling his fingers. "You . . . you can call me Uncle Prospero." Out of the corner of his eye he catches the two fighting girls, still shoving and scratching at each other, now both covered in mud. "Young *ladies!*" he barks, and the girls freeze in a tangled tableau, finger in mouth and hand over face. He turns to one of the gold-plated mechanical women and says, "Would you take these two and get them spruced up in time for lunch?" His words are accompanied by an intricate series of hand gestures, and the mechanical woman nods briefly, walks across the hall (and note her movement: not the jerky all-over-the-place clanking of her male counterparts, but a gentle saunter with a barely perceptible sway in the hips), picks up a girl by the leg with each arm, and takes them through an enormous set of double doors and out of the banquet hall, a spindly girl-leg grasped in each hand, the giggling girls swinging pendulum-like back and forth, their long, matted hair brushing the carpet, their baggy bloomers showing, the hems of their ruined dresses tickling their noses.

"Well," says Prospero, "those two will just have to miss the tour. But the rest of you, even though *many* of you have misbehaved, won't have to. Come, and I will show you" (and he tries to be majestic here—he knows that the children dream that he is a magician) "the wonders of my Tower! Then we'll come back here for a lovely lunch, and Miranda will get her birthday present."

THIRTY-TWO

Where is Miranda?

A party is being held for Miranda with a hundred guests, and she sleeps. She sleeps alone, her head on an enormous eiderdown pillow, in the middle of a mattress that seems large enough to her to sleep ten little girls, beneath layer upon layer of silken sheets the color of blood. Not the color of blood that we imagine it to be as it courses through our arteries, but the color it is at the moment it's spilled. (A difficult lesson to learn: Miranda remembers how Prospero taught it to her, holding the jack-knife's blade to the inside of her elbow, quickly making the cut, shallow and perhaps a half inch long... "Don't flinch... don't *flinch* or you'll only make this harder, this is something you have to see... there. See? I can look at your face and tell you were expecting to see a pure bright liquid burst forth, the color of an unfurling rose or a piece of cherry-flavored candy... but it's not. You see? Impure. Imperfect. See now? You learn important lessons when you bleed." Three years later she still carries the tiny scar, and runs her finger over it when she's nervous.) Miranda sleeps, and her blood moves sluggishly inside her.

The noises of all the Tower's machines are muffled to a murmur by the bedroom's thick obsidian walls. The lights are incandescent, and soft and yellow, and dim. The sheets are nice and warm: silk, with heavy quilted blankets over them. In sleep, it feels good to have silk against the skin.

The calling voice of her father intrudes as a whisper, coming from a speaker set in the ceiling, growing in volume until it is strong enough to gently pull Miranda up and out of her slumber. "Darling. Miri. Miri. Darling."

The little girl rubs her eyes. "Father."

"It's time to wake up. Time for the concert, and the party. Time for smiles and songs."

Miranda yawns and stretches. "Time to wake up," she says. But her blood does not believe it.

THIRTY-THREE

An endless row of steel torsos travels past the children's wide eyes as they peer through a window into one of the assembly rooms. The torsos emerge on a conveyor belt from a featureless circular hole in the wall on the right side of the room. They pass under a series of skeletal parodies of human arms that dangle from the ceiling, elongated spidery steel things ending in hands with digits twice as long as those of a normal adult's. Quickly, each pair of arms hanging over the belt performs a different task, tossing components from hand to hand with the unerring dexterity of professional jugglers: lifting the torso from the belt; picking up a stainless-steel head from a second belt that runs perpendicular to the first and beneath it; deftly screwing the head onto the torso; placing the new head-torso assemblage back onto the belt, where it goes into a hole in the opposite wall to be routed to other rooms, where arms and legs will be added.

"I'll bet you thought the *stork* brought your mechanical servants to your offices and homes," Prospero says to the boys and girls whose jaws are gaping (and Prospero is remembering what his publicist told him just this morning: *Remember, when you're taking the kids on the tour and you're talking to them, to put a smile in your voice.* The expression seems stupid to him: he's not good with literary devices. He wouldn't know how to begin to make a voice that has the shape of a smile: that seems absurd. But he figures that if he smiles when he's speaking, his voice will somehow come out right, will not be frightening as it can sometimes be: he is trying his best). He forces a chuckle out of his throat: "Haw *hah*! You see now: they're made *here*, in factories like this all over Xeroville, and in other distant cities, too, where people speak strange languages!"

The boy standing next to Harold stares through the glass. He is fat-faced and freckled, his head topped with a mop of chaotically curly deep red hair that his rakishly skewed checkered cap can't manage to tame. He is clearly troubled: his lower lip quivers as if he's about to cry. "Uncle Prospero?" he says.

"What's . . . what's your name. Little one."

"Sebastian." The boy turns away from the window, away from the seemingly infinite parade of torsos and heads, to face Prospero. Harold remains transfixed by the scene on the other side of the glass, pressing his palms to the window to feel the rhythmic thunder and throb of the machines as they build the tin men. Beats nested within beats flange and come into sync as the machines whisper a percussive song to the tips of his fingers. He feels it, and by feeling it, he hears it. It is one of the most beautiful things he has ever heard.

"Well, Sebastian," Prospero says, "do you have a question for me?"

Sebastian balks for a moment, the other boys and girls (except for the mesmerized Harold) staring at him, then says, "Does this mean I can't be a mechanical man when I grow up?"

Naïve children's questions like this make Prospero acutely uncomfortable. *Smile in the voice. Smile in the voice.* "I'm afraid so," he says. "But don't let that make you feel like you're not special. Sure, mechanical men might have superhuman strength, and inexhaustible stamina, but do you know what you have, that they don't?"

"What?" Sebastian asks, hands clasped behind his back, innocent eyes looking up.

Prospero bends to look Sebastian in the eye. "A soul," he says, his voice just above a whisper now, with a hint of a tremor in it. "Our company files five new patent applications each week, and our technology advances faster than we can keep up with it, but we still—"

—extending one of his narrow, bony fingers and placing its tip on Sebastian's chest—

"—haven't been able to duplicate *this*."

Prospero rises and turns, gazing through the plate glass at the movements of the automatic assembly line. The sets of arms hanging from the ceiling sway back and forth, going about their tasks with inhuman grace, conducting a symphony born from the thrumming of the conveyor belts beneath them and the muffled noises of machines in nearby chambers.

"Not yet," he says.

THIRTY-FOUR

An excerpt from the sixth of the seventeen notebooks of Caliban Taligent (which sit before me in a stack on the desk in the zeppelin's observation room, both sides of their pages filled with line after line of his single-spaced script, his letters cramped and careful, almost as if they issued from a typewriter instead of a human hand):

> —I sometimes fear that when my father's name receives its final, indelible inscription in History's long and unforgiving ledger, it will only be with the additional notation that he was a man without a soul. This is not so. As much as I hate my father, I must admit that Prospero Taligent is an extremely soulful person, even more so than most of us blundering our way through this new twentieth century. But Father refuses to believe that there is something in the world, some idea, that can be understood by none but a God dreamed up by humankind and defined in terms of his own unimaginability. The idea that a blueprint for the human spirit lies locked in a treasure-chest in Heaven, its codes indecipherable to all eyes but those of angels, is revolting to him. If this makes Father soulless, would that we were all men without souls.
>
> For example. I have pointed out to Father on several

occasions that perhaps a machine that desires to mimic the human form, with the greatest accuracy possible with our current technology and construction methods, is not a device that would have optimal design efficiency. Perhaps we might add a third leg for greater stability, or fashion the neck so that the head could swivel about completely, instead of being limited to some hundred fifty degrees of arc. However, Father is as much an aesthete as he is a technician. He desires to build the best machine that he can, but it also seems that he desires to construct a human being, with a soul, from scratch. To his mind, these desires are not incompatible; in fact, they are one and the same.

If Father ever does manage to achieve his grand design, he will have proved two things: that souls exist (a belief that has been considered more or less heretical in respectable intellectual circles for a good many years); and that they are not inexplicable or beyond our comprehension, as those who lived during the long-forgotten age of miracles believed, but that they are objects that can be observed, measured, under-stood, and constructed.

My father does have a soul. He just thinks of souls in a different way. I myself am living proof of that.

THIRTY-FIVE

"Once upon a time," Uncle Prospero says, "there was a virgin queen."

The children are in the Tower's library. Shelf after shelf of books parade orderly before their sensation-gorged eyes: books bound in leather with metal clasps holding them shut; books with spines of glass, their titles delicately etched in frost; ancient books so large they require three strong men to take them down and open them, with lavish, photo-realistic illustrations that are twice the size of life. Mechanical men sort and shelve texts that have lost their places, cradling volumes in their

spindly but strong arms, climbing up and down varnished wooden lad-
ders with casters on their bases that can be moved along the shelves.

"A virgin queen," Prospero says to the children, who are gathered
together around a small circular table on the library's floor, illuminated
by a shimmering pool of white light from a high-powered ceiling lamp
several stories above. The lamp casts its beam downward in a brilliant
column defined by the dust motes floating through it, and on the table
beneath it lies a book that seems several centuries old to Harold, the
edges of its pages covered with gilding and mold. Harold is at the back
of the crowd of children, having lagged behind them on the tour, and so
he is jumping as high as he can, catching glimpses of the book bathing
luxuriously in its pool of light (and, yes, the light is indeed doing irrepa-
rable damage to the aged volume, but never fear: Prospero normally
keeps it in climate-controlled darkness with the other copies he owns,
but for this moment, with the children, he believes that theatrics are
warranted). The book is open to one of its first pages: —Bote-ſwaine. —
Heere Maſter: What cheere? To Harold the language seems like his own,
but also somehow different, and he wonders what happened to the
meaning of these old words in the meantime that made them shift their
shapes. —Tend to th'Maſters whiſtle: Blow till thou burſt thy winde, if
roome enough. —Mercy on vs. Weſplit.

"A virgin queen," Uncle Prospero says, "and every last man in the
kingdom she ruled was her aspiring paramour. They were born loving
her, and they continued to love her from cradle to grave, though none of
them could ever have her, and they knew it. This is the root of the beautiful paradox. All the men in the kingdom knew that, if they were ever to
convince the virgin queen to love them, in the moment she was kissed, in
the moment she was touched, she would cease to be what they desired.
Not a virgin queen; just an ordinary queen, like any other."

—we run ourſelues a ground—

Prospero reaches out and runs a finger along the green gilded edge of
the folio's page, his face entranced. "There was an agreement between all
the men, and it was never spoken of, because no one ever needed to speak
of it. The agreement was this: they could hold contests and duels and
chess matches to decide who loved and deserved her the most; they could
compose songs and dances; they could boast of their prowess and they

could abase themselves at her feet. But never, *never*, could they touch her. For the moment one of them laid a finger on her, brushed a tear from her eye, caressed the space on her neck where the hair was too short to be combed and too fine to be seen: at that moment there would be no more contests, and no more dances, and no more songs, and the dances and songs were what made the world beautiful, and the virgin queen was what made it possible for the world to be beautiful. This was the power, and the curse, of their undying love."

Prospero removes his finger from the book, lifting his gaze to look into the eyes of a wisp of a dark-haired girl facing him on the other side of the table. "This," he says, "is a book of lovesongs, composed for the virgin queen by one of her most talented and fervent admirers. It is a catalog of all the many forms of love that one human being can have for another. There is the love between father and son, of mother for daughter; love between soldiers bleeding to death in each other's arms; love possessive, love obsessive; love of men for women, and for power, and for the mirror images they see in other men's faces; and there is jealousy as well, and hatred, for these, too, are forms of love: twisted, but true all the same—"

(The children are completely bewildered. It was real neat at first, being in the Tower, I mean, what are the kids back at school gonna say about *this*, we were in the Taligent *Tower*, we saw all kinds of *crazy* stuff, lots of cool *machines*, aw holy cripes we saw them *putting together mechanical men*, but now this guy has us in his dumb old library and he's going on about this book and love and stuff, and every time he says the word *love* it's weird, like when your mother tells you she loves you it's weird enough, but it's your mother, you know, but when your *father* says he loves you it's *really* weird, like maybe he's drunk or getting ready to die or something, but no, he just *said* it, this *word*, and this old guy just keeps saying it over and over again, I wish he would stop—)

—*Have mercy on vs. We ſplit. We ſplit. We ſplit.*

THIRTY-SIX

From the sixth notebook of Caliban Taligent:

—By day I am worse than a beast, but at night . . . oh, at night I have the loveliest dreams. At night the chessmaster and the poet within me combine to give me fantasies of such rampant hubris that I am shamed upon waking from them. In my dreams legions come to worship me, and they gather before me and cry out with one voice, "What have we done to deserve you as a deity, you, Caliban, whose name is used as a curse, you with your twisted face and your blackened, shriveled heart?" And I must reply to them, "You made me. God made man in his own image, so man returns the favor by remaking the face of God again and again, changing His image to suit constantly shifting faith and fashion. This is what you have done to me. You made me. You."

THIRTY-SEVEN

The tour of the Taligent Tower has reached its final stop, and the children have still not seen Miranda, their hostess. They are seated in the five front rows of a concert hall, intimately designed, but still large enough to hold a few hundred. The lights in the house are up. Prospero stands in front of a deep-red velvet curtain hanging in front of the stage. An enormous tarpaulin covers the entire orchestra pit, and oddly shaped lumps beneath the canvas suggest some things beneath it that are clearly not musical instruments.

"Supersonic-train conductor." "Firefighter." "Flying car pilot."

"Typewriter girl." "Dollmaker." Prospero has asked the children to tell him what they want to be when they grow up, and they are naming off occupations, one by one. Harold is sitting next to Sebastian in the back row: he will be the last. "Policeman." "Pawnshop owner." "Numbers runner." "Hired assassin." "Psychotherapist."

It is almost Harold's turn to speak, and he can't think of what to say. "Sebastian," Prospero says. "You can't be a mechanical man, and I'm sorry about that. But is there anything else you want to be?"

"We-e-e-ell," says Sebastian nervously, kicking his legs back and forth in the oversized seat, "the *other* thing I want to be when I grow up is a *vitrioleur*, b-b-but my mom, she said already that she ain't gonna send me to school for that, 'cause she said it's too expensive and only a few of 'em can get steady work."

Prospero recalls what his publicist said: *Remember, you have to inspire them.* "You shouldn't give up on your dream, just because of something silly like money," he says. This sounds inspirational, he thinks. "You're young, and you have the future in front of you, and you can have *anything you want* if you want it enough. You can even have all the perfect things in the world that could ever be, all at once. Because that's what the future is: *possibility.*"

"But my mom, she said the people always sayin' stuff like that is the same people that's got all the money anyway and they don't know what it is to have to live hand to mouth paycheck to paycheck—"

"—ahem that's very nice. And you."

"Harry. Harry Winslow."

"Harry. What do you want to be? When you grow up."

The thing is, up to now, Harold hasn't really given much thought to what he wants to be. Strange: it seems that all the other children in the audience, rattling off their responses so easily, are already thinking of themselves as adults. But Harold hasn't made that cognitive leap yet. The things that adults do aren't things he imagines himself doing: reading the newspaper; making things with his hands and selling them for money; touching parts of women's bodies. For Harold there are no newspapers, and the radio tells him the news of the world; money appears whenever it wants, dropping from his father's hand into his; girls would be just like boys, if they didn't insist on acting so strange.

But everyone in the hall is waiting—the children are turned around, looking over the high backs of their chairs at him, and now he's getting nervous. He needs to come up with something. He thinks back to what his father said to him a few days ago: *So be on your best behavior. Remember everything you see. When you come back, write it down. I'll buy you some pens and some clean new paper, and you can sit at my desk and write down everything you remember.* Maybe that can be a job. Maybe you can make a job out of writing things down? Yes. "I want to write things down!" Harold blurts. "I want to write stories down. I like"—and now it dawns on him, really occurs to him for the first time, that all stories have makers as well as listeners—"listening to stories. So maybe I might like telling them, too. Sir!"

"Beautiful," Prospero says. "Fantastic. It's good to have ambition, and in the past age of miracles there were indeed many professional storytellers who traveled from town to town, paying for their room and board with tales of the lands they'd come from, or lands they'd just imagined. But those days are gone, child, and this is the age of machines. Have you thought of what will happen to you if you want to tell a tale and no one can hear you or has the time to listen? Have you thought about trying to tell a tale in a crowded room, where everyone is shouting to be heard?

"Storytelling—that's not the future. The future, I'm afraid, is flashes and impulses. It's made up of moments and fragments, and stories won't survive."

THIRTY-EIGHT

"Well," Prospero says to the audience of children, "you all seem to have *wonderful* aspirations for the future, but none of you have fallen into my trap! I was hoping that one of you boys and girls would say that you wanted to be a *musician*, because then I would get to tell you that you had better find another line of work, and fast!" He calls offstage: "Gideon! Martin! Uncover my mechanical orchestra!"

At this summons the two men, wearing spotless laboratory gowns,

emerge from one of the hall's side doors. With some struggle they remove the tarpaulin from the orchestra pit, rolling it into a tube which
they carry out the way they came in, one of them supporting either end.
Gideon waves at the group of kids in the auditorium as he leaves, and
Harold wonders which of the other children in the crowd had directly
been subjected to his hustle.

With its cover gone, the children can now see in the pit a machine of
ludicrously sprawling complexity. It has all of the instruments of a conventional orchestra, arranged in their traditional positions, but the instruments are all inextricably entangled in a nest of levers and pulleys
and rods, along with many mechanical devices that resemble the spidery
elongated arms that Harold had seen earlier, hanging from the ceiling of
the room where the mechanical men were being assembled. Bellows are
attached to the horns and woodwinds; mechanical hands with pencil-
thin fingers are poised over the strings of a pair of harps.

In the center of the orchestra pit is a large, ornately carved cabinet
from whose back a hundred levers sprout, each in a different direction.
Each lever is indirectly connected through a chain of devices to one of
the mechanical orchestra's instruments. Installed in the front of the cabinet is a scroll housed on an enormous wooden rod; it is about ten feet
wide and seems as if it might be a mile long if unrolled. The scroll is
punched with thousands of holes in a series of lines that appear to run
its length, in parallel.

A crank with a large, filigreed brass handle protrudes from the side of
the cabinet; its purpose is to turn the enormous scroll in its housing. Sitting next to the crank is a plushly cushioned, wooden three-legged stool,
for its operator.

"Nowadays," Prospero says, "when people wish to hear music that is
live, instead of phonographic, they have to hire several, sometimes *hundreds* of performers. It is extremely expensive and impractical, is it not?
One finds oneself wondering if the expenditure is worth the reward. But
my mechanical orchestra will change all that. Encoded within the scroll
that you see in this cabinet, here, is an entire piece of music. And just
the way that a human musician has a scoresheet that tells him what notes
to play and how to play them, this scroll tells the mechanical orchestra
what notes to play. The difference is that where it once took many, many

people to perform a piece of music, people who had to be sent to school for training, wasting years of life in the process that might be spent in more productive ways: now it only takes one person, turning that crank, right there."

Prospero smiles. "Ladies and gentlemen, performing Jean Sibelius's Opus 109, *The Tempest*: my daughter, Miranda Taligent." And the girl comes onto the stage.

Her clothing is odd: first, because it is several centuries out of fashion; second, because it seems to be the sort of thing one might wear if one is the guest of honor at a coronation, rather than a birthday party. Every inch of Miranda's spare body is concealed except for her tiny hands, which peek forth from the billowing sleeves of an overdress, elegantly embroidered and decorated in a pattern of entangled vines of ivy, flirting with the concept of tessellation without actually repeating itself. The overdress opens down the middle, revealing a second dress, a forepart, decorated with a complex pattern of silvery intermeshing gears of different sizes. This pattern also refuses to repeat itself, as if in imitation of the intricately entwining vines of the overdress. A white ruff a yard across encircles the little girl's neck, and its effect is to make Miranda's head, with her porcelain-powdered face and her shimmering red-gold hair piled atop it in a series of intertwining braids, seem as if it is a solitary gourmet delicacy on a plate, waiting to be devoured.

She moves awkwardly across the stage, as if her clothing is reinforced with hoops of iron, and comes to stand next to her father, facing the bedazzled children. "Good day," she says, her vowels perfect and discrete, her consonants sharp and clipped. "My name is Miranda. Today is my birthday. Welcome to my Tower. I will perform for you."

And with that, the little girl turns stiffly, winces as if she is in pain, leaves the stage, and descends into the pit.

THIRTY-NINE

A mechanical Prospero moves toward center stage, in front of a backdrop upon which is painted an impressionistic image of a tranquil island shore populated by palm trees, the sun a perfect yellow suspended in a field of cloudless blue. Unlike the mechanical men seen thus far (which were clearly made from one kind of metal or another), the mechanical Prospero is almost indistinguishable from the real one (now seated next to Harold to watch Miranda's performance). From this distance, indescribable, but still somehow perceptible, irregularities in its movements and gait are the only signs that the automaton is less, or other, than human. "The skin is rubber," Prospero says. "The hair is from human heads. These are our best mechanical men. Prototypes: you wouldn't *believe* how expensive they are to manufacture." For the duration of the performance Prospero talks to Harold nonstop, raising his voice to compete with the music and the voices (yes, the voices) of the mechanical performers on the stage. "We only have a very few so far, some of which are on this stage, the rest of which populate Miranda's playroom. I know they may look more like living humans than you may be used to, but there's no need to be afraid. We're just now learning how to mechanically duplicate the subtler movements of the human body. Do you have any idea how complicated a larynx is? A device that you use countless times each day without even having to give a single thought to the complexity of its construction? It's taken us years to find the proper combination of strings and weights—look. Here's Ariel, the sprite. He's going to sing."

"Hør, hør, hvor kjæk og kry hanen galer højt i sky, højt i Sky! Kykke-liky!" sings Ariel in a mezzo-soprano with slight undertones that speak of tin and clockwork. The androgynous machine, child-sized, naked, and covered in glittering golden paint, hangs suspended by cables above the stage, a windup key grinding in its back. "Hør, hør! Vov, vov! Hunden gjøer; Vov, vov!" But Harold's ears are attuned to something else, a second symphony playing itself out under the harmonies of the Sibelius, composed of the rumbling trundling of the coded scroll as it rotates in its housing in the central cabinet, the clicks and snicks of the levers and drivers that move the bows across the strings, and the motors that grumble sullenly in the guts of the singers.

Now a new automatic actor comes onto the stage, capering and stumbling on all fours like a damned idiot, covered in dirt, grasping the scarred, barren space in its crotch where its genitalia ought to be. Its hair is made from shining twisted copper wires, and its head is turned around backward on its neck. "Ban! Ban! Caliban!" it yells, out of time with the music, falling to the floor and clumsily picking itself up. "Ban! Ban! Caliban!" On the opposite side of the stage, the fake Prospero in his necromancer's robes and the fake Miranda in her outgrown swaddling rags shrink away in mock-theatrical terror, turning their heads and throwing their arms in front of their faces. The flesh-and-blood Miranda in the pit goes on patiently turning the crank at the heart of the orchestral machine, staring at nothing.

"Ban! Ban! Caliban! Ban! Ban! Caliban!"

"There he is," Prospero whispers to Harold, his voice trembling. "The beast."

FORTY

"Harry," Prospero says later, placing his hand on the boy's shoulder, "perhaps I shouldn't have been so hard on you when you told me of your wishes. It isn't nice to have someone else dash your dreams for you, is it? It gives you the same feeling you get when you've been caught doing something shamefully wrong. The feeling that you've been exposed. As if you're reciting a poem to a roomful of great-aunts and your trousers drop.

"Harry, there is something I like about you, but I can't put my finger on it yet. I've made a mistake, but let me try to fix it. There are no preterite storytellers, Harry; remember that. I'll make the storyteller the luckiest boy, so he'll have a story to tell the other boys at school. I want you to meet my daughter. At the birthday banquet you will sit at my daughter's right hand."

FORTY-ONE

And so, at Prospero's request, Harold Winslow sits to the right of Miranda Taligent at her fabulous birthday banquet. The children are back in the banquet hall where they began today's adventure. The two mudslinging girls that had messed up their clothing with fighting have returned, wearing brand-new, beautiful dresses that look like they were bought off the rack at the same establishment where Miranda's coronation gown was handmade: the embroidery is not quite as elaborate, and the ruffs are not quite as large, but they are still most impressive. "We watched these *made* for us," the formerly squabbling girls sing in harmony to envious onlookers. "Mechanical seamsters measured us and *made* them to fit us and no one else, all in a snap and a flash. It was *worth* getting in trouble." The girls sit across the table from Harold, swinging their legs back and forth, holding hands.

Miranda's body, already ensconced in layers of clothing, is swallowed up by the thronelike chair in which she sits at the head of the banquet table. All the girls are seated in a long line of fifty on Miranda's left; the boys are facing them on her right. Prospero sits opposite Miranda at the far end of the long table, in silence. Keeping up his charm with the children has cost him a good deal of energy, so he quietly eats, serving himself from the bowls and platters of colorful vegetables, fresh breads, succulent meats, and decadent sweets that cover the table. As soon at the children sat down they started in on the food with abandon. No preliminary pauses for decorum, no saying grace, no toasts with goblets of seltzer water: they are too young yet to feel the need for rituals and politeness. No chemical solutions and essences for them: they know the pleasure of the texture of food on the tongue and the pain of an overfilled stomach.

Harold is so nervous that he doesn't know if he can keep his food down. This close up, Miranda looks really weird. Her face is covered with a thick layer of powder, as white as the banquet table's cloth. Her lips are painted bright red, and she stares in front of her, her bright blue eyes unblinking, mechanically placing forkfuls of food in her mouth. The girl's manners are impeccable.

He feels uncomfortable. The boy sitting next to him, named William, is forgoing the use of utensils and shoveling food down his throat with both hands. He is larger than Harold, and he has curly, tousled black hair that hangs over his forehead in front of his eyes, and thick eyebrows that join above his nose. More hairs are scattered across his cheeks and chin, not enough to merit shaving, but enough to mark him as older than Harold, and old enough to have nothing to say to him. Miranda is weird, and he was half hoping that the girls who now look like Miranda's handmaidens would at least try to talk to Miranda, leaving him to listen to girlish conversations in puzzlement or sink into a brown study. But the handmaidens are busy becoming the best of friends, entwining their arms together and placing spoonfuls of food into each other's mouths, whispering into each other's ears, swearing eternal fealty to each other in a secret language they've just now invented, that only the two of them speak. They laugh in a dozen different ways at private jokes: giggles; guffaws; snorts that make milk fly out their noses. Boys don't make friends like this, Harold thinks—not so close, not so quickly. Girls don't understand that friendships are a risk. Ill-chosen loyalties will earn you split lips during recess. Girls don't do due diligence.

He has to talk to Miranda. What will his father and Astrid and the boys at school say when he tells them that he couldn't talk to Miranda? First, though, he has to get her attention. "Hey," he says. He means to speak in a normal voice, but the word comes out as a croak. A pit forms in his stomach. "Hey."

Miranda says nothing; she doesn't even look at him.

Carefully, then, as if risking electric shock, Harold reaches out and taps Miranda with one finger, on the large white ruff that surrounds her neck.

Miranda's head swivels forty-five degrees on its neck to face Harold. She stretches her neck and swallows the food in her mouth like a bird. "Do not touch me," she says. "Don't."

He snatches his hand back, as if from open flame. "Sorry?" he says. "Sorry!" This is all turning out wrong.

Miranda stares at Harold, pursing her lips. She holds her fork in midair. Her gaze is boring a hole through him.

Hello, Miranda. That's it. That's all you need to say to start.

But it isn't that easy, is it?

"Huh," says Harold. "Hey."

Miranda blinks, once, slowly.

"Hey!" says Harold. "D—"

Miranda frowns.

"Hey?" says Harold.

Not even a blink this time.

"Hey," says Harold. "Do you like stuff?"

Miranda blinks. Doing better.

Emboldened, Harold tries again. "Do you like to *do* stuff?"

Miranda blinks, twice.

"I like all *kinds* of stuff," Harold says. "I like taking pictures of things with stereoscopic cameras, and listening to stories about captains of industry, and watching my father make dolls. What kinds of stuff do *you* like to do?"

Miranda opens her mouth and monotone words tumble out of it. "I like to sleep. I like all the different varieties of sleep: dozes, slumbers, stupors, comas . . . I like dreams, because they are stronger than memories. I have a recurring dream; in it, I am asleep, sleeping a sleep that is too deep for dreams. It is my favorite dream." She closes her mouth. She blinks.

"You talk funny for a little girl," Harold says.

"You will have to forgive me," says Miranda. "I have not yet learned the ways in which words work. I have not yet comprehended their rhythms and rules: I do not know which words are best for secrets, and which for advertisements."

"It's adver*tise*ments," Harold says, exasperated. "Not ad*ver*tisements."

There is a pause, during which Miranda continues to stare at Harold, blinking and occasionally cocking her head winsomely to one side, still holding her fork in the air above the plate, while the other guests, the ones *not* sitting at Miranda's right hand, gnaw on jellied candies, and sticks of dark chocolate dusted with powdered sugar and dipped in caramel.

The doll! Maybe it's time to show her the doll. "Do you want to see something my father made?" Harold sinks down into the seat so he can reach into the pocket of his pants.

Miranda looks distressed. "My father makes lots of things!" She drops the fork and it clangs against the plate. At the other end of the table Prospero looks up from his food, at his daughter.

"My dad's not an inventor, like your dad," Harold says, clutching his hand around the little windup doll his father gave him. "He makes things with plans someone else gives him. But he made this." Harold places the doll on the table, turns the windup key in its back, and lets it go. The tin Miranda lifts its arms and begins to totter across the table toward its namesake.

"It's Miranda!" Harold says. "You can have it."

Miranda, the real one, looks horrified. "Take it away!" she cries.

The doll trips on a fold in the tablecloth and falls on its face. Miranda puts her hand to her mouth and makes a noise somewhere between a yelp and a wail. Her eyes are stretched to the size of saucers.

"Okay, okay!" Harold picks up the doll, its metal legs still scissor-kicking, and puts it in his lap, out of sight.

"I do not *like* you!" Miranda says. "Don't!"

Harold says nothing.

For a minute or two, Harold and Miranda both look down at their plates, pushing around stray bits of cold food. Harold reaches over to a silver tray full of chocolate sticks, takes one, and chews on it. It tastes bitter, not the way he feels that chocolate should. He wants to go home and listen to the radio. He wishes he'd never come here.

"I am not yet very good at conversations," Miranda says.

"No kiddin'," Harold says.

At the other end of the table, Prospero Taligent rises and gently taps the blade of his knife against his glass. It's finest crystal, and one clear ring from it cuts through all the high-pitched chatter in the hall and brings all the boys and girls to silence.

FORTY-TWO

"Children," Prospero says. "My guests. I've shown you wonders and stuffed your bellies, and now it is time for the giving of gifts. It is time, for a moment, for each of us to have the thing that we desire.

"You boys and girls are too young to understand this yet, but it's endless unsatisfied desire that makes us human, that binds our spirits to flesh that it would rather do without. Even now, at this young age, you know the discontent of wanting something and not yet having it, and not even knowing the name of the thing that you want. This is why it's good manners to give gifts in wrappers: so that, for a moment, that beast in all of us that makes us feel alive and keeps us from becoming angels can be satisfied. While a gift is in its wrapper, it can be anything, even that one indescribable thing that will make us happy enough to die in peace."

(The boys and girls look at each other in stunned confusion, crumbs in their laps and chocolate smeared across their faces. Now he's talking about dying. This is such a weird birthday party.)

"If I were the kind of man who believed in God, I would tell you that Miranda, my adopted daughter, the only person in this world who I can truly claim to love, is that gift from God to me. And because I am so happy that you have all come to be guests in my Tower to celebrate her birthday, I want to give each of you a gift, as well as Miranda. You will not receive these gifts today. However, I and my many servants visible and invisible have been watching each and every one of you for the entire day. And we will continue to watch over you from shadows, all one hundred of you, after you leave this place; even after you've become adults, perhaps with little boys and girls of your own.

"Sometime, in the future, my gift to you will come. It may not be for several days; it may not be for many years; it may not be until I myself am long dead and you in your old age have long forgotten about me. Perhaps my gift to you will be something as simple as a single word, whispered into your ear by one of my servants as you lie on your deathbed, a word that solves a final mystery and makes it easy for you to slip quietly into the dark. But, in honor of this day, and in honor of Miranda, I promise you that each and every one of you will have your heart's desires fulfilled."

William, the boy sitting next to Harold, turns to him and sneers, "I wouldn't get your hopes up. It's just fairy stories for children, to keep us entertained. He doesn't mean a thing he says." William makes a nasty face and shows Harold a tongue laden with chewed mush. Miranda frowns in disgust.

"But now," Prospero says, "it is my daughter's turn." He strides past the banquet table, to the large double doors at the opposite end of the hall. With a flourish, he throws open the huge doors simultaneously and steps back.

"Bring it in," he says.

FORTY-THREE

A spiraling ivory horn emerges from the center of its skull, just beneath the forelock. The unicorn, its eyes the color of black coffee, trots slowly across the parquet of the banquet hall, past the children who are so oversaturated with the day's wonders that they can do nothing but stare. Its coat is an unblemished white, and its mane streams white behind it; its hooves are shod in gleaming steel. It obediently follows the man who's leading it by its gem-encrusted halter and stops in the center of the hall.

Miranda pushes back her little throne and rises. She turns in seeming slow motion and glides across the hall to the unicorn, close enough to touch it, then places her tiny ear to its broad chest, running her fingers along the gentle indentations of its ribs, caressing its croup and its flank.

"See," Prospero says, joining her, placing his hand on her shoulder. "It's real. It's not a machine. You can feel its warmth and the beat of its heart. I didn't lie to you, even though I looked in your eyes and saw that you didn't believe me. It's as real as you and me."

"Father," Miranda says, her ear pressed up against the horse's side, her arms spread across it in an attempted embrace. A falling tear draws a narrow track in the powder that covers her face, revealing the flesh-tone beneath. "You shouldn't have. You shouldn't."

FORTY-FOUR

To Harold's relief, he's returned to his apartment from the Taligent Tower by a garden-variety taxicab instead of a perilous flying mechanical contraption. He runs upstairs and through the door. Allan has the pen and paper waiting for him as he promised—he's cleared off the desk where he makes his dolls, and a stack of fifty sheets of paper is there, next to a bottle of ink in which sits a pen with a newly sharpened nib.

But when Harold starts to write down a recount of the events of the day, they start to slip through his fingers. His mind feels like a sieve through which his experience is draining out, too quick for him to stop it. He captures a few fine details, here and there—*its metal legs still scissor-kicking; there was a virgin queen; uncover my mechanical orchestra*—but no matter how he tries he can't make the ink marks on the page represent the things he's seen with enough fidelity to be certain that someone else might read the words and be certain of the things he saw. Even worse than this is that he can feel his mind actively making up events from whole cloth to fill the blank spaces of his story that lie between those few things he *does* remember, and that as soon as it does this, he can't distinguish between the truths of his memory and the fictions of his necessary fantasies. After seven double-sided pages covered with his cramped script, he slams the pen down in frustration, spattering drops of ink across the desk.

"You can't get it down fast enough?" his father says.

"I can't," says Harold, rubbing his eyes. "It's all gone. Or it might not be. I don't even know. It was all so strange."

"It doesn't matter, really," says his father. "I no longer know whether my memory of the past is something I made up to please myself, or something that actually happened. I sometimes think on my childhood and how *wonderful* it was, and how mundane the time in which I now live seems by comparison. I *seem* to remember mornings playing games alone at the edge of a forest, and one of these mornings during which my noisy boy's antics startled a flock of angels to break from the cover of the nearby trees, and that as they rose to fly away one of them shed a single feather that fell right into my open hand, and that as I placed the feather in my mouth as village custom dictated: the taste, dear God, as it melted like a spun-sugar confection there was this indescribable, never-to-be-replicated *taste*—

"Did that really happen? Or do I merely believe that it happened? If the thought of this thing that I think is a memory consoles me at night when I lie in darkness, and the empty space and coldness of the bed reminds me of the vanished miracle of the woman I once loved, does it matter, one way or the other?

"Son: write down what you think happened, or what you believe happened, or something like what might have happened. All of these are better in the end than writing down nothing at all; all are true, in their own way."

FORTY-FIVE

When Astrid finishes reading Harold's fourteen handwritten pages, she looks at him and frowns. She is lying on her bed, surrounded by scattered colored pencils and the strange drawings on store-bought parchment paper with which she's been spending an increasing amount of her time in recent months. They are distant cousins of the drawings that Harold remembers himself making with crayons when he was much younger, of flying cars and mechanical men that he'd imagined before others had done the hard work to bring them into existence, but these pictures are much more obsessively detailed and disturbing—an old man whose left eye has been replaced with a telescopic camera lens, the wound of the apparently recent surgery still suppurating ichor; another grimacing man looking upward with the muscles of his neck stretched taut, who is nude and has a third mechanical leg joined to the space between his two real legs; a disgustingly corpulent woman with gimlet eyes who has a V-shaped flap cut into her stomach, pulled back to reveal a baby made of metal, nestled in a cocoon of its mother's fatty yellow flesh. The pictures don't make sense to Harold, and he tries his best not to look at them, though it's clear that gruesomeness aside, she has talent that exceeds her age. Maybe Astrid's drawing the things she says are inside her head, that she mentions sometimes. Their father explains them away by claiming that she's merely "going through a phase."

"Are you telling me this happened?" says Astrid, throwing the pages down.

"Yeah," says Harold. He doesn't tell her about the conversation that he just had with his father, nor that he feels he may have reason to doubt his own memory, at least a little. He read it back just after he finished writing it, and what was set down seemed true, or true enough.

"This doesn't seem like something that would happen to anybody," Astrid says. "The whole thing seems made-up."

"But you saw the demon," Harold says. "You saw it." *You talked to it and kissed it*, he doesn't say.

"Well I know, I know," says Astrid. "And I guess *that* must have been true, and if that was true, then the rest of it could be also. But what I'm saying—what I'm saying is this story here sounds like something that happens in a kid's book. Not something that happens to real people."

"Well, why?"

"It's like . . . it's like you left out all the meanness and the nastiness that's inside and under everything. If this had been something that really happened, then when something like this unicorn showed up here at the end, there would have been something mean and twisted behind it. Nothing's ever all-the-time happy or beautiful like this. It just isn't. Either you didn't understand what you were looking at today, or you just want to remember it all happily like this because it makes you feel better."

Harold protests, "But it *was*—"

"Get out of here and do some homework or go to sleep or something!" barks Astrid suddenly, giving Harold's writing back to him. She looks a little irritated now. "Get out of here—I'm drawing!" He obediently leaves and closes her bedroom door behind him.

She stays shut up in her room for the rest of the night, and well into the next day.

FORTY-SIX

Teaching helmets hang from cables over each desk of the classroom, ready to descend and dispense their knowledge. The desks themselves are barren. There is little or no paper in the twentieth-century classroom, and no paper means no idle, naughty games: no tic-tac-toe, no spitballs, no passing notes, no paper airplanes. Writing by hand is becoming a lost art.

The students in Harold's class sit discussing schoolyard happenings: who has a crush on whom, or blow-by-blow details of sandbox battles. It has been four months since Harold Winslow was a guest in the Taligent Tower. On his return to school he was asked a million different questions. ("Was Prospero mean? On newsreels he looks mean." "No. He was pretty nice." "Can he fly?" "No." "Did you see Miranda? Did you *kiss her*? Did you touch her—" *"No!"*) He recounted the tale of his adventure over and over until it sounded like a mindless litany in his own ears, devoid of meaning. Now, however, he is no longer famous, not even by schoolyard standards. He does not even have the half-decent reputation of a has-been, not like that other kid in the class who still carries disfiguring scars across his face, earned during some misadventures in forbidden culs-de-sac of a local chocolate factory.

Now the teacher comes into the room, grumbling: "—don't know why they don't fire us all, cutting our salaries whick-whack, may as well hire goddamned tin men, see what the little whelps learn from—good *morning*, kids." As always, she is frazzled and disheveled, but teaching doesn't really take much these days. She goes over to her desk, removes a large bag from her shoulder, and fishes a book out of it, seemingly at random. "Okay, then," she sighs. "Whose turn is it to help me operate the teaching machine."

Six children raise their hands and squeal. The teacher picks one, a girl in blond pigtails who springs to her feet with a grin and bounds over to the teaching machine, a contraption that takes up most of the back wall of the classroom. Its major discernible features are a wide, funnel-shaped chute on its top, a series of incandescent lamps of different bright colors, and a crank, which the student in pigtails is to turn. A huge bundle of cables leads out of the top of the machine to the ceiling, and each cable in the bundle leads to one of the helmets that hang over the children's heads, ready to descend.

The pigtailed girl begins to turn the crank industriously, slowly at first, then faster as she builds up momentum. The bank of lights on the side of the machine begin to flicker, then brightly burn. The teacher then pulls a lever on the side of the machine, and as a mechanism plays out the bundle of cables, the teaching helmets, which look something like colanders with steel earmuffs attached, drop snugly over the students' heads. Harold hates this moment, when the learning begins: it's always the worst, and never fails to make him nauseous.

The teacher opens the large volume in her hand, tears out a random page, and drops it into the teaching machine's chute.

With a suddenness, the world goes black and things are known. "Sometime in the 1540s, the nature of English costume drifted away from German influences, becoming significantly transformed in the process by styles of dress that were emigrating from Spain." There is no way to avoid the knowledge being seared into his mind by the teaching machine, no escape to daydream. Sometimes Harold comes awake at four a.m., his bedclothes drenched in sweat, reciting lengthy passages from Shakespeare, manuals for the operation of mechanical men, whole books whose words he knows but cannot even comprehend. "Not even the hostility felt towards Spain in England could weaken the influence of Spanish fashions; the tendency toward solemnity symbolized by the ruff and farthingale had its origin in the Spanish court."

The girl in pigtails continues to turn the crank with a smile. She is happy because she does not have to learn. The teacher drops in another page: "Under the rule of Elizabeth I, luxurious, expensively decorated garments still remained under Spanish influence, lending them a stiff, artificial appearance. Many historians judge that women's costume of this period, more elaborately worked and tending to be made in fresh spring colors, may reflect, at least in part, the Virgin Queen's efforts to recapture her fading charms God damn it I don't know how they expect me to conduct a class with all these interruptions." A blinding bolt of pure pain arcs across Harold's skull as the teacher yanks the helmet off his head and grabs him by his tiny arm. "What are you *doing*?" Harold yells. The rest of the students, held captive by the teaching machine, stare straight ahead in their seats with glazed eyes and perfect posture, hands on their desks with their fingers interlocked. "Come on," the teacher says, jerking Harold from his chair, halfway pulling his arm out of its socket. "There's a car for you outside. From Miss La-di-da Miranda Taligent. You bigheaded brat." She spits at him: "You've been *summoned*."

FORTY-SEVEN

PLAYROOM

is the single word stenciled on the single door in the center of the long hallway in which Harold finds himself. The hallway is otherwise feature-less: white-tiled walls; white ceiling; white floor. The corridor stretches interminably and turns at either end, just before the vanishing point. Other than Harold, the hallway is empty, and dead quiet. He is alone.

Harold surveys his options and decides that they are limited: to enter the door, or to wander down the hallway until he finds some other exit. Being lost inside the Taligent Tower does not appeal to him.

The playroom door has a large spherical polished brass knob, which Harold grasps clumsily in both hands. The door is heavy and oaken, but weighted to swing open easily, and as Harold slowly pushes it, a breeze beckons from the other side, smelling of sea salt.

FORTY-EIGHT

Island beach sun sky tree wheel around him. He is dizzy and sick. Beach sun sky tree island bird bright girl unicorn. This is worse than the teaching machine. The door behind him has swung shut. Too much to see. Leaf sand glare yellow blue. It is like reading two books, one with each eye, and understanding them both. There's too much to see, and smell, and touch beneath him as he drops weakly to his knees in the seashore sand, and too much to hear. Someone, a comforter, is at his side, small and dressed in white: white fedora, white suit, white shirt, white tie, white slacks, white socks, smartly polished white leather shoes. Her reddish golden hair is loosely knotted in a strand of white lace and falls from beneath her hat, streaming down her back. Her unicorn stands reined to a palm tree, sleeping on its feet.

Sun beach sky island tree. Green grainy bright unicorn girl white. Harold is puking on his knees by the island seashore. Miranda has a gentle hand on his back, stroking it. "It always hurts like this the first time. My father made this place more real than the places you're used to being in, and it's hard to get used to so many new and different sights and sounds and smells all at once. You'll be fine soon. I've learned to use contractions better since we spoke last."

"They pulled me out of school," Harold stammers. Only when he speaks these words aloud does he begin to comprehend the full magnitude of Prospero Taligent's power. He has done the unthinkable. "They pulled me out of *school*. In the middle of a lesson. And then I went through a door and now I'm on a desert island."

"No, it's not a desert island, silly," Miranda says, giggling. "You're still here, in the Tower. This place just looks like a desert island, but it's all done with illusions and mirrors and the cleverest machines. My father can't make people vanish and reappear somewhere else, like in storybooks you buy for a dime, and he doesn't have the power to banish or exile anyone. Some people think he's a magician, but he's not."

Gently, Miranda takes Harold in her arms and lays him on his back on the sand. She looks into his eyes, unsmiling, unblinking. Harold hears the sound of waves lapping against the beach. Miranda is silhouetted by the sun shining behind her.

"I don't want you to get the impression that, because you are my guest, you are my friend," she says. "I said that I don't like you, and I still don't. But we may as well make the best of things.

"This is my playroom, that my father made for me. This is where I learn my lessons. My father brought you here. And from now on you'll take your lessons with me."

FORTY-NINE

It is easy to see how one who did not know the entire story of the strange relationship between Prospero and Miranda Taligent might think that he did not love his daughter, or that he had no idea how to. But such a miraculous place as Miranda's playroom, which stretched to take up an entire floor of his Tower and fill it wall-to-wall with wonders, could only have been created out of love. It wore, of course, the guise of an island, but if a visitor to the playroom wished to deny himself the pleasure of self-deception, he could reach out and touch the walls on which were painted photo-realistic verdant landscapes with accurate vanishing perspectives, or swim a few hundred yards out into a false salt sea and, ducking his head beneath the surface, see the huge pumps that generated the waves that broke rhythmically across the island shore.

The contents of the playroom were never exactly the same from one day to the next. The ivy-covered walls of miniature labyrinths uprooted themselves in the small hours of the morning and, rolling around on metal casters and communicating to each other by means of radios implanted within them, rearranged themselves to create new patterns and produce new puzzles. Professional actors and actresses were paid to play the parts of island inhabitants that had been washed ashore, and mixed in with these were Prospero's finest mechanical men, so cleverly constructed that, unless one touched them and felt the absence of the warmth of human flesh, one would not easily be able to discern their difference.

An entire department of Taligent Industries was formed for the sole purpose of devising new entertainments for Prospero's daughter as she wandered her indoor island. At its heart were five men and five women who spent fifteen hours a day lying on their backs in beds of feather mattresses while a delicately balanced concoction of intravenous drugs kept them perpetually suspended in a state of dream. An additional hour was given over to recording the recollections of their dreams, which a team of engineers and artisans immediately began to realize within the space of the playroom. The other eight hours of each of their days was left to them, to indulge in the restfulness of staying awake. The ten dreamers never left the Tower, and sometimes the workers who pulled the graveyard shifts would see one of them, clad in a thick soft white terry-cloth robe, face sallow, muscles atrophied, running her fingers in confusion over a wall that obstinately refused to dissolve to allow passage through it, or walking repeatedly in wide-eyed bewilderment back and forth through a doorway that utterly failed to lead to another dimension.

FIFTY

And so, instead of attending classes in one of Xeroville's public schools, Harold was picked up at his home each day by an automobile with its doors embossed with the Taligent Industries logo, its driver sitting in silence behind the wheel, waiting each morning for the boy to come cautiously downstairs and out of the apartment building. He was then driven through the city to the Tower, whisked up by elevator to the playroom, and left there, to keep Miranda company. At the end of the day that same driver would pick him up at the playroom's entrance and return him home, where his father waited.

There were no lessons in Miranda's playroom in the formal sense, none of the rigorous daily structure imposed by the public school's instructors and teaching machines. Sometimes, as the two children wandered the island, either on foot or seated on the back of Miranda's unicorn, they would be presented with sudden conundrums, but they would be pleasures to solve, not tasks, and more like games than homework. As when the savage hurled himself out of a dense grove of palms and into their path, his face covered in symmetrical patterns of brightly colored paint, brandishing a long serrated knife with nicks and bloodstains along its edges, yelling, "Grrr! Arrgh! Quick now: man or machine—which are you? Only men can pass this way—which are you?"

"Silly savage," Miranda said, and giggled. "I'm not a man *or* a machine. I'm a *girl*." She deftly jumped from the unicorn's back and curtsied politely in her white linen dress. "And my companion is a boy. But he'll be a man, given time."

"Well, I wouldn't be so *sure* about that," the savage said, pointing his knife warily at Harold, who had by now removed himself clumsily from the back of the unicorn to stand beside the girl. The trunks of palm trees curved apselike over their heads, and shafts of sunlight cut through the fronds as they waved in a light wind, playing tiny spotlights across their faces. "They're getting better and better at making those machines every day. Why, I hear that some of the newest mechanical men don't even have any metal *parts* in them these days, but hearts that beat like ours, and skin that feels soft and warm to the touch. . . . *I* hear that in the future, they won't even need *factories* to make mechanical men; that instead, they'll come out of the wombs of real live screaming women, just like *you* did! And what will be the difference then? And how will I know who should be allowed to pass this way?"

Quickly, the savage inverted the blade in his hand and nicked himself in the upper arm with it. The three of them paused, watching silently as a small thick line of blood welled up from the cut. "See?" the savage said, licking his lips as, without warning, a shower of electric sparks sputtered from his ear, dying out as it descended. "Prick me: do I not bleed?"

FIFTY-ONE

It did not take long for Harold to commit the unforgivable sin that angered the ever-watching Prospero enough to have him banished from the playroom, and the Tower. Although Harold would return to the playroom briefly ten years later, he would not have the opportunity to look Prospero in the eye for twenty years after the banishment (and then, when the two of them are on the roof of the Taligent Tower, with the good ship *Chrysalis* ready to lift off, Prospero, with the barrel of the pistol in Harold's hand pressed against his stomach, will say, "You do realize that I couldn't make it easy for you. That would have been unfair to you, and her, and *me*. You do understand that?"). But for now, Harold and Miranda have the freedom not to worry about the gray-skied future: they simply let Time bring it to them, as it surely will, in time. They live moment by moment, in a world without clocks. They wander hand in hand through Paradise.

FIFTY-TWO

The playroom was a kind of paradise, but it had monsters, as if its designers felt that the absence of evil could only be appreciated when contrasted with its presence. But the monsters were toys, more or less: built to scare, but never to harm.

Harold and Miranda would play a game sometimes that they made up, called Damsel in Distress. They would separate, and while Miranda would hide herself, Harold would go down to the island's beach and brood, as idle heroes do when nothing is around to be vanquished. In his hand he would have a long metal sword, hollow, but weighted at the tip to give it a simultaneous sense of lightness and heft. It wasn't sharp enough to cut a stick of butter. This was play, after all.

Miranda's screams would come to Harold from somewhere on the island then, high-pitched and horror-film vixenish. "Help! *Hellllp!* The monster!" And Harold would jump to his feet and start running, following her gleeful yells, tracing them to the source. And there would be Miranda, in an ankle-length white dress, her back against a tree, and menacingly approaching her would be the monster, an eight-foot-tall jabberwock of a beast with a large, lumbering gait, and reddish green metallic scaly skin, and a long thick tail, and large yellow spherical rolling eyes, and jets of steam shooting out of its ears and nostrils and mouth, and both its clawed three-fingered hands raised over its head, as if to grab the girl and commit all manner of dastardly deeds.

At this point, Harold, the boy in short pants, screams, "Unhand her, knave!" or some equally heroic challenge, in a register about the same as Miranda's. Then the monster swivels to face him and they fight, Harold swinging with his dull sword at the monster's knees, each hit accompanied by the *whing* of metal on metal, the monster growling and sputtering and tottering around and randomly waving its arms, until the key in its back runs down and the monster falls over, inert. Then red-cheeked Miranda runs to Harold with a sighed "My hero!" and puts her arms around him and holds him close.

Once, though, something different happens. The game starts out in the same way, with Harold sitting at the shore, gripping the hilt of his toy sword in both his hands, pondering the eternal grave questions that concern heroes, until he hears the screams. But when he finds her, no beast is waiting to be obediently slain: there's just Miranda, alone in the middle of the copse, sitting cross-legged on the ground, weeping, both fists holding long frayed strands of her own hair, ripped out at the root. "He thinks he can get me," she says, "in *here*," and she begins to repeatedly thump the side of her skull with her index finger, as if she's trying to punch a hole through it. "But I know how to escape." She winds a turn of her red-gold hair into her chubby little fist and pulls it clean out. Beads of blood bloom in the newly bald spot. Harold, with a boy's simplicity, reaches out to touch her, not knowing what to say, but she jumps away from him: "Don't *touch* me! I'm going to escape. I'll weave my hair into a rope, and then I'll climb out of *here*." Tapping her head again. "Miranda," says Harold, "you're *scaring* me. Stop it." *Yank* and out comes another chunk of locks.

"I told you don't you *touch me!*" Backing off from him, stumbling and falling and getting up again, grabbing another hunk of hair in her hand. Harold, panicked, clumsily tackles her before she can do any more damage to herself, and as soon as he grabs her slender little sleeveless arm he feels the answering coldness of stainless steel. He touches his finger to a tear running down the girl's face, and then to his tongue: it's machine oil. "Silly boy," the real Miranda says, peeking out from behind a tree, laughing gaily. "You were trying to rescue the *monster.*"

FIFTY-THREE

The tip of a knife is buried the smallest fraction of an inch into the woman's skin, not even deep enough to draw blood, just at the place on her chest where the gentle swell of her breast begins. The knife is grasped by a hand; the hand belongs to a man who sits with his legs crossed in the sand, opposite his lover. His shirt is loosely buttoned, as is hers. The tip of a knife is buried the smallest fraction of an inch into his skin, not deep enough to draw blood. The knife is grasped by a hand; the hand belongs to a woman who sits with her legs crossed in the sand, opposite her lover. Her shirt is loosely buttoned, as is his. The tip of a knife is buried the smallest fraction of an inch into the woman's skin, not deep enough to draw blood, just at the place on her chest where the gentle swell of her breast begins.

They sit this way, in symmetry, in a circle drawn in the sand, and the boy and the girl stand outside the boundary, timid, hand in hand. No one moves.

The man in the circle has to pee, badly. He has had to pee for some time now.

"They weren't here yesterday," Miranda says.

"We are here," the woman says through clenched teeth, not daring to move a muscle, not willing to take her eyes off her lover's, even to look at Miranda, "because we are in love."

"Ain't love grand?" the man says.

"You shut up," the woman hisses. "You just close your mouth."

The man flexes his grip on his knife ever so slightly, gaze flicking down to the point of the blade lying on his own chest. "I'm gonna do it. I swear I'm gonna do it."

"We are in love," the woman says. "I am deeply in love with this man. In my mind I carve our names in the bark of imaginary oak trees, encircled in cartoon hearts. I have wanted to kill him for many months."

"I have wanted to kill her for many months," the man says. "In my mind I write her name with endless flourishes in the margins of copybooks. I am deeply in love with this woman. We are in love. I was so careful, honing the knife's edge while she was asleep."

"I was so careful," the woman says, "honing the knife's edge while he was asleep. But when I'd secretly sharpened it so much that the tip was invisible to the naked eye—"

"—and I reached out," the man says, "ever so quietly in the dark, to cut out her heart and end it for good—"

"—I looked down—"

"—and there she was with her own secret knife—"

"—at my own heart—"

"—even as my knife," says the man.

"—was at his," says the woman. "One of the pleasures of being long in love is that you come to know each other."

"You come to be like each other."

"Hand in glove."

"Sleeping together like spoons lying in a drawer."

They are all silent for a while. Harold is afraid. He wants to take his clammy sweaty hand out of Miranda's and run, off the island, out of the Tower, to a place where rhythm and symmetry don't hurt. Miranda is not holding his hand tightly enough to resist his withdrawal, but if he moves, if he even flinches, then she'll *know*, and that will be worse.

"Hey, kid," the man says to Harold.

"What?" says Harold weakly. He flinches. And feels the subtle answering tremor in Miranda's hand, bespeaking recognition, understanding, disappointment, sorrow.

"Hey, kid," the man says. "I *really* have to take a leak. My eyeballs are floating, over here."

FIFTY-FOUR

She scurries frantically between several piles of arms and legs and torsos and hands and fingers and toes and feet and heads with dead lamps
for eyes, lying on the seashore just out of reach of the lapping waves. They
are scavenged from the bodies of defunct mechanical men, defective
and obsolete models, silvery steel scarred with burns and scratches,
freckled with spots of rust.

Farther up the beach,.in the shade of a tree, an incomplete, mismatched, disconnected set of these scrap parts is arranged in an approximation of a human form. The arrangement of parts recalls the position
that the dead take in sarcophagi.

As Harold and Miranda stand in the cover of the shade tree that
shelters the mechanical corpse, they watch the woman shuffle quickly
back and forth between the piles of components. She is still young, but
age is creeping up on her before it's due, evidencing itself in places like
the network of veins stretched taut over the birdlike bones of her hands,
and the gentle curve of her upper back where it slopes into her neck. Her
eyes are large and mercury gray and would be beautiful if they didn't
have spots of discolor beneath them, and if they weren't glazed and unfocused, and if they blinked. She is muttering to herself, a continual
stream of chatter too soft for the children to hear. Her mouth does not
stop moving. Her hands shake.

Suddenly, she reaches deep into a pile of forearms and yanks one
out, a long, slender, rust-covered rod. Then she runs up the beach toward the mechanical corpse (and Harold and Miranda, not wishing to
speak or be seen, withdraw quietly into the shadows of the palms that
line the beachfront). Kneeling at the corpse's side, the woman removes
its left forearm, replacing it with the one she has in her hand. She tries,
futilely, to connect it to both the hand and the upper arm, then gives up
and simply lies the disconnected part in its proper place in the arrangement.

"Not it," she says softly, "not quite it. Close. But . . . no. Not it." She comes to her feet and turns, as if to return to the pile of derelict parts arrayed on the shore, but pauses for a moment, tilting her head quizzically as if she senses she is being watched.

Then she proceeds down to the shore again, shuffling and mumbling, but, as if for the benefit of her unseen audience, she raises her voice.

"—and if you stood behind him and whispered his name, he'd startle and spin around to face you, as if you'd snatched him out of a dream. I don't expect you to understand. I know that all the words I use fall flat. But he was such a *powerful* person. We had conversations! He would talk, and I would talk, and he would talk, and each of our words sounded out the deepest secret depths inside us. There are some forms of love that words can do no justice to. There are some scars that cannot be seen. Perfection is in itself an imperfection. He had flaws. He was sick. He needed help. Is not everyone sick, at one time or another? That was part of his beauty, his sickness. If he had not been sick, he would not have been beautiful, in the way that consumptives are, burning themselves up in brilliant flashes of light. You don't know. He would eat the tarts from the inside out, breaking off the crusty edges, setting them aside and saving them for last. You don't know. I don't expect you to be able to understand. Love is strong enough to resurrect the dead. I don't like the word *scar*, because it implies intent and blame. A soul as powerful as his had to burn. I have never known a love like this. You will never know a love like this. You don't know. I would have done anything at all for him. You don't know. It feels so goddamn good to be needed, to have someone tell you that he has a gaping hole in him whose shape is made to fit you. Not that I had any power. He had it all. He needed me when he burned, and when he burned me that first time, I looked right into his eyes and read the apology there that he didn't know how to speak. A lucky thing for me. He never wanted to hurt me. It was in his beautiful nature to burn. And the mark that he left on me was not something that I chose to call a scar, because that would have implied intent and blame. And when future marks came to join that one, I saw that he was burning a piece of art on me, a signature on my psyche because it filled the hole in his own, and he wanted to make me his. And it hurt, yes, but I never blamed him, even when the burns lost their pattern and became random, and too much to bear. I would tell him that he was hurting me, but the tone of his voice was enough to absolve him in my eyes. There are some forms of love that words can do no justice to. Don't think that I haven't come to my senses and seen him for what he was. No—that's not right. The person he was, the beautiful person I fell in love with, is gone, and now he only knows how to burn. I tried to bring him back, tried to remind him how and why he needed me so much, but he'd hurt me every time. He's gone now, somewhere, with someone else that I'm left to imagine, and I am here, trying to resurrect the dead, with his scars on me—no, I must remember, they're not scars—like a signature and a blueprint. No one can ever have what I had. No one in the whole wide world will ever have what I had with him. Never ever. Never. You don't know. It makes me so unhappy to think of him, away somewhere else, unhappy with someone else and missing me. Trying to make someone else's face into mine, as he must be. Without me the person he was must be dead. He can't be the same person he was before. The feelings I had were so strong that they could not have been wrong. Without my love he must be little more than a walking corpse, a tin man. But I knew him, and I loved him, and I can bring him back to me, re-create him out of memory with the blueprint he burned onto me like a last desperate love letter, find and rescue him, show him that he needs me, even if I have to lie to myself sometimes and say I've forgotten him. I can bring him back to me," she says, looking up the beach at the mechanical corpse lying in the sand (and if she'd been able to peer into the shadows, she might have seen Harold and Miranda hiding apart, huddled and holding themselves, struck dumb). "Love is strong enough to resurrect the dead," she says. "I can bring him back."

FIFTY-FIVE

And it's slipping away. Miranda can feel it slipping away, and she says:

Come with me. Father has set us some difficult lessons, and I can feel them working their way into me, making me learn and making me forget. I have already lost the knowledge of the word whose sound has the shape of a soul. But perhaps it's not too late. Come with me. Hurry now. We still have a chance to be young.

FIFTY-SIX

From the eighth notebook of Caliban Taligent:

—You, my hypothetical reader, perusing these pages long after what, based on events thus far, is likely to be my painful and ignominious death: you must think it hubris of the greatest sort for me to have believed that my thousands of pages of acute social observations and razor-sharp philosophical musings would be preserved, sheltered from the indiscriminate ravages of Time so that they would come before your glazed, uncomprehending eyes. Yet work your thoughts and you will see: my ugly athlete dancer's body has gone to dust and here you are, enchanted, just as I foresaw centuries ago! Ha!

I know you, I think, and because I know you, I will have mercy on you. A steady diet of ideas of the magnitude of those contained in these notebooks (especially notebooks seven and sixteen, which are especially theoretical and dense) must be far too rich for you. It must be leavened with cheap cardboard narrative to make it palatable, and easier to swallow. You need the lone gunman hiding in the shadows; you need the first hesitant childhood kiss; you need the simplicity of "happily ever after" and "once upon a time." So I shall let you rest for a moment. I shall describe to you the place where I live.

The Taligent Tower has one hundred fifty floors; my accommodations are on the 101st. At least this is what I am told by my father. My cage, fifteen feet by fifteen feet, hangs by a chain a few inches above the floor of the slightly larger room in which it is enclosed. The room is of a size such that, by reaching through the bars of the cage (which are iron, and doubly reinforced) I can touch any part of any wall. There is a single small double-paned glass window, through which someone on the opposite side may observe me, and a door that is kept securely locked, through which my mechanical servants bring meals, along with pen and ink and fresh notebooks, so that I may continue my memoirs.

I have already said that, by reaching through the bars of my cage, I can touch any part of any wall of the room that encloses it. I can now tell you that three of the four walls of this room are covered with thin, tiny rubber tubes, densely packed against each other. Each of these tubes is individually labeled with a white tag, and by grasping any one of them I choose, I can pull it through the bars of the cage and stick it into my ear.

This room is a listening post: a father's gift to a son he could never publicly acknowledge. Each of the tubes in this room snakes through the superstructure of the Taligent Tower to find its end in a different room, concealed by a wall clock or secret panel, so that, by placing the proper tube in my ear, I can hear the sounds in any room of the Tower, day or night. (No: any room in the Tower but one. But that is for later.) No one in the Tower knows of this room but my father and myself, and since my existence is also an equally well-kept secret, I sit here at the center of this world, like an omniscient God Who persistently carries on His duties, in spite of the knowledge that His subjects no longer believe in Him.

FIFTY-SEVEN

And Miranda feels it slipping away, and she says:

This is the first time in my life that I've had the feeling that I'm running out of time. We have to hurry. This will be simple if we get there in time, but we have to hurry. I used to spend days lost in this playroom, wandering safe beneath the trees in simulated night, and surprised by the slow rise of my father's artificial sun. Now I worry, and I wish that I had a mindless machine strapped to my wrist to measure out seconds one by one, to save me the trouble and relieve me of my new obsession. I no longer wish to be surprised by sunrise, which is the first clear sign, I think, that I am no longer a child.

Don't stand there looking! Hurry! Soon we will split, and it'll be too late. My father will have you stoking the fires in his boiler room if he finds out.

FIFTY-EIGHT

From the eighth notebook of Caliban Taligent:

—Despite what you may think from reading of the circumstances of my existence, it is not true that I have not known love, although I have not experienced it in the base, traditional sense in which it seems the word is most often used. In my cage at the heart of this Tower I have listened to hundreds of fools claim that their love for one another knew no bounds, that it lay beyond the expression of words, that the only way it could be expressed was in the touch of flesh on secret flesh. But to mistake simple touch for love? If this is love, then it is the love of the dumb. Reflex and orgasm are what the machines that imprison our souls need to remind themselves of their existence. My beautiful body is one of the ugliest in the world, but I have been fortunate enough to have been granted the knowledge of a love that transcends it. In my sleep the flesh machine that holds me in its cage sweats and writhes and proclaims its loneliness, but I know better.

I have already spoken of my father's desire to build a mechanical man with a soul. His fiercest critics say that he seeks to deny the right of human beings to be mysteries to themselves. I suppose they are correct. But I pose a question: why should it be considered a right to believe oneself a miracle, just because one does not understand oneself and the motives for one's actions? Just as I hear of my father's mechanical men and know that they are not golems animated by magic, so I also know that this thing I call a "soul" within me is nothing more than the evidence of a machine whose complexity is of such a high degree that it is presently out of my power to grasp.

I am aware that most people are not as intelligent as myself, and that their primary sensations in life arise from little else than dumb impulse and desire. I suppose that, for those unfortunate people, physical sensation must suffice as a simple substitute for love. What has troubled me more in this cage, though, is those who claim that touch is more than the crudest of pleasures at best: that it is a viable form of communication. Perhaps some small bits of information can be divined from the length and nature of a kiss, but for such highly evolved beings as ourselves to debase ourselves by settling for mere instinct? When we could write treatises and sing songs to declare our higher love? Horrifying. The possession of a sense of self is the prize we won when our ancestors crawled out of the sea, and to succumb to basic instinct when so much better is available to us is to squander our hard-earned reward. I fail to see how a thinking being in love can desire to touch the object of his desire. Wouldn't the fear that the touch would be taken as an insult be enough to dampen that dumb physical ache?

I want to murder my father. I have many reasons why, not the least of which is that he sometimes reaches into this cage to touch me, not speaking, pretending pity; now I shall tell you another. Love, no matter how high or low its form, must be requited, or the lover suffers. This is the nature of the beast. I have already described the rubber tubes that cover the walls of my residence. One tube, however, differs from the others; it is stopped with cotton and glue, so that I can't hear what goes on in the room at the other end. And as if to taunt me, this tube is labeled with a bloodred tag, and on this tag is written: MIRANDA.

Not that I can never hear the voice of my sister. I can hear her in the playroom, in the library, in my father's study seated on his lap, or running gaily up and down the Tower's corridors. But I want to be with her in the place that she sleeps, and this my father has forbidden. I have heard the evidence of the most intimate moments of the lives of those in this Tower, all the sounds that we pretend to be deaf to each day because they remind us of our own filthy human-ness: heard farts and belches; heard the plops and hissing streams of toilet stalls; heard the moans of executives cavort-ing in closets with typewriter girls. But I have never heard the gentle sound of my sister's snoring. This alone is forbid-den me.

I would like to be able to put my mouth to this stoppered tube and sing a song to her. (Lest you think I could not ac-complish this, you should know that not only am I an accomplished composer, but I have trained my vocal cords so that I can sing with multiple overtones. I refer you to the aleatoric symphony that comprises most of notebook thir-teen.) I would like to sing a song to my sister, that creeps into her dreams to keep her warm while she sleeps. But this is a love that can never be consummated. In the past age of mir-acles, beasts that were not yet human freed their lust of shame by calling it love and mounted one another atop the altar of a God that represented all they didn't understand; in my dreams, I imagine myself speaking a poem of unbearable beauty to my sister, nestled warm in the belly of a vast and wonderful machine of infinite size and complexity. This is why I want to murder my father: because he has forever forbidden me the chance to sing a simple, sweet lovesong to my sister.

Oh, God—Miranda!

FIFTY-NINE

And Miranda says:

Now. Here we are, in this secret place. Sit down, in the grass, and feel its cold morning dampness beneath you. Listen to the wind blowing through the leaves of the trees that make this bower.

Listen. We are running out of time. Soon we won't be able to speak without worrying about whether we're understood. We won't be able to dream without it meaning something when we awake. We won't be able to look into mirrors without wishing that they had the power to lie. Hurry.

It's simple. Look at me. Come close and look at me, closer: see that I have a smell that is my very own, like a fingerprint or a signature. Look at the wrinkles of fat that are disappearing from my hands, at my fingers, which will soon be long and slender. Look at the curve of my chin where it becomes my neck. The imperfections of color in my iris, with flecks of green suspended in their blue. The flare of my nostrils. The golden red sheen of my hair. The gentle shape of my mouth, and the way I stretch one side of it into a smile as I shrink away and blush, revealing a single dimple. Simple. Like this: kiss.

INTERLUDE

aboard the good ship *chrysalis*

—*I remember what happened next! Father barged in on our child wedding all upset, eyes red as hot coals, jets of steam shooting from his ears. "Why, Harold Winslow! What are you doing?! Are you ... are you kissing my daughter!? The nerve of you! Next you'll have your trousers down! Get out of my Tower!" Grabbing you by the scrawny scruff of your neck, shaking you like a rag doll while I looked on and you complained, "But I didn't mean anything! It's not what you think!" "Get out!" I'm surprised he didn't throw you straight through a window, letting you rethink your poor behavior while you plummeted to the ground. "Get out! GET OUT OF MY TOWER!"*

I can hear what you have to say: it's not clear whom I think I'm fooling, with this business about "searching for Miranda." Perhaps you think this is some kind of dumb fable, a means to evoke the rhetorical question "Ah, but can one person ever really *know* another? Are we not all mysteries to each other? Is not Woman an eternal mystery to Man?" It's all very profound, and at the end of the story we discover that Miranda (Woman) was just an objectified fragment of Harold's (Man's) imagination, just like the voices from his past. All very academic. Poor crazy Harold Winslow. No.

The question at hand isn't "Where's Miranda?"; it's "Why can't Harold find her?" Though this ship dwarfs all other zeppelins in size, it is not infinitely large, and it obeys conventional laws of physics, even in the heart of its malfunctioning perpetual motion machine. The ship is not a place of magic. In fact, by now I've searched it from stem to stern dozens of times. I've gone through the galley, the bedrooms, the hold, the steel garden, the laboratory, the observation deck, the boiler room. I've discovered every secret panel and hidden hatchway large enough to hold a woman. I've spent weeks poring over blueprints. I've been everywhere on this ship, and I *cannot find her.* And yet, from her secret place, she continues to speak to me.

Why do I not speak back? you're asking. What deception could be so enormous that its perpetration would sew a man's lips shut?

Again—all in good time.

I have not yet told you that there is another man's voice, here in the zeppelin with us. Like mine, it prefers to speak of the past.

Next to the obsidian desk in the observation room, within reach of my hand when I sit in its chair and look out at the clouds and stars, there patiently stands a little mechanical boy, about three feet tall, its body plated in gold and inlaid with bronze. Unlike all the other mechanical men on this ship, whose functional designs betray their factory origins, this one features irregularities and filigrees that signal handmade craft. Implanted between its shoulder blades is a ten-digit keypad, and beneath the keypad is etched the flowing signature of its artisan, Prospero Taligent.

Most of the time it's silent and still, but pressing a series of three digits on its back brings the mechanical child to life with the cheerful sound of a cash register ringing up a sale. Then it turns smartly and walks over to a wall of the observation room, where an array of compartments are labeled with three-digit numbers, each one holding a wooden cylinder about two inches in diameter and six inches long. The cylinders are covered in bloodred wax that is finely scored with grooves from end to end.

Delicately, the tin child retrieves the cylinder from the compartment; then it marches to stand before me, on the other side of the desk.
With its left hand it lifts the latch of a small square hatch that has been
set into its stomach where its navel should be; then with its right it swivels the hatch open and plunges the cylinder into its guts.

Once it closes the hatch again, it makes the cash-register sound again
and cups its hands to its mouth, which is frozen open in a permanent O
of surprise. It stands there for a moment, as if drawing breath in prepara-
tion to hail someone in the distance; then, out of its mouth comes, tinny
and scratchy, the voice of its maker.

The one thousand wax cylinders constitute Prospero Taligent's dia-
ries, recorded intermittently over a span of fifteen years. How far back
did he envision all this—the zeppelin that serves as his tomb, the shining
tin boy speaking with his voice, and someone imprisoned here to listen
to him? When he started drawing up the plans for the mechanical boy,
he must have foreseen his own death. He was already thinking, back
then, that I would find him and kill him, and that later I would sit at this
desk to hear his tales.

I have a recurring dream that goes something like this. It is a variation
on a theme: this time I have made it to the top of the obsidian tower, and
I can see the back of the virgin queen as she stands on the edge of the
tower's roof, contemplating the long fall.

"It's not me that wants to jump," she says. "It's the shoes. They have a
curse on them that makes them kill their owner. I didn't know until I
slipped them on and felt the fresh warm blood of the newly dead between my toes. They've carried me up this tower's spiraling staircase
against my will, and now they're going to throw me off.

"You can save me. The way to break the spell is this: I have to hear the
voice of the person I love the most, which is you." The sunlight shines off
her crystalline crown. "It can be any word. Any word at all: nothing
beautiful, nothing poetic. I just need to hear the sound of your voice. But
don't you touch me: if you reach out to touch me, then I'll jump. Now.
Save me."

The cursed shoes are dancing now, bringing her closer to thin air. The cheers of the crowd below come to my ears, faint and distorted. It is about this time that I become aware of the presence of my inverse, on the roof of the tower with me. This is hard to explain, but the best way is to say that he is my opposite in an axiomatic, fundamental way, a kind of wolsniW dloraH. It's as if, just by being present on the roof of the tower, he makes me invisible and worthless, even though, in most ways, we are identical twins.

As I open my mouth to tell the virgin queen that I love her, he opens his. My inverse is not malicious or evil. His face wears the same expression as mine, of concern and despair and fear. As I speak the words "I love you," he speaks them as well, but *in his own language*, which is the inverse of mine. "uoy evol I," he says, and as the sounds from our mouths merge in the air, the result is dead silence.

The virgin queen waits patiently on the edge for me to save her. "Don't jump!" I yell. "pmuj t'noD!" yells my inverse, equally frustrated. Again both of us hear nothing. "Wait!" "tiaW!" "Listen!" "netsiL!" "Please!" "esaelP!" We move our mouths like mutes or mimes and throw our hands in the air. It's not that my inverse is deliberately using his inverse-speech to trip me up for his motivelessly malign ends; he just can't help it, because, except for being my inverse, *he is me*. The queen is asking questions now, and I can hear the sobs in her voice, and I dearly wish that she would turn around to look at me: "Why won't you speak to me? Do you *want* me to die? Are you *trying* to kill me?" "Let me explain," I shout, but of course my inverse shouts "nialpxe em teL" equally loudly, which does no good. At last, in frustration, I run across the roof to try to stop her in spite of her warning, and just as she said, when I reach out to grab her my hand closes on a hint of skin and empty air, and she is on her way down, falling on her back so that she can pierce me with her gaze full of blame.

I want to thank you, Harold, for beginning to speak to me, even though you claim to have sworn yourself to silence. There's no real reason for you to speak your sentences aloud as you beat them into shape, but you do it, and I like to think that I might fill the shoes of that invisible reader you seem to long for. So continue. If we can't have a conversation, at least we can have this. Everything left in the twentieth century is artifice and simulation, anyway; I don't see why this should be any different. But I do wish that you could at least admit to yourself that you're telling this story to me, and not yourself or any of those past selves that you're always going on about. I hope you'll think about including these words I speak right now; that'll be a start.

Besides, my love, I must admit that you have a bit of a knack for spinning a tale. I think I'm due to show up again soon, aren't I? The world changed so much in those intervening years, and my father and his company were single-handedly responsible for much of that change. That was when I finally got the nerve to run away from home. I remember your face when you recognized me in the deserted warehouse. You were so surprised. Shy little virgin that you were, you suddenly had a pair of women to deal with. It couldn't have been easy. Not between me and Astrid.

Astrid.
Beautiful bronze Astrid. Dearest, only sister.
Lovely suicide girl.
What have you done.

THREE

music for an

automatic

bronzing

ONE

The bars of Picturetown are nearly always empty on weekday afternoons, and so Harold prefers them as meeting places, on those rare occasions when he has people whom he wishes to meet. Even when he doesn't, they are good places to get a head start on a day's worth of steady drinking—one can purchase a generous shot of no-name blended whiskey and nurse it in a corner, scribbling acidic aphorisms in a notebook with un-lined pages, playing at being a writer or, worse, an intellectual.

He is waiting at this particular bar for his sister, Astrid, whom he hasn't seen in months, though they both still live in the same city. She will be late, as she almost always is for all appointments, since it seems that those few people in the world who are lucky or savvy enough to earn a living from making art are allowed to ignore the hands of clocks. This isn't as bad as it might be—if he applies himself, he can be a pint ahead of her when she arrives, and this will make her easier to tolerate. Astrid and Harold have changed a great deal in ten years, and it became clear to him some time ago that were she not his sister, he would not choose to be her friend. Still, though, out of honor of a genetic commonality, he calls her on her birthday and on holidays, and every once in a while he meets her at a bar or restaurant, to listen to her chatter or to shrive her if necessary (which, for her, it usually is).

The bartender comes up to Harold and points at the gigantic pictographic menu that takes up most of the wall behind him; Harold indicates a pint of lager (or at least that's what he guesses it is, judging from the color of the beer in the glass—it's a painting, though, and lifelike as it is, with a healthy froth of head and beads of moisture running down the glass's sides, who knows if the portrayal is anywhere near accurate to what he'll get). In silence the bartender trudges over to the tap and starts the pour, and Harold slaps down the proper number of coins on the bar, plus a tip—as custom dictates in the bars of Picturetown, the ringing smack of the coins against the wood instead of their silent placement indicates that change is to be kept, and when the bartender hears this, he nods at Harold and smiles. He takes care with filling the pint glass to the top then, making a show of it.

It's noon, and the bar has just opened—the place isn't even fully cleaned up yet from the night before. One boy silently mops the canting wooden tables with a damp, dingy rag, while another uses a push broom to pile up the hundreds and hundreds of index cards left on the floor from the night before, the detritus of pickups and drunk talk. Harold looks down at a bunch of the cards that are strewn beneath his barstool: some have symbols that he thinks he understands, such as hearts with arrows drawn through them or daggers clutched in disembodied hands; some are covered with those odd picturelike words that remind Harold of the instructions that accompanied the components of the windup dolls that his father used to make before his eyesight went; some have words in English, likely penned by patrons like himself who wish to obey the custom of the country; some of the messages appear to be in codes that he has no hope of deciphering, the means of their decryption known by two at most.

Some critics view the refusal of the residents of Picturetown to speak aloud under all but the direst of circumstances as primitive, or barbaric, or as evidence of a religious impulse that, lacking an easy outlet in a godless world, has shunted itself into this bizarre secular mode of expression. They point to its children, who fail to thrive in the city's public schools, and at the severe underrepresentation of the district in city politics. But to Harold this behavior is a kind of common sense, a straight-forward acknowledgment of what language has become in a mechanical age. In the age of miracles that his father used to talk of, spoken words had an infinitesimally temporary existence, as their speakers used their mouths to change the motion of molecules for just long enough a time to hold a message; in this age, like the index cards lying on the floor beneath him, all messages have the potential to be permanent, no matter their medium or their triviality. The palimpsests of molecules need not be overwritten, for machines make once-ephemeral words persist: they collect in gutters; they pile up and require sweeping; they hang in air like morning fog.

TWO

The only other people in the bar at this early hour are a man and a woman, seated at the bar a few stools away from Harold. She wears a short tight apple-green dress and matching pillbox hat, and grease-pencil lines are drawn down the backs of her calves to simulate stockings; he wears a suit and loosened tie and huddles over his martini. Their body language speaks of assignation. They both have stacks of index cards in front of them and are scribbling away with ballpoint pens, furiously trading endearments back and forth, passionately flinging ink-splotched cards to the floor. Perhaps later this afternoon a private eye will sift through them, looking for evidence against one lover or the other, or third-rate rakes with leaden tongues will steal their words to use as their own. Perhaps trash-can scavengers will give their lovesongs second lives.

Astrid arrives just as Harold is finishing his beer. "Harold!" she cries as soon as she's entered the bar, her shrill voice piercing the silence, and the other two patrons both tense their shoulders as the bartender favors Astrid with a nasty glare. So oblivious. So goddamn rude. "Harold, it is so, *so* good to see you." She struts toward him, kicking aside clouds of index cards. "Mwah. *Mwah.*"

What's happened to her? The person that she is seems like a shell designed to cover up the person that Harold once knew her to be. For a professional artist she has little sense in sartorial matters—her blouse looks cut to reveal cleavage that she doesn't have; her fishnet stockings are out of fashion, if indeed they were ever in; her lipstick's on crooked. Her gawky gait, held over from childhood, is grievously ill-suited for her three-inch stilettos. "Could I have a beer!" she screeches at the bartender. "A. Beer." Harold realizes that given the choice between offending his sister by telling her to shut her mouth and offending the other patrons of the bar by carrying on an audible conversation, he'll be forced to pick the latter. He won't be able to return here for months. Thanks a million, Astrid.

Fortunately, once they order a round and remove to a booth, she lowers her voice a bit. "I had a devil of a time getting here, I have to say," she says. "I took a cab, but it was one of those new ones that's got a tin man for a driver—easier to hail since no one trusts them, you know, but half the time who *knows* where you'll end up. So it gets me about a dozen blocks away from here, and I've got my fingers crossed, then—get this—it just pulls over to a parking space and the top of its skull just *pops right off* and lands in the passenger seat. And little gears and bolts start spewing out of the damn thing's brainpan, pinging against the windshield, flying all over the place. I thought, well fuck *this*, I'll just walk. And here I am! I sure could use some weed, you know?"

The bartender brings over two stacks of index cards and two ballpoint pens, courtesy of the house, but Astrid cheerfully waves them away: "We won't be needing those. My brother and I have not seen each other in some time, and when we *do* see each other we prefer to *talk* to each other. We are going to *talk*. Thank. You." The bartender frowns and leaves the cards there anyway. "Don't people speak English here?" Astrid says, all shifty-eyed.

After a sufficient pause in the conversation, during which Harold clandestinely grinds his teeth while clenching his fists beneath the table, he asks after Astrid's welfare. She's doing well: at twenty-four she's regarded as a prodigy, and skipping college in favor of a two-year tenure in art school seems to have been the right decision for her, though her father went to war over it. Her larger, more expensive pieces are selling, and her dealer has begun treating her to the occasional dinner out to keep her mollified. There is talk that in a few months she may get one of the smaller rooms of one of the city's museums to herself for a little while—most of the pieces will be on loan from other patrons, none of them for sale or "courtesy of the artist." A ten-dollar art magazine just had a two-page spread that featured two of her recent sculptures, from a series of stainless-steel German shepherds sporting extravagantly erect penises welded together from springs and ball bearings. An article in the society section of the *Xeroville Courier-Post* (circulation six thousand) covering a fund-raising fete reported the presence of **Astrid**, the single given name in bold.

She sighs, and the tenor of the sigh tells Harold that she's about to start in on her personal life. "Okay," she says. "Okay. So I've been fucking this guy, you know." Like many of Astrid's sentences, its breathless hasty blurt is meant to disguise its careful, long-premeditated composition—the word *fucking* intended to shock, though most of Harold's college friends use such obscenities as standard punctuation; the *you know* to finish off the sentence while emphasizing the shockingly casual nature of the supposedly shocking fucking. "I've been fucking this guy," says Astrid. "I'm still living with my ex-boyfriend, which hasn't been easy but he's having trouble finding a place and damned if I'm giving this one up, I don't care whose name is on the lease, there's fair and then there's fair. It hasn't been easy, because the reason we broke up is because he cheated on me and every time I see him I want to rip out his guts and make them into chitterlings and feed them back to him, but I cheated on him, too, so I guess it's kind of even, but it's still horrible. And sometimes I think the hate sex since we broke up is just about worth the breaking up, to be honest. But anyway. There's this guy. And my *jackass* ex-boyfriend and I never thought to make any rules about whether we can have people over and when, since we haven't been talking much, and when we do talk, we spend most of our time arguing about what we mean by what we say. So we never came up with any rules; we never set any boundaries. But this guy? He's stuck in an apartment with his ex-girlfriend, except they *do* have rules. So that pretty much means he has to come over to my place if we want to get together. Right? Right. And he's kind of loud. And I'm kind of loud."

La-la-la, shouts Harold's mind in an attempt to drown out Astrid's voice and do him a favor. *La-la-la; la-la—*

"So we're really loud in bed," says Astrid, "and for some reason I'm louder with him than I am with my ex-boyfriend, maybe because my ex-boyfriend is an *asshole*. And so one night the asshole finds this girl and brings her over, I swear she was a whore because she looked like one, she looked like the queen mother of Whoreovia, and he *knew* my guy was going to be over because he's over *every* Friday night and Saturday night, and I'm sitting on the couch with him listening to the radio shows and trying to have a quiet romantic moment and he and this whore go into his bedroom and slam the door and start going at it, screaming like a couple of crazy people. It sounded like five porn movies. And my guy just gets up and leaves without saying *one word*. I was so angry, Harold. I was *so angry*. I went in my room and smoked two bowls and I was *still* angry. Okay, so I'm loud. Fine. I get the point. But not *that* loud."

Harold says nothing.

"I told him the next morning that if that's the score, then he can either pay to get his bedroom soundproofed or he can get the hell out," says Astrid. "Like it'll do any good. But I had to say it. It was something that had to be said."

They sit there silently for a while, and Harold picks up a pen, takes an index card from a stack, and begins to doodle absently, drawing a series of five-pointed stars over some waves that look like the humps of abstract sea monsters. Then Astrid slaps the table with her palms. "It doesn't get *easy*," she says. "You'd think that as smart as people are, we could figure out a way to make simple problems like this go away. But we've got tin men and flying cars and it still hasn't gotten any easier. And the tin men we've got can't do the simplest things half the time like get someone from one place to another in a cab, so what good is any of it. What good is a flying car to me if I still have boyfriend trouble."

Now the lines that Harold draws across the card beneath the stars look like waves of water in a child's diorama of the sea. He keeps his eyes cast down.

"Like I'd like to just be able to sit next to someone and look at them and just know how they feel, you know?" says Astrid. "Isn't that the way it's supposed to work? And not some science-fiction bullshit like telepathy or mind control. Just to look at somebody's face and understand what the face is trying to tell me for once, without wondering whether the person I'm looking at bought a five-cent pamphlet off a street salesman that told him what look he's supposed to have on his face if he wants to pick up a girl, and what he's supposed to say. You know?

"You don't know," says Astrid to Harold. "You wouldn't know."

Now the waves that Harold draws become more pronounced as he digs the tip of the pen into the index card, and the once-calm water beneath the stars becomes a sea disturbed by a tempest.

"Not that you'd know anything about this kind of thing." Astrid tries to strike a jocular, buddy-buddy tone, leaning conspiratorially toward him. "Have you—you know, are you inserting tab A into slot B? College days and all, you know—pussy, falling from the sky."

"Can we talk about something *else*?" says Harold, throwing down the pen.

THREE

In order to get off the subject of his personal life, or, more accurately, his startling lack of one, Harold goes into a droning monologue about his classes and how he's doing in them. He gives Astrid the dutiful rundown that other college students might have given their mothers.

Some classes are going better than others. He's majoring in English and his grades are best in creative-writing courses, though he has a sneaking suspicion that the professors prefer to reward competence and mediocrity instead of innovation—the A's he gets may well be backhanded compliments. He is doing the worst in Physics for Poets, the last science course he plans to take at the university if he can help it. Harold is learning to hate science. At first he liked it fine enough, and he pretty much aced the physics concepts that practically hailed from the dawn of time—levers and balls that roll down inclines and other things like that.

But later sessions of the course dealt with more recent, abstract subjects—optics; sound waves; E and M—and, like many others who are destined not to make the cut, he lost his way, puzzling over equations that had too many letters and not enough numbers. The only girl in the class runs circles around them all and jeers at the boys when the problem sets are returned. But Harold cannot fathom how white light bends or separates; he wraps his fingers hitchhiker's-style around imaginary wires, but can't seem to get their electrons moving in correct directions.

"The girl in the class says it helps to have an eye for art to get the problems right," says Harold. "She's always going on about elegant solutions and symmetry and things like that. And sometimes I see something like that, and I get it, but where I guess I'm supposed to feel some sort of universal awe at the order of things, instead I feel—I don't know. Nervous. Terrified. Take—take destructive interference. Now here is one of the things I kind of get," he says, feeling once again the pleasure of having *got* it. He takes a fresh index card from the stack on the table and draws a wave across it, nothing like a sine wave, but close enough to get the point across:

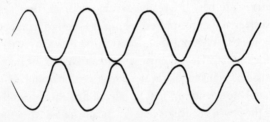

"That's the shape of a sound," says Harold. "But every sound has an enemy. And to discover the shape of a sound's enemy, you hold a mirror up to it." Harold scribbles on the card some more, adding to the original drawing:

"Now take this sound on the other side of the mirror and pull it into your own world:

"And if you add these sounds together, this is what you get." Flipping the card over and drawing a straight line across it from corner to corner:

"Nothing."

"Well, what's so god-awfully scary about that?" asks Astrid.

"It's scary because every day thousands of new sounds are born into the world: new machines with new rhythms; new words to name those new machines. Every day there are *more sounds*, and I'm afraid that, some day in the future, every sound that's possible to make will be in the world *at the same time*. And since every sound has its opposite, they will cancel each other out, and at the end of the day there'll be billions of machines with their percussive rhythms, and billions of words in a language that doesn't work anymore, and billions of people trying to be heard, screaming their lungs out, hurling their impotent noises into a world so saturated with noise that it might as well be deaf, and dumb, and blind."

Now it's Astrid's turn to say nothing.

"All the noises of the world add up to silence," says Harold. "This world will begin and end in silence."

"Can I make a suggestion?" says Astrid.

"What?" says Harold, his voice cracking.

"A toke or two would do you wonders. Also: tab A, slot B."

But as they're finishing up their conversation her eye lingers on the diagram that Harold's drawn, and as they're settling the bill and leaving she casually lifts the card from the table and slides it into her purse.

On the front steps of the bar there are triple air-kisses, and empty pleasantries, and assertions that all this must be done again soon. But he doesn't see her again for the better part of a year.

FOUR

A restricted memorandum, written by Prospero Taligent and distributed to the directors and vice presidents of Taligent Industries, September 8, 19—:

. . . Essentially, I have decided to restructure and reorganize the research divisions of Taligent Industries completely, consolidating them significantly. Most of the workers in these divisions can expect to keep their current positions at their current salaries; however, most can also expect to abandon their current projects indefinitely. From now on, the research divisions will devote themselves entirely to two projects. If our researchers continue to perform at their current rates of productivity, Taligent Industries will be able to deliver the fruits of their labors to the general public within ten to fifteen years.

The two projects, listed in order of expected time of completion from least to greatest, are:

1. Next-generation mechanical men, with significant technological advantages over current models.

2. Perpetual motion.

1. Next-generation mechanical men. *Taligent Industries has made significant advancements in mechanical-man technology in the last ten years (e.g., miniaturization of components, aesthetic realism, and the increasingly convincing illusion of "intelligence"). Though proof-of-concept models have inhabited the playroom of my daughter Miranda for some time now, the company has not released mass-produced versions of these advanced mechanical men to the general public, for fear of a hostile response. Humans still prefer to believe in their own irreproducible uniqueness, and*

mechanical men with these technological advantages built into their construction could be considered a challenge to this uniqueness.

The further miniaturization of individual components is of paramount importance. Many of the traits that separate mechanical from nonmechanical men (e.g., creativity, spontaneity, hypergraphia, the development of "hunches," hyperreligiosity, etc.) are a by-product of untraceable random elements introduced into construction as a result of complexity. In other words, as the complexity of a design increases, unpreventable random elements appear in the construction of each individual device, which manifest themselves in unpredictable ways. (See Table 1: Comparisons of Certain Internal Systems of Homo sapiens, Various Extinct Hominids, and Grand Pianos.) It is expected that a sufficient decrease in the size of each individual component of a mechanical man will lead to a corresponding increase in the number of the possible components that can be contained within one mechanical man, which will in turn lead to an increase in complexity of construction that will (if the failure rate of parts is held constant) give spontaneous rise to the forms of behavior cited above in nonmechanical men. The next-generation mechanical men resulting from these developments will be indistinguishable from nonmechanical men to the naked eye. They will write epic poems in Spenserian stanzas, embrace each other on meeting, sing scat solos, pray, and have an understanding of their own impending obsolescence.

2. Perpetual motion. As the details regarding the research path that will lead to the perpetual motion machine are nebulous at best, I have less to say about this topic at this time. I am fully aware, however, that a perpetual motion machine would violate the laws of thermodynamics as we presently understand them.

You will permit me to describe to you an exceptionally lucid dream that I had on the night of August 31 that began with me flying through the air high above this city, propelling myself by spreading my robes wide and quickly waving my arms up and down as if they were wings. After what seemed to be an impossibly long and impossibly high flight, I landed in a giant nest, made from the branches of redwoods and perched on the edge *of a cliff whose base was shrouded by clouds. In the nest were several baby origami cranes, who immediately mistook me for their mother and swarmed around me, chirping and begging for food. At this point I removed the top of my skull and pulled from my head a fistful of long squirming worms, which I tossed to them. These they hungrily devoured. One of the baby cranes made from bright blue paper then approached me and unfolded himself at my feet. He was made from a blueprint, for a perpetual motion machine. He allowed me to examine him for several seconds before I awoke. On waking I was not able to duplicate the blueprint in its entirety; however, I have made sketches that bear what I believe is a faint resemblance, and I will assemble a team of engineers, hypnotists, psychologists, sculptors, and psychics in the coming weeks to assist me personally in pursuing this line of research.*

I will soon schedule a meeting of all vice presidents and directors to discuss the far-reaching implications of these admittedly ambitious plans. . . .

FIVE

From an article printed above the fold on the front page of the Business section of the *Xeroville Free Press*, September 30, 19—:

TALIGENT INDUSTRIES STOCK DIVES AFTER SECRET MEMORANDUM LEAKED TO PUBLIC

Rumors Surface That CEO Has "Gone Insane"

XEROVILLE—**Taligent Industries** stock dropped eleven points yesterday as leaked copies of a lengthy secret memorandum, unintended for public viewing, made the rounds of the business district. The memo, confirmed to the *Free Press* by several anonymous sources as authored by CEO Prospero Taligent, details his plans for the company's future, which, in all apparent seriousness, include the development of "perpetual motion."

SIX

A transcription from the diary of Prospero Taligent, cylinder #338:

—History is replete with tales of men who were considered mad in life, their genius only appreciated by the public long after their death. I realize that more often than not genius and madness are indissolubly linked, and indistinguishable from one another to the untutored; still, though, I cannot help but be distressed and saddened by the allegations of my insanity appearing in the newspapers in these past days, for they come earlier than I expected, and with far less provocation. Clearly, someone in the upper echelons of the corporate structure of Taligent Industries cannot be trusted, and house will have to be cleaned.

Even though I have been granted the dubious gift of a clearer foresight than my contemporaries, the drastic changes in Miranda are still beyond my understanding. She is quiet, moody, and sullen. She has a certain walk, and a new smell that I do not like. Moreover, Caliban tells me that he has overheard men in my employ make certain remarks about her that are too indecent to record here. While I cannot say that her developments over the past few years are entirely unforeseen, I must say that I find them frustrating, and disheartening.

Recently, for example, she has developed an inexplicable desire to *leave the Tower*. I myself have not left this place in five years, making my necessary communications with the outside world through press releases and radio interviews. When a man has as much power over his environment as I do, he has no need to leave it; not only can he shape it to resemble anything that exists outside it, but he can alter it to bring to life his fantasies as well. In Miranda's playroom I can simulate any place in Xeroville or beyond, real or fictional, and fill it with mechanical representations of any living being, past, present, or future. So why should she want to leave?

But she does. She complains to me that this hundred-fifty-story tower is "cramped," and that she wants some "fresh air." She is an adult and not a prisoner here, of course. But if she does finally manage to leave this place, I cannot let her do so without, somehow, watching over her.

The world sullies, and by keeping parts of it from her, I have tried my best to make Miranda into the best, most beautiful person a human being can be. I am on my way to concluding that, as an experiment, she is a failure. I had high hopes for her as a child, with her delicate mix of innocence and precocity, but in her waning adolescence such a combination of personality traits seems unstable. I made my own mistakes in bringing her up (for example, it was foolish of me to allow prolonged and repeated contact with the child Harold Winslow, despite her need for friendship and the company of a human male of her own age; I should have known that such contact would inevitably lead to an instance of osculation). However, such incidents, no matter their number, cannot account fully for the radical change in Miranda's behavior and appearance in these past few years. I fear I must conclude that, as a result of several irredeemable flaws in their makeup, it is impossible for even the most beautiful children to retain their inborn, "God-given" beauty into adulthood.

Still, I cannot help but feel a twinge of pity when, walking insomniac through the corridors of my Tower, I come silently across her, face and hands pressed to the glass of a high window, staring at the grids of light and movement in the city below. Darling daughter. Too dumb to know that nothing in this world really matters to me but her.

SEVEN

"Students, believe me when I tell you this: everything in the twentieth century is dead. Everything has already been said. Every color of paint has been ground and every canvas covered. Every sculpture has been sculpted and fired. Every combination of notes on every possible musical instrument has been generated and performed. There is nothing new left for you to say. All we have left to us are possible permutations of the building blocks of fossilized ideas and dead sentences."

At the front of the classroom sits the newest teaching tool of the Creative Writing department of Xeroville University, the Taligent Industries Critic-O-Matic. Its principal component is a single-occupant sensory-deprivation chamber, a seven-foot-tall glass cylinder with a swiveling steel lid, filled to the top with water. In the cylinder floats a blindfolded undergraduate girl in a one-piece bathing suit with a pleated skirt, who is volunteering for this job to work off a chunk of her university tuition. Electrical nodes are attached to various places on her forehead and body, with insulated wires leading out of the chamber in a bundle through an airtight hole in the lid. The wires terminate in a large machine sitting against the wall, a rectangular metal box featuring several meters with quivering needles, along with the requisite bank of frantically blinking lamps. Rubber tubes jammed into the girl's nostrils also lead out of the chamber to an oxygen tank. The steel lid has a microphone fastened to it by a cable, so that the machine's operator can stand in front of the chamber, holding the mike, and speak to the girl floating weightless and limp inside. So, when a student's composition is read into the microphone, the mass of circuits in the bank attached to the chamber measures the physiological responses of the girl inside; the machine then uses this data to evaluate the text for style and marketability and recommends a grade, thereby saving the class's teacher from the unverifiability and the inaccuracy of subjective judgment.

Each of the twelve students in the classroom has on his or her desk a twenty-cent paperbound copy of *The Tempest*, a bottle of glue, and a pair of scissors. Their assignment is to dismantle and reconstruct: that is, they are to cut words out of the pages of the book with scissors, then, as if they are writing ransom notes, they must rearrange the words into another work that is to "reflect the spirit of the twentieth century," according to the professor standing at the front of the classroom. He continues to lecture, pacing back and forth as the students busily cut and paste. In the sensory-deprivation chamber, the girl's long black hair has come loose and swirls about her head, Medusa-like. Her fingertips are shriveling. "Just as every single word has been spoken, so has every single life been lived. In the twentieth century we have no choice but to walk in the footsteps of the dead. What better example have we for this phenomenon than the great Prospero Taligent, who has used this *very* play you take apart as the source material for the story of his life, just as Shakespeare himself takes his inspiration, or plagiarizes, if you will, from a folktale of a magician and his daughter that is now lost to us? We can see that Taligent has consciously modeled his life after his fictional namesake: naming his adopted daughter Miranda, secluding himself from society, wearing embroidered robes decorated with cryptic symbols in his increasingly infrequent public appearances. . . . What motivation might we hazard for such behavior? I suggest that, like all of us, Prospero Taligent wishes to make a piece of art from his own life, to give a random series of events the comforting shape of narrative and destiny, creating evidence of pattern and predestination in a modern, godless world. An impulse born out of a need to believe in miracles, even though miracles in this world are no more—"

At a desk in the back of the room Harold's hands move deftly, ripping pages out of the binding, folding and cutting, scattering random words across his desk: *ridiculous thee Sycorax weak i' Stephano mouth Ferdinand neither a Caliban.* He cuts, and he pastes, and he slips into daydream.

EIGHT

—Tonight I'm the devil again. Why do they need a human devil when a tin man will do just as well for the job? Still, it pays part of my tuition, so I guess I shouldn't complain. That day I tripped with the tray of type and all those inverted letters scattered across the floor, under all the desks and machines, the mechanical men slipping and falling on them . . . the boss was mad enough to spit. Hours needed to get them sorted again. Why I'm on the graveyard shift now. Not too much to screw up there. Watch the tin men cast and set the type and cut and bind and stack. All I have to make do is make sure that one doesn't (gasp) *run amok*! I don't know what I'm supposed to do since I'm there alone. Imagine that: tin man clutching me by the throat with its superstrong grip, cramming slugs and backward letters into my mouth with its metal fingers until I choke to death. Like the nightmares that Dad says he has sometimes. I should visit him. So much pain in him now. Everything went to hell after I left. Eighteen. Time to move out: bildungsroman. No, son. Stay. Please. Sit next to me here and we can both stay warm.

A piece of art of his own life. Prospero. I've seen the man in the flesh. But childhood seems like something out of a book now. Miranda. Simple like this kiss. But it isn't that simple, is it. There's one thing Astrid was right about, wrong as she often is, deaf as she is to the meanings of things. Nearly done with college and I'm still a virgin, virgin, virgin. My roommate takes a drag from the lip of a drugstore vodka bottle and claims that he hopes to do something with a woman that he'll later come to regret, but I can't square his grin and the leering look in his eye with what little I know of regret—partly because those things at which men leer only seem to disgust me, partly because I've managed to do so little in life that has any more than a negligible chance of invoking this regret, so dearly sought. I am a virgin, virgin, virgin. The blind-eyed true love that arose between couples that met during their first semester and stayed together ever since passed me by; the drunken fumbling of fingers at bra straps in a darkened corner of a fraternity house continues to elude me. A bleary-eyed pixie holding a glass of swill concocted in a frat boy's bathtub struts up to me as I stand against a wall; she slurs a flirty greeting, and I fail to say whatever thing in response that would be interpreted in her alcohol-pickled brain as the password. She squints at me in puzzlement, idly lifting her arm to reveal a black patch of stubble in its pit where she's let her shaving go for a second day, and I am revolted. She sees my grimace and she leaves me alone. I see the callousness with which the big man on campus walks up to a woman whom he's never met and places his hand on her shoulder as he introduces himself; she giggles because she doesn't seem to know what else to do, and it makes my gorge rise. And yet if I could speak this secret language of drug-mangled speech and insincere touch. And yet if I did not pray to be spared the knowledge of the shapes and smells of other bodies. And yet if shyness did not rivet my tongue to my palate those few times when I see an unattended woman at whom I can stand to look. I would not be a virgin, virgin, virgin—

NINE

"—Winslow."

"Mmmmnah. Uh. Wha."

"Are you finished? It looks like you have something finished here."

"Well, I guess, but . . . it's not something I really want the rest of the class to hear, I mean, I've just been pushing words around, thinking about something else entirely, haven't been keeping my mind on my work, daydreaming, letting the words arrange themselves—"

Snatching the sheet of paper up before Harold can grab it. Words are stuck crookedly all over it, along with superfluous crusty blotches of dried glue. "This shyness is something you'll have to get *over*, Winslow." Walking up to the front of the room where the Critic-O-Matic waits. "How do you expect to *improve* your work without constructive *criticism*?" He takes the microphone and, looking at the paper in his hand and turning it this way and that, begins to read. The girl in the chamber stirs:

—As I hope
For quiet days, fair issue, and long life
Which such love as 'tis now, the murkiest den
The most opportune place, the strong'st suggestion
Our worser genius can, shall never melt
Mine honour into lust, to take away
The edge of that day's celebration
When I shall think or Phœbus's steeds are founder'd
Or Night kept chain'd below.

When the professor finishes, the bank of circuits attached to the chamber wakes up. Lights flicker on and off in mysterious patterns. The needles on the meters wiggle crazily back and forth. Buzzes sound in different pitches. Finally, a high-pitched bell rings and a slot in the side of the machine spits out a printed piece of paper, like a fortune cookie's fortune:

BRILLIANT! ABSOLUTELY BRILLIANT. A+.

"Well, Mr. Winslow," the professor says, peering over the lenses of his spectacles at the little slip of paper, "it seems your work is improving. There's hope for you yet."

TEN

A mechanical man can compose type at a rate slightly less than that of a veteran typesetter. However, a tin man doesn't need smoke breaks, doesn't care about monotony, and doesn't mind working through the worst hours of the night. This is why typesetting is an ideal task to assign to mechanical men on a press's graveyard shift, for they can perform it with almost no human supervision (although many other important chores that keep a press running are beyond them). Although human typesetters are in no danger of being entirely replaced by their mechanical counterparts, it is admittedly a great convenience to be able to place a sheaf of typewritten pages in front of a mechanical man when the human pressmen are knocking off for the day (the pages must be typewritten, for mechanical men can't decipher even a child's clean block letters; nor can they set type involving musical notations or mathematical equations). Open up shop in the morning, and the type is composed and justified, in the forms and nearly ready to go. A human compositor then looks over the forms for errors, corrects them, and takes them to the press.

In addition to thirty workers, the Xeroville University Press employs four mechanical men, leased from Taligent Industries. Only two are working under Harold's supervision tonight; the other two stand in shadows against a back wall as if at attention, the lights in their eyes gone dark. One is setting type, the pinpoint light from its gaze moving slowly from left to right across the page on the desk in front of it, then dropping down to the next line and scanning right to left. A composing stick is in its left hand, and its right, fitted with specially elongated fingers, darts among the irregularly arranged trays of type at its side, placing mirrored letters into the stick.

When Harold is paying attention to anything at all, he is watching the other tin man, whose job tonight is to melt down some type and recast it into another font. Its hands move back and forth over an array of devices surrounding a bath of molten metal, glowing golden red. Tiny lead blocks with inverted letters carved on them in relief are dropped into the bath one at a time, and the letters twist out of shape and disappear amidst bubbles that slowly rise to the surface and explode, each one releasing the whiff of a lost word.

The room has a large radio that Harold turns on during his shift, its shape and speaker grille reminiscent of the interior of a cathedral ruin. It is the closest thing to company that he has while he is at work: these low-end models of tin men are not capable of speech, and would not indulge in small talk if they were.

He sits in a chair with his arms folded, looking at the inert presses with their huge cylinders, at the tin men going quietly about their labors. The radio plays some instrumental pop music, mutters a goodnight and signoff, performs the Xeroville city anthem, and, without taking a breath first, whispers static.

Harold's legs splay and stretch out, and his head drops onto his chest. He snores. A string of drool begins to creep out of the corner of his mouth.

The reversed letters melt into hot nothing, one after another.

The quiet *snickety-snick* of slugs dropped in the composing stick.

". . . sssssfffello. Hello." Harold snaps awake whatwhowhat nearly falling out of the little wooden chair. "Hello. Is anyone listening?" A voice. Strangely familiar. Where coming from. Radio. "Anyone. Is there anybody out there. This is Miranda Taligent.

"Hello. This is Miranda Taligent. I'm a twenty-one-year-old girl . . . woman. I live in the Taligent Tower. I . . . I know that there's no way for you to talk back to me, but . . . even if there isn't, I just need to feel like there's someone out there. Listening."

ELEVEN

The gallery where Astrid's newest exhibition is premiering is a single room of a dealer's home, in one of the tonier Xeroville suburbs. The four walls are shining white and completely barren, except for Astrid's eight paintings, two of which hang on each wall. About thirty people are here to look at the works: some are here to buy; some are here to envy Astrid for obtaining this particular dealer; some (such as Harold) are here who feel obligated to come; and some (like Harold's college roommate, Marlon Giddings) are here to hit on women. "Women who buy black hair dye off the shelf," Marlon says, "and dye every single strand of hair the same black color. Women who wear eyeglasses with wire frames in perfect circles. And the glasses slide down to the tips of their noses, and they reach up with a manicured index finger to push them back up. That's what I'm here for, Harry." Marlon stuffs an hors d'oeuvre into his mouth without looking at it, and Harold thinks that someone in a kitchen spent time giving that bit of food a singular flavor and shape, perhaps hoping against hope that whoever came across it would be so bedeviled by its intricate appearance that they'd take it home and place it on a mantel instead of eating it. "Hey, Harry," Marlon says as crumbs fly out of his mouth onto Harold's lapel, "your sister's paintings are crap, and you know it and I know it and damned if *she* doesn't know it too. I do believe that she is running some kind of clever shyster's racket."

Each of the eight paintings is on a white square canvas, eighteen inches on a side. In the center of each canvas, a phrase is lettered in black paint, so carefully that the words appear to have been printed by machines. They all have the same font, a lowercase lettering without serifs, formed out of simple geometric shapes.

One of the paintings looks like this:

destructive interference

Another looks like this:

the shape of a sound's enemy

A third looks like this:

new machines with new rhythms

"Oh my god with a lowercase *g*, Astrid," a young woman wearing a tight-fitting black turtleneck sweater, black slacks, and wire-framed glasses with perfectly circular lenses is saying to Astrid, who is standing about ten feet away from Harold and Marlon, in the middle of a small crowd. "This is just—this is just—oh my god. Among these *works* I *feel* as if I am in the *presence* of the *uncanny*." This is Charmaine Saint Claire, one of Astrid's graduate-student friends. "So *young* and yet so *talented*. You have the *aura* of *election* about you, Astrid."

"*You have the* aura *of* election *about you*," Marlon mimics, flourishing with his hand while he says it. "Harry, I just found my next pickup line."

TWELVE

"Listen. This is Miranda Taligent. Listen. What am I going to talk about? I know what I want to talk about tonight. I'm going to talk about speaking. I'm going to talk about what the difference is between speaking *with* someone, and speaking *to* someone, and speaking *at* someone.

"Sometimes when I wander through this Tower, I have conversations with the people that work here, or live here, or work here so much that they seem as if they live here. I say something like 'Hello' to them, and then they say, 'Hello, Miranda,' and then I say something to them that causes much surprise and then their faces light up and then we *converse*, because there is one of them, and one of the other person, and we take turns. But now I'm in a room full of machines, and I speak into a microphone and then my voice has ten thousand mouths. This is an ability that only angels should have, or queens. So if I say 'Hello' in my mechanical queen's voice, you could all say 'Hello, Miranda,' at the same time, and here in the Tower I'd be able to understand it, because it would be as if the city has the voice of a giant and the giant is saying my name. But if I say something to you that causes surprise, or even say, 'What is your name?' then you'd all say something different because you all have different names and different ways of being surprised and I guess then the city's giant voice would sound something like 'Harmahrrmahhamah!' So I'm not speaking *with* you, I'm speaking *to* you because you can't always speak back, and I have to remember to think about this when I talk, that you all hear the same thing but you are all thinking different things.

"Speaking *at* someone is when you're standing in front of someone, but you talk to them like you're broadcasting on the radio and they're listening. My father speaks at me most of the time. He says, 'I am your father.' And he says, 'Come here, darling daughter.' And he says, 'I believe that this article of clothing will allow you to properly bind your breasts.' Maybe the next time he speaks at me I'll just say 'Harmahrrmahhamah!' and I wonder what he will think then. Good night."

THIRTEEN

"These paintings are bullshit," Marlon says. "She just took stuff that somebody said in a bar one night after a couple of beers, painted it on a canvas, and hung it on a wall. Now people are lining up to pay eight hundred dollars a pop for these things just because she's an ar-*teest*—"

"Shush," Harold says. "Here she comes."

Astrid sashays over to Harold with two hangers-on, wineglass in her hand, slightly tipsy, and slips her arm into his. "I want you all to meet my *brother*," she trills. "Harold," Astrid says, motioning to her companions one at a time, "this is Charmaine Saint Claire, and she's a *brilliant* graduate student that is positively going to be one of the leaders in her field. I just read this brilliant paper she just published that was on—what was that?"

"Bodies, and commodities," Charmaine Saint Claire says. "And the uncanny."

"And *this*," Astrid says, gesturing at a wiry gentleman wearing eyeglasses and a houndstooth suit in need of pressing, standing a little distance away from the rest of the group, looking slightly uncomfortable, "is Dexter Palmer, and he's a—what?"

"I," says Dexter Palmer. "Um."

"He's a *novelist*," Astrid brays, and Harold looks at Dexter, at his right arm rubbing his threadbare left elbow. Harold sees the oaken trunk in the corner of Dexter's filthy downtown loft with an enormous padlock on it, sees the tens of thousands of pages of handwritten manuscript that fill it. He sees the stub of the tallow candle on Dexter's rickety wooden desk, purchased for a dollar-fifty at a rummage sale. He sees the short leg of the desk propped up with a seven-hundred-page study of phrenology, printed during the age of miracles. He sees Dexter's eyes going bad by candlelight, a whole diopter lost with each late night. "Zounds, I am working on my *masterpiece*," Dexter Palmer yells hoarsely, disturbing the neighbors. He slings a cup half-full of tepid chamomile tea at the wall, where it shatters.

"Dexter's writing a *novel*," Astrid says brightly.

After a few minutes of introductory cross-talk, the group of five splits into separate conversations: Harold talks with his sister and Charmaine, while Marlon ends up with Dexter. To Harold, Marlon looks cornered—Harold can't hear what Dexter's saying, but whatever he's talking about, he's clearly going on about it at length and in fine detail. Maybe Marlon is getting to hear all about the novel. Every once in a while Marlon will look at Harold and theatrically roll his eyes and sigh, but Dexter, who's frantically gesticulating, wrapped up in whatever he's chattering about, doesn't notice.

"It's positively *stunning*, what you've done here, Astrid," Charmaine says yet again. She turns to Harold. "What Astrid's doing here is *liberating language* from the *patriarchy*." Is this how critics talk? Harold's idea of an art critic is someone who wanders through a gallery and waves his arm in the general direction of a painting while saying, "Notice the diagonal." "Astrid," Charmaine says to Harold, "realizes that we live in a world in which an enduring *patriarchal hegemony* has transformed the *woman's voice* into a *commodity*. By *re-presenting* her own language and giving it a *body*, as Astrid has done here, she *embraces* that *patriarchal* desire to *commodify*, while subversively reaping the *benefits* of that commodification. You saw the men here this evening with their wads of money, wallowing in *anality*—not only were they *reading bodies*, in that they themselves were *bodies* that were *reading* Astrid's work, but they were also *reading bodies*, in that they were interpreting and *reifying* Astrid's literal and figurative *body* of work, and in turn attempting to *possess* and *circumscribe* her *own desirable* body. And when they *bought* the paintings, not realizing that the *price tags* were *themselves* part of the work—"

"They were?" says Astrid. "Yes. Yes, they were."

"—you saw their faces, saw that they believed that Astrid was *selling* her language, saw that they believed her to be a *prostitute*, a woman who *whores out* her *speech*, not realizing the *subversively uncanny* nature of her work, not realizing that when they *placed* these *embodied words* in their homes, they would begin to *striate* their *previously smooth patriar-chal spaces.*"

"What does that mean?" Harold says. "I don't know what the hell that means."

FOURTEEN

"Listen. This is Miranda Taligent. Tonight I'm going to talk about the pet unicorn that I used to have. Have any of you ever had a unicorn? I got one as a gift for my tenth birthday, but now I'm older, and now it's dead. One day I went looking for him in my playroom so I could go for a ride on him, but when I found him he was lying on his side with a dozen flies dancing on his flank. When I saw him I cried like a little girl. Then I asked my father to take it away, but he was in one of his moods and he wouldn't do anything about it. He just left it there, and it made my playroom stink. He made me watch it decay day after day until it stopped smelling bad and turned into a skeleton with an ivory horn sticking out of its skull. He said, 'This is all your fault. You could have had a mechanical unicorn that would have lived forever. But you wanted flesh and blood. You got it: now you sit there and watch it fester and go to dust. And this will teach you not to turn your nose up at immortality when it's offered to you.' I hate my father. Good night."

FIFTEEN

"I must say, Astrid," says Charmaine Saint Claire, "that this is lovely, lovely work. And it pleases me to see women succeed in the arts, much as it pains me beyond words to see women who shamefully take up the patriarchal weapons of Science. This is the subject of my forthcoming article—you see, it is obvious that we have been trained by the *patriar-*

chal hegemony to conflate *that which is masculine* with *that which is objective,* and since Science itself bears the *standard* of *objectivity,* it is also our primary cause of *patriarchal oppression.* You must have observed the inherent sexist bias in the study of physics, which deals *ever so well* with *rigid masculine solids,* but *breaks down* when it is accosted with the *paradox* of the *feminine fluid,* which can *shift its shape* and become sometimes a *solid,* sometimes a *liquid,* and sometimes a *gas.* You must have also observed the masculine bias in the *English language itself,* in which women—literally, 'not-men'—are daily confronted with the terror, unknowable to men, of concepts which they can imagine, but which an *inherently patriarchal* language does not allow them to express. These women who engage in the practice of Science, and choose to give their lives over to this most supposedly *objective* and most *masculine* of languages, do so because they wish to *escape* that *uniquely feminine* terror that *gives them their identity,* instead of *grappling* with it and *mastering it,* as you and I have, Astrid. These *not-men* scientists are held up as models of *feminist progression* by the *untutored,* but they are *slaves* to the *capitalist pig-dog patriarchy* as surely as if they were incessant *baby-breeders* and *bakers of pies,* with *strands of pearls* about their necks like *chains—*"

"Holy shit!" says Harold, looking at his watch. "I do believe I must be going!" He says a hurried good-bye to Astrid, smiles politely at Charmaine Saint Claire, drags Marlon away from Dexter Palmer (who's been going on and on for an hour now), and hightails it out of there.

"Christ, I thought that was *never* going to end," Marlon says later, in the cab that's taking them downtown, back to the university. He smells like wine. "This crowd you run with—completely full of hot air. Blabbering on and on about this and that, and half of it doesn't make any sense, and the rest has nothing to do with the real world anyway. What do you and Astrid talk about, anyway? I mean, I know you're brother and sister, but you guys are so different you must barely even talk."

"We don't see each other much," Harold says. "We talk now and again, about her, mostly. The pieces she's working on, things like that. Thoughts that she has. Every once in a while she mentions this big thing she's working on these days, some kind of installation in a building that's eventually supposed to house a planetarium, but somehow when she describes it, I can't visualize it—I think it's something you have to see for yourself. She's been working on it for months now—it's apparently this ridiculous thing that needs, I think she said, a soundproof room, and two dozen phonographs, and a bunch of other stuff. . . . This showing was supposed to raise the money she needed to finish that thing, but I don't know how many of those paintings she sold this evening, or what.

"I'll admit it—her head's a little in the clouds sometimes, but she's not so bad when I don't spend that much time around her. That friend of hers has got to go, though. You're lucky you got stuck with that Dexter guy instead of her."

"Yeah, but that Dexter couldn't shut *his* piehole either," Marlon says. "I mean, Christ. Artists and writers—let them kill each other off in cage matches; let God sort 'em out." Then he fell, with an almost audible *clunk*, into an alcohol-induced sleep.

SIXTEEN

From the diary of Prospero Taligent, cylinder #343:

—A number of terrible things about falling in love make it not worth the time and the effort. But the worst of these is that we can never truly fall in love with a person, but only what we think that person is—more precisely, we fall in love with an image of a person that we create in our minds based on a few inconsequential traits: hair color; bloodline; timbre of voice; preference in music or literature. We are so quick to make a judgment on first sight, and it is so easy for us to decide that the object of our love is unquestionably perfect. And while people can only be human at best, these same fallible humans are more than capable of imagining each other to be infallible gods.

Any relationship we have with another human being is an ongoing process of error correction, altering this image that we see in our mind's eye whenever we lay love-blinded eyes on our beloved. It changes bit by bit until it matches the beloved herself, who is invariably less than perfect, often unworthy of love, and often incapable of giving love. This is why any extended interpersonal relationship other than the most superficial, be it a friendship, a romance, or a tie between father and daughter, must by necessity involve disappointment and pain. When the woman you worship behaves as a human being eventually will, she does not merely disappoint: she commits sacrilege, as if the God we worship were to somehow damn Himself.

The realization that Miranda has deceived me as to her true nature for all these years is the most painful of my life. Of course I know about the radio transmissions: Caliban has told me everything (and I suspect that she knows that I know as well, but for some reason, perhaps to keep up appearances, it's important for both of us to pretend innocence). Of course it hurts to hear her say these things about me. But to know that this spiteful, ungrateful woman was looking out at me from behind the eyes of my beloved virgin queen, in her coronation gown for her tenth birthday party—this is unbearable. Caliban has never disappointed me in this way. He has always been what he pretended to be—if anyone has been deceptive about his true identity, it's me, not him. Unlike Miranda, he has never been shy about expressing his desire to murder me; he has told me to my face, and I have seen his notebooks. We both know that he is cordial to me only because he is in a cage and I am his warden, and that he lives at my pleasure. But at least I can say in truth that he has never tried to deceive me.

Caliban also tells me that he has heard rumors that Miranda is planning to run away from home. Part of me wants to lock her in chains and keep her here for her own good, until she learns to love this place and me; part of me wants to throw her to the wolves and see her come back to me wounded by the world, on her knees to beg for shelter. She never believes me when I tell her how terrible the world is.

If she wants to leave, then she can go. I'll have to resign myself to keeping an eye on her from afar, as best I can. And when she comes back to the Tower covered with scars, I will gather her in my arms, as a good father should. And I will read the hieroglyphics in those scars, and use the words written there as the evidence that I may someday need against her.

SEVENTEEN

"Listen. This is Miranda Taligent. This will be my last broadcast. I'm leaving.

"Maybe you'll see me, on a sidewalk, or in the back rows of a cinema, or purchasing a sundae in an ice-cream parlor. There are other people in the world who look the way that I look sometimes in pictures, but they won't be me.

"What do I look like? So that you can say 'Hello' to me when you see me.

"I look just like what you think I look like. I look just like the sound of my voice, which does not lie.

"I'm leaving now.

"Good night."

EIGHTEEN

On the increasingly rare occasions when Harold visits his father, who lives alone in the same apartment that the Winslow family occupied when Harold was a boy, the first reminder to him that his father's life has changed over these past years are the newspapers. Allan Winslow used to fastidiously throw his daily paper away once he'd finished reading it, disposing of it section by section. But now, as Harold opens the front door, piles of out-of-date and yellowed news have to be kicked aside so he can make his way inside: the mess covers the floor, a half inch deep. And not just issues from a single subscription: the pile of refuse includes legitimate Papers of Record, set in small austere fonts, their articles illustrated with stippled pointillistic portraits of men with high collars and grimly pursed lips; and half-sized tabloids, their head-lines large, bold, vulgar, and shamelessly speculative, selling an imag-ined future to gullible readers as if it's the present day ("INTERSTELLAR TRAVEL BY 1985?" "CITY COUNCIL TESTS NEW DEATH RAY! WE HAVE RESULTS!" "THE TALIGENT PERPETUAL MOTION EN-GINE: FACT OR FICTION?"). Earlier issues from several years back are folded neatly, stacked in bundles, and bound in twine, and they sit against a wall. After Allan Winslow's sight started to go, though, he couldn't sort them so diligently anymore. Now he opens the paper, squints at the words, gets frustrated, and throws it to the floor.

"I'm getting worse," Allan says. Now Harold and Allan sit in the liv-ing room amid the sea of old news, facing each other. Allan is in his ha-bitual rocking chair with his feet propped up on an ottoman, its cushion leaking stuffing; Harold sits precariously perched on a small three-legged stool, his fedora clutched in his hands and his knees halfway up to his chest. Harold knows that Allan is looking at him because Allan's gaze is pointed over Harold's shoulder, at the stacks of old papers against the wall behind him. "I can only see the edges and corners of things," Allan says. "Whenever I try to look right *at* something, it's like an imp is hold-ing something in front of my face to stop me from seeing it. But if I look at things out the corner of my eye, I can sometimes *just* make them out. I have to fight my curiosity, though. I can't look right at you, to see you as clearly as I'd like. Are you growing a little beard?"

"No, Dad," says Harold, whose new goatee is in an awkward phase, poorly trimmed and manifesting itself in patches.

"Good. You've always looked good clean-shaven. Beards are for pre-tentious students. 'Look at me—I want you to know that I'm a student.' That's what a beard says."

"Of course, Dad."

"And boys with weak chins who want you to think they're men— they wear beards," Allan says.

There's some awkward silence for a time. Allan's gaze turns to face Harold, signaling that he's looking into the distance, in some sort of reverie. Harold thinks about blindness, and wonders how his father's began. Perhaps just a pinprick in his field of vision, not always there, and easy enough to blink away. But it keeps coming back, becoming larger, growing from a flea-sized dot to a penny-sized disc. Too large to ignore then, but it keeps getting bigger, the rods and cones in the backs of his eyes burning out one at a time.

I should stay here with him, Harold thinks. But he doesn't.

"The thing I miss the most," Allan says, looking over Harold's shoulder again, "is the sound of the voice in my head that used to read the news back to me, when I'd sit silently in the afternoons with the paper, in this rocking chair. You know—that voice that's always in the back of your mind and loudest just before sleep, the one that replays fragments of old conversations or sings verses of popular songs over and over. When I opened the paper and that voice read the news back to me, I knew that I could trust it, that it would always find the meanings of words that were the most true. When the radio would tell me the news of the world, or when someone else reads the paper aloud—those are different things. As if the way you pause between words or change your pitch to say certain things gives the words a meaning they weren't meant to have. I know you can't help it—you have to read things *some* way. But I can't bring myself to trust your voice in the way that I trusted my own.

"Did I tell you that a tube burned out in the radio some time ago? Don't bother with it—I don't want to get it fixed. I used to leave it on, just to have sounds in the place. But once it stopped working I learned to prefer silence.

"All the same, I suppose you can read something to me." Allan gestures toward the floor. "Just anything will do—all the news is the same to me now, no matter when it's happened. What's lying on the top should all be fairly recent."

As Harold leans over and roots around through the pile, looking for something interesting, Allan's mind begins to drift, and he starts to ramble. This happens more often these days—the recurring themes of his monologues are events of the past that he has coated with a nostalgic patina, and his long-gone wife, the mother of Harold and Astrid. He almost never talked about her when Harold was a child, so one would think that Allan's newfound loquacity on the subject would be an endless source of crucial revelations. One would expect that after each conversation with his father, the son would return home to see in his mirror a little bit more of the ghost of the woman before him, hovering behind his own face as if they are the subjects of a twice-exposed photograph.

But the problem with this is that Allan's memories are too fluid—the truth of the past stopped mattering to him long ago, since the past's only useful purposes were to help him make sense of his own wretched present, and to entertain him while he whiled away the days until he reached whatever miserable future was in store for him.

And so when he has told Harold tales of his mother, she has taken fifty different faces, and been taken from Allan in fifty different ways. Allan has told his son of the morning when he discovered a pillar of brown sugar with her shape in the midst of a wheat field, the ants already crawling on it, and that as the clouds above split open he feverishly kissed her to get the last sweet taste of her before she washed away. She has vanished before his eyes, with only discarded clothing and a neat conical pile of blue powder to mark the spot of her rapture. She has screamed as her eyes burst into flames and light burned her shadow into the wall behind her. She has joined the circus; she has absconded with the milkman. She has died alone in an insane asylum, and when the doctors performed the autopsy they scooped dollops of chocolate pudding out of her skull.

"When I lived in the age of miracles," Allan said, "your mother was the greatest miracle of all. Just by standing near me she made me better than I am. She brought out that in me that makes me best. I'd think, *I don't deserve her*, and then I'd think again and say, *wait, yes I do*. Because her mere presence made me become someone who deserved her love. Do you see?

"And we used to just *talk*." He always comes back to the talking—this is what all the tales of her have in common. "I miss her voice, or what her voice was before everything changed. Not *everything* we said was a flat-out love letter—we pointed out the shapes of clouds and related the unchanging details of passing days like anyone else. I can't remember much of what we said. But it was the music in our voices that mattered. That was a kind of miracle, too—that a simple description of her troubling bunion could serve as a confession of her love, when she said it to me, and when she spoke in the way that she did.

"I don't know how to explain this to you. I'm not sure you're able to understand what I'm saying.

"I don't know why what happened next happened. It may have been because miracles were leaving the world and machines were taking their place; it may have been that the horrible half-sight I have now was secretly preceded by a blindness of the mind. But all at once she seemed to change into a creature made of edges and corners—nothing in the middle of her. The music of her voice became corrupted by sawtooth waves. Everything she said slashed and tore. Some of the words she spoke made lacerations erupt across my back just as surely as she'd taken a whip to me. Everything went bad then. She was edges and corners and emptiness, and it was beyond me to fill her again.

"I forget what happened to her in the end. . . . Oh yes. She turned to glass. One morning I awoke to find lying next to me in the bed a life-sized glass sculpture in her place, every detail worked with care, the seeming product of a master blower. Sunlight shone through the curtains and straight through her hollow body, refracting into rainbows on the opposite wall. I touched her once and your mother shattered to fragments. That was it. That was it.

"But before that . . . before that she was a miracle.

"You're not listening to what I say, are you. You can't hear what I say."

"I'm listening, Dad." Harold has a section of a paper clutched in his hand.

Curtly Allan says, "Read."

"Taligent heir still missing," Harold reads. "Search enters second week. Rumors abound. Foul play feared. Xeroville. Some fear the worst as Miranda Taligent, sole heir to the Taligent Industries business conglomerate, has been missing now for eight days. This morning a visibly distraught Prospero Taligent made a rare public appearance at the gates of the Taligent Tower, pleading for his daughter's safe return. The tone of Mr. Taligent's brief address seemed to confirm the speculations of sources inside the Tower that what was formerly seen as a simple case of a malcontented child running away from home is now suspected to be a kidnapping, perhaps a murder. 'If she's being held captive, I'll pay any price for my daughter's return,' Mr. Taligent said to reporters, and then addressed his missing daughter directly: 'Miranda, if you can come home, if you're able to, then please come back to me. I know you as well as I know myself, and I know that you are alone, and afraid. That's understandable; the world is a place of terror, and it's not a place you were made for. So listen to me. Please come home.'" Harold puts the paper down and waits for his father to speak.

Allan is looking at the floor. "Miranda," he says quietly, and smiles. "Weren't you and she supposed to fall in love? Why couldn't you manage that?"

"I'm not as good as you are with women, Dad," Harold says. "And I was only ten."

Allan laughs, once: "Heh. That was a missed opportunity. You might have married her, and her father might have become my patron. I might have served out the rest of my days in his Tower of riches and wonders, instead of in this place, subsisting off the paltry alms tossed to me by the city fathers. . . ." Allan trails off into silence for a few moments, but when he begins talking again, his voice has more life in it. "Do you think—here's an idea. Perhaps he might've made mechanical eyes for me, with lamps that would never go out, that could only see the world in black and white. Or built a machine that could read the paper aloud, in a voice with no color, but one that could only say true things. That would've been nice, I think. Not a miracle, but I would have settled for it. And you might have known something like what I knew with your mother. Perhaps. If that's still possible these days. . . .

"Son. What's happened to your voice? I hear something new in it when you read the papers. There used to be music in it; now there's metal in its place. Not something strong and forged, like steel—something cheap that breaks when you bend it. Tin, or the gilding on a cheap thing that makes it look like gold. Yes—there's metal in your voice now." Allan's gaze drifts, and he looks confused.

I don't know what he's talking about, Harold thinks. But he does.

"To tell the truth, it wasn't sudden," Allan said. "For years I've heard it creeping in, more and more, a cheap tin noise coming from something cheap and made of tin. Wait—that's too harsh. I'm sorry. I'm sorry

I said that. If I said it it's because I'm sitting here in these empty rooms and turning to tin as well. Just like everyone else.

"But your voice had music in it when you were a child! I remember when you were so excited about that silly roller coaster. Spinning yourself dizzy. *Tornadoooo!* I'd never hear high notes like that out of you now; haven't for years. You haven't felt like that in a long time, have you?

"All the high notes have left your voice. Mine too."

Harold says nothing and looks at the floor.

"I can't blame you," says Allan. "Soft hearts provide poor harbor; tin hearts can better stand against time and bad weather, thin and hollow as they are. So you pray to change from flesh to metal, and the dying Author of this world hears your plea and performs his final miracle. He lays His hand on you and then He vanishes. And what mortal man can undo that? What human on this earth has the power to change a tin man back to flesh?"

Allan's lip curls in a sudden snarl. "Read something else." He is fidgeting and wringing his hands, near tears.

Harold doesn't know what to do. He flips over the sheet of newsprint in his hands, clears his throat, and reads something from the other side. "Acts of vandalism increase sharply in industrial district. Xeroville. An organized gang is thought to be responsible for a sudden epidemic of vandalism that has erupted in the past two weeks in Xeroville's industrial district. The objective of the gangs seems to be to destroy the machines and the mechanical men they target, generally ignoring any occupants. 'Vandalism is a child's crime with a child's punishment,' said Xeroville police chief Stephen Smollett in a press conference yesterday afternoon. 'By attacking only mechanical men, who have no rights or legal standing, they're keeping the charge from escalating to assault or attempted murder—'"

But Allan is out of his chair now, an expression of clear pain on his face, walking on unsure feet toward his son. He stands over Harold, who is perched on his little stool. "Will you come closer to me? Don't ask questions."

"Jesus. Sure, Dad." Harold stands and holds his father in a weak embrace, barely touching him, his fingertips resting lightly on his back, beneath his shoulder blades. This close he smells. Allan is gripping

Harold as if to crush the breath from him. They stand there in silence, Harold wishing that he were somewhere else, away from his family, away from Astrid, away from himself; his father thinking who knows what. "Loss of signal," Allan whispers. "If you touch me, then there'll be no loss of signal. Tell me: do you think I've gone crazy?"

Harold decides that there's no use in lying. "Maybe," he says. "You may have."

"It's okay," Allan says. "Everyone goes insane eventually, sometime or other. Hold me."

So they stand in each other's arms for a while, and lose track of time.

NINETEEN

I look just like the sound of my voice, which does not lie. That is Miranda Taligent's final broadcast. It doesn't take long for the rumors to start up concerning her whereabouts: the woman is silenced; the woman is dead; the woman lives among us with a secret face.

As for Harold, whose graveyard shifts in the press are silent again, he feels as if he has lost a friend, as do so many others across the city. Her voice over the airwaves was soothing and human, and with its lingering hints of the stilted speech of the girl that Harold knew at age ten, it seemed familiar to him in a way that radio voices rarely do. And there is no melancholy like that we feel when our favorite radio program is canceled without warning: at that special time of the night we prepare to receive a friendly, dependable visitor, who loves unconditionally and never fails to entertain, only to find that she will never come to us again, that she is forced to spurn us by powers higher than our own.

With nothing to keep his attention during the night shift, Harold goes back to napping on the job, slumping in his chair, letting the syncopated soft mechanical rhythms of the room lull him into slumber. It is then that he starts to have a recurring dream; it goes something like this. He walks down an infinitely long corridor that vanishes to a point before and behind; its walls are lined with open doors. The floor is covered with plush red carpeting; the ceiling and walls are also painted a bright pure red, the color of a rose whose petals have just begun to unfurl. The doors and doorframes are golden, and each opens onto a small, featureless room whose walls are all a gleaming white.

On the floor of each of these rooms lies a naked man in pain. As Harold walks down the corridor, looking in the open doors to his left and right, he sees that all the men are different, but they are all doing the same thing: clutching their crotches, with blood seeping between their fingers. Some of the men are being tended to by gentle cherub-faced little boys in spotless white nurse's uniforms, their stickshaped hairless boy-legs sticking out of skirts; some of the boys sport hooves, or idly flapping angel's wings. . . . "You have to understand," one of the boys is saying, gently but firmly pulling his patient's hands away from himself, bandaging the wounded, empty space they once protected. "The queen needs singers for the high parts, and women aren't allowed. So what else is she supposed to do? Hush now. Hush . . . you are performing an inestimable service for this nation."

Now the virgin queen is beside Harold, walking down the corridor with her arm slipped into his, as if he were escorting her to a ball. Her billowing gown is dyed with deep and brilliant blues and greens, the colors of a peacock's feathers; indeed, a fan of blue-green feathers, each a yard long, spreads behind her, slowly waving in a light breeze that drifts down the hallway. But the woman is old. Her face is shriveled; her breasts are fallen; her teeth are blackened and gone; a glass eye rolls like a gyroscope in her skull. "I still get love letters from strangers," she says, "and a line of paramours winds around this castle three times, waiting for an audience. I allow one to enter my presence each day; today it is you.

"Few in the kingdom know of my decay. In the future, perhaps there will be machines that record my image as it truly is and disseminate it to the public for their disillusionment, but for now there are only painters, whom I hire and whom I hang if I find their work displeasing. And the miracle is that when these paramours come before me, they see me not as I am, but as I was—no. Better yet, they see me as I never was. But I bring only the best, only the cleverest, only the strongest, to this corridor, the home of the knights that defend my name and my honor.

"Have you come to be knighted?" The virgin queen giggles obscenely and thrusts a shaking liver-spotted hand into Harold's trousers. "A practical man. You brought your sword along, and you're prepared. Come." She ushers him into an empty room. Up and down the corridor resonate the echoes of screams.

The old woman shuts the door, leaving the two of them alone, in silence. She turns to him, and the long feathers attached to her gown quiver and spread. "Ever made it with a *virgin*?" she says. "Here in my kingdom we go about the process a bit differently than you may have heard of. Now drop your pants." She gets down on her knees and opens her mouth, and now it is not a human mouth but something else, the mouth of a sea monster drawn into an uncharted space on an ancient map, a lipless perfect circle ringed with fangs. A snake's tongue flits out of it and back again. "Now," she says. "Come, and lose yourself inside me."

TWENTY

Harold starts awake to the irregular sound of metal violently striking metal. Bang. Bang . . . *dong*. Huh? Whazzat. Someone's in here.

The room he's in is empty, except for himself and a single typesetting mechanical man that is quietly going about its business, seemingly oblivious of the nearby clamor. From where he is sitting, Harold can see through the doorway into the next room, where the presses are. Two men are in there, moving back and forth in front of the door, in and out of shadow. Something about their silhouettes is strange: their heads are oddly geometrical, the tops of them shaped like perfect cones, tapering to a point with some kind of tube sticking on top. One wields a double-bladed axe; the other has what looks like a length of lead pipe. "I swear to Christ if there's one thing I *hate*," he screams, "it's movable type! Seems to me that type is meant to *stay put*! You know?! So that you can get a *good clear look* at it. So you can take the *time* that you need"—(ssswishCLANK!)—"to figure out what it's *saying*. But some crazy sons of bitches who think that everything that *can* be invented *ought* to be came up with this *bullshit* movable type: you try to read a book made out of it, and it says one thing, then you put it down because you have to answer the door or go pee or something, and when you come back to it the type's gone and moved all around and it says something else entirely! But I swear that tonight, *tonight* my friend, I am going to teach that shit to stay"—*ssswishDONK!*—"*put!*"

Common sense says to run. The duties of a security guard are not in Harold's job description, and the idea of getting beaten to a pulp is not appealing, by axe or by pipe. But the room's one exit is blocked, and when the two thugs finish tearing apart the merchandise in the room they're in, they'll come in here, and that'll be it.

So he can hide. But where? There's no room for him in any of the closets; crawling under a table is a dumb idea. Then he has it: a clever man in this situation would *hide in plain sight*! The lighting in the room is dim, and most of the walls are in shadow. Against one of the walls are two mechanical men, standing at attention in the dark. Harold quietly tiptoes around and cuts off the few lights in the room, feeling a little brave now, feeling *sly*, even (and the typesetting tin man goes on working in the dark, the only illumination in the room now coming from his scanning eye, moving across the page from left to right and right to left).

Harold runs over to the wall and stands still next to the rigid tin men, wedged between one of them and a locker. He can't see three feet in front of him. *This is going to work*, he thinks. But just as he hears one of the thugs enter the room, he realizes that, when most people enter a darkened room, the first thing they think of doing is turning on a—

He hears his enemy fumble along the wall for a switch, then an overhead lamp flickers on. Not bright enough to illuminate Harold's hiding place, but bright enough to see. Now Harold can see the two toughs clearly. Their faces are caked with bright silver paint, as if they are mimicking the appearance of mechanical men, and they have funnels strapped to their heads for hats, which would make them seem somewhat comical if they weren't carrying weapons with malicious intent. The ringleader, who's wearing a dingy cotton shirt with its sleeves ripped off and hypertrophied muscles bulging beneath it, shifts his grip on the length of pipe. "Hey, watch this. Batter up," he says as he sees the mechanical man at its table, still composing. He takes aim at its head with his pipe: "*Swing batter!*" and the head goes flying off the neck and rolling across the floor, coming to a stop near Harold's feet. Decapitated, the tin man's hands go through a few more measured motions as it unerringly places a last piece of type; then it is still.

Now the leader is peering into the dark, in Harold's direction, but not at him. He squints and his eyes jitter back and forth in his silvery face. Then he turns to face his comrade and says, "Oh, me! Oh my! Oh goodness gracious! Do you think there's someone in here *besides us*?" The other silver-faced man looks at the leader, nodding and shrugging. The leader cups a hand to his ear. "I know one thing," he says, approaching Harold (but still not looking straight at him), "if there's one thing I *haaaaate*, even *more* than movable type, it's a tin man! And if I were to do to a real person *accidentally* what I'm about to do to one of these *three tin men* that are over here, why, that person would be one sorry black-and-blue decapitated son of a bitch's bastard when I was done!" The leader swings at the head of the first mechanical man and takes it clean off. *"Bickety-bam!"* he yells. "That *satisifies!*" He takes aim again, and a second head, of the mechanical man standing next to Harold, goes flying off. "Oh, I would *hate* to have to—"

Harold steps forward. "Okay. That's enough. I'm here."

The ringleader looks at Harold with positively manic glee. "And now, my friend"—he points one end of the pipe at Harold's forehead—"you have *got* to get knocked *out*—"

Out.

TWENTY-ONE

From the diary of Prospero Taligent, cylinder #361:

—After I'm laid to rest I want to be remembered as a man who keeps his promises, even those that might have been considered rash or fantastic. The tens of millions of dollars I've spent fulfilling the heart's desires of those hundred boys and girls that attended Miranda's tenth birthday party,

money spent retaining the services of dozens of private de-
tectives, cosmetic surgeons, parlor magicians, professional
actors, barbershop singers, fortune-tellers, prostitutes, and,
yes, the occasional hit man—most others would look at it as
a waste, I imagine. I could have sent them all gift certificates
to a department store, for fifty-dollar shopping sprees, and
no one would have raised an eyebrow. But I want to keep my
promise. Thirty-four have been satisfied; sixty-six remain. I
think there's still time enough.

But as those children grow older, and more complicated,
and their hearts become darker and harder to see into, as
they learn the wretched talents of inscrutability and subter-
fuge that my own daughter seems to have mastered, seeing
what their hearts want for them becomes so difficult. More
care has to be taken; more money must be spent. My guesses
of the things they need to complete their lives are becoming
slightly less certain.

Except for that hundredth child, that luckiest storytelling boy. I know just the thing that he wants, as well as I
know myself, and it hasn't changed since those days in the
playroom. His gift will be my masterpiece, I think.

I wonder if he'll begin to guess, when he awakes to see
the girl in peril? Will it make him feel like the boy he was,
on the magic island, ready to rescue the damsel in distress?
Will his heart race, as mine would?

This entry will have to be cut short—I'd like to spend
some time with Caliban this evening. But it is to be hoped
that Harold Winslow's return to Miranda's life, after ten
years, will remind her of what she once was, or at least of
what she pretended to be for my benefit. I think that, if she
chose to take up the mantle of the virgin queen once again
upon her return, I could find it in myself to forgive her. I still
think the girl can remain pure.

And if Gideon performs as he's been instructed, then
Miranda will hear those words at last that I don't have the
nerve or the strength to say to her myself.

TWENTY-TWO

"—don't touch me."

"But I don't want to—"

"I told you don't you *touch me*."

Harold comes back to consciousness, feeling a rickety wooden chair beneath him, its back digging into his own. He opens his eyes, groggy, and lifts his head to take in his surroundings. He doesn't know where he is. He can hear two people nearby, a man and a woman, having words.

"Stay over there."

"But I—"

"You *get* over there and you *stay* over there. *Away from me*." She's shrieking.

"Okay. Okay. I'm stepping back. I'm over here. You're safe."

What's this? He can't move his arms. He's tied to a chair with each of his wrists bound to one of its legs, firmly enough so that twisting his fists in an attempt to slip the knots does no good. He is in some sort of cavernous room—it looks almost as if it used to be some kind of warehouse, a simple shotgun structure whose only entrance is a pair of garage doors in front of him, at the opposite end. The walls are plated with warped aluminum panels. Low-powered lights that hang from the steel crossbeams of the high ceiling strain to illuminate the place, but do little more than make shadows. Moonlight shines murkily through high windows smudged with grime.

On the wall near Harold hangs an out-of-date pinup calendar from a dozen years ago—it features a painting of a curvaceous woman in a bathing dress. The dress's former deep red has been faded by the yellowing and bleaching of the calendar's pages. The woman leans suggestively against the side of what must have been next year's model of automobile, back then, smirking coyly with her back arched. Her eyebrows are cocked devilishly above a pair of goggles. The artist, not the most skilled, has given her a bright spot of rouge on either cheek, as if she were a marionette. Everything about the image seems dated: the numbers on the calendar itself and the decay of its paper; the automobile, whose long lines and gleaming metal curves are naïvely meant to suggest some dead engineer's idea of a capital-*F* Future; the cheesecake woman, whose knees are apparently meant to be titillating, but whose supposedly immodest clothing wouldn't even merit a second look on the street today. This building hasn't regularly been inhabited for a while, it seems.

Across the room, on the other side, are the two people arguing. One is one of the two costumed tin men who broke into the printing press and, apparently, kidnapped Harold (who, by the way, is done performing his little exegesis of the pinup calendar, and is now wondering why exactly he merits the honor of kidnapping). Though the man is wearing a similar outfit, complete with silver facepaint and the metal funnel fastened to his head, he's not made out of pure muscle like the thug who took a pipe to Harold's forehead—he's lithe and birdboned and fey, and the tone of his voice has a certain gentleness. To Harold he seems as if he'd really rather not be kidnapping this woman, as if his heart isn't in it.

Both of the men seem familiar to him, but he can't figure out where he would have seen them before. Some other guise, without the silver faces. Some long time ago. Tip of the tongue. Can't figure it.

The woman, Harold realizes all at once, is none other than Miranda Taligent, grown-up. It seems as if, in ten years, she wouldn't be the same person she was before, and different enough to be a stranger to him. But without a doubt he's sure. *I look just like my voice, which does not lie.* She's dressed as she was in the playroom the first time Harold entered it ten years ago, in a larger, adult version of the same outfit—white seersucker suit jacket, white slacks, white tie, a white fedora clutched tightly in her hands. Her red-blond hair is long, tangled, and matted, and her formerly sharp white suit, perfect for stylish traveling, is soiled. She's standing with her back against the wall, and she looks terrified.

No one seems to notice or care that Harold is conscious, with his eyes open. Then a door opens behind him, and though he can't see him with his back to the doorway, he recognizes the bellow: *"Talus!"* It's the thug who knocked him out. *"Taaaaalus! Get over here!"*

Talus spins to face the man, looking over Harold's shoulder. "I'm in charge here," he says, his voice slightly quivering. "I'm the one in charge, is what the boss said. You're in charge in the streets, but I'm in charge here. I am the only one who is allowed to talk to the girl. If *you* speak to her by name he'll cut your *tongue* out. He pointed at your face and said this to you."

"Oh, I ain't sayin' a *thing* to *her*, you better believe I got no interest in *talking* to her, if I do *anything* with her you bet your ass it ain't gonna involve much *talking*, except for: uh. Uh. *Uh!*" The thug is walking up behind Harold now. "But don't you go thinking you're the boss of me. The boots are on the ground now, and the *fact* of the *matter* is I weigh *two sixty-five* and I am *so tough* that I can swallow *coal* and shit *diamonds*. Now I don't give a *shit* what the big boss said, *I* think that makes *me* the boss of *you*! Now get *over here!*"

Talus throws up his hands in frustration and feeble protest and crosses the wide room to approach the other man. It's now that Miranda sees Harold, and just like him, she feels the sudden shock of recognition. Her eyebrows furrow, and she mouths a word involuntarily: *What?*

The two men are standing just behind Harold now, and he can't see either of them. "Artegall," Harold hears Talus say in a low voice. "We have to be gentle with her."

"To *hell* with gentle," says Artegall loudly. "Get her out of those clothes and we'll see about who's gentle."

"Artegall, we can't—"

"Hey—ho-ho-hold it. You know what?"

"What?"

Artegall lowers his voice. "I'll tell you a secret."

"What."

"I think," says Artegall, "that our other guest over here just woke up, and he's playing possum."

Talus says nothing.

"Why," Artegall says, "don't I," placing his hand on the back of Harold's chair, "give him another love tap. Just to make sure."

—Out.

TWENTY-THREE

Again, it is dreamtime.

It took two full-grown men to usher the struggling spitting girl into the operating theater, her fingernails raking welts down their arms. *Get her into the chair.* The room was dimly lit and almost empty, its principal feature being a dentist's chair in which the girl was being restrained, her wrists and ankles tightly bound to it by turns of electrical tape, the broken halves of toothpicks slid under her eyelids to keep them open. A wooden stall of some kind was on the other side of the room, fitted with ropes and chains, apparently meant for the confinement of some large animal. Next to it was a surgical tray with tools too large for use on humans, and some of them better suited for carpenters than surgeons: pairs of pliers of different sizes, a large rubber mallet, a drill fitted with a long thick bit . . . Father came into the chamber with a spiraling horn in his hand, carved out of ivory. *Father. What are you doing. Do not. Don't.*

Darling daughter. I'm giving you your heart's desire. Tomorrow you will be ten. Do you remember what I said about desire?

Bring in the horse.

They brought the white horse into the operating theater and harnessed it into the little stable, lashing it to the walls with ropes, fixing its head in a vise. Its eyes rolled in its head; foam spilled from its mouth. *Now do what I told you to do. In front of the girl? Yes.* He stuffed a snotty pocket handkerchief in her mouth to keep her from screaming. The splintered ends of the toothpick halves dug into the insides of her eyelids. *Do what I told you to do. She has to learn. Without anesthesia? It doesn't need an anesthetic. It's a beast. I won't do it. Then God damn it I'll do it myself. Stand aside. Give that drill to me. Now darling daughter watch.* A thick deep red jet of blood spurted out of the new hole in the horse's head, drenching its white mane and spattering Father's face and arms. Three sharp raps of the mallet drove the ivory horn home. *There! That's*

your birthday present a day in advance! Now you've learned what happens
when you make wishes for miracles! There's your unicorn. Flesh and blood,
Miranda.

Miranda.

TWENTY-FOUR

"Harold."

He starts awake again to find himself still in the chair. The ropes
binding his wrists have begun to chafe. Before he opens his eyes, he
stretches as much as he can, given the circumstances, rolling his head
around on his stiff neck, extending his legs and wiggling his toes inside
his shoes.

When he opens his eyes he finds Talus before him, seated on the floor
with his legs crossed beneath him. He's removed the silver paint from his
face and changed out of his costume into a loosely fitted linen shirt and
slacks. Out of the costume he seems aged, but oddly elfin, with large
watery pale green eyes, a beak for a nose, and an impish cast to his mouth.
The shrinking shyness that Harold saw in him a few hours ago, when he
was attempting to address Miranda, is entirely gone.

"How do you know my name?" Harold says. Where *has* he seen this
man before? Not Talus. Another name. Long ago.

"How . . . do I know your name. Hm." Talus cocks his head and
strokes his chin in a mock-scholarly way, pondering the conundrum.
"How. Do I know. Your name." He isn't much help.

On the opposite side of the room, Miranda is curled on a pile of
blankets, sleeping. Her hands are balled into fists, and her arms are
folded and clenched to her chest. In her sleep she mumbles and shivers,
as if she is deep in nightmare.

"I won't have done my job," Talus says quietly, "if this whole experience, the kidnapping, doesn't get your adrenaline running. If it doesn't
make you feel young again. Is this not an exciting thing, to imagine

happening to oneself? *I've* certainly never been kidnapped." He lowers his head. "I'm not important enough."

"I'm not important," Harold says.

"You're important enough to be *kidnapped*. I think that says *something*. Frankly, I'm jealous."

Now Talus jumps to his feet in a single smooth motion. "We're all playing a part here!" he says. "Me, um, Artegall—you, too. Miranda, too. Speak your lines."

Harold looks at Talus in confusion.

"Imagine this," Talus says. "I'm offstage in the wings, watching you, distressed because the play's going all wrong. Because you're up to your next line and you've drawn a blank. We can't just skip it. You've got to play the hero here. You've got to give the villain the chance to reveal his motives. You've got to say—say it with me. *Why—*"

"Why."

"Not enough righteous outrage. Try again. *Why—*"

"Why—"

"—have you *kidnapped*—"

"—have you kidnapped—"

"—*Miranda!?* Finish it off with indignation."

"Miranda," Harold sighs.

Talus rolls his eyes. "Close enough," he says in exasperation, then sits back down on the floor to look up at Harold. "Let me tell you," he says, "the tale of when I was a child and the century was turning, and my father took me to the Exposition of the Future. Then you'll understand."

TWENTY-FIVE

—By the time the touring Exposition of the Future came to our town, all the signs were in the air that the age of miracles was almost at its end. It wasn't uncommon to see sights like an angel staggering down the middle of a street in broad daylight, weaving like a drunkard, clutching its hand to its stomach and vomiting up blood. My father was a metal-

smith, and more than half his income in those last days came from demons, who'd come to the back door of his establishment under cover of
night, sacks of silver coins clutched in their clawed hands, begging him to
use his tools to file off their magnificent curling horns.

We had to clear out all the rooms in the city hall, our town's largest
building, to house the Exposition, plus a nearby barn that became the
fabulous Hall of Dynamos. The century was about to turn, and though
machines weren't nearly as prevalent as they are now, they were still
common enough not to take us entirely by surprise when we saw them,
even though things with engines were primarily owned by the rich. But
the single declared purpose of the Exposition of the Future was to awe
us common men, to terrify us with visions of the coming twentieth century in the way that we were terrified of an inscrutable God Who killed
and bestowed gifts according to His own unknowable logic.

Most of the Exposition was fantasy, though—smoke and hot air,
drawings and models, based more on artist's fancy than scientific fact. I
remember staring for minutes on end at a diorama of what was supposed to be an automobile driving on the barren landscape of the Moon,
with little figures meticulously carved out of balsa wood behind the
wheel and in the passenger's seat, perhaps a husband and wife on an
afternoon joyride. They were driving toward a symmetrically arrayed
phalanx of Moon people led by a balsa-wood King, who wore a tiny brass
crown and royal finery stitched out of a couple of scraps of velvet and
lace, and who was accompanied by two dozen equally well-dressed
handmaidens. His arms were outstretched in greeting, as if the two
smiling people in the fast-approaching car were welcome guests, not
colonizers. This was to be the Future.

Of course, nothing like the scene depicted in that diorama has
happened—the Moon and its inhabitants are just as far away from us
now as they were in the days when angels and demons still had some life
left in them. Half of the things I saw at that Exposition have never come
to pass and probably never will. But amidst the flights of fancy there
were more sensible exhibits, and technological wonders that seemed
like they belonged to the future, but that, to our surprise (and remember,
we were common men), *already existed*. Nothing as elaborate as the
mechanical men that are now commonplace, but still, to my eyes, they

were wondrous. In one room of the Exposition there was a mechanical device like an oversized typewriter whose keys were all labeled with numbers and symbols, and when you pressed a series of numbers and a final key labeled with a mathematical sign, the device's gears would click and whirl and it would spit a slip of paper out of its side with the solution to the equation you'd made up stamped on it. In another room my father saw experimental ways to forge new kinds of metal, easily malleable and amazingly strong, that he feared would put him out of business. They did, and my father died penniless after all the demons lost their horns, and those new metals make up the bones of this building in which we sit. But nothing we saw that day held the terror of the Hall of Dynamos.

The Hall of Dynamos was designed to be the last stop on the tour, after you'd gone through all the exhibits in the city hall. You'd go out the city hall's back door and get in a line to enter an enormous barn that had originally been built to house hundreds of head of cattle, and a young girl would hand you a pair of earplugs made out of beeswax. As you got closer to the barn's entrance, you'd see people stumbling past you in the opposite direction, having already seen the things that lay in wait inside. All the color would be drained from their faces, and if you asked them to describe what they'd seen, they'd either refuse or, worse, they'd try and be unable and break down into stammers and sniffling sobs.

When you finally reached the barn door, another attendant would caution you to insert the beeswax plugs in your ears. Then you'd step through the door, and you'd see *engines*. Dozens upon dozens of engines crammed into every available space, even lining the walls all the way up to the roof, some smaller than your fist, some big as houses. Intermeshed gears and fans with blades as long as I was tall turned so quickly that they were blurs to the eye. Electric arcs traveled back and forth across the barn's ceiling, excess power burning itself off in bright blue light. It took ten men shoveling coal into an enormous furnace at top speed to keep it all running.

The roar of the whirring and grinding was unbelievable, and deafening even through the beeswax; as an unwise child I thought that the noise of all those engines must have been what the true voice of God sounded like, the one He only used when speaking to His seraphim. As my father held my hand and stood there quivering, wanting to run from the place but not wanting to show cowardice in front of his son, I watched one man piss his pants, and another dare to remove a beeswax plug to hear the sounds of engines undiluted: a few drops of blood spurted out of his ear as its drum ruptured. I saw him scream as he clutched the side of his head and collapsed to his knees in supplication, but I couldn't hear him.

Engines, you're thinking, modern man that you are, and you roll your eyes with boredom and make snide remarks about my age. *I've seen engines: nothing to be afraid of.* But those of us who entered the Hall of Dynamos saw those engines with eyes that you can never have, and we learned something that you'll never truly know, even if I tell it to you now as clearly and directly as I can: that what we were afraid of wasn't the mechanical power of the engines, and their seeming ability to make anything happen that you could imagine, even before you'd finished fully imagining it. It was instantly clear to all of us, standing there in the Hall of Dynamos, that we were in the presence of an unstoppable *moral force*, and that this force would not rest until it did us in, all of us, even if it didn't mean to.

TWENTY-SIX

—Two moral forces shaped how we think and live in this shining twentieth century: the Virgin, and the Dynamo. The Dynamo represents the desire to know; the Virgin represents the freedom not to know.

What's the Virgin made of? Things that we think are silly, mostly. The peculiar logic of dreams, or the inexplicable stirring we feel when we look on someone that's beautiful not in a way that we all agree is beautiful, but the unique way in which a single person is. The Virgin is faith and mysticism; miracle and instinct; art and randomness.

On the other hand, you have the Dynamo: the unstoppable engine. It finds the logic behind a seeming miracle and explains that miracle away; it finds the order in randomness to which we're blind; it takes a caliper to a young woman's head and quantifies her beauty in terms of pleasing mathematical ratios; it accounts for the secret stirring you felt by discoursing at length on the nervous systems of animals.

These forces aren't diametrically opposed, and it's not correct to say that one's good and the other's evil, despite the prejudices we might have toward one or the other. When we're at our best, both the Virgin and the Dynamo govern what we think and what we do. But the fear that we felt standing in the Hall of Dynamos stemmed from the certainty that the Virgin was in trouble, and that we *needed* her, just as much as we needed and even *wanted* the Dynamo. What the Dynamo threatened to do was to murder the Virgin by explaining her to us, because it was its nature to explain. To us common men it wasn't worth the pleasure of looking at a woman and knowing that we found her beautiful because of the distance between the tip of her nose and her top lip and the size of her eyes, if it meant losing the equally wonderful pleasure of looking at that same woman and finding her beautiful *without knowing why.*

Imagine a damsel in distress, tied to a train track and screaming. Her impending death would be unfortunate, but would you call the engine that drives the oncoming train evil? You have to ask: how did the damsel get there? Where's the black-cowled dastard in the top hat and the handlebar mustache who did the tying? He is one who forces us to view the damsel and the engine as moral opposites when, in fact, they're nothing of the kind. He is a person who believes that all of our human problems can be solved by the all-knowing Dynamo. And if the Dynamo has to run over a Virgin or two as it barrels unerringly toward its final destination: no great loss, really, in the end.

TWENTY-SEVEN

"Instead of seeing these two kingdoms of force as diametric opposites, always in conflict, as this industrial age has taught us," Talus says, "we have to find a way to allow them to coexist. We have to find a way to marry the Virgin to the Dynamo."

"And Miranda will help you do this?" Harold says.

"The daughter of the inventor of the mechanical man is going to be our Queen," Talus says. "It's just me and Artegall right now, and a couple of others. But once we have a Queen the movement will grow.

"Unless you manage to rescue her, of course. That's what young heroes do, after all. Hey—is the adrenaline running yet? You'll need it to pull off your *hairbreadth escape*."

Suddenly Talus rises and looks around to see if anyone else is listening. But Miranda is still sleeping, and Artegall is presumably in the back room. Then he leans over and whispers to Harold, "All jokes aside, you have to do something soon. I don't know how long I can keep Artegall off of her."

TWENTY-EIGHT

Meanwhile, how is Astrid doing? Not so well. No one has seen her for days now except the delivery boys from fast-food restaurants who pedal to the planetarium door on their bicycles, knock sharply four times per instructions, quickly trade their package (a greasy paper bag or a cardboard box) for purchase price plus a generous tip, then pedal away to the next delivery site, no questions asked. Astrid is at work, and she does not want to be disturbed.

The planetarium under construction on the Xeroville University campus is the ideal exhibition space for Astrid's sculpture: a building whose interior space is a nearly perfect hemisphere. Moreover, with its thick concrete walls and almost no mechanical equipment yet installed, it is completely soundproof, making it a wonderful acoustic space. She managed to talk the university trustees into delaying the opening of the planetarium for a few months while she built the sculpture and exhibited it, giving them a slightly modified version of her plans for the thing (but leaving out what police investigators would later consider to be a rather important detail), and so, opening in this space in less than two weeks will be Astrid Winslow's greatest work, *Music for an Automatic Bronzing*.

Strewn across the planetarium floor are a cot, where Astrid gets five hours of sleep out of every twenty-four; the remains of dozens of fast-food orders that have been her breakfast, lunch, and dinner since she started work on the sculpture in earnest, moving out of her apartment away from the ex-boyfriend du jour and into the exhibition space; expired marijuana roaches and cigarette butts; scraps of paper featuring sketches of the final product; huge coils of wire, along with a welder and cutting tool that Astrid is using to construct some kind of cage; an enormous metal bathtub, big enough to comfortably bathe four, with six feet in the shape of a gryphon's claws; an electrical generator; burners to provide gas flames beneath the bathtub; crates filled with hundreds of defective bronze figurines bought wholesale, screaming cherubs and madonnas with twisted faces; more wires and cables and all the other gears and things necessary to make machines in the twentieth century; the guts and cabinets of two dozen top-of-the-line phonographs; and a recording rig that Astrid is using right now to engrave the discs that will be played on the phonographs when the sculpture is completed. The recording rig works like this: A microphone is connected to the arm of a phonograph, whose needle sits on a disc that spins as long as the phonograph's crank is properly wound, so that any vibrations from the microphone are scratched onto the disc, to be replayed later. The phonograph's arm is also connected by a wire to a small black box with a motor inside it and a lever sticking out of it. The lever has a pencil fastened to it; the point of the pencil is in contact with a long rolling sheet of paper wound around two dowels, powered by small motors. So the vibrations from the phonograph arm are translated through the black box into waveforms drawn by the pencil as the lever to which it is attached swivels back and forth. In addition to being attached to the lever, the pencil is connected to a second lever, which is attached to a second pencil; this second lever pivots on a pin, on an axis halfway between the two pencils to which the lever is attached. The second half of the recording rig is a mirror image of the first: the pencil etching waveforms on paper; the black box; the wire leading to the arm of a second recording phonograph. However, because of the pivoting lever arm that connects the two halves of the recording rig, the waves drawn on the second rolling spool of paper are the inverse of the waves drawn on the first spool. The result, then, is that the sounds recorded on the second phonograph are the inverse of the sounds of the words that Astrid, this malnourished and bedraggled young woman living on a steady diet of carbonated water, salt, and starches, speaks into the microphone over and over, holding her cracked lips close: "This world will begin and end in silence. This world will begin and end in silence."

TWENTY-NINE

Harold awakes again to find himself *starving*, his stomach stabbing itself with knives. He flexes his stiff wrists and finds that his arms have been untied: the ropes lie coiled about the chair's feet. Strange. Why?

He hears Talus and Artegall arguing heatedly through the door of the room that's behind him. Talus's high-pitched words alternate with Artegall's abrasive bellow: they are quarreling, apparently, about Miranda. "You ain't got what it *takes* to get with that high-class girl!" Artegall says. "You ain't *got* it! You ain't goin' to do nothing but sit and *talk* to her! You and her sitting there drinking tea in the *gazebo* with your pinky fingers sticking out, you going on all genteel about important events of the day when all the girl wants is for you to shut your mouth and get to *laying pipe*. You ain't—"

"The *boss* said that it's *me* that talks to her, and you that stays away—"

"I told you that the boss isn't *shit* to us now! He said all we're supposed to do is act this stuff out! Well we aren't *acting* anymore! We aren't *pretending* that we want us a Queen! This is one hundred percent for *real* now. *We've* got the girl, and *I've* got what this situation requires, and I can damn well tell you this: I am going to shuck that girl out of that seersucker suit so fast it'll take her back to her senior prom—"

On the other side of the warehouse, Miranda is curled on the blankets, sleeping, her body trembling. It's time to move, Harold realizes, and he leaves the chair and moves across the warehouse to her as quickly as he can, without making any noise. *You have to do something soon. I don't know how long I can keep Artegall off of her.*

"I don't understand what you're about," Harold hears Artegall say to Talus. "Because, seriously, I don't see how you could look at that woman and *not* want to jump her ASAP. I wouldn't care if she was writing me a traffic ticket or giving me communion."

Bent over Miranda, Harold reaches out a hand to shake her into wakefulness, but then thinks better of it. He hesitates for a long moment with his hand in the air above her, thinking of what he should do (and ten years from now, when Harold Winslow is about to murder Miranda's father, Prospero Taligent will tell him that this moment of hesitation, which in retrospect seemed not too different to Harold than any other, was the happiest of Harold's life). He hates to scare her like this, but instead of touching her shoulder, he takes his hand and firmly clamps it over her mouth. This much he's learned from movies.

The girl's eyes snap open.

Artegall's voice comes clearly to them through the metal door: "I have doubts about you."

Harold keeps Miranda pinned down as she screams and kicks and flails her arms for a moment; then she stops as she realizes who Harold is. Her eyes are stretched wide and unblinking in pure terror, her gaze darting back and forth. "Miranda," Harold hisses. "It's me. We have to get out of here."

"Artegall," Talus says behind the door, "have you lost your mind? What are you doing?"

"You see *this*?" Artegall says. "You see this *magnificence*? This is what I got waiting for the girl. Some of this, and some of this. You want to see some of this? You want—oh no you *don't*. You get back here. I'm going to show you some of this. I'm going to give you some of this."

Miranda looks over to the door on the opposite side of the warehouse. Harold takes his hand away from her mouth and she whispers, "What's happening?"

"We don't have time to worry about them. Leave them to it. We have to go." Harold gestures toward the crumpled white fedora on the floor: "Don't forget your hat."

Behind the door, there's the dull painful smack of something solid and metallic colliding with soft flesh. "Agh," Talus says.

Miranda rises, brushes off her clothes, straightens her suit and tie, and places her hat on her head; then the two of them run over to one of the wide garage doors and try to lift it. To Miranda's surprise (but not Harold's, not really) it's not even locked, and rises easily.

"Do you like that?" growls Artegall. "That's what you like. This is what you like, isn't it. You *know* you like the pipe! Everybody likes the *pipe!*" He's hysterical. There is another soft thud, and another, then the ringing clang of some hollow things falling off shelves.

Talus screams. "*Help me.*" Harold hears his hands scrabbling against the inside of the closed door.

It's a pity when one has to turn one's back on another in distress, but this time it has to be done. Together, Miranda and Harold lift the door of the warehouse just high enough for the two of them to scurry under it and lower it behind them. In another moment they are running down the street, out into the night of the city's industrial district, leaving the two living tin men to their ministrations.

THIRTY

Two hours later, it's three o'clock in the morning and Harold finds himself in a twenty-four-hour automatic restaurant, sitting in a booth across a table from Miranda. He is only now beginning to think clearly, after their escape. At first all he could think of was that they needed to get away from people, and that he was nearly faint from hunger, so he hailed a passing cab and had it drop them here, sixty blocks north of the warehouse and far enough away so that Talus and Artegall won't be able to find them.

Miranda is a nervous wreck, crying her eyes out, her hands shaking too much to hold her coffee cup to her lips without spilling it on her already stained white suit. Harold doesn't know how to deal with Miranda just yet. He feels that he's not quite performing as well as he might in this situation. But given that he's managed to extract them both from the custody of kidnappers, he thinks that on balance he's doing okay, even if there wasn't much to the escape attempt in the end but walking straight out of the place—no fisticuffs; no outfoxing.

He looks at everything else he can in the automatic restaurant except Miranda: if she catches his eye, then he feels that his clear inability to say something sufficiently comforting will make things even worse for her. He puts a good deal of effort into trying to figure out how the device works that operates his "bottomless cup of coffee." The cup, it appears, is perfectly ordinary, but its saucer is bolted to the table—whenever he sets his empty cup down on the saucer, a nozzle shoots out of a hatch on the wall, squirts a few ounces of lukewarm brown sludge into the cup, and goes back whence it came. Maybe the saucer is attached to a plate that measures the weight of the cup sitting on it, and the plate's calibrated so that it activates the nozzle once the cup is sufficiently light. Then why doesn't the nozzle appear whenever there's no cup on the saucer at all, and spray coffee all over the table? Like much modern technology, it's a mystery to him.

Maybe he should get Miranda some food? Yes. Maybe he should place some food in front of her, as a gesture of care. He has a few coins in his pocket, enough to get them both something to eat. Miranda is still vacillating between looking around her surroundings all wild-eyed and bursting into tears, so asking her what she wants probably isn't the best idea. He'll pick it himself, he decides.

"I'll be right back with some food," he says quietly, touching the woman's hand, and Miranda nods her head feverishly and rubs her bloodshot eyes, her chest hitching with sobs. Some communication is better than none at all: she's settling down. He gets out of the booth and approaches the back wall of the restaurant, which is made up of an array of hundreds of tiny glass windows, each one with some sort of foodstuff behind it. All of the dishes are concealed within identical white cardboard boxes, each printed with its name. All of the names of the dishes end with exclamation points, as if to convey some halfhearted sense of exuberance that's meant to be felt when consuming twentieth-century mass-produced convenience food. Harold drops a few coins into a slot next to a window displaying a SLICE OF PECAN PIE!, lifts the window, and takes the box; that'll be for Miranda. He wants something a little more substantial for himself, though. The PORK SANDWICH! seems a little questionable: he can already see spots of pink-tinged grease blooming through its box. The CHICKEN SANDWICH! looks safe enough, though.

He slides his last few coins into the proper slot and takes the chicken sandwich. Through the empty window he can see the back room of the restaurant, where a single mechanical man stands at attention, surrounded by pallets holding stacks of little white boxes that tower to the ceiling. Harold supposes that in a few moments, once it's worth its while, the tin man will go into action and refill the newly emptied windows with the proper, missing dishes. So this place *is* entirely automatic, then: there's really not a soul in the building except for Miranda and himself. He carries the boxes of food back to the booth and places the piece of pie before Miranda. "Thank you," she murmurs hoarsely, and she picks away the box's seal and opens the lid. Inside there is a slender slice of pie with a dark brown glistening filling, with a single pecan-half placed on top of it for decoration. The package also contains a paper napkin, and a disposable fork made of tin that'll last just long enough to finish off the pie before it's too bent out of shape to be useful.

She places a bite of pie in her mouth. "It's really really sweet," she says.

The chicken sandwich turns out to be composed of two stale pieces of bread that hold together an overcooked slice of chicken breast and a pile of lettuce that has been shredded to the consistency of confetti. A nondescript yellowish white sauce is smeared over it all.

"It's hard to be in the world," Miranda says.

Harold says nothing and bites into his sandwich. The flavor of the sauce takes him by surprise; it's rancid, and it turns his stomach. He still doesn't know what to say. To him Miranda seems like a girl trapped in an adult's body. The suit she's wearing conceals her shape—the only visible sign that she might be female is her unkempt gold-red hair, which falls nearly to her waist. What must it have been like for her to grow into adulthood, never leaving the safety of her father's Tower, spending away the days of her adolescence in that playroom made for little children, filled with fantasies custom-built from scratch? She can't be normal, Harold thinks; she certainly can't think like normal women who go through the laundry list of difficult things that women go through, growing up in the outside world. If you locked her in an empty room with Astrid, or with Charmaine Saint Claire, what would they have to talk about? Not much. Even though Harold and Miranda are the same age, Harold looks at Miranda and thinks to himself that she isn't much more than a little girl, really.

Should he say to Miranda that he's nearly certain that this whole incident was rigged by her father, possibly even including his own kidnapping, and it all went wrong in the end because Artegall decided to go off the script that had been provided to him by Prospero? If Artegall hadn't gone off on his own, what would have happened? Or maybe *this* is what was supposed to happen—Harold and Miranda, sitting here in this deserted automatic restaurant, with Miranda feeling like a rescued damsel and Harold experiencing that incomparable rush of heroism, just as in the game they played together years ago? Is Prospero Taligent really *that* smart, to be able to pull that off?

Maybe when Artegall was saying to Talus that he wasn't acting, he was still acting? Harold didn't actually see what happened behind the door where they were, even though he could hear their voices. Perhaps they were faking it all, like actors in a radio play who know they won't be seen.

What should Harold say to Miranda? He doesn't know what to say.

Miranda puts down her fork, her pecan pie half-finished. Harold has his hand on the table, and she reaches out and grips two of his outstretched fingers in her fist, in the way a small child holds a parent's hand.

They sit like that for several long minutes in silence in the empty restaurant, then Miranda takes a breath and gets herself together. "I'm going to tell you something now," she says.

THIRTY-ONE

"When I got my first period I was twelve and a half years old, and I thought I was bleeding to death. It's not like I knew what was happening to me, and Father had never sat me down to have the talk that I assume normal fathers have with their daughters about their bodies. He didn't notice anything for two days, and I took the time to put my affairs in order: making a will out with a blue crayon, apologizing to Father for the times I'd thrown temper tantrums. He found out because of the sheets. This is kind of embarrassing. He told my maid only to put white sheets on my bed soon after my tenth birthday—soon after you got kicked out of the playroom for kissing me: remember that? He never explained it to me; he just said that it was a matter of trust after that little kissing incident, that he needed to regain my trust. And five or six times during any month he'd come wake me up himself, and he'd inspect the sheets while I got ready for the day, looking over every inch of them. Then he'd say something like 'Clean as can be. She's still pure. The girl is still pure. Good.' But then he saw the blood that one morning, and he looked at me with what I still think today was an expression of absolute undiluted fright, his magnifying glass slipping out of his hand and shattering on the floor, and he *screamed*. He said, 'You see what happens! When you *kiss boys*? One thing leads to another and now you're ruined!' And I broke and told him everything, in hysterical words that I'm sure didn't make much sense.

"He started crying, right there, and he gathered me into his arms and carried me down to the Tower's infirmary. It was the closest I'd ever felt to my father: my arms around his neck, his broad hand splayed against my shaking back, my head tucked into the slope of his shoulder, my tears running down my face and making a damp spot on his shirt. And when he entered the infirmary, this room that was full of cleanness and bright light, a nurse looked up from her desk to see the two of us, and my father said, not in the voice he uses when he's trying to humor me and shield me from some unknown terror, but a voice I'd never heard before, giving out that he himself was genuinely terrified, 'You have to save my daughter. She's bleeding to death.' As if that was easier for him to believe than what I later found out from the nurse was the truth of the matter.

"Sometimes my father comes into my room when he thinks I'm sleeping, and he just stares at me. It makes me feel like he's trying to will me back into the body I had ten years ago, when he used to talk to me and play little games while I sat on his desk in his office. I don't understand why it is that we never want anything to get old. No, that's not true: we think that bottles of wine are better the older they are, not like little girls.

But in that case we're just whetting our appetites, waiting for the right time to consume them.

"There's something very wrong—wrong with my father, and wrong with me. I wake up every morning and I feel wrong, and when he looks at me it makes me want to run somewhere and hide. But it's not just us . . . it's you, too. I can look at you and be certain that you can't tell me the thing I need to hear to save me, but it's hard for me to hold it against you, because I can't tell you the thing you need to hear, either. There's no way for me to warn you about the terrible things that I know are going to happen.

"Every desire has a price; the price of being young is growing old; the price of knowledge is the loss of innocence. These are not new truths. But knowing this still doesn't take the sting out of the fact that things were so different when we were young, in that place that we both believed was somehow full of magic, even though it was built with machines. Do you remember, we'd spend long minutes just sitting next to each other, your arm just touching mine, and neither of us speaking? Not worrying about whether we'd be able to say the thing we need to say; not trying to fill up the air with stupid noises to relieve us of the responsibility of dealing with what was going on in our heads? Do you think then that we were willing the world to stand still? Do you think we knew, even though we never could have said it aloud for fear of breaking the spell, that those last innocent moments of our youth were burning themselves up one at a time?"

"I have something to say to you," says Harold when Miranda stops speaking. Then, again, hesitantly, clearing his throat first: "I have something to say?" The inside of his throat feels as if it's lined with sand.

THIRTY-TWO

And that is all he can make himself say to her: that he has something to say. After he stammers that out, his voice trails off into silence and his gaze drops to the tabletop.

What he can't bring himself to say to Miranda is:

"When I was a child, I used to look at adults half with confusion, half with envy, trying and failing to imagine the nature of the mysteries to which they'd been initiated, the pleasures they were keeping to themselves. Have you ever watched the swings of moods that toddlers go through, the way they act as if they're attending their own funeral if the axle falls off a favored toy car, or the rapturous expressions that show up on their faces when they suck on sweet things? Though the memory's fading, I can still *remember* feeling like that, and I thought that being an adult would be even more like that—that the emotions that make us human got more intense, the older you grew. Even at the age of ten, simple surprise gifts could be enough to make me feel like my heart and my brain were both about to burst. I couldn't imagine how people even survived to the age of twenty when such pleasures were lying in wait, out in the world.

"But that hasn't turned out to be what happened—instead, my own father tells me that he thinks I'm turning into tin. Something inside me is dying, and I don't know what to do to save it; something inside me is slipping away, and somehow my memories of what you were as a child have come to stand in for all the things I want to keep alive inside myself and don't know how. In dreams I see you as a queen, standing at the roof's edge; again and again you beckon to me, and again and again I watch you fall, and with you fall all those things within me that make me best.

"There has to be a spell to speak to save you, and myself. But for the life of me I can't come up with the words."

THIRTY-THREE

Harold says none of that, though: he just sits there. Then, after a while, Miranda speaks.

"Harold," Miranda says. "Harry. I want to go back."

"Back to the Tower?"

"Back to my playroom, whose door is likely rusted shut. Back to our magic island."

THIRTY-FOUR

Harold had the idea that getting back into the Taligent Tower with Miranda would involve some kind of exciting covert operation, like knocking out a pair of guards and taking their uniforms, or scaling the Tower's obsidian walls with rubber suction cups attached to their hands and feet. It turned out, though, that they showed up at the Tower's gates in the early morning when the workers were arriving, marching into the Tower in their habitual neat rows and columns, wearing identical overalls and singing one of those proletarian songs in three-part harmony while they swung their gleaming lunch buckets in synchrony. They joined the crowd, and Miranda flashed her identification to the gate guard, taking in Harold as her personal guest ("Hey there, Miranda!" the gate guard said, and beamed a smile at her. "It's very nice to see you again!"). Then Miranda let the two of them into the Tower through one of its side entrances, to which she had a long silver key hanging around her neck on a chain.

But.

This is what Harold expected to happen when he and Miranda reached the playroom and Miranda swung open its door:

A miasmatic decay blasted them in the face as soon as the door opened. Everything in the playroom was dead, dead: vines and leaves of plants gone brown; a small and formerly iris-blue lake turned foul with a thick layer of deep green pond scum covering its surface; mechanical corpses sprawled on the ground in unnatural positions with spots of rust blooming on them; the skeleton of a horse with its bones picked clean and a neat little hole drilled into its skull. "O!" said Miranda. "O, how could I ever have expected to reclaim the innocent pastoral world of my long-vanished youth?? O, we have learned a *most important lesson*, Harold: that the innocence and beauty of our younger years can never be valued enough, for it is lost too soon, O, *all too soon*. Now

I shall sit here in the dead grass and weep until I can weep no more, mourning the loss of all my illusions. Boo-hoo-hoo!" wept Miranda. *"Boo-hoo-hoooo!!"*

But that is not what happened.

THIRTY-FIVE

This is what really happened, which was worse.

"Everything is exactly like I left it," Miranda said. "I haven't come into this place in years, but he kept everything exactly the same for me. In case I ever wanted to come back."

They stood together on the seashore, hand in hand, in a child's place. Waves from an ice-blue sea beat gently against a beach with sand the color of newly made paper, waiting to be written on. A brace of palm trees with perfectly parabolic trunks and bright green leaves stood behind them, waving gently in a light cold wind that carried the sharp smell of salt. A lightbulb sun, deep red turning to yellow, rose on the island's false horizon.

"No footprints here but our own," Miranda said. "It's our own little paradise." She looked up at Harold and drew a smile across her face.

Something is wrong here, Harold thought. He'd felt disoriented like this the first time he'd entered the playroom ten years ago; back then Miranda said that it had something to do with this place being "more real" than the places he was used to being in. *It always hurts like this the first time*, she'd said. But now something else was wrong in an altogether different way. Something to do with the way time was moving here, or that this place seemed less real to him now than anywhere he'd ever been, even in dreams.

"Do you remember all of those troublesome tin men that Father put on the island, to give us lessons?" Miranda said. "To constantly remind us that the world wasn't perfect, and that outside the special secluded places that some of us can manage to make for ourselves there's nothing but suffering? All those tin men are gone now. We don't need lessons anymore, because we've grown up. Now we can come to this place in peace, because we were smart enough to find it. Most people stop believing in things like paradise once they grow up, and their hearts encase themselves in ice and armor. But paradise never goes away. You just have to be able to find your way back to it."

"There's something wrong," Harold said.

"There's *nothing* wrong!" Miranda spat back at him. "Nothing, except that I neglected this place for all this time because I thought I was too grown up for it, and now that time is wasted. There's no evil here, except for that we bring with us. And we didn't bring any evil with us, did we?" She glared at Harold, her hand on her hip, speaking with the tone of a chiding mother. *"Did we?"*

"No," said Harold. "We didn't."

"Then lie down with me in the sand," Miranda said, "and put your arms around me."

And this is what he did, the sun already high in the sky, shortening the island's shadows to nothing.

THIRTY-SIX

"There's something wrong with time here," Harold said a minute later as the afternoon sun began its downward arc. "It's moving faster than it should."

"It's all the time that's built up in this place unspent, burning itself away," Miranda said quietly, her arms around him. "Hurry. We still have a chance to be young."

"I'm tired," said Harold. "I don't know why."

"Sleep, then," said Miranda.

Hurry; sleep, thought Harold. *It doesn't make sense.*

He slept.

THIRTY-SEVEN

When he awoke again five minutes later, Miranda was naked and lying on top of him. Evening had come, and some of the golden tone had gone out of her hair in the light from the full moon over the sea, leaving it the color of newly forged copper. Her white suit lay shed like a second skin in a pile farther down the shore, just out of reach of the tide.

"I wanted to be naked with you," Miranda said.

Harold looked at her and squinted drowsily. He felt drunk.

"Harry," Miranda whispered, straddling him now and cupping his chin in her hands, silhouetted in moonlight, "there is something very important that I have to tell you, but I cannot say it with words. But I think that it will be the most important thing I will ever say. Before I can tell you, I need to have your body inside mine.

"Did I say that right?" she said, bending over him, her lips brushing against his ear, her hands at the top button of his shirt, slipping it open.

"Did I sound silly when I said that?

"It's hard to talk about this kind of thing without sounding silly.

"Did I . . .

"Can I—"

THIRTY-EIGHT

And so Harold Winslow and Miranda Taligent made love, on the shore of that pastoral place where they'd played their childhood games so long ago. First there was the problem with the condom. When Harold finally fumbled his way out of his clothes, removed the condom from his wallet (where it had spent the last year and a half), opened its wrapper with a great deal of difficulty (he finally had to use his teeth), and sheathed himself with it, it split right down the shaft, shrinking in a flash to a little ring of rubber. Fortunately, he had a second, but Miranda, noting that it was the same brand as the first and, moreover, a brand she'd never heard of, became gun-shy. "But I thought you had something to *tell* me," said Harold, all hot and bothered—virgin, virgin, virgin. "Well, *yeah*," said Miranda, "I like you fine enough, and I have something that it'd be very *nice* to tell you, but it's not worth me getting *pregnant* because of a crap condom made by the—what? The . . . the Happy Family Toy Company? They make *rubbers*?" But after a few minutes of coaxing and explaining that maybe he *tore* that first condom with his teeth trying to get the package open, she reluctantly acquiesced. Then they argued for a good half hour about which position to use, as each carried certain symbolic overtones of dominance and submission with which one or the other was uncomfortable. By the time they settled on a position (missionary, if you're interested, because it allows the deepest possible penetration and contact between the male pubic bone and clitoris, according to a radio program that Harold had heard one afternoon on the subject), Miranda had lost any trace of sexual arousal, and so Harold had to go through this elaborate business of foreplay (which he was already finding he hated) in order to get her "turned on" (to coin a phrase) again. So. When he finally entered her, Miranda was just realizing that she might have to fake it (having already judged Harold against the standard set by her other lovers and found him sorely wanting, especially next to that Ferdinand fellow, a muscle-bound dullard who worked in the Tower's boiler room, shirtless chest begrimed with soot and slick shining sweat . . . mmmmyes Ferdinand. *There are many men that shovel coal in this boiler room. But I am their master.*) when Harold saved her the trouble by climaxing, having thrust against her for approximately forty seconds: gasp, grunt, done. "It was because I passed my peak," he said by way of vague apology, citing the above-mentioned time-consuming foreplay. And as he stripped off the rubber and threw it down the shore to be taken away by the morning tide, Harold turned on his side away from Miranda, frustrated and exhausted, wondering if this was the secret thing that Miranda had been trying to tell him all along, even though she hadn't known it: that everything in the twentieth century was dead, and we'd built shields between all of us, and that there was nothing really worth saying that one person could say to another anymore, nothing, nothing further, nothing more.

THIRTY-NINE

Before the incident that cost him his job and landed his image on the front page of every major paper in Xeroville, Jason Fenman, eighteen years old, was the best pizza delivery boy the Xeroville Famous Pizza Company had ever had in its four years of existence. His two shining virtues were especially strong calves (good for pedaling his bicycle up hills that would have sent lesser delivery boys sprawling to the ground ready to spit up a lung, their shipments spilled in the street and devoured by stray dogs) and a finely honed sense of balance that allowed him to carry his cargo by hand instead of stowing it in the rear rack of his bike, where it'd be tossed around inside its box until it was transformed into an unrecognizable mass of dough and tomato sauce and several varieties of cured meat. By holding the pizza in the air as he pedaled, balanced on a platform made from the splayed fingers of his open right hand, he could compensate for continually changing tilt and inertia with slight movements of his wrist, leaning the pizza a hair to the right when making a left turn, or tipping it a bit backward when flying down a steep slope. Jason Fenman could deliver a seven-topping, extralarge special from downtown to uptown and never have its crust touch the inside wall of its box once. He was a savant.

Because of his unparalleled pizza-delivering capabilities, Jason Fenman is always given the Astrid Winslow order, whenever it comes through. She orders an extralarge three-topping pizza every other day (pepperoni, sausage, black olives), asking for it to be delivered to the Xeroville University Planetarium, which sits at the top of one of the steepest hills in the city. Jason doesn't know much about Astrid, except that she's not a vegetarian. He likes that about her. (Vegetarian pizza gives him the shivers: all the water from those toppings, green and red peppers and onions and broccoli and carrot slices and whatever the hell else those vegetarians eat—what is that stuff, *tofu*? The *curd*? Wouldn't trust that stuff one bit, anything that looks like that has *got* to have some fish lips and worm ears mixed into it—all the water from those vegetables soaking through the crust, utterly ruining its crispy flaky flavor, unlike the grease from meat, which not only *adds* flavor but acts as a handy congealing agent.) When he comes to the planetarium's double doors he knocks four times per instructions and Astrid comes, opening the doors just wide enough to take the box through them (and she doesn't tilt the box at all when she takes it, notice that, she appreciates an undamaged pizza as much as Jason; they have a common bond, he thinks), giving Jason the price of the pizza plus a 30 percent tip, shutting the doors quickly before he can get out a word other than *thank you*. She looks beautiful, he thinks, if a bit older than she should, but perhaps that's just because he's only seen her for ten seconds at a time at the most. He could be filling in most of the details of her appearance from memories and fantasies. People often do that, he thinks.

But on this particular evening, the evening that would ruin Jason Fenman's life, when he made his way up the hill to the planetarium with his three-topping extralarge pizza in hand, got off his bike, and approached the planetarium's entrance, a neatly lettered sign was taped to one of the double doors:

It's unlocked.
Come on in.
Astrid.

Jason thought that was just a little weird at first, then changed his mind: maybe Astrid was finally going to let him see what she was up to in here. It wasn't unheard of for a pizza delivery boy and his customer to form a casual friendship, or sometimes a relationship that was a bit more intimate. He recalled fragments of the stories of older, more experienced delivery boys, who claimed that sometimes lonely housewives picked up their pizzas topless or asked them to come up to their bedroom to repair a malfunctioning mechanical phallus, but Jason suspected that nothing like that would cross Astrid's mind. Probably. He suspected that Astrid was some kind of artist, and artists think it's okay to be naked in all kinds of strange places. You never know.

So Jason broke the first and most important rule of pizza delivery—he crossed the threshold. He found himself in a short, dimly lit corridor, its walls sparsely decorated with building blueprints and curling yellowed posters depicting paintings of other planets. At the other end of the corridor was the door that let onto the planetarium's central dome, where the shows would be held when the place was finished. The door was open just a crack, and a brightly flickering yellow light spilled from it, cutting a thin line across the corridor's floor.

Jason approached the door and rapped on it four times, sharply. He didn't like this. The pizza was starting to get cold; he could feel its heat bleeding out of the box through his fingers. Cold pizza meant a stiff tip on the next delivery—bad. "Ms. Winslow?" he said. "Pizza: I got your pizza."

"It's open," hollered a woman from somewhere deep in the room, her voice distorted a bit by echo. "Just open the door and come on in!"

Jason took the doorknob to his hand and pulled it to him. It resisted a bit at first, as if something was attached to it from the other side.

He shifted his grip on the knob, yanked on the door, threw it wide open to a bright light and the sound of applause, and killed Astrid Winslow.

FORTY

When Harold opens his eyes, he cannot make the time told by the wall clock square with the lines of light on the wall, shining through the window blinds. Either the clock has stopped, or the earth shifted its orbit while he slept, or he is misremembering the season, or he is still in Miranda's playroom, burning through time like a fire through tissue paper.

But he is in his dormitory room, the yellowed posters advertising jazz concerts and movie serials tacked to its dingy walls, his dirty clothes from a week before scattered across the floor, and now he is remembering his escape from the Taligent Tower, his journey back to the university, his disoriented crawl into bed. It's not four a.m., but four p.m.: he's slept the clock round. And kidnapped before that. How long has he been gone? Was he even missed? Some sort of manhunt under way, begun when the morning shift came in and saw the damaged press and headless tin men? The whole affair couldn't have taken more than a day or two.

Those two men with the silver faces. So familiar. Seen them before—the answer is lodged in his throat and won't come out. Where? Some time ago—the Tower?

That's it. Ten years ago. The camera obscura. And the day he was cradled in the tin demon's arms.

One of them thin and scrawny, the other one fat. Like a vaudeville team.

Talus? Artegall? No.

Martin. Gideon.

Taligent's men.

FORTY-ONE

He expects, having lost his virginity the night before, to feel somehow profoundly different; he used to look around at passengers on buses, or at the queues in front of movie theaters, and think that all of those people had knowledge to which he was uninitiated, that all of them but him had done a wonderful thing that animals do. He imagined that the double entendres that peppered romantic comedies and frat-boy boasts were like words in a foreign language that couldn't directly be translated into his own—he might get the gist of them and know what was being spoken of, but without recourse to the memories that he assumed everyone else in the theater had, they were like describing color to the blind from birth, or music to the deaf.

But he feels exactly the same as he did the day before, and the day before that. There is a distinct lack of romanticized specialness to his memory of last night's encounter with Miranda. As he stands naked before the bathroom mirror his body still looks the same; no film of sin sticks to his skin, refusing to be scrubbed off in the shower. His heart is neither light nor heavy. He has not become enlightened.

When he returns to his room and starts to dress, he notices that the answering device attached to his telephone has recorded a message. The wax cylinder lying in the device's tray is engraved with grooves from end to end—not just someone saying *hey, call me*, but a long message. A salesman at best, prattling on about matchmaking services or opportunities for low-interest loans; likely something more inconvenient. Or his roommate, Marlon, a drunken ramble letting him know that he's staying the night with some girl.

Harold places the cylinder on the playback dowel, drops the needle onto it, and starts to turn the crank. It's hard to get the speed properly matched, and even then there's a crackle that obscures a third of the words, due partly to recording technology that seems as if it's not going to get its kinks worked out until the end of time, and partly to what must have been a bad telephone connection. But it isn't a salesman who placed the call—it's a policeman. "Hello. This is Officer—" What is that name? Scythe? Smythe. "Smythe. You may want to—" Unintelligible. "—we think your sister may have—" Unintelligible. "—automatic bronzing. Please call—" Unintelligible. "—no note. We've kept everyone out so you—" Unintelligible. "—send someone out to bring you to the planetarium if you need it—" Unintelligible. "—as soon as possible. Thank—"

The needle slides off the end of the cylinder, and the reedy voice of the cop goes silent.

It makes sense for the police to call his apartment, he thinks—he's reassured that someone cares about his disappearance. And maybe it's Astrid who's been looking for him and alerted the cops, though it's hard for him to imagine her being that concerned about his welfare. But fragments of the message don't quite fit that hypothesis: *automatic bronzing*; *no note*; *bring you to the planetarium*. Strange.

As he picks up the phone to call the police department, he still can't make sense of it.

FORTY-TWO

But he's disappointed to find that the police don't seem to care much about his kidnapping, which is one of the most unusual events to have happened to him in some time—it seems to him that everyone else should be at least as excited about it as he is. In fact, after he's relayed from person to person upon calling the department, he ends up talking to this same Officer Smythe, who fails to be forthcoming with much of anything at all—though he presumably wears a badge, he speaks in riddles, like a pulp-fiction master criminal. Over the telephone line his voice sounds less tinny—it doesn't grate against the ear like it does when it's carved into wax. But there's still something strange about the way he speaks, as if he's composing his sentences from beginning to end in close consultation with an editor and a lawyer, and reciting them into the handset fully formed.

"I am to ask you," says Officer Smythe, "if you're well."

"I'm fine," says Harold. "As well as can be expected, considering that I just got back from—"

"I am to *ask* you," interrupts Officer Smythe, "if you made them *shove off.*"

"I don't understand—"

"I am to ask if you made them *shove off,*" Officer Smythe repeats, sounding like a hostage reading his own ransom note.

"Yeah. Yeah—sure I did. You bet. They shoved off. You betcha."

"It's going to be a difficult time for you soon," says Officer Smythe, his voice becoming slightly more relaxed. "If it could have been managed another way, be assured that it would have been. The timing of this could not be worse."

"Officer, I don't know what—"

"Where are you right now?"

"In my dormitory room at the university. Hey, Officer! Hey did I mention that I just got back from being kid—"

"We're going to send an officer over immediately to escort you to the university's planetarium."

"What for?" Planetarium? Sure, there's that project that Astrid's been working on there, but—

Smythe pauses, then says in a measured voice: "There's a crime scene."

"A *what*?" Hey what—

A pause; a sigh.

"We need you to identify a body," says Officer Smythe.

FORTY-THREE

There are four police cars near the entrance to the planetarium when Harold and the police officer with him ascend the hill; they are parked at various careless angles, the lights on their roofs flashing blue. Most of the cops in the area are just milling around the place, writing things on notepads and engaging in idle conversation; two of them are brandishing nightsticks, holding back a small gang of hipsters that look as if they're trying to get inside the planetarium, whose entrance is cordoned off with rope. Harold recognizes one of the people in the crowd—it's Charmaine Saint Claire, the graduate student he met at Astrid's exhibition. She is screaming bloody murder at the policeman standing before her. "The visual is *essentially* pornographic," she yells, and the cop flinches as her spittle flies into his face. "And how *ironic* that you with your *fetishized uniform* are attempting to repress Astrid's *reification*—indeed, her *potentiation*—of the *pornographic impulse*. But her subversive *embodiment* of the *scriptible* will *not* be stopped." With her index finger she points at her own eye. "*I think the visual*," she shouts. "History sharpens the female gaze; it brings it into being—"

The policeman with Harold escorts him past Charmaine and her accompanying rabble-rousers and over to the planetarium's entrance. They both duck under the rope, and another officer approaches Harold, introducing himself as Officer Smythe.

Smythe nods at the cop next to Harold, and he leaves the two of them alone.

"I'm really sorry about this," Smythe says in a low voice. "We haven't let anyone in since we got the place cleared out."

"Thanks," says Harold, not knowing if that's the right thing to say.

"Would you like to go in alone?"

Would he? "Yes," says Harold. "I'd like that. I think that might be best."

FORTY-FOUR

He enters the double doors and walks down the silent corridor. The door at the other end is closed tight shut, and an engraved bronze plaque is affixed to it, a polished square four inches on a side:

ASTRID WINSLOW.

MUSIC FOR AN AUTOMATIC BRONZING.

MIXED MEDIA.

19—.

Beneath this plaque, a second:

ARTIST'S STATEMENT.

Under that, taped to the door by its top, is a spindled, smudged index card with a series of crude waves drawn across it in ink. Harold lifts it to look at its back side: a straight line is drawn from corner to corner. He'd drawn it himself a year ago in the bar in Picturetown, when he wanted to illustrate his limited understanding of destructive interference.

He lets the card drop and takes a breath, then pulls the door open and enters the exhibition space.

The door shuts behind him; the lights come up; the sound nearly knocks him down.

FORTY-FIVE

An excerpt from an article appearing on the first page of the Arts, Leisure, and Society section of the *Xeroville Times*, November 2, 19—, entitled, "Astrid Winslow's Final Work Premieres at Xeroville Planetarium":

A cacophony of sound assaults the viewer of the piece when she enters the soundproof, hemispherical dome and shuts the door. Arranged around the inner wall of the dome at precisely measured intervals are twenty-four phonographs with their doors thrown wide, each of them playing a different recording. Each of the phonographs has an apparatus attached to it, a disembodied mechanical arm and four-fingered hand projecting from a black box. The mechanical hands continuously reset the recordings when they finish playing and wind the phonograph cranks to keep them running, and these apparatuses are all powered by an electric generator that sits in a recessed pit near the circular wall. The mechanical hands are synchronized together to make identical movements simultaneously, and the overall visual effect is beautiful and balletic.

The twenty-four phonographs are all pointed toward the center of the room and are oriented to take advantage of the principle of destructive interference (see sidebar), which Ms. Winslow has used to miraculous effect. Because of this principle of sound, when one stands in certain geometrically defined spots of the floor of the dome, elements of the noise initially encountered upon entry suddenly resolve themselves, the inverted sound waves canceling each other out. It is a most unusual sight to see other viewers of the piece drifting through the exhibition space with their eyes closed, letting their feet direct them to the spaces in the chamber where the volume suddenly dips, revealing a simple repetitive melody played on a wind instrument, or a looping series of whispered phrases in a dead language.

At the exact center of the chamber, where viewers of the piece tend to clump together, there is complete silence (this being the spot in the room where all of the sound waves coming from the phonographs meet their inversions and die). Looking up to the ceiling, one sees a cage hanging from a cable about nine feet off the ground, made from heavy-gauge wire and encompassing a space about six feet wide, eight feet long, and eighteen inches high. Enclosed in the cage is the corpse of the artist, Ms. Winslow. The corpse is cast in bronze. Its gleaming fingers clutch the wires of the cage in which it is interred, and its frozen face stares down on the viewers, contorted into a scream.

In a final stroke of genius, the door by which one enters the exhibit has a time-release lock, set for ten minutes. Once you have entered the space and the door closes behind you, you have no choice but to endure the sculpture's maddening beauty, at least until the ghost of the artist who haunts the planetarium grants you her begrudging permission to leave.

FORTY-SIX

All the noises of the world are in here with him; all the news of the world is in here and he cannot get away from it.

The door to the outside world is barred; the only silent space in the hall is directly beneath the bronzed corpse of his sister, whose presence that close to him he cannot bear. He stumbles around the sculpture like a man possessed, and the twenty-four phonographs assault him with the spatter of rain against glass, the rustle of wind through pines, the crack of a lightning strike just overhead, the rumble of an earth tremor, the grinding of continental plates as they pass each other, a rottweiler's howl, the plaintive roar of a lion with a thorn in its paw, the unholy keening of cicadas that return every seventeen years, the bray of a donkey, the crack of a cheetah's leg breaking, the buzz of a wasp nest disturbed by a stick, the sunrise songs of sixty different birds, a gryphon's squawk, a unicorn's neigh, the caw of a phoenix, the crunch of a baby's bones in the mouth of the thing beneath your bed, the sizzle of ichor dripping from the wound of a movie monster, the snap of a violin string as it breaks, the ringing shatter of a crystal glass broken by a soprano's voice, the melody of a player piano performing a wedding march, the bleating honk of a tenor saxophone in the hands of a man with a poor embouchure, the cacophony of a child slamming his fists against a harpsichord's keys, the gentle strum of a mandolin performing a lovesong, the ditty of a slot machine announcing a winning pull, a march drummed out on the bottom of an overturned garbage can, the song of the nine choirs of seraphim in the tenth crystal sphere, the fanfare announcing the entrance of a professional boxer into the ring, the scratch of a quill pen writing a poison-pen letter, the *snick* of the lock of a prison cell's door, the explosion of a firecracker, the snap of a bullet sliding into the chamber of a revolver, the twang of a bowstring, the pop of a cork sliding out of a bottle of chardonnay, the *tchank* of a beer bottle as its top is popped off, the slice of a box cutter gliding through corrugated cardboard, the burble of hot chicken soup on the stove, the smack of a baseball bat impacting with a skull, the beep of an automobile's horn, the ring of a telephone, the splintering of a door to a drug den as the cops come crashing through, the loop of a phonograph recording with a scratch, the drill of a jackhammer cracking asphalt, the tick of a grandfather clock, the rattle of a flying car's malfunctioning engine, the trundle of a railway car, the creak of a first-generation tin man's rusted joints, the tick of a bicycle's gears, the whir of a film in its projector, the scream as a hammer comes down on a finger, the squall of a thirsty newborn babe, the nonsensical words of a toddler, the tentative stutter of a ten-year-old learning to swear, the giggle of a teenager looking at his first pornographic woodcuts, the smack of a fist as it breaks a man's jaw, the pop of an eyeball punctured by a sharpened pencil, the gasp preceding a faked orgasm, the snore of a sleeping mother, the fart of a drunken bum, the death rattle of an invalid, the unanimous cheer of a stadium crowd, the unintelligible barks of a cheerleading squad, the sneeze of a cook who's dropped the pepper pot, the cries of the crew of a tempest-wrecked ship, the dots and dashes of an SOS, the curse laid by a warlock on a wayward lover, the prayer of a supplicant to a god with stopped ears and closed eyes, an erotic poem written in a forgotten language, a declaration of war against a state that does not exist on maps, a five-year-old boy's recitation of a nursery rhyme, the closing argument of a murder trial, the valedictorian's speech for a technical school's graduation, a funeral oration full of well-meant lies, and the unending monotony of a man listing all the names of all the sounds in the world, but among all the noises Harold never hears the instructions that he dearly needs to hear: how to feel and how to know you feel; how to love and how to honor love; how to grieve the death of one who shares your blood, but whom you barely knew.

By the time he finds his way out of the chamber and the planetarium, he has become me.

FORTY-SEVEN

"It's a magnificent piece as it stands now; there's no question about that. But it pales next to the experience of actually seeing *Music for an Automatic Bronzing* when it was in the final stage of execution—"

"Excuse me, Miss—"

"Charmaine Saint Claire. *Ms.*"

"—you do realize that you're being charged as an accomplice to murder?"

"Murder? Who murdered? None of the twelve people who watched Astrid go down into the bath. Not the pizza boy: he didn't know what he was doing. He just opened a door, as Astrid asked him to. You can say that either Astrid killed herself, or that the machines in the room killed her, but I'd like to see you prosecute either of them.

"Besides, it's not murder, so much as preservation. When you look at it in the correct way."

"Preservation."

"Yes. You have to understand that this is Astrid's way of preserving herself as a piece of art, but in a much more elemental, meaningful way than a poet composing a hundred-sonnet cycle, for example. She's cheating death by rendering it meaningless. She's saying that humanity is the sum of its artistic endeavors. She's laughing at the game and thereby winning the game by subverting it to her own ends. She's thrusting the burning brand of the modern into the cyclopean eye of the mind-body problem. It's all very complicated."

"Well, why don't we go over it one more time, then. . . . There was a specially constructed machine, rigged to activate when the door to the planetarium opened."

"Yes. We prepared it a few hours before we ordered the pizza, to give the bronze statuettes in the bath enough time to melt. We locked Astrid into the cage and hoisted it off the ground. It was hanging from the ceiling by a pulley, you see. The cable attached to the cage looped over the pulley and back down to a motor, which was connected by a trip wire to the knob of the door to the planetarium."

"So . . . when the door opened, the motor would come on and lower the woman into the . . . bath."

"Right."

"And she was still alive then."

"Oh, yes, of course. She was alive right up until the end."

"So, after you hoisted the cage up—"

"Then we pushed the tub under it, this gigantic tub filled with bronze statuettes, cheap stuff, madonnas and valkyries. And we lit the flames beneath the tub, and after a few hours, the statuettes melted into a beautiful pool of hot liquid bronze, with occasional bubbles coming to the surface and bursting."

"And she hung over this pool of bronze in her cage for . . . ?"

"Five hours, probably. It couldn't have been comfortable, but she never complained. No one spoke much while we were waiting. We stayed alone with our thoughts. It was a quiet time. And kind of religious, I imagine."

"So then there was a knock on the door—the pizza delivery boy."

"And Astrid said, 'Open the door and come in!' Then the delivery guy pulled the door open, and that started everything: the phonographs blaring—but they were quiet where we were standing, because of the destructive interference—and the cage descending into the bath.

"She looked so happy as she was going down. Her face had a cheery red glow that, frankly, I'd never seen in it before. And just before she disappeared beneath the surface of the bronze pool, she spoke her beautiful final words."

"Which were?"

"Oh, they were so beautiful! And rather profound!"

"It's okay, Mizz Saint Claire, take your time, here's a tissue, get yourself together."

"Yes. Yes. I'm sorry."

"Now then. Her last words."

"... Her last words were 'Hot buttered spleen! Hot buttered spleen!' With a positively beatific smile on her face. Rapturous."

"Excuse me?"

"I wouldn't expect you to understand."

"Wait ... wait one moment. That doesn't correlate with the information we have, not to mention common sense. It doesn't make sense. Let me read you part of the deposition of the pizza delivery boy, Jason Fenman ... here it is. 'It all happened so fast and it was so weird I didn't know what to do. I almost dropped the pizza, even. She was hanging over the tub, rattling the cage she was in and screaming her effing head off. "Stop the machine! Stop the machine!" And then she went under and then she burned.'"

"He must have heard wrong. I can see how he might think he heard that, but remember: he was disoriented and had two phonographs playing at full volume on either side of him. But I was with Astrid when she died, in the silent space where all the sound dropped out. I think you can trust my recollection over his. And I knew Astrid personally—it wasn't in her nature to finish off her life by saying something as mundane as you think. She was an artist."

"... So. Let's say, for the sake of argument, that she did say 'Hot buttered spleen' instead of 'Stop the machine.' What do you suppose that means?"

"Don't ask stupid questions."

"I'll ask whatever questions I like, stupid or no."

"Well, it's all very complicated."

"Why don't you try to give me an explanation that's simple enough for my average intellect, then."

"Well, um . . . you see, Astrid was making a mock-comic request to the bronze bath to *cook* her, to preserve her by cooking her and cooking her well, to make her delicious. Especially her spleen . . . the spleen being, in her opinion, where the soul of an artist resides, instead of her heart. It's a cryptic and provocative statement, you see . . . you see how she has her mouth as wide-open as it can go, in the final version of the piece? It's because she wants her work to preserve her, inside and out, even if it scalds her throat and turns her lungs to ash. She looks so happy hanging there. She's received her own art. It's come inside her."

FORTY-EIGHT

And now, at long last, Miranda Taligent, the shining light of her father's life, has come back home.

Sleep doesn't come to her as easily as it used to. It seemed when she was young that she could actually *summon* sleep at will to put her under, no matter how long or how recently she'd slept before, or whether she'd gorged herself on so many sweets that the tips of her fingers tingled. Now, on this particular night, the best that she can manage is a fitful eyelid flickering, letting her unconscious dispiritedly rearrange the building blocks of her memories into mildly disquieting and mostly unimaginative dreams. This lasts for a few minutes, a quarter of an hour at the most; then she snaps awake again, staring wide-eyed into the total darkness of this room where she has slept since she first came to the Tower as an infant, the room in this place that is most, to her, like home.

Naked beneath the sheets, she stretches both her arms out as far as she can; she can *just* touch both edges of the mattress with the tips of her fingers. When she was younger, the surface of the bed seemed immense, like a sea to be sailed across or an island to be explored. She remembers jumping up and down in a candy-fueled frenzy, nearly rupturing the box springs, yelling nonsense, trying to hit her head on the ceiling. But space shrinks when you get old, and things lose their wonder, and the wisest thing to do then is to try your best to sleep.

Now a rectangle of white light appears and widens on the opposite side of the darkened room. Father is here. He closes the door and approaches the bed, his long robes rustling quietly against the floor. When he reaches the edge of the bed, he silently sinks to his knees.

"Father," Miranda says.

"Miranda."

There is more silence for a time after this naming, and then Prospero breaks down into a full-throated sob. "I *missed* you," he weeps, and coming to his feet, he leans over the bed to embrace his daughter. He feels her long slender arms come out and clasp him awkwardly around the waist, and he is careful to keep the bedsheet between them and covering her (because he can't touch her, ever again. No matter what happens, he can never let her dirty skin touch his. She has been ruined. In one of his desk drawers he has saved something that he found when he was wandering alone through Miranda's playroom, a condom wrapper ripped open and empty, illustrated with a silhouette of a couple in congress, the outlines of their pelvises mingled into a shadowy blur, but it's best not to bring that up right now, he thinks. It's probably best forgotten. But she is ruined).

"Miranda," he says. "My little girl's all grown-up. . . . Do you know how hard this kind of thing is on a father? You're not angry, are you? Tell me you're not angry with me."

"No, Father," Miranda replies. "Of course not."

"If I could somehow stop time and keep you from moving into the future . . ." He holds her tightly for a stretch of seconds, then, slowly, lets her go. "I . . . I didn't mean to hurt you. I'll never hurt you, ever again. Just . . . just stay. Be the company of a loving father in his old age." He is backing away from her as he speaks, toward the door. Making distance.

Sleep is coming on for Miranda at last, welcome and long sought. "I'll stay," she says, starting to go under. Ludicrous, to leave home to search for what you want, when all you want is sleep and peace. No place like home.

Now the rectangle of light is back and Prospero stands silhouetted in it, shoulders slumped, looking down at the floor. "Miranda?" he says, his voice cracking and just above a whisper.

"Father," the woman in the bed replies. She's almost gone now.

"I'm going to do terrible things to you," Prospero says, and quietly shuts the door.

INTERLUDE

aboard the good ship *chrysalis*.

My failure to grieve my sister's death is harder to bear than grief itself. Or at least that's what I believe I'd say, were it the case that I knew something of grief that would assist me in making the comparison.

Gentle reader: if I am allowed the liberty of imagining your existence in some far future, perhaps you might grant me the further liberty of imagining that you've found some way to record your voice and send it back through time to me. In that case, tell me this: grief. What is it like; what does it do to you? Does it change your heart from gold to lead? Does it pin the corners of your mouth back past your ears? Does it stiffen your prick, or line your stomach with acid? Does it send you stumbling against your will down an alley lined with bars and brothels? What?

I truly do not know, and that unnameable feeling that comes with not knowing: it must be worse than grief. It must.

Not just grief, but ecstasies as well—there have been times that should have taken me as high as grief should have brought me low, and those have been just as unremarkable. The twelve hours during which I lost my virginity to Miranda and discovered Astrid's suicide should have been a roller coaster for me, but the roller coaster that I rode with Astrid in the Nickel Empire was much more terrifying; I'm sad to say that it's likely to be the most terrifying moment that I will experience in these pages.

Never fear, though: even though such thrills are forbidden me, you, my imaginary gentle reader, will get your vicarious excitement. There will be a last grand adventure before this comes to an end—you'll get your love, and your murder.

My father used to talk about a God Who was an Author of the universe, who lent order to it by the simple fact of His existence. Looking back on what he said, it seems as if he felt that it did not really matter whether that Author-God truly did exist, so long as people believed that He did: as long as they believed, then they would believe that the world had order, even if they could not perceive that order for themselves.

The existence of such a God must have lent a certain surety to language that's now unknown to us. I imagine that the entries of the dictionary that lies on the desk in God's study must have one-to-one correspondences between words and their definitions, so that when God sends directives to his angels, they are completely free from ambiguity. Each sentence that He speaks or writes must be perfect, and therefore a miracle.

With faith in God comes faith in language; if God made us, then it is language that makes us better things than animals. If those who lived in the age of miracles could not be Authors of the world in the manner that God was, then they must have believed that authorship in a lesser sense had a similar, if lesser, power—if we could not be makers of worlds, then we could at least be makers of words that described worlds, be they worlds in which we lived, or future worlds, or worlds that could never exist. And listeners must have had the same if lesser faith in speakers as they did in the unassailable truth of the words of God when they drifted down from heaven to earth.

But in the absence of some sort of Godlike author or poet whose every word is clear and perfect, whose speech we'd measure our own against and always find it wanting, it is so much harder to have the faith in language that belief in God affords us—we are forced to see that words are not themselves ideas, but merely strings of ink marks; we see that sounds are nothing more than waves. In a modern age without an Author looking down on us from heaven, language is not a thing of definite certainty, but infinite possibility; without the comforting illusion of meaningful order we have no choice but to stare into the face of meaningless disorder; without the feeling that meaning can be certain, we find ourselves overwhelmed by all the things that words *might* mean.

Whether God exists, or whether this certainty of meaning is fact or fantasy, is moot: without the feeling of such certainty we move from a common present into our own exclusive futures, none of which exist; our eyes see all things and are therefore blinded; our ears hear all things and make us deaf; our hearts are neither lead nor gold, but soundproof. They must be so, to keep us sane.

Does grief bring up the bile in the throat? Does it twist the spine in the shape of an *S*? Tell me, future gentle reader, because it might be that if I simulate grief for long enough and make the proper motions, then I might be able to take a better stab at guessing what grief is like, and so this horrible feeling brought on by the endless absence of grief would come to an end.

But if I cannot be certain of the words and motions that signal grief in others, then I cannot learn to recognize grief in myself. And without the recognition of grief, or any other emotion for that matter, it may as well not exist.

This is the feeling, then: that without faith in language I am no better than or different from a tin man. Without certainty in meaning, nothing I say has any meaning, and the hundreds of pages' worth of words I've written here are passionless nonsense: they're little more than strings of obsessive decorations.

This may not be the worst of things. In all honesty, the primary purpose of this tale is to help me while away the time, since I'm sure that it will never be read—this zeppelin is not supplied with machines to duplicate and distribute texts, and this copy of my memoirs is doomed to be the only one. Still, at my best I take the same pride in what I'm writing that a carpenter might take in a well-constructed table, with a level surface and four legs of a matching length.

Such pride does afford a dim form of pleasure, though, the best available to me.

My sister left me a message at the entrance to her tomb—my own drawing on an index card, returned to me. And perhaps you, gentle reader, read of the message and said to yourself, "I knew what she meant by that." And you thought that her final statement to her brother was either profound or silly.

Would you tell me what she meant, then? Because I can't be certain. I don't know. I feel that I should, and it kills me.

At least I presume that the message was left for me. It may not have been.

Too much writing for tonight. Tired; time for bed.

More to this part later—description, and suspense.

Now then.

Though this story up to now has covered twenty years, the rest of it will be a tale of only twenty hours. I suppose that this interlude between decades past and the almost-present is as good a time as any to tell you, my imaginary reader, of my life aboard this zeppelin from day to day.

Though my voice in these pages is the voice of a gentleman, I must confess that in the past year I have come to live like an animal. For the first month or so of my imprisonment I kept up the ingrained habits of civilization, maintaining my hygiene and wearing the only suit of clothes

I had on hand (the same ones I wore when I boarded this ship, and which were stained in spots with Prospero Taligent's blood). But after some time my clothes became too soiled to tolerate, and I didn't see the point in wearing them anyway, so I began to wander the corridors naked. The only other person aboard this vessel is Miranda, and though I'm certain she can hear me, I'm equally certain she can't see me, so there's not much need for modesty. I bathe whenever my own odor becomes too much for me to bear, but that is probably less often than might satisfy the sensibilities of others, were they in my presence.

I take what passes for my meals irregularly from the steel garden, which is maintained by the mechanical men. It is a small room near the bottom of the gondola that has an array of windows that afford the usual spectacular views of cloud formations and starlight to which I've become accustomed. Fruits and vegetables grow there on potted vines— tomatoes, eggplants, corn, grapes, melons. (There are also plots of hundreds of flowers with walkways weaving between them, but these are made of metal, with painted wires for stems and shining lacquered petals.) I pull the fruit off the vine and pound it on the floor until it splits or bite straight into it if its skin is thin enough. When I finish my meal, I place the leftover seeds in a receptacle that has thoughtfully been labeled by the makers of the ship. Other receptacles in various places are meant for my urine and feces, and I assume that the mechanical men are collecting it all, to purify and recycle.

I am part of a machine that transfers energy from one place to another. It is not a perpetual motion machine, but it is still failing, slowly but surely. The plants in the steel garden soak up energy from the sunlight coming through its windows; I ingest the food from the plants and expend the energy contained in them in order to keep myself alive; the waste I expel is used along with the seeds and more sunlight to make more plants, and more food. But over the past year the tomatoes have been becoming less red, the melons less sweet, the harvest less plentiful. I've had to ration out the food to myself, and I've become used to a slight but constant hunger through most of the day, until the evening when I allow myself the indulgence of a full stomach. And I miss the taste of fresh meat—I have dreams of the $2.99 special advertised in a diner's grimy flyspecked window, the slab of pan-broiled cow flesh slapped down on a cracked china plate, covered with black pepper and still bleeding.

Recently I have taken up the habit of taking a pen and paper to the steel garden and composing there, instead of writing in the room with the obsidian desk where Prospero Taligent's corpse is interred. Though he's dead, and his eyes are closed, I just don't like the feeling of him there. Part of the reason for the change is also that I'm getting closer in my story to the point where I murdered him.

It's become important to me now, for some reason, that the story of my life should sound pleasant to the ear when read aloud. I find myself going back and changing words in passages a hundred pages before, not because the new version of a given sentence has more sense, but because it sounds nicer for reasons I can't put my finger on. And, as egotistical as it may seem, I like to hear the sound of my voice again, after a year of silence. Muscles in my throat and my chest that had gone soft are becoming strong again, and this feels good.

When I read this manuscript back to myself, Miranda becomes quiet. I said that I wouldn't speak to her, and I will not. But I have decided not to let this refusal force me to deny myself the freedom to speak. If Miranda chooses to comment on my work, as she often does, then I have the freedom of ignoring her, or even including her words in my manuscript whether or not she wants me to. I'll do as I wish, whatever she says.

I'll say that I do like hearing your tale, Harold, but there's not enough of yourself in it, and this is ruining whatever attempts you might be making at total truth. You're stitching things together from your own memories and the documents stored aboard the ship, and those cause enough problems in and of themselves. But where's the "I" in this story? That's what I'm expecting. I want you. Even when you don't rely on those papers and choose to tell your story for yourself, it's always "Harold" that does this or

that: not you. As if the person you are can disassociate himself from the
persons you were. That's not the way it works at all, I'm afraid.

I. I kissed Miranda Taligent. I lay half-asleep on a false beach and
mourned the loss of my spent seed while Astrid dipped herself into the
bronze bath. I killed Prospero Taligent. Each of those people was you. That's
what I want you to admit to me. That's what I want to hear.

There is not much left to tell now. The only part of the story that remains
is the chronicle of the hours before I boarded the good ship *Chrysalis.*

All of us have days in our lives, perhaps three or four at the most,
when what we might call disparate events converge. These are the times
when we sit down for an uncomfortable holiday dinner with our long-
absent and best-forgotten past selves and dine on embarrassment and
remorse until we are stuffed. Mostly, we deliberately make these messy
moments for ourselves: the wedding to a wife whom your parents hate
because she hails from an enemy nation; the high school reunion at
which the guests immediately fall into the cliques that were the cause of
your childhood torment.

This was part of Prospero Taligent's most elaborate final gift to me,
the one that he promised all us birthday-party children twenty years ago,
the fulfillment of our heart's desires: he gave me one of those days, when
my former selves pursued me like hounds running a fox to ground. I
ended up boarding this ship to escape from those ghosts of myself that
he summoned. But they were already aboard when the *Chrysalis* lifted
off, waiting for me to reckon with them.

I'll make the storyteller the luckiest boy, so he'll have a story to tell the
other boys at school. That is what he promised me twenty years ago, and
that is what he did, whether I wanted it or not. That son of a bitch is the
Author of my life.

Miranda is partially right about one thing, I think. I cannot escape what
I am and what I have done. My earlier mistakes I can disown by ascrib-
ing them to youth, but before I boarded this ship I killed Miranda's

father. It is the people I once was that made me what I am. I must admit to that.

Not yet, though. I have to record the events of that Christmas Eve, the day before the good ship *Chrysalis* was launched on its first and only voyage. This was the day when the whole world began to fall apart.

FOUR

romance in a

mechanical

dancehall

ONE

What was her name—Minerva? Melinda, maybe. I was never sure—the noise of the dancehall drowned out the music of her name as she said it, and with just the movement of her mouth to go on, I could only make out the pursed lips of her *M* and the tentative accompanying smile of the final *a* as she spoke it. It didn't matter, though—in retrospect there was a sweet naïveté in the way she gave her name to me unasked, as though we were in a place where the names of people mattered.

The two of us were wedged together, shoulder to shoulder, in the midst of a milling throng of sweating, panting people who were trying either to work their way to a bar to order drinks whose value was best measured in days of pay, or to return to the dance floor without spilling their glasses or taking inadvertent elbows to the chest. The women in the crowd kept their eyes to the floor, inching forward on clunky high-heeled shoes and clutching impractically tiny purses slung just beneath their armpits; the men's gazes roved and darted and crawled, dazzled by tricks of makeup that made cheeks seem redder and eyes seem larger, by clothes that changed the shapes of bodies from pears to hourglasses. The music that echoed from the dance floor was all rhythm and no

melody, an endlessly transforming, looping, layered series of drumbeats
that numbed the ears and made jittering ripples in the surfaces of gingerly held martinis.

When we made our way to the bar at last we exhaled with relief. The
bartender was clearly going to take a while to get to us—he was in the
middle of mixing four doses of a drink that seemed to involve more craft
than alcohol, pouring one neon-bright liqueur after another into a row of
Erlenmeyer flasks while a group of giggling sorority sisters watched, en-
raptured. "Always the little girls that hold things up, isn't it!" the woman
said in my ear, standing on tiptoe. "Always the girls with their girly
drinks!"

I gave her a wide smile and the slightest of winks—Marlon Giddings
would have been proud. That was when she offered her hand and gave
her name—Melinda, maybe. Or Melissa. I clasped her cold fingers briefly,
then drew away—I didn't yet have enough liquor in me that evening not
to find the touch of other humans revolting.

Her smile faltered slightly, then returned, flashing two hundred watts'
worth of white teeth. She seemed pretty, though in the ever-shifting
lighting of the club it was hard to determine the details of faces with certainty. Her close-cropped hair was dyed fire-engine red and dusted with
the tiniest of metallic specks, and her freckled face had a pallor that suggested that she spent high summer days shielded by an umbrella. She was
simply but stylishly dressed—well-worn jeans and a shirt featuring what
seemed to be a hand-painted portrait of a bygone film starlet I didn't
recognize.

The bartender poured a final shot of some imported drink into each
of the four flasks that turned their contents from a pale blue to a seemingly pulsing neon green, then finished off the drinks by dropping a
small pebble of dry ice into each. The faces of the girls lit up as white
smoke bloomed out of the necks of the flasks, drifted down their sides,
and began to pool on the surface of the bar. "Four Mad Scientists," the
bartender said, and after conferring with each other and fiddling with the
contents of their purses, the girls handed him a small pile of crumpled
bills. They collected their beakers, took prim sips from them, and began
to burrow back through the crowd, chattering to each other and trailing
four thin dissipating tendrils of smoke behind them.

When the bartender approached Melissa (or Minerva) he seemed to recognize her on sight; at least he gave her the hearty greeting that bartenders tend to reserve for regulars who tip well and don't cause any trouble. "Gripe water!" she ordered, and I moved in (most likely as expected) and offered to pick up the tab for her drink, tacking on an order for a gin and tonic for myself. "Gripe water" turned out to be what looked like five or six shots of vodka poured into a tumbler that was better suited for orange juice than hard liquor, with a single mint leaf tossed on top to give the enterprise the appearance of legitimacy. "Well, *thank you*," she said, tilting her head and smiling winsomely as she hoisted her glass. "Now what do you say we get these in us and *dance*?"

TWO

The dance floor of the nightclub was made up of an enormous array of hexagonal panels of clear glass; just beneath the glass we could see the sprawling conglomeration of machines that drove the dancers, an amalgamation of percussive instruments tangled together with decades-old mechanical men whose bodies had been endlessly deformed by the aftermarket modifications of talented amateurs. Beneath us a tin man with three legs performed a lazy leper's shuffle, clicking castanets in its hands as it limped around in slow ellipses. Another mechanical man had had its hands severed from its arms and replaced with the heads of sledgehammers, with which it rang changes on an arrangement of giant brass bells. A tin man whose hands fanned out into two dozen slender, mallet-tipped fingers tickled the bars of three xylophones; a tin man whose rust-covered torso was riddled with jagged holes mindlessly banged together two concussion stones to make the sound of thunder. A tin creature formed more like a spider than a human skittered over the surface of a kettledrum; another tin man with extraordinarily long arms twirled calabashes so fast that they seemed like blurs. Ten more tin men surrounded a medicine drum, beaing out ten different shifting rhythms with their iron fists.

The mechanical contraption beneath us sounded so different from the automatic orchestra that I'd heard in the Taligent Tower as a child, with young Miranda nestled within a cocoon of violins and pianos and harps, laboring away at the single crank that ran it all. The orchestra had had noise beneath its music, but in the dancehall noise and rhythm were everything. We listened with our instinct and our sex instead of our hearts and our minds; we responded not with polite applause after a moment of considered silence, but with the increasingly frenetic movements of our bodies in time to the beats.

The gin and tonic that I'd downed had gotten to me, loosening up my muscles and deadening the disgust that I often felt on contact with the flesh of others. Melissa (or Minerva) was coming closer to me, gracing me here and there with occasional touches that neither of us thought were accidental, though they were meant to seem so. Every once in a while some slick shyster would try to cut in on me, but I'd long ago mastered the kind of unblinking stare that made other men shove off.

With flirts and come-ons the woman drew me farther into the middle of the floor, where the beats were stronger and deeper and the crowd was packed closer together, and I began to lose myself a little, the hamster wheels of my most persistent thoughts spinning down to rest. Certain parts of me became a little bit forgotten, a little bit numb, a little bit dead, and it was nice to have some dead places in me for a little while, to lose a little bit of my broken mind.

After a while Minerva (or Melinda) waved her open palm fanlike in front of her face—*phew!*—gently took my hand in hers—*mine.*—and led me over to the edge of the dance floor, where a dais held a few bar tables. From here we could see the crowd of dancers, though not the machinery beneath them that made them move. On a canvas hanging on the opposite wall I could see a projected image, a heavily scratched print of vintage pornography from the early days of the century that was playing at the wrong speed: a plump nude brunette with a pageboy haircut and a rictus pasted on her face performed an odd jackknifing dance, while a group of cigar-smoking dandies in white suits looked on from the edge of the frame, grinning salaciously and nudging each other in the ribs. Near the edge of the dance floor were the four sorority girls, huddled together in a tight circle with their purses piled in the middle;

they were surrounded by twice as many men, all of whom were trying awkward strategies intended to separate one of them from the rest of the flock and draw her off alone.

It was quieter here, so Melinda (or Melissa) and I could talk without shoving our lips against each other's ear. "What do you do?" she said to me.

"I'm in publishing," I said, leaving it at that. "What about you?"

"What do *I* do?" she said. "I *fail*. I get red marks on report cards, letters of the alphabet you haven't ever even seen—they only show up when you're spelling the most obscene swear words. I can wither plants with a touch. I can't follow the simplest directions even if they're tattooed on the insides of my eyelids. Which is to say that I'm forever unemployed. I fail, is what I do, and then I spend my nights spinning on barstools and flirting with only the most *handsome* men." She tilted her head again and flashed an impish grin.

A waiter came by and asked us if we wanted drinks. "Gripe water," M. said, "and *he* wants gripe water."

"I don't—"

"Oh for God's sake take off your *skirt*," she said. Then to the waiter, two fingers extended: "Trust me, if he doesn't drink it, it'll *get* drunk."

"Understood," said the waiter, and drifted off.

We performed the act of conversation, rather than conversing—neither of us was meant to be left altered by what we said to each other, since we were merely marking time. We mostly discussed the recent events of radio serials—like most modern people, we no longer bothered to make the distinction between events in real life and the dramas of fictional worlds, and so the cliff-hanger that inevitably, reliably ended the hour held just as much or more importance to us as the newspaper that usually went from doorstep to garbage bin unread, and we speculated about the future lives of the characters that populated decayed mansions or desert isles as if they weren't inventions of other human minds. As M. chattered she slid her chair closer to me, and I held her small, short-fingered hand in mine, gently sliding my thumb back and forth across its back. The waiter brought our drinks and we downed them directly ("Good man," she said, pounding me on the back, "getting rid of your skirt and your girly pink panties"), then we returned to the dance floor.

Now my limbs were weightless; now my joints had turned to rubber; now my inhibition was gone. Parts of the floor were packed so tightly that dancing could only consist of little more than a constricted movement of the elbows. M. and I ground against each other as if we were ill-fitting jigsaw pieces determined to jam together, even though one showed sidewalk, the other sky.

I was almost there. I was almost to the point where, for a few moments, I'd be able to forget the one failure of my life to which all the smaller failures of this other woman's life could not compare. It was long past midnight, and time to cut deals. Soon we would strike a speechless bargain, with a long slow gaze copied from the third act of a romantic comedy, or a comically leering wink, or a hand slid surreptitiously beneath a shirt to caress the bones at the base of the spine. She would tacitly allow me to let her face and body stand in for those I saw in a recurring dream of someone else, and I would perhaps unwittingly do the same for her; I would wake the following morning and see, outlined beneath the sheets, the shape of an unfamiliar shoulder, and though I'd be revolted by it I'd remember that, for a few moments a few hours before, I'd almost been there.

But that was when the music went wrong.

We felt rather than heard it at first, an arrhythmia creeping into the beats that made the music increasingly difficult to dance to. One of the four sorority girls had fallen into the embrace of a middle-aged man with a mustache that'd been trimmed to a pencil line sitting atop his upper lip, and she yelped in surprise as he clumsily stepped on her open-toed shoe. A couple, drunk out of their minds and mock-rutting in a darkened corner, paused to gaze around them querulously, their eyes glazed. The pornographic film began to jitter in its projector, the nude woman's image stretching and smearing into abstraction.

M. paused, drew her arms from around my waist, and looked up at me. "Something's not right," she said. The music was even more offbeat now, and through it we could feel the trembling of malfunctioning machinery beneath us, of gears about to become unthreaded and belts about to snap.

It was then that I looked over M.'s shoulder and saw another dancer scream as the panel of glass he stood on shattered. He tried to clutch at anyone within his reach as he fell, but a moment later he was caught in the conglomeration of machines that lay under us, seemingly unable to extricate himself no matter how much he twisted and writhed.

As the nearby dancers cleared a space around him, I watched him sink deeper, hollering and fumbling as if mired in quicksand to the waist; then I looked down past my own feet. If it could be said that tin men have minds to go mad with, then the tin musicians beneath us were going mad. One with sledgehammers for hands had given up bell ringing in favor of bashing in his own misshapen skull; another was scrabbling at the glass above it, and I could see a crack appear in a nearby panel as a xylophone bar was hurled against it from below. The massive percussive machine beneath us was flying apart, arrhythmia racing through it now like a contagion, and I began to sense even through my drunkenness that all of us here in the club were in danger.

But it was the harsh, blinding lights coming up in the club that made everyone start to panic. I could hear the voice of someone attempting to sound authoritative, telling us to stay calm and stand where we were, and that repairmen would be handling this directly, but at that moment another pane of glass exploded upward with the loud *pop* of an expiring lightbulb, scattering shards everywhere. A snare drum with a ruptured head flew out of the new hole in the floor, catching a young woman under the chin so hard that she bit down on her tongue and collapsed, her eyelids fluttering.

"Stay calm," the voice of authority pleaded, "will you all *please* stay calm," and the pencil-mustached man bodychecked his dance partner, sending her sprawling as he ran toward the single exit, shoving people out of the way. That started the stampede. As the dance floor's panels began to fracture more quickly, M. and I found ourselves swept up in a mob whose members had become bereft of their sense of honor and self. They shoved and swore and bit, their eyes all fixed on the single exit door. Slivers of glass rained down around us, catching and refracting the light; broken glass crunched beneath our feet.

Suddenly I couldn't move—M. had tightly gripped me around the waist, and just keeping my footing in the midst of the panicked herd of dancers was hard enough. She buried her face in my chest. "I can't," she said incoherently as I tried ineffectively to drag her along with me. "I can't. Just—" I could see a series of cracks spiderwebbing through the pane beneath me as a malfunctioning mechanical man (with four arms welded onto its torso in addition to the standard two) pounded on its underside, its six steel fists banging out stuttering tattoos as sparks spilled out of its joints. Nearby a bawling girl lay prone on the floor, shielding her head with her arms and frantically kicking with her legs to save herself from being trampled.

M. looked up at me, her lip quivering, her face tear-streaked. In the former darkness of the nightclub it had been impossible to determine her age—a best guess would make her one of those small, pixielike women who seem forever seventeen—but in the bright emergency lights I could tell that she was forty years old if a day. The creases at the corners of her eyes told of too many nights spent squinting them shut as she sobbed; the twin divots between her brows had been hewn there by the frustration of endless failure. And still there was something in her face that hadn't yet been spoiled, something that reminded me of someone else, a pure girl I'd once known who'd grown over twenty years of reimagining into a pure woman I dreamed of every single night—falling from the tower; calling out to me.

"Just—" she said. "I can't—oh *God*—"

A steel hand burst through the glass that held us up, latching onto her leg and starting to drag her down. I struggled with her for a moment as the rest of the pane we stood on began to fracture and fall away.

But I was not good enough. You should understand this about me—I am not a hero; not one to tap unknown reserves of courage; not one to rise to circumstance. I am the understudy who chokes on his lines when he is forced onto the stage. I am never, ever good enough.

So I let her go. I jumped to the adjacent and still solid pane of glass, and even as I made the leap, the panel I'd been standing on disintegrated. M. was being drawn down into a roiling mass of broken musical instruments and machines gone haywire. The six-armed tin man gripped her legs with four of its hands, while its fifth and sixth banged on her back with a pair of drumsticks. She stretched out a hand to me—*Save me*—and even though I couldn't (or didn't care to) reach her and we both knew it, I did the same, thinking it good manners at the least to make the gesture.

And then, not being good enough, not even good enough to spit out the halfhearted apology lodged in my throat, I turned and ran from the club like all the rest.

"Howard!" she hollered as the machines pulled her under. *"Howard!"* At least she didn't remember my name, either.

THREE

A light snow was falling as I found my way out of the club, melting as soon as it touched the concrete. A pair of fire trucks were parked at the club's entrance, though there was no evidence of flame; they seemed to be there out of either caution or boredom, and most of the firemen were lazily smoking cigarettes and critiquing the outlandish appearances of some of the escaped clubgoers. A few flying police cars banked in slow figure eights above the crowd, pinning random revelers with their spot-lights. A few men in crisp white jackets with bright red crosses on their backs climbed out of the back of an ambulance, pushing their way past the last of the escapees to see to whatever wounded remained inside.

I didn't stick around. The snow began to fall more heavily and stick to the sidewalk, so I headed to the nearest subway station, walking down the middle of the empty street. If I wasn't going to take a woman home that evening, the next best thing would be a good night's sleep. At first a police car left the formation above to follow along with me, illuminating me with its light from behind as if I were an actor striding onto a stage to deliver a play's central soliloquy, but after I turned around and cheerfully waved up at it, it peeled away after flicking its headlights to rejoin the rest.

The subway car on which I eventually found myself was nearly empty—a few ne'er-do-well late-night partygoers like myself, who'd try to squeeze in an hour or two of sleep before heading to their offices and impersonating responsible citizens, along with a couple of service types who had started their day an hour before, who would soon begin all the tasks that mechanical man were still too expensive or too ill-suited for, stoking the boilers and firing the ovens that made the city run.

This is the time of night just before sunrise, the time that no one owns, and if you have found yourself awake and alone during this time, out in the city, outside the safety of the walls you call your own, then you know me, and you have felt what I have felt. This is the hour of the night it's best to sleep through, for if it catches you awake then it will force you to face what is true. This is when you look into the half-dead eyes of those who are either wishing for sleep or shaking off its final remnants, and you see the signs of the twilight in which your own mind is suspended.

At any other time it's better. You can do the things you feel you should; you're an expert at going through the motions. Your handshakes with strangers are firm and your gaze never wavers; you think of steel and diamonds when you stare. In a monotone you repeat the legendary words of long-dead lovers to those you claim to love; you take them into bed with you, and you mimic the rhythmic motions you're read of in manuals. When protocol demands it you dutifully drop to your knees and pray to a god who no longer exists. But in this hour you must admit to yourself that this is not enough, that you are not good enough. And when you knock your fist against your chest you hear a hollow ringing echo, and all your thoughts are accompanied by the ticks of clockwork spinning behind your eyes, and everything you eat and drink has the aftertaste of rust.

FOUR

When I was still earthbound, in the days before I boarded the zeppelin, the most precious moments of my life were those fractions of seconds between the moment when I awoke each morning, and the moment when I realized that I was awake. In those halves of seconds the world was silent, and I was at rest. The patterns on my bedroom ceiling had not yet resolved into meaninglessness, and the incessant sounds of the world's machines had not yet intruded upon my consciousness. But after no time at all, a second at the most if I was lucky, they'd come: the drone of the air conditioner humming harmonically through a rattling vent; the arrhythmic rapping of the headboard of my neighbor's bed against the wall behind my head; the honks of hundreds of horns from automobiles ensnarled in gridlock on the street twenty floors below; the intermittent, high-pitched wheedling buzz of a flying car whizzing by my window. If you add up all the fragments of time when I was deaf to the noise of the world, these halves and three-fourths of seconds between sleeping and waking, over my life they might come to about ninety minutes. For an hour and a half of my life I have been allowed glimpses of the silent world that once was, before the machines came, when there were still miracles.

On this particular morning, which would prove to be the last in which my feet touched earth, the sound that ruptured the bubble of my pastoral semiconsciousness was a sharp knocking, which at first seemed unfamiliar. Coming up out of the dark, still hungover from the night before, I tried to locate it in the catalog of ambient noises that make up the din of the world, but I couldn't place it: three sharp irregular raps, then a pause, then four more. Then, wide-awake now, I had it: someone was knocking on the door, and the noise was magnified by the hollow metal door of my studio apartment.

The knocking at the door grew louder, and the man on the other side was saying, "Sir! Harold Winslow! I got an urgent *message*! You gotta let me in! I got an urgent message, and *also*, I'm fuckin' *bleedin'* all over the place out here! I got an urgent message!" I stumbled out of bed and took a couple of moments to clear my head; then I shuffled over to the door of my apartment and opened it.

On the other side, with a large cream-colored envelope in his right hand and a shallow gash running the length of his left forearm, stood a winged messenger.

I had no idea what message anyone would have for me that would actually require a private, human courier. He stepped past me into the threshold, a wiry, pale, stubble-headed, sweat-covered man wearing a close-fitting cap with red cardboard wings affixed to either side with cellophane, a black short-sleeved shirt and short pants, and red leather boots with more cardboard wings glued to them, just above the ankles. "Fuck *me*," he said, gesturing at the wound on his arm. "Jackass *cut* me.

With a broken beer bottle. Comin' at me all screamin' *aaaaah!* In the street down below. It's the fucking end of days, friend. You got anything I can put on this?"

The only thing I had on hand to bind the wound was an old thread-bare tie, which I retrieved from a drawer and began to clumsily wrap around his arm. He was seated on my unmade bed, still holding the large envelope. "That's unusual," I said to him. "This is generally a safe neighborhood."

"There *ain't* no safe neighborhoods this morning, sir," the courier said. "The whole city's been a giant scream since sunup. I tell you when Taligent lowers the boom he lowers it but good. Oh, yeah," he said as I finished bandaging him. "Here's your message. Extra-urgent and paranoid-secret. Given to me by double blind. I don't know what you did to rate *that*. And I don't even know who it's from, so don't ask. And I'm supposed to instruct you not to open it until I'm off the premises, and that's what I just did."

I took the envelope from him and asked, "What do you mean? About Taligent. Lowering the boom, you said. End of days?"

The courier looked at me in confusion. "You don't *know*? Oh, you just got up. You ain't turned on the radio or been out of the house yet. The old man is stickin' it to us and there ain't nothing we can do." Lying back on the bed, he ran his hand into the pocket of his pants and began to search for something. "Fleets of Taligent's flying cars have been dropping these leaflets over the city, all in different colors. They're stuck in all the gutters and caught in the updrafts. They got people pissing mad and shitting bricks. I never seen anything like it. I wanna try to get out of here." He pulled out a wrinkled, soiled sheet of paper and began to unfold it. "We've been sleeping. Not paying attention to where the power was."

He handed me the piece of paper, and this is what it said:

Citizens of Xeroville!
Loyal Subjects!
Happy Days for You!

I, Prospero Taligent, am proud to announce at long
last that the perpetual motion machine that has been

in development at Taligent Industries for the past ten years is now complete. It is, and will be, the only one of its kind. The completion of the device signals the time for me to harvest the ripening fruits of my own boundless genius. As of tomorrow, I will assume the title that now belongs to me by right, of Ruler of the Known World.

As you read this, the perpetual motion machine is being installed aboard a specially fitted zeppelin, the good ship *Chrysalis*, moored on the roof of the Taligent Tower. Once the installation is complete, my daughter, Miranda, and I will leave this earthly sphere and spend the rest of our days among the clouds. The airship contains a completely self-sufficient environment, with a self-perpetuating food and water supply large enough for two, so that our feet will never have to touch this filthy earth again. When we pass over the city at regular intervals, you will have the opportunity to offer your tributes to me in the form of poems, gold ingots, or self-abasement. I will also use the flying cars you see above you to distribute leaflets printed with written commands, which you will cheerfully obey in the interest of your own happiness and self-betterment. Occasionally, for my personal amusement, I will relieve hundreds of you of the tiresome burden of your lives at a single stroke, vaporizing you instantaneously with the batteries of death rays with which my zeppelin is liberally equipped.

In conclusion: henceforth you may view me as your Ruler, though those few of you who choose to will still be permitted to attend your regular houses of worship. Good day to you!

"You don't really believe this, do you?" I said to the courier, handing the paper back to him. "That rumor of the perpetual motion machine has been going around for at least ten years. At least since I was in college. Everyone knows he's crazy, right?"

"Have you looked *outside*?" the messenger asked, on his way out the door with my tie knotted around his skinny arm, soaking up blood. "Maybe you don't believe it, but everyone *else* believes he's the real thing. So you can't afford not to be careful—the rioting down there is *fierce*. Death rays. I swear. What the fuck." He walked through the doorway and turned to face me.

"Man," he said, "fuck *that* noise," and slammed the door shut.

FIVE

In accordance with the messenger's instructions, I waited for a few minutes until I could be reasonably sure that he was gone from the building. Then I opened the envelope.

Inside were two things: an entrance pass to the Taligent Tower with my name printed on it, and a single sheet of cream-colored, heavy-gauge paper. Holding the paper up to the light revealed a watermark, the logo of Taligent Industries, and the handwritten message said:

Dear Harold,

I don't know if you've found out yet about Father's plans to KIDNAP me and keep me prisoner FOREVER aboard his airship, the Chrysalis. *He has terrible things in mind for me— that's what he said. He's gone completely crazy! Everything in here (the Tower) is total chaos. Father just runs around laughing all the time, like the mad scientists in movies. I don't know what to do. I'm really scared. I've never been so scared, even that time when we first kissed (and I mightn't've looked scared then, but let me tell you, I was nervous. I'd never kissed a guy before!). I was scared, too, a little, that other time, when we— you know.*

I need you to come save me! I put an entrance pass into the envelope so you can get into the Tower. That was all I could do—you'll have to figure out the rest yourself. I know it sounds weird to ask a favor like this of someone you haven't seen in

*about ten years, but I'm trapped here, and I can't trust anyone
and you're my only hope, which is why you have to come save
me yourself and don't bring anyone with you. I know you'll
figure out a way to come rescue me! You were so good at it the
last time when we were in that warehouse! There's not much
time left. Tonight he's going to put me aboard the zeppelin,
and after that it'll lift off and then it'll be all over. Right now I
think I'm being kept somewhere on the 101st floor. You have to
get there with the entrance pass. Then you can figure out how
to get me out of here!*

*This is a noisy, filthy place and I DON'T WANT TO BE
WITH FATHER ANYMORE!!!*

I need you to come save me, Harold.

Love, Miranda.

SIX

I took the subway to work that morning, as none of my various neuroses
seemed demanding enough to required a shrinkcabbie that day, and I
was low on money at any rate. Christmas was coming to the city, and despite what the courier had said about what was happening in the streets, I
still looked forward to the holiday with some anticipation.

One of the luxuries of my apartment building was a tunnel, connected to its basement parking garage, that let directly onto a subway
platform. It meant that, if I wished, I could go straight to the greeting-
card works without ever having to go outside (since a similar tunnel at
the platform where I got off the subway led into the bowels of the enormous building). However, the elevator nearest my apartment stopped
at the lobby without descending into the basement, so that I had to get
out there and take a flight of stairs down. When I stepped out of the
elevator, I briefly looked through the lobby's plate-glass windows into
the street. A pair of automobiles were overturned, one of them being
quickly consumed by flames, the other already a charred and smoking

shell; a gang of identically clothed thugs in jeans and black leather jackets were goose-stepping down the sidewalk in formation; a grizzled old
man dressed in rags was staggering down the street's yellow dividing
line under the burden of a yard-tall stack of phonograph records, still
in their paper wrappers. Some kind of a severed human limb flung itself against a lobby window and fell to the ground, leaving a wide red
smear, but whether it was the arm of an adult or the leg of a child was
hard to tell, as what had once been either its hand or foot had been removed.

I had a list of minor tasks to complete on that Christmas Eve, and I
went over them in my head as I sat in the subway car, trying my best, as
always, to ignore all the noises: the trundling of the wheels against the
track; the bansheelike screaming of the blood-spattered woman seated
at the other end of the car; the rattling whirr of the fan struggling to
recycle the air; the mechanical self-winding gramophones that crawled
up and down the aisle on their eight slender spidery legs, tinnily trum-
peting advertisements through their horns for absinthe and cleaning
products and love-philters. First I had to put in a half day at work, but as
it was Christmas Eve, I got the afternoon off. And I was going to have
Christmas Day to myself. Christmas morning is the only time each year
when the city is quiet. I suppose that those with families have a different
perspective, sitting under their metal pine trees and reading each other
the words I scripted for them six months ago, or simply tearing open the
card to get at the bill or the check folded inside. Meanwhile, greedy children coming off a sleepless night rip open boxes and pull out clever little
machines, automatons that dance and chirp gibberish.

But all the threads that had once bound me to those who shared my
blood had snapped. I wasn't present years before when my father's body
was discovered in his apartment, so all I have remaining to me are memories of the dreams I had back then—of doctors and policemen donning
deep-sea suits and diving down through layer after layer of newspapers,
heading farther back in time the deeper they descended, until at the bottom of an ocean of information they found my father's floating corpse, its
mouth stuffed with wood pulp, its irisless eyes the color of spoiled cream,
its hand clutching a faded piece of parchment chronicling the mundane
events of ancient days.

And those dreams were free of grief, or at least I believe they were; and the waking hours that followed those dreams were filled with that nameless feeling that must be a dozen times worse than all the other emotions to which we've given names. I dutifully stood alone one sunrise and tossed my father's ashes to the wind that blew across the city's bay, forcing all the facial expressions I could think of onto my face to find the one that would identify itself with grief and let the grieving start. But nothing worked, and nothing has since.

And if I could have prayed to the God that ordered the world in which my father had come of age, I would have, hoping that He'd deign to descend from heaven and breathe life and heat back into the metal of which I was made. But He was long gone, like Father and like Astrid and like a mother who was little more than a fiction, left back in a past I'd almost lost the capacity to even imagine.

At any rate, I was free to walk the streets on Christmas morning. There is nothing so beautiful as the quiet mechanical city, with everyone inside their homes and everything gone still. There are messages scrawled across skyscrapers with letters five stories tall, and no one there to read them. You can stand still for minutes in places where you'd have been run over fifty times in ten seconds twelve hours before. Christmas morning is the best time to indulge in the luxury of loneliness.

The letter from Miranda Taligent seemed as if it might change my plans, though. Memory is strange. I suppose that for most people, memories carry traces of the emotional colors associated with them from the time that past events occurred, so that the photograph of a particular woman or the mention of her name is enough to make one wince and clench one's fists; at least, that is how the behavior of others often seems to me.

For me, though, recalling an event that happened six months ago is like reading about it in a used paperback book. As I look back on my past, as I have tried to in this narrative, it seems as if I've shed the skins of a series of selves (or grew a series of shells; either metaphor is equally appropriate, I think). And, looking at the letter that Miranda sent, it seemed silly to me that she would write to the Harold Winslow that had kissed her in her playroom twenty years ago, or made love with her there ten years after that, and expect the person I was on this Christmas Eve to answer. As if I had to honor the obligations of my past selves that they had incurred by falling in love.

Not to mention the impossibility of fulfilling the request of this damsel in distress. Whisking the girl out of the Tower under the noses of hundreds of guards: that was the stuff of serial short films. I didn't think I was up to it.

It never came to that, though. And it turned out that I had a little more courage than I thought. But not enough. If I'd had enough courage, I would have turned my back on the *Chrysalis* and never boarded her. And I wouldn't be here, on the zeppelin, with Miranda.

SEVEN

I spent the morning working in my cubicle at the greeting-card works. It was almost completely devoid of decorations, the way I liked it. Most other workers had daguerreotypes of loved ones taped to the walls, or cynical cartoons about office life cut out of the morning paper, or little rhyming maxims about teamwork and success, or vain prayers to God: *Dear Lord, give me the strength to accept the things I cannot change. Dear Lord, if you can't make me thin, at least make everyone else fat!* I didn't know how they could stand it. Those little scraps of paper tacked all over the place with their edges curled, saying the same dumb puerile things to them each and every time they looked at them. Frozen girlsmiles and put-upon stick figures. Staying the same.

I had a single sheet of paper attached to the wall of my cubicle, the same sheet of paper that everyone else had in every cubicle in the writing department, in one form or another. A series of rhymes were written on it. You need rhymes at hand to work quickly, and certain sets lend themselves to the genre: day/way; love/dove/above; breath/death; sunny/money; you/do/new/blue/true. Some workers chose to write blank verse, but they never wrote the top sellers. I knew better than that, though. People are more likely to assign emotional meaning to statements when they rhyme. Rhymes touch what the potential purchaser thinks of as his or her heart.

I had my briefcase with me as well, which contained the envelope with Miranda's letter and the entrance pass to the Tower. I still hadn't made up my mind about what to do with them. The letter kept calling to me, and every half hour or so I would pull it out of my briefcase to read it over, as if it would say something different or new.

So we wrote, I and Ophelia Flavin in the cubicle on my right, and Marlon Giddings in the cubicle on my left, and a host of other writers in their separate cubicles in a large, windowless, poorly lit room, with walls painted in various shades of gray. We scribbled our little ditties, and our supervisors came by our cubicles regularly, looked over our work, and harvested what they liked. The supervisors sent our scribbles to the marketing division; there they were matched up with an artist that would draw a suitable series of accompanying images: seascapes, or still lifes, or cartoonish, goggle-eyed beasts with pastel skins that behave as humans do. Then the finished cards were delivered into the bowels of the greeting-card works, where the presses deafened their caretakers with their noise and stained their faces black with ink, churning out apologies and condolences and lovesongs by the tens of thousands, minting simulations of the motions of the heart.

Time was out of joint. Outside the temperature was below freezing, with the threat of snow and a brutal, skyscraper-accelerated wind whipping down streets, strong enough to tear through overcoats and chill the flesh. Inside the greeting-card works it was June, and stifling hot. Because of the six-month production time for greeting cards, during the winter months there is no particular holiday to write for that demands all of our attention, like Christmas or Valentine's Day. So we used those months to fill out the demand for cards that celebrate personal holidays, like birthdays and anniversaries, as well as those nondescript declarations of love that one sees in drugstore aisles, filed under labels like FOR A NEW FRIEND and I LOVE YOU!

We were all burning up. Marlon and I had removed our coats and loosened our ties. Beneath the roar of the rows of ceiling fans balancing out the effects of the building's heaters, I could hear an occasional strangled scream from the street below, or the firing of a weapon.

The word had come down from marketing that we were short of multiple-purpose couplets on the generic subject of love, so those were what Marlon and Ophelia and I were writing. The lines of all the couplets needed to be iambic, with seven feet each; this way, couplets from different writers could easily be mixed and matched.

I hadn't come up with much of anything after two hours; Ophelia, on the other hand, was just plugging away. She'd written more than thirty couplets since she'd clocked in. She'd sit at her desk for about five minutes, humming arpeggios to herself with the tip of her index finger between her lips; then she'd rip one out. Then she'd look over the shared wall of our two cubicles, dripping with sweat, and show it to me.

"Look!" she said, handing a piece of paper over the cubicle wall for the thirty-fourth time. "I got another one."

I took the paper from her and read it:

> *I loved you so darned muchly when our love was fresh and new.*
> *But a love that's even better is a love that's tried and true!*

"This one would be good for endings," Ophelia said. "To end something with."

Ophelia Flavin was six and a half feet tall, and beautiful. But she was a horrible writer. "That's good," I said to Ophelia, giving the paper back. "You're really cranking them out today."

"Yeah," Ophelia replied. "You seem to be stuck today. You ought to try writing down the things you see in dreams. That's how I'm inspired."

"You got that from a dream," I said. "What kind of dreams do you usually have?"

"Nothing fraught with meaning," said Ophelia. "Nothing *complicated*. People embracing, with faces that I can't make out; certain shades of pink invisible to the eye. Dreams where I don't grow old. You have to believe in your dreams if you want to practice this art. This is a special thing that we do, that everyone takes for granted: people need us to say the things for them that they wish they could say themselves, because wishes aren't enough to make words out of desires. We need to be there when those important times come, when the woman looks her lover in his eye, and her hands shake and her lips lock. This is when we step in, to save her. We can be there for her, if we just believe in our dreams—"

"For God's sake," Marlon broke in from the cubicle on my left, "will somebody please deliver me from this creeping *bullshit*?" He stood up to look over the cubicle walls at Ophelia. "Believe. Do you actually believe the bullshit that just came out of your mouth. Do you. Do you know what I've gotten in exchange for true love, and knights in shining armor, and damsels locked in stone penthouses waiting for escape? Shit. And you're dining out on dreams and wishes. I've gotten shit, and hangovers, and kicks in the balls and cigarette smoke mixed with the stink of seven different brands of stale perfume. And you're flinging a bunch of shit at me about the truth of rhyming couplets! Pieced together like jigsaw puzzles! You believe. For God's sake. Have you looked outside. Have you looked at what's going on outside. On the way to work this morning I saw a woman wandering down the middle of the street in a ripped wedding gown and both her ring fingers sliced down to stumps. Smile and believe *that* shit. You believe. You're dumb enough to believe that people actually *read* greeting cards. You think they get *interpreted*. They're just placeholders for thoughts that people didn't have the balls to think for themselves. Their eyes just *slide* over the words, and maybe if the words make a nice shape on the page then they say something about that. Then they throw the thing on the floor and go to dinner in their skimpy little dresses with their tits falling out or go to their silly little musicals with the flashing lights at the end or blow out the candles or screw their tin men or whatever it is that people do. The things we write here are *disposable*.

"You believe. Well if you believe then for Christ's sake don't *tell* anyone. I'd be ashamed to be so goddamn stupid if I were you. Shit. I've gotten shit." And he sat down.

EIGHT

My manager came by my cubicle fifteen minutes before I was supposed to leave work. I only had one couplet to show him. He read, squinting at the sheet of paper in his hand:

I love you when I'm throwing up on roller-coaster rides
I love you when I'm dancing on the brink of suicide.

"See," the manager said, sighing and handing the paper back to me, "see . . . the problem with *this* is, there's a forced rhyme. *Rides, suicide.* It doesn't work. Forced rhymes cause disquiet in the stomach of the potential purchaser. Let's see . . . maybe we can fix it. You could perhaps pluralize *suicide*, but then you can't really have one person killing himself over and over again, can you? That is unintelligible. But if you put *ride* in the singular then it makes it sound like caveman talk. No . . . no. This one won't work. Tell you what . . . you're off your game today. Why don't you knock off a few minutes early. Try to have a merry Christmas." He tentatively patted me on the shoulder, as if what I had were catching; then he walked away.

NINE

After work, I boarded the subway that went back to my apartment. It was half past noon by the time I entered the car, and its floor was covered with copies of Taligent's proclamation. I imagined that a million of them must have been dumped onto the city by now, with still more raining between the skyscrapers and onto the streets.

I still hadn't made up my mind completely about the letter I received from Miranda. But before I left for home, I stopped off at a nearby liquor store and purchased a small flask of single-malt Scotch. I figured that if I decided not to rescue Miranda, I'd drink the whiskey myself the next day. It would be a Christmas present to myself.

My train didn't make it all the way to its intended stop, unfortunately—as we were pulling off from the station just before mine, the train jerked to a sudden halt as all its lights went dark. Its passengers sat there in silence for a few moments; then the car's emergency lights came up, a few flickering red bulbs screwed into sockets in the ceiling.

We looked at each other in the dim crimson light, our faces indistinct. Shadows made black holes of our eye sockets.

"What happened?" said one person.

"He cut the power," said another. "I bet that crazy son of a bitch just cut the power to the whole city. I bet you."

"He can't just cut the power, can he? I don't understand how he can do that. Isn't electricity something that's everyone's? Like, you know, water? Air?"

"He can do anything he wants," said a small boy.

"Well somebody for damn sure needs to do something about that guy. The son of a bitch goes too far."

"Don't swear," said the small boy. "It's Christmastime."

"Dinglepep!" chattered the automatic gramophone as it continued to patrol the aisle in darkness. "What puts pride in your stride and pep in your step? Dinglepep."

After we waited long enough to be certain that the car wouldn't be moving anytime soon, and that official sorts of people in uniforms wouldn't be coming along to save us, we made our way carefully to the rear car of the train, which was still adjacent to the platform. With a good deal of work four of us managed to jimmy its door open wide enough for all of us to work our way through it, one at a time. The only light we could make out was the daylight shining from a nearby stairway, which we moved toward. I was going to have to walk the rest of the way back to my apartment, a few blocks.

When I emerged from the subway tunnel into the street above, I found that the ground was littered with more of Taligent's flyers, in seven different colors. I could see phalanxes of his flying cars whizzing across the sky, dumping their messages, following a half second later by their own Dopplering buzz. The storefronts of the buildings on the opposite side of the street from the parking lot were all shattered, their contents looted. Looking down the street, I could see three curling plumes of ink-black smoke on the horizon, their sources obscured from view by sky-scrapers.

No traffic moved on the street itself. Along with the flyers from Taligent's flying cars, the road was littered with the remnants of broken machines, many of them taken from the shop windows: radio dials; the limbs and skulls of tin men; wristwatches with missing hands and shattered faces; phonographs with their cabinets stove in; toaster ovens trying to hold in their guts. A totaled automobile was turned on its side in the middle of the narrow road, in a position such that it would have blocked traffic in both directions had there been any. A group of about fifty people was gathered around it, most of them young, most of them men. They were all looking up at the three mechanical men that were standing precariously atop the automobile, screaming.

At least my first impression was that the men standing on the automobile were mechanical. But, as I approached the crowd gathered around it, I realized that they were, in fact, artificial tin men. The three of them were dressed almost exactly like those who'd kidnapped Miranda after she ran away from home ten years ago: their faces were painted silver, and they wore the same funnels atop their heads. In their hands they wielded double-bladed axes.

The one in the center was speaking. I recognized his oversized, hypertrophied build, and his voice. I'd seen him twice before, in different guises. Martin. Artegall.

"—ask you," he said as I came close enough to hear him, "are we gonna allow ourselves to be ruled by Dynamos?"

"No!" the crowd screamed.

"Are we gonna allow this *man* to tell us what to do?"

"No!"

"I tell you—I let him tell me what to do for long enough. He used to look me in the *eye* and tell me what to do, and I'd do it. But I've had enough. Have you had enough? Tell me."

"We've had enough!" they responded.

"Then we gotta act *now*! Not tomorrow—*now*! We've been sleeping for *too* long! Now we have to *wake up*! We have to *storm Prospero Taligent's citadel*! We have to break down the doors of his Tower and search it floor by floor until we find him! Then we'll throttle him with our *bare hands*!

"He's kept us under his thumb for too long! *We have to take this city back!*"

(*He said all we're supposed to do is act this stuff out! Well we aren't* acting *anymore!*)

The crowd let loose a collective yell, turned as one, and began to run down the deserted street toward the obsidian tower that dominated the eastern skyline, the false tin men leading them with their axes held high.

(*This is one hundred percent for* real *now*.)

TEN

Given the commotion in front of the entrance to my apartment building (a man with an unkempt beard and a thousand-yard stare pressing a pamphlet describing the end-times into the hands of hurried passersby; a panicked doorman brandishing a rusty jackknife at a gang of jeering hooligans; a pile of defunct mechanical men in the middle of the empty street that a couple of cops in full riot gear were lighting up with flame-throwers), I thought it would be safest to enter the building through the parking garage beneath it.

As I walked down one of the dimly lit aisles (for the power was out here, too, with only a few lights running off an emergency generator), an automobile prowling for a parking space kept pace with me, a shiny affair in black and chrome, polished to a mirror's likeness, large and low to the ground. I couldn't make out the driver's face in the failing light; only that he wore a black fedora and a black trench coat with its collar turned up.

We traveled down the aisle together for a short time, until someone vacated a parking space almost at the aisle's head. The black automobile

pulled ahead of me to swing into the spot, but before he could execute
the turn, a hot-pink finned behemoth of a car came out of nowhere and
whipped into the space, parking crookedly, nearly clipping off the black
automobile's front fender.

As I approached the scene of the near accident, I could see the driver
of the black automobile pounding his steering wheel repeatedly with his
fists and quickly moving his lips with a grimace on his face. He'd barely
managed to avoid a collision. The driver of the pink car opened her door
and stepped out. She looked to be in her sixties, short, scrawny, wrinkled,
and heavily made-up, with drawn-on eyebrows and twin spots of deep
red rouge ground into her sagging cheeks. Her tight knee-length dress
gave the clear impression that she'd just been inside a paint factory while
it was imploding. In her jewelry-burdened hands she held a small, white,
and unreasonably furry dog, its eyes obscured by its own hair.

She let the dog drop to the ground and it began to run around frantically in tight circles, yapping hysterically. "Oh my *gosh*," she said, approaching the black automobile as its driver shoved open its door. "Oh
my gosh, I'm *sorry*? Oh I didn't mean to cut you off like that—"

"If you were really sorry about it, then you wouldn't have done it," the
automobile driver whispered. He reached into a pocket of his trousers
with his right hand and pulled out a keyring closed in his fist, tightly
gripping one of the keys between his index and middle fingers.

"I didn't mean to cut you off?" the woman continued. "It's just that
I'm in a hurry? I want to get safe and sound in my bed before this business with the death rays starts! And also it's *such* a good parking space,
you can't blame—"

"If you were really sorry about it, then *you wouldn't have done it!*"
the automobile driver screamed. "Why do you say you did not mean to do
something when you know that you *did* mean to? 'I do not mean to hurt
you as I am hurting you': What is this? How's *this*?" He ran up to her car
and ripped a long ragged gash into its pink paint with the key in his fist.
"Oh, I'm *sorry* I ruined your paint job!" He then strode over to the woman
and spat cleanly in her eye. "I didn't mean to spit in your eye, either! And
I'm sorry I killed your *dog*, too," he said, reaching into the folds of his vo-
luminous trench coat and removing a revolver, which he used to pump six
bullets into the dog's body, mowing it down. "And I didn't mean to *ruin*

your looks for life, either," he said, holstering the revolver, reaching into his trench coat again, and pulling out a corked glass vial with a fluorescent green liquid inside; he deftly removed the cork with his thumb and, with an adept flick of the wrist, slung the contents of the tube into the woman's face. "Acid?" she yelled. "Oh my God *acid*?" She put her hands to the smoking remains of her face and collapsed to the ground, weeping. "There, now!" said the man in the trench coat, stabbing a finger at the woman lying prone on the ground. "This will teach you to say what you *mean* in the future!"

As the *vitrioleur* turned to look at me, I got a clear look at his face: round and ruddy, freckled, with a shock of curly carroty hair creeping from under the brim of his hat. He pointed a finger at me. "You remind me of someone I don't think I like," he said, "but I can't remember who. But when I do, there's going to be hell to pay—who are you. Tell me who you are."

"I'm Harold Winslow," I stammered as he approached me, reaching into his trench coat again to pull out who knew what. "I don't know you. I write greeting cards."

I was afraid for a moment that the man standing before me was a dissatisfied customer, seeking revenge. It wouldn't have been the first time this kind of thing happened. For instance, the cards that I wrote for the company's "I'd Like to Declare My Confused and Ambiguous Fondness for You" line were all notorious failures, some of which were blamed as the single direct cause of several nasty divorces, and some of their purchasers had actually taken the effort to discover the identity of their anonymous author, sending me hate mail, dead fish, and poorly wrapped, oil-stained packages emitting ticking noises.

But the *vitrioleur* paused. "Wait a second. Harold Winslow." He squinted. "Are you . . . this seems silly, but were you at a birthday party, about twenty years ago, for Miranda Taligent? You . . . you were the story-teller."

"Yes. Yes. That was me."

"So was *I*!" He pointed at himself. "I'm Sebastian! I sat next to you at the concert with the mechanical orchestra, remember?"

That placed it for me. His face still looked the same.

His hand came out of his trench coat, empty and offered in greeting.

He shook my hand firmly, with a grip just short of being painful. The driver of the pink car was rolling back and forth on the ground and wailing. "Oh my God my face. Oh God my face."

"You know, I still think about that party," Sebastian said. "Hey, you'll like this! Remember when I said I wanted to be a *vitrioleur* when I grew up? And then Prospero Taligent said all that creepy stuff about how he'd watch all of us our whole lives and make our dreams come true?"

I could hear the letter from Miranda in my briefcase, reading itself to me. "Yes," I said.

"Well, imagine my surprise when, on the day I graduated from high school, I received a letter in the mail saying that, in recognition of my stellar academic achievement, Taligent Industries was awarding me a full scholarship to the Xeroville College of Vitriol!"

"There's a school for that kind of thing?"

"Why, sure! You don't think you can just go around throwing acid in people's faces without a degree, do you? Hundreds of hours of training are required before a man can don the black trench coat!"

"Oh, really."

"Well, *yes*. It's a two-year program. The first year is all chemistry, you know: mixing the acid, procedures for preservation and containment, things like that. A lot of people wash out in that first year. They like the *image* of the *vitrioleur*, the *glamour*, but not the work they have to put in, see? But if you can make it to that second year, that's when the fun starts. That's when you learn *technique*."

"Technique."

"Oh, yes. You try to sling acid without the proper technique, it could end up all over your hand; hell, it could end up in your *own* face for that matter!"

"So this is your job, then." I started to edge away from Sebastian, but he kept following me, his twitching hand nervously sliding into his trench coat and coming out empty, then going back in.

"Yes, it's great, isn't it? I get hired by rich old men, mostly: revenge on squirrelly second wives that run off with a suitcase full of money and the plumber. It's got a real sense of drama, more so than the usual stuff with guns and knives. First I track the victim for a few days, to figure out the pattern of their lives; then I come up to them when they're stepping out of their apartment in their bathrobe to pick up the newspaper in the morning, or when they're waiting for a cab in the afternoon, and then I spring it on them! And just so they understand who's doing them in, I'll say something just beforehand like 'This bile comes to you from the tongue of Jeremiah Smith!' Like *this*!" And quicker than my eyes could follow, his hand snaked into his trench coat, came out with a vial, uncorked it, and threw its contents into my face.

I yelped and staggered backward, putting my hands to my face, but noticed that I felt none of the intense stinging that one normally associates with caustic liquids in contact with the skin. I dropped my hands and looked at Sebastian, confused. "Ho ho!" he laughed. "That was merely colored water! That is a little trick I like to play on new friends! You see the drama of it now? Some of the newer *vitrioleurs* like to fake their way through that part of it. They have these rigged-out vials that have a mechanical *delivery system* inside, so that the acid just shoots out through a tiny hole in the cork. But where's the glory in that? If you're going to do that then you might as well get a little toy *squirt gun*, is what I say."

He looked behind him at the woman, still lying on the ground, moaning incoherently. "Miss Priss is no longer the cat's meow when her face is made ugly," he said between clenched teeth. He turned back to me, and an honest-to-God tear glistened in the corner of his eye. "Prospero Taligent made my dream come true," he said. "He really did."

ELEVEN

After climbing twenty flights of stairs in darkness, I let myself into my apartment and shut the door, double-bolting it. Then I opened my briefcase, removed the bottle of Scotch, uncorked it, and took a swig straight from the bottle. From the street below I could hear screams, the cracks of firing rifles and revolvers, and the shattering of window glass.

I sat in silence as the afternoon passed and the light dimmed, sipping from the bottle of Scotch, reading the letter from Miranda again, thinking, reading the letter again, thinking, sipping from the bottle of

Scotch. Soon enough night began to come on, heralded by the early, man-made, gloomy sunset that descends on a city full of skyscrapers, made of sharply defined mile-long swaths of light and shadow. The city was refusing to sleep as it should have on the night of Christmas Eve, with the last presents wrapped in foil and placed in the closet to be trotted out at three o'clock in the morning, and the last of the greeting cards I'd written in midsummer snatched hurriedly off drugstore racks unread. It seemed that Xeroville was heading for a full-scale riot.

With the power gone out in the building it was strangely quiet, with all its machines shut down. That was good—the quiet was rare, and it let me mull things over.

The thing is—I'd just gone about my business today. The winged messenger; the letter from a lost love; the proclamation of the madman; the riots in the streets—and I'd just gone about my business, trying to ignore it all as if it were just so much noise. And everyone else in the city who could carry it off was probably trying to do the same. Nothing less than acid thrown straight in our faces would turn us from our predetermined paths, or our quibbles over quality parking spaces.

Outside my window I could see the nearly full moon rising in deepening twilight over the Xeroville skyline. The stars were coming out, and as they shone above the dark city they looked the way they must have looked in the age of miracles that my father used to speak of—thousands of twinkling pinpricks in the sky, the distant indicators of forbidden planets. Hundreds of flying cars were circling aimlessly around the upper floors of skyscrapers like clouds of insects, their headlamps painting circles of white light that slowly floated across the rows of plate-glass windows.

The only building in the city that still had lights in its windows was the tallest: the Taligent Tower. Moored atop it I could see what appeared to be an enormous white cigar-shaped bladder, moving almost imperceptibly back and forth as if it were being tossed by a strong wind. That must have been the zeppelin *Chrysalis*.

All the other buildings in the city looked like tombstones for giants.

TWELVE

Even now, as I sit here aboard the zeppelin, having had a year to think about it, I am not entirely sure why I decided, then, to take up the task of charging into the Taligent Tower and single-handedly rescuing Miranda, as if I were some kind of serial-film space pirate, clad in sequined tights with a Röntgen gun charged and ready to fire. I have guesses for my own motivations, but I can't be certain. I know what I wish to be true about my character, but I don't know that it is.

Perhaps you know the kind of man I am, dear imaginary reader. I have never felt as if I have known anyone well. I have never had that sense of instinctive empathy that I am told comes to lovers, or brothers and sisters, or parents and children. I have never been able to finish a sentence that someone else starts. I have never been able to give a gift to someone that they have liked, one that surprises them even as they secretly expected it.

Whenever I looked into faces and tried to discern the thoughts that lay behind them I had to make best guesses, and more often than not it seemed that my guesses were wrong. And one of my greatest fears in life has been that I might, sometime, receive the call of a damsel in distress, and *not know it for what it is*—that I might mistake it for an insult or the punch line of a poorly told joke. Or worse, that I would recognize it and fail, miserably, repeatedly, to respond.

Why did I enter the Tower? (Prospero Taligent, on the roof of the Tower a few hours later, gave me his own reasons. But I'm getting ahead of myself.) It may have been as simple as that Miranda's message to me was handwritten. The message in it was unique. It wasn't written by a committee; it wasn't one of ten million machine-made copies; it wasn't blaring out the speaker of every radio in the city; it wasn't printed on the inside of a greeting card in a script choking on its own flourishes and curlicues. It was composed by a single person, for the express purpose of communicating an original message to another, specific person. It was composed with that person, me, in mind. And so few messages like that were left in the world.

In the middle of all the world's incessant noise, her message was music, and music was a thing that I'd mostly lived my life without. In the ten years since I'd last seen Miranda she'd come to somehow stand in for all the things I didn't have in life that were thought to make us human, all the absent music and touch and sympathy; in my mind she lived a separate life apart from her real one, and there she grew more pure and perfect with each passing day. Silly, perhaps, given what's passed and what's to come, but if you know the kind of man I am, then you cannot blame me for this, no more than I could blame my father for his addled daily rewrites of my mother's life before he passed away. In my mind Miranda had become a miracle.

And if she was a miracle, then for once in my life I could behave as if I still lived in a time of miracles. I could try for once to be the kind of hero that people used to read about in books, leaping chasms or running through flames, rescuing the woman from the tracks just before the train blew by. I'd done it once; I could do it again.

Granted, I'd never touched a gun in my life, or even a knife outside a kitchen, and heaven knows I didn't have a killer's instinct. But I had language—that could be my weapon. I saw myself forcing my way through the Tower's obsidian doors with a dirge for a sword and a sonnet for a shield. I'd hurl one-liners at Prospero's guards that would cripple them with laughter, and once I reached the villain himself, I'd vanquish him with a spirited and rigorous philosophical debate that would last till sunrise, at which time he would willingly hand the girl over to me and commit an honorable suicide.

Then I would take Miranda somewhere, I don't know where, some place where there weren't machines, and I would write lovesongs for her, a different one each day. Each one would have a new melody, and their rhymes would never be forced; every time I sang one to her, she would understand just what it meant; every morning I would wake before her and read her face as she slept, and I would know her thoughts and feelings with absolute certainty before she opened her eyes.

And at my command the woman would assume the age that I wished her to be—thirty, or twenty, or ten. At thirty we'd talk of higher things and make each other wiser; at twenty we'd strip off our clothes and tangle together a half dozen times a day; and at ten she would take me in hand and resurrect those things in me that had been dead for so long that I'd even forgotten they existed—when we'd finished with each other, I'd use her eyes for mirrors and I'd see a boy's wide eyes staring out of my own face. Her touch would give me the thrill of a child riding a roller coaster for the first time, and the meanings of the words she spoke to me would always be beyond doubt.

Of course, it bears mentioning that by then I had finished off more than half of the bottle of Scotch, and I was good and drunk.

INTERLUDE

aboard the good ship *chrysalis*

—we don't have much time left, do we?

I have a recurring dream: it goes something like this. I am standing at the base of an obsidian tower that rises out of a field of newly mown grass stretching to the horizon in all directions, crosshatched patterns of light and dark green making it into an infinitely large chessboard. Unlike this dream's other variations, no crowd is waiting to watch the woman fall. There is only me, looking up at the queen dancing drunkenly along the edge of the roof in a bloodred gown.

Now the wizard appears, standing behind me, whispering in my ear. "She's going to fall," he says. "And even though you have seen this death in uncounted previous dreams, it will still be the most horrific thing you have ever witnessed in your life, and it will be the stuff of nightmares for years to come. Let me give you a *mathematical demonstration.*"

The wizard waves his hands and mumbles something in the back of his throat, and a chalkboard in a weathered wooden frame materializes in front of me, accompanied by a burst of sparks and the quickly disappearing sound of a harp. The wizard, who wears a pointy purple hat and a robe decorated with golden stars and moons and comets, scurries over to the chalkboard, trailing his improbably long white beard behind him, and draws a rough diagram of the tower, and a long curved arrow going from the roof of the tower to the ground, depicting the trajectory of the queen's body once she commits to suicide. The queen is a faceless stick figure atop the tower, with a sawtooth crown and a hollow triangle standing in for her hips and thighs. "First she has to fall half the distance between the tower's roof and the ground," he says. "Then she has to fall half the distance that's left. And then half again. And so on. She has to fall past an infinite series of halfway marks, you see, stretching in front of her like all of unspent time. So although you'd be inclined to think that she'd dash her brains out on the ground a few seconds after she jumped, in truth, she will perpetually fall, but she will *never reach the ground*. And you will have to stand here and watch her fall (tee-hee) *forever!*" The wizard seems to think that this is all very funny. On the roof of the tower the queen briefly loses her footing and almost slips off, but after frantically windmilling her arms she goes back to precariously traipsing along the edge. "You can save her," the wizard says. "All you have to do is erase the drawing of the queen on the chalkboard and draw yourself in her place."

He hands me a piece of chalk, and with my open hand I rub out the woman's image, turning it into a smear of white, and draw a male stick figure in its place. There is a flash of light as I finish the final stroke, and more sparks, and the harp, and maybe a choir of girls performing a little ditty. And I am standing on the roof, where the woman was. But instead of my own clothes, I am wearing the queen's red gown, and no matter how hard I try to will myself back to safety, I cannot stop myself from stepping over the edge.

The wizard is striking the same deal with the queen now, who stands where I once stood, wearing the suit and hat that I once wore, her long reddish gold hair spilling out from beneath the fedora's brim. It occurs to me that this could go on forever, this switching of names and identities, each of us perpetually rescuing the other. There is not much time left for me; my feet are carrying me too close to the edge. "But if he falls forever, and never hits the ground, then that means he'll never die," the queen says. "So the best way for me to show my love for him is to let him fall, and grant him immortality."

Then I step off the roof. I always wake up just before I hit the ground.

FIVE

the dream

of perpetual

motion

ONE

Girls are angels of goodness and light. Boys are demons with malice and spite. And little girls get marriage plots and tales of spiteful stepsisters to fuel their fantasies of adulthood. But the stories that men tell their sons are stories of men with weapons, standing alone in places where men do not belong. *And so, with his dagger clenched between his teeth, he swam into the mouth of the giant whale. And brandishing the great sword he charged into the cavern, where the dragon lay sleeping atop his pile of gold. And he lived for five years among the merfolk that whiled away their days in a city of ivory beneath the waves, and he took one of their women for his wife.*

When I was a child and I listened to my father as he sat behind his desk and made his little dolls, before everything happened with the Taligents and before my sister's suicide, the stories he told me of the past age of miracles made it seem as if every single boy who grew up in those days was a hero at some point in his life. I never knew whether any or all of the things my father said were true or false, but he had me half-believing that schools of giant fish would swim up to the shores of seacoast towns back then, beaching themselves and opening their mouths wide in invitations for exploration, as if they were patients at the dentist's office. Looking back on it, I'm sure that he looked at me and felt that, in this age of machines and skyscrapers, I never had a chance to be young, in the way that he did. Even in Miranda's playroom I never had that child's thrill of feeling myself in mortal peril: any monstrous fish we might have found there would have obligingly kept its jaws agape until we'd gotten bored with dancing jigs on its tongue and prodding at its molars.

But when I made my way through the mob that crowded the city streets and finally set foot in the rapidly emptying obsidian Taligent Tower, in its cavernous central lobby filled with the descending pitches of thousands of machines winding down, I felt as if I'd stepped into one of those stories of supermen conquering forbidden fictional spaces, and even through the haze of my drunkenness, even running off four hours of sleep in the past twenty-four, I felt young. It is nice enough to be a child, but it is far rarer, and much more precious, to no longer be young, and to truly feel young again.

TWO

And so the young hero charged into the tower, to save the woman and the world with her. And on his last journey to vanquish the dastardly villain he heard the tales of three storytellers who lay in wait, all of whom had been touched by the woman he believed he loved: the master of the boiler room; the portraitmaker; and the beast.

Listen.

THREE

The lobby was filled with hundreds of people running in dozens of different directions: panicked employees attempting to escape from the building with sheaves of documents clutched in either hand; young secretaries in high heels and ripped stockings struggling with boxes of filched office supplies; a gang of silver-faced men dressed like Artegall, pushing through the crowd with fire axes at the ready, looking for something to break; people who had stumbled into the Tower from nearby streets just to observe the rioting and get a secondhand adrenaline rush. The building's security guards were present in the crowd, but there were not nearly enough to keep order; whenever I was accosted by one, I'd show the security pass that had been in the courier envelope I'd received that morning, and the guard would glance at it for half a second, send me on my way with a nod, and hassle someone else. Nightstick-wielding policemen in sharp, deep blue uniforms were already starting to trickle into the lobby, though there weren't yet enough of them to lock the building down. I figured that it would be prudent to make my way up to the 101st floor of the Tower, rescue the girl in some suitably valiant fashion, and somehow bring her out of the building before there were too many authorities to stop me. I felt young. I felt like I could do this.

I made my way toward the bank of elevator cars at the rear of the lobby, taking a swig of whiskey and trying not to let all the sounds in the place get to me. There was the noise of all the building's dying machines; of the mob at the Tower's doors, pushing their way inside behind me; of the throng of employees inside the hall; of an engineer who cradled in his arm a large folder stamped SECRET in bloodred ink, screaming technical data at the top of his lungs; of a shirtless toothless urchin in overalls, weaving quickly between the legs of all the adults, barking nonsense and banging a pair of cymbals together as if he were a windup tin monkey.

When I reached the elevator door, one of the false tin men was standing there as well, resting the handle of his axe on his shoulder like some kind of lumberjack, waiting for the elevator to reach the lobby and the door to open. "Hey there!" he said to me as I stood next to him to wait, his white teeth glimmering in a shining silver face.

"Hello," I said.

"Nice night, isn't it?" He motioned at the mayhem going on around him, at the lobby full of noise. "The new forebrain components will be composed of a nickel-platinum alloy!" yelled the engineer. "Capable of withstanding a Beaumont pressure of two hundred pounds squared per square inch squared!" "Yah yah yah!" screamed the urchin, banging his cymbals for all he was worth. "Yah yah yah *yah*!" Then a deep voice came out of the ceiling, heralded by the earsplitting whine of speaker feedback, lent an echo by the hall's acoustics: "—ughter. Darling daughter. My daughter was raped by a god. Transformed into a brute." His voice trembled with madness. "I thought I'd lost her. I couldn't recognize her. When she opened her mouth to speak all that would come out of her was the dumb sound of a beast. She had to draw letters in the dust with her newfound hoof to tell me the tale of her altered shape—" The voice suddenly shut off.

"What brings you here?" said the imitation tin man.

"I'm here to rescue a damsel in distress," I said.

"That's a nice way to spend an evening like this," said the tin man. "Noble of you. Me, I'm just here to cause trouble. Hey—I can't help but notice that you positively *reek* of alcohol. Got any on you?"

I took the flask of Scotch out of my coat pocket, and since it only had a couple of gulps left in it, I handed it over. "Keep it."

"That's nice of you," the tin man said. "You have the Christmas spirit." He placed the bottle to his lips and tilted his whole head back theatrically, swallowing until it was empty. "In times like this, we have to stick together. Small favors, and all." He pitched the empty bottle away with an underhand throw, and it went sliding across the floor. "Hey, after you finish doing whatever you're doing," he said, "you ought to meet us on the roof of the Tower. A bunch of us guys are making our way up there, one way or another. Splitting up so the cops can't catch us all. That's where it's all going to go down, I think. He's gotta be up there, I think— the old man, getting his ship ready. I don't have any intention of letting that happen, you know? You just heard what he said? The man is clearly stone-cold crazy." The tin man slung the fire axe off his shoulder and thwacked its handle in his open palm. "I think *this* will have something to say about the matter first. If you're feeling the way we do about this, maybe you can help us out—what do you say?"

A policeman barged out of a crowd of people and came toward us, waving his nightstick in the air. "Hey. Hey, you two." We turned, and while I protectively showed him the entrance pass to the Tower, the tin man merely smiled, not even dropping his axe.

"You," the cop said, pointing his nightstick at me, "you got ID: you're okay. You," he said to the tin man, "look here. We can't have you guys running around in here like this. How would that look, if the cops just started letting vigilantes run around in the place willy-nilly, huh? Even if maybe some of these cops, or maybe even just about all of them, wouldn't mind if some of these vigilantes happened to make their way to the *roof of the building*, where some *rich crazy evil genius* is almost ready to take off in what from all appearances is some kind of *death-dealing zeppelin*, and said vigilantes happened to sink a couple of *axe-heads* into this guy's *skull*. After this is over there's going to be an investigation, the whole works. You know? People are going to get subpoenaed; people are going to ask questions. The force will be under the microscope."

"Sure," the tin man said. "I get you."

"All I'm saying," the cop said, "is that if I *were* a vigilante, running around this place, and not that I approve of such behavior, personally, I think it's despicable, I think somebody ought to arrest you guys—I wouldn't take the *elevator* up to the roof, like this guy. I'd take the *fire stairs*, over there, which seem to have somehow been left unattended by a couple of security guards, who I may or may not have had conversations with about the evening's exciting events, and who may or may not exactly mind if their employer, who is the *crazy genius* I just mentioned, befell some kind of *mishap*. Okay? See the guys headed over that way, dressed like you? They know that by taking the *stairs*, which no one's watching, they're unlikely to run into *hassle*, since they don't exactly have *passes* like this guy, right? Maybe it'll take a long time to climb those flights, but I'm hearing, from the same security guards who would never cut it on the force because they are carelessly *letting crucial information slip*, that this guy's scheduled time to take off is in *three hours*. So you've got time. Not that I approve of you going up to the roof of the building just as fast as you can make it and kicking every bit of ass that you can find to kick, especially if it is the ass of a crazy genius. You guys oughta go home and wipe that stupid paint off your faces and let the law take care of this.

"I hope I've made myself clear, that I don't appreciate this vigilante business," the cop said, tapping the tin man on the shoulder with his nightstick. Then he walked away.

"Well," the false tin man said to me with a sigh as the elevator doors opened, "I've got a hundred and fifty flights to climb. I may as well get started." He still seemed to be in his unusual good humor. I stepped into the car and pressed the button marked 101, and as I looked at the silver-faced man he lifted his hand, as if in benediction.

"Good luck, my friend," he said as the doors slid shut. "Thanks for the whiskey. Three hours. I'll see you on the roof."

FOUR

A few minutes later, the elevator glided to a stop, and its doors slid quietly open. I looked out onto the 101st floor of the Taligent Tower.

Years of experience with reading signs on doors had taught me that a door's sign was usually indicative of what lay on its other side. But the signs on the closely spaced doors that lined both sides of the labyrinthine hallways that branched crazily before me at all angles could mean nothing, unless Prospero had somehow developed the ability to bottle dreams and wishes: AWKWARD read one, all in capital letters. NORTH read another. TUESDAY. NOT. IMPAIR. VERSIONS. MIRACLE. HEAT. EARLY. THE. CANDLELIGHT. I stepped cautiously out of the elevator, and it shut and went whizzing down to the bottom floor. Then it was dead quiet.

I didn't know what to do. Which one of the doors concealed the woman? Was there a door here that read DAMSEL? If so, how would I find it? If the rooms weren't in alphabetical order, what order were they in? I had never before felt so lost in my life as I did then. MELTED. SIN. EAST. SOUNDPROOF. ESSENCE. DUNE. AN. It was as if the building had gone mad along with its owner.

The feedback whine erupted out of the ceiling again, and I jumped as I felt my heart dump adrenaline into my body. "—odeon of alternate pasts. People think they want to see the future. But do they not truly desire to see a past that never existed when they speak of this future? Do they in their old age not want to return to some misremembered pastoral childhood, full of daisies and innocence, censored of its beatings and suffering? The nickelodeon of alternate pasts will show films custommade for each viewer, films of *what might have been*: had you taken a left instead of a right at a certain crosswalk; had you not walked in on your parents in the midst of sexual congress at the age of eight; had you introduced yourself to the plain Jane at the wedding reception instead of the temptress with the startling décolletage. Each film will end identically: the customer enters the nickelodeon and sits rapt at the viewer, watching himself watching himself watching himself dine on regret, unable to leave—"

Quiet again. After a few more moments, I decided that the only course of action available was to try a door at random. I turned to a door next to me; it wouldn't open when I tried the knob, but embedded in the door's frame was a device with a blinking light and a small slot. I slipped the identification card into it. It swallowed the card and spat it back out; the light stopped blinking and glowed cleanly; the door swung open, revealing darkness on the other side. It was labeled with the single word HEAT.

FIVE

When the door shut behind me, it took a few moments for my eyes to adjust to the light. In pitch darkness I felt my way down a narrow corridor until it opened out into what seemed like a spacious room with a high ceiling; the only light came from an odd reddish orange rectangle at the far end, which flickered like a fire and was occasionally obscured. As my pupils widened I began to take in more details: a glinting line of light on a wide metal pipe descending from the ceiling; piles of something, rocks perhaps, five times as high as I was tall; a large metallic egglike structure mounted against a wall, twice as tall as myself, with a dark rectangular hole cut into it like a gaping mouth.

It was a furnace, with the fire inside it gone out. And the piles of rocks in front of me were piles of coal. This was one of the Tower's boiler rooms.

The dead furnace I saw was one of many, perhaps a hundred, scattered irregularly throughout the boiler room like forgotten totems. Pipes led out of them to twist like nests of metal pythons and disappear into the ceiling and floor. The dancing light at the chamber's end came from the only burning furnace in the entire room, and as I slowly approached it, clumsily making my way past pipes and clambering around mountains of coal, I saw a stockily built man standing in front of the furnace, frantically slinging shovelfuls of coal down its throat.

I got close enough to shout a greeting to him, and he spun to face me. He was shirtless and muscular, and covered in coal dust. With an enormous upper body, thick stout legs, and no neck or waist to speak of, he looked like a child's drawing of a strongman.

He took a step toward me, holding his shovel in a pose suggesting that he could use it either as a tool or a weapon. A grin dawned on his coal-smudged face.

"You came for the heat," he said.

I stumbled backward, nearly slipping on a nugget of coal lying beneath my foot. "I'm looking for a damsel in distress," I managed to spit out. "Her name is Miranda."

He stood there for a moment, backlit by furnace glow. "Miranda?" he said, and his grin widened. "I screwed her."

He turned away from me then, picked up a shovelful of coal from a nearby mound, and threw it into the furnace, which spoke with a deep *whoomph* from its gullet as the coal ignited. "I'm Ferdinand," he said, continuing to feed the furnace. "I'm the master of this boiler room. You picked the wrong time to come if you came for the heat. Usually there's a hundred men here. All of us shoveling. Keeping things hot. Tin men can't work here. They can't take the heat. It's constant. Their insides gum up. They freeze. They choke on coal dust.

"One hundred men. Shoveling coal and singing bawdy songs to keep the beat and pass the time. Sweating to make your heat and your light. But ninety-nine men were cowards tonight. They ran away because they were afraid." He stopped shoveling for a moment to look at me and pound his chest with a meaty fist. "Not me. Not Ferdinand. I'm staying until the end. Because men have to take responsibility."

"I'm looking for Miranda," I said, and it sounded crazy as soon as it came out of my mouth. "If you know, please tell me where I can find her."

"When I touched her," Ferdinand said, "I would leave a handprint in coal dust on her perfect porcelain flesh." He went back to shoveling as he spoke, punctuating his words with the swings of the shovel and the sound of the coal's ignition. "I found her wandering among the furnaces." *Whoomph.* "Through the mountains of coal." *Whoomph.* "The girl wore a thin nightgown." *Whoomph.* "She huddled on the slope of a coal mountain. She held a lump of coal in her hand. She was chewing on it. Her other arm was drawn around her. Hiding her breasts from me. She shook. Two heat spots of red on her cheeks.

"I said that's not how you get the heat out of it. Not by eating it. You have to heat it up. It takes heat to make more heat. That's science. She said I'm cold. I said come here then. She climbed down from the coal pile. I could see through her nightgown. Her nipples were hard and the color of wine. She put her arms around me. She laid her cheek against my chest. She shivered. My cock sprang up like a dowsing rod. She said I'm so cold. I'm very cold. All around me I could hear the slicing sound of shovel blades sliding into piles of coal. Like swords sliding into sheaths. We were hidden from the other men. In the mountains of coal. They sang as they worked. Love Meg Moll Marian and Margery. But none of us cared for Kate. For she had a tongue with a tang. I said are you maid or no. She said haven't you heard the news. I'm a little virgin queen. She said I'm unmade. She said I want you to make me.

"I tasted the coal on her tongue then. I took her up to the top of one of the coal mountains. The lumps skittered beneath our feet as we crawled upward. I had her there lying on my back. My hands gripping her waist. Impaling her on me.

"After that she came to me again and again. For five years. Sometimes not for months at a time. Sometimes every day. We would screw in the coal mountains. The other men found out about her soon enough. But none of them tried to take her. Because the girl was mine by right. There are many men that shovel coal in this boiler room. But I am their master. They would raise their voices in song to drown out our screams.

"Afterward we would lie at the top of the mountain of coal. Sweat drying to a thin film of salt on our bodies. I would try to tell her I loved her. But I have trouble with making words do the things I want. I said things to her that I found in books. Love better than wine. Name like ointment poured forth. Doves' eyes in your locks. Hair like a flock of goats. She'd place a hand over my mouth. She said don't speak. Every time you speak you sound like a barking animal. Bark bark bark. I don't come to you to hear words. I don't want words from you. I'm sick of hearing words to tell me what I am. She started crying. I tried to say something. She said shut up shut up. She called me nasty names. She said every time I spoke it was like a hammer driving a nail home.

"Days turned to years. She got older. Once she went away and didn't come back for months. Then she came. And we did what we always did. The men were happy when she came back. Because it gave them a reason to sing loud. But I could smell another man on her.

"Afterward she said Father—. I said I—. She said I told you to be quiet. Be quiet and listen now. She said, 'Father has terrible things in mind for me. I don't know what they are. At first I thought he was just going to punish me for running away from home, but now I think he has something worse in store. It's going to be something that hurts me—I can tell from the way he looks at me. The worst thing is that, when he finally does it, this awful thing, he'll *know* it's hurting me, but he won't be able to stop himself. Because he loves me so very, very much. His face is chiseled into a permanent scowl. But he is drowning in his own love.'

"Once afterward she said, 'There is something I do that isn't permitted, when I am alone and I know Father won't find out. And while I'm doing it I think of straddling you, holding a needle and thread, sewing your lips tight shut. Sometimes I think of you with no mouth at all—just a blank stretch of skin beneath your nose that's as unmarked as the top of your foot or your buttock. Sometimes I think of you without a face, and I imagine that I have a lump of coal in my hand and I'm drawing on your blank skull with it. And I can draw any face on you that I want. The face of an architect or a demolition man, or a strongman or an invalid, or an angel or a devil, or a rocket scientist or a court fool. That's how I wish you were. That's how you should be.'

"Once afterward she said, 'Stay with me, atop this mountain of coal, and let your furnace go out. I wish there were one of me for every man that shovels coal in this Tower's boiler rooms, so that they could learn the thing that you have learned. Then they would climb atop their own coal beds with me, and drop their shovels and hold me in their arms, and spend themselves and drowse in silence. Then all of the fires in all of the furnaces would die. And the Tower would freeze. Films of frost covering the walls and windows; frost coating the metal keys of the secretaries' typewriters. Frost killing all the colorful plants in my playroom. Everything would freeze. The machines and the mechanical men would freeze. The secretaries would look down at their typewriters and see that there were no more letters anymore, and they would freeze, and frost would coat the lenses of their spectacles. And Father would freeze with his cup of morning coffee halfway to his lips. And everything would get quiet. Then all the Mirandas could leave this place and go out into the world. One Miranda by herself is always a girl in danger, and has to come back to this place. But a hundred of me would be safe.'

"I said I have to go back to the furnace. I said a man has responsibilities. I climbed down from the coal mountain. I left her there.

"I didn't see her anymore after that.

"I don't want to talk anymore."

Ferdinand continued to sling coal into the furnace in silence; then, after a few moments, he spun around and said, "Are you just going to stand there *staring*? Or are you going to help me *shovel*? A man's got *responsibility*! We've got to keep things *hot*!"

"I'm looking for Miranda," I said, because it was all I knew to say. "She told me that I have to save her. But there are too many doors outside, and they all have signs I don't know how to read."

Ferdinand raised his shovel over his head and then threw it clattering to the ground. He stepped toward me and grabbed me by the shoulders with his huge, slablike hands. I thought he was going to crush me. Spit flew from his coal-smeared mouth into my face as he screamed: "Doors with signs you do not understand are *not for you!*" He released me with a shove, and I stumbled backward and nearly fell to the floor. "Did you look for a door that said MIRANDA?" he sneered, picking up his shovel again, turning back to his work. "Dumbass."

SIX

When I reentered the labyrinth of twisting corridors and oddly labeled doors, I decided that I needed a much better plan than wandering around randomly if I was to locate Miranda before she was taken from the 101st floor to the airship (if, in fact, she wasn't already on board). I sat down with my back against a door (with a sign that read QUIXOTIC) for a few moments, to get the coal dust out of my lungs and throat, and to think.

I decided that the best thing to do would be to walk down the left side of the hallway, sticking to the left wall as if I were a blind man trapped in a labyrinth. I would mark each door with the lump of coal as I passed it; in that way, I wasn't guaranteed to pass all of the doors on the 101st floor, but any system of elimination was better than none. When I found a door that spoke to me and told me to open it, then I would. Simple enough.

IT. FINGER. BARTER. SUBURB. The doors passed by me with X's marked in coal. I soon realized that I could save time by cutting the two strokes of an X down to one, so later doors were marked with simple, messy smears. NEEDFUL. VISIONARY. PUNCTUATE. OF. GET.

MIRANDA.

I stood before the door with her name on it. I hadn't actually believed that finding her would be as easy as this, but seeing Miranda's name emblazoned there made me happy that I hadn't listened to Ferdinand's message for nothing.

I pulled out my identification card and slid it into the receptacle next to the door. It swallowed the card, but held it for several seconds while it

made grinding noises and its light blinked irregularly, as if it were de-
ciding whether to shred the card and vomit it up in pieces. Finally,
though, the card ejected, a bit bent and chewed up on the edges, and the
door marked MIRANDA swung quietly open.

SEVEN

I stepped through the door and found myself in what appeared to be a
museum of some kind, a large room lit by electric lamps that were affixed
to the ceiling and arranged to shine spotlights at various angles onto
hundreds of pedestals of different heights, scattered throughout the hall.
Some of the pedestals had sculptures atop them, but most were barren.

I took a few steps forward into the room and heard a crunching
sound beneath my feet, as if I were walking over gravel. I looked down at
the floor then, and saw that it was strewn with the remnants of broken
women's bodies, arms and legs and feet and breasts and slender hands
and halves of heads, of women made from wax and bronze and marble. I
knelt and picked up a split wax head and turned it over in my hands.
When I saw its single ice-blue eye staring at me, and the locks of fake red-
gold hair that clung to its skull, I understood. All of the sculptures in this
museum were portraits of Miranda Taligent, or had been. Someone else
was in here, destroying them.

My heart skipped. I called Miranda's name, as if one of the sculptures on the pedestals would uncurl itself from its frozen pose and come
running to me with its arms outstretched. But none of them moved.

I noticed then that in the center of the room was a small, cylindrical
chamber, with two large glass doors framed in silver. The doors appeared to be coated on the inside with a layer of frost, and through it I
thought I could discern the silhouette of a man, pacing back and forth.
I started to make my way there, stepping gingerly over the broken statue
fragments.

The sculptures that remained on their pedestals were all unique, and
made of completely different, more exotic materials than the broken

ones whose remains covered the museum floor, as if the vandal working his way through this room had decided to save these works for last, to let them live just a bit longer. There was a tiny carving out of balsa wood of Miranda as a little girl astride her unicorn; it sat on a pedestal at eye level, and couldn't have been more than four inches high. There was a Miranda made out of papier-mâché applied to a wire frame bent to the shape of a young woman's body; covered in newsprint, she had a downcast expression on her face as she held her lips to the microphone in her hand. One of the pedestals held what looked like a child's toy; it was a housing that held a vertically oriented wheel with a crank connected to it. The wheel had dozens of photographs attached to it, and as I turned the crank I saw an animated image of the young Miranda asleep in her bed; then, silently, with only the riffling sound of the photographs flipping past to accompany her, she awoke, rolled over, sat on the bed's edge, yawned, and stretched her arms. . . . Then the photographs looped, and quicker than a finger snap she was back in bed, her eyes tight shut. There was a hollow sculpture of Miranda in the brilliant gown she wore when she operated the mechanical orchestra at that birthday party twenty years ago; the sculpture was made from nine different colors of stained glass, and each of the hairs on its head was made from an individually spun golden red glass fiber. Its face was clear and completely transparent, and an electric lamp shone warmly in its heart.

    I passed wonderstruck by these figures as I approached the little frozen room at the center of the museum. But what made my heart skip once again was what lay at my feet before the room's glass doors, amidst the fragments of broken girls. It was the mechanical Miranda that I had first encountered when I played at being a hero as a child, in the girl's playroom. I could still see the dried fake blood on its half-bald skull. It was naked, its legs were missing, and its chestplate was ripped off, so that I could see the motors and gears and levers inside the body that powered it.

    Nestled among all of these components was what looked like a turntable for a miniature gramophone, with a tiny record atop it and a needle poised above it. As I nudged the metal Miranda aside with my foot, the needle dropped onto the record, which began to spin. "Don't touch me," the legless false Miranda said, its voice crackling. "Don't touch—" It flailed its arms around, pawing idiotically at its scalp; then it suddenly stopped dead.

I stood there for a few moments to catch my breath; then, with what I hoped would pass for resolve, I pulled open the glass doors and, buffeted by a blast of cold air, I entered the chamber of frost.

The interior of the chamber was lined with scored and dented plates of sheet metal, and long icicles dangled from its ceiling. Dozens of mesh-covered grates were embedded in the floor, and beneath them whirring fans blew bone-chilling drafts of air into the little cylindrical room. On the opposite side of the chamber stood the figure whose shadow I had seen from outside, and between us, in the center of the chamber, with a ceiling spotlight shining straight through it and lighting it up from the inside, was another statue of Miranda Taligent, larger than life and hewn from a single immense block of ice. In this rendering of her she wore the traveling suit with matching hat that I had seen her in when I rescued her from the abandoned warehouse, ten years ago. The statue was nine feet tall, and with the woman's hands in her pockets, a slight slouch to her posture, narrowed eyes, pursed lips, and the brim of her fedora riding low on her forehead, there seemed to be some indefinable sense of masculinity in this representation of the woman that I could never recall seeing in the woman herself.

And the statue was so *detailed*. How could you carve something with so much detail out of ice? Each individual button of Miranda's suit was represented, and the threads that fastened the buttons to the fabric. The statue's eyes had eyelashes. Hundreds of fine, transparent hairs were dusted across its lower arms. Why did whatever artist who made this thing have such an obsessive concern with realism? And what kind of tools could accomplish such feats with frozen water?

The other man in the chamber watched me warily. He was old, with his face fallen and his hair gone white, its few remaining thin strands peeking from beneath the gray beret that sat stylishly askew on his head. He wore an artist's smock smeared with stains of paint and handprints of clay, and in his hands he held a flamethrower, with a blue pilot light flickering nervously at its nozzle and its gas tanks strapped to his back.

"Why have you come here?" he barked in a high voice. "Everyone's leaving. I have to break everything, and then I'll be gone myself."

"I'm looking for Miranda," I said. "Do you—"

"Miranda!" the man said, and the pilot light of his flamethrower erupted briefly, then went back to its jittering. "I especially appreciate the naïve manner in which you just *say her name*, and expect her to be summoned. As if a name can say what someone *is*. As if a few syllables can signify what that woman has *become*.

"Forgive me. My manners. I should have introduced myself. You'll have to excuse me if I don't shake hands, but I don't want this flame-thrower to get away from me. I am Miranda Taligent's official portrait-maker. And the works in this museum that I have shattered with hammers and put to the torch are my life's work, the unceasing effort of twenty-five years. But now we have the perfect woman. So tonight all the rest must burn."

EIGHT

"I'm looking for Miranda Taligent," I said once again.

"What is *that* supposed to mean?" the portraitmaker said. "Looking for Miranda. We were all *looking* for Miranda. I was, and so was her father, and so were the surgeons who wielded the knives. Even Miranda herself. There's nothing new in that. Did you look outside at all of the women I broke? All that time I spent looking for her, and I never even got close, not once, until now. But now everything in this museum has to go."

"Why?"

"Because it's an *affront*," the portraitmaker said. "After what we've finally achieved, it's a sin to have those things in the world. My entire career is gone. But it's worth it. It's worth it; had damned well better be—"

"So," I said, backing away from him against the wall of the chamber, "you've done nothing for the past twenty-five years—"

"—but make sculptures of Miranda: yes. But we have the one we want now. So there's no point in all the others. They're an *insult*—how can I make you understand? If only you were an artist, so that we could speak the same language—"

"I write greeting cards," I offered.

The portraitmaker sighed, then said, "Fine. We'll pretend that those count as art. Now suppose, through some miracle, you were able to write the *perfect* greeting card. One that would be suitable for absolutely any occasion. Guaranteed to completely convey and magnify the spirit in which it was given."

"What does it say?"

"Who knows what it says. But listen: this greeting card. You can give it to a new widower, and he will break into tears and find the consolation that eluded him. You can give this same card to a strange woman you see on the street that you're sweet on and she'll propose to marry you, on the spot. You can give it to your sick sister, get well soon, and the next day her consumption will vanish and her cancer will go into remission. The card will cure junkies of their addictions. If you give it to a madman he will read it and become sane. This card does everything you could *ever* want a greeting card to do. Now, if you wrote that greeting card, and you finished setting down the final rhyme and you read it and knew it for the miracle it was, wouldn't you look back on all the other cards you'd written, all those stupid little verses, and realize that there was no need for them in the world anymore? That they no longer served a purpose? That their existence was a sacrilege against the purity of your art?"

"I don't understand," I said.

"Look," said the portraitmaker, tracing figure eights in the air with the nozzle of his flamethrower. "Can I tell you a special story? Imagine it set off with a centered heading in capital letters, three points smaller than the principal text. This is the portraitmaker's tale.

"I'll tell you this story, the last I'll ever tell, and you'll listen. Then at the end you'll know where the woman is, and you can try your hand at whatever heroics you have in mind, if you think they'll do any good.

"That's the deal, my friend.

"Now then—"

NINE

THE PORTRAITMAKER'S TALE.

—My first Miranda [the portraitmaker began] was hewn out of a block of granite, studded with tiny crystals of quartz. I was thirty-five years old when Prospero Taligent commissioned it. It was an unusual request of me: he should have known from my portfolio that I didn't habitually work with stone that hard. I'd usually stuck to marble, using limestone on the rarest occasions, because you could make more precise, finer movements with the tools. When you hack into something like granite you never know half the time what's going to happen—it might break lucky, it might not. Granite doesn't want to change what it is.

But granite was what Prospero requested, and he said, moreover, that he wanted the sculpture to look exactly like his daughter. Not "something like," he took care to say. Exactly. Back then my work was all about abstraction and essence, female forms with just the suggestions of a bust or a face: you were meant, when you looked at them, not to think of whatever women I had in my mind when I was at work, but to be reminded of women whom you yourself once knew, but whom I myself had never seen. But the promise of a ridiculously high payment for the work, many times my going rate, plus the added opportunity to work with a large, heavy block of stone without having to go out to a quarry to carve it—he said he would supply the stone himself and have it brought to the Tower—was enough to induce me into trying to change my materials and style.

You might wonder, as I did, what Prospero meant by the word *exact*; after all, his daughter was made from flesh and blood, not stone, and granite as a medium has its limitations. And art deals in impressions, not exactitude. But *exact* is the word that he used again when he ushered me into the room on the 101st floor of the Taligent Tower that was to serve as my studio. There were six mechanical men laboring to shove an eight-foot-tall block of stone into place in the center of the room, narrow jets of steam shooting out of the joints in their knees and elbows.

I tried, unsuccessfully, to explain the fundamental nature of art to my newfound patron. He had Miranda with him, and he sat in the studio's only chair, bouncing the nightgown-clad little girl up and down on his knee. "Igneous," he was saying, tickling Miranda under his chin with his index finger, then pointing at the block of pink granite. "Can you say *igneous*? It's perfect for you. It's not even the least bit metamorphic—not one tiny bit." "Listen," I said. "Exactness as I think you're thinking of it is not within the capabilities of art. Not even so-called realist art. Not even stereographs, whose status as legitimate art is still contested. Yes, they have the illusion of three dimensions, but is Miranda the size of a postcard, colored entirely in shades of gray? When we look at a piece of art and say that it is exactly like the thing it resembles, we mean that it gives us a strong impression that reminds us of that thing, be it an apple or a woman or an emotion or whatever—not that we are fooled into responding to it as if it's the thing it pretends to be. I fear that's what you want, and with granite, or with any other stone in fact, I can't give it to you."

"What is all this sophistry you are going on with? Why are you quibbling with the meanings of words so much—to wriggle out of your contract? I don't know much about art—why, your little essay just flew right over my head," Prospero said, his lips smiling, but his gaze giving them the lie. "Exact is what I want, and exact is what you'll give me. You know what I mean."

The little girl on his knee looked at me then, and giggled.

Before I began the sculpture in earnest, I took a few photographs of Miranda to have some images to work from. Normally I would have just done some sketches, but I thought that letting my patron see me as I photographed the girl would give him some reassurance that I was considering his idea of "exactness," whatever that was.

Miranda Taligent was a terrible model. She fretted and squirmed on her little stool; she crawled under it and placed it on her head as if it were a hat; she would spontaneously burst into tears that would disappear inside of a minute, like the rain from a lone storm cloud blown past by a high wind. Sometimes she would point at me with her chubby finger and laugh, for no reason I could see.

I am not good with children. I tried every little hack photographer's trick I could think of to try to make her sit still: throwing my voice to a hand puppet with the head of a unicorn; singing silly jingles in a squeaky falsetto; promising sweets to her if she won the "be-a-statue" game. But nothing could induce her to remain still for the sixty seconds that my plates took to expose. Looking back, I think that she might have somehow understood the nature of the camera, for I think that she made some of her motions, like imperceptible movements of her hand over the course of a minute, to deliberately confound my attempt to capture her image. So in the photographs I had pinned to the walls of my studio, all of the images of Miranda sported aberrations, like multiple heads or arms, or translucent eyelids, or halos, or angel's wings made by flapping arms, or nimbuses of light that surrounded her entire body.

Prospero was there on the morning when I began to knock the corners off the block of granite that he'd provided for me. I don't like being observed when I work, and the prospect of my patron dropping in unannounced at all stages of the process over the following months was extremely unsettling to me. While I paced around the block, trying to see the possible sculpture of the little girl buried within it, Prospero examined the flawed photographs of the girl that I had tacked to the walls, turning his head this way and that, making little noises under his breath. Then he turned his attention to the tools that I'd laid out on a metal cart, the chisels of varying shapes and the hammers.

He picked up one of the heaviest hammers and turned it over, hefting its weight. "Is *this* what you're going to use to render my darling daughter?" he asked. He seemed shocked, even a little horrified, as if he thought I was going to take the hammer to Miranda's head instead of to the stone.

"Yes," I replied, trying not to sound too patronizing. "That, and the other tools."

He snorted. "*Tools* are what you call these?" He placed the hammer on the cart. "I clearly don't understand these. Explain them to me."

I suppose I should have been flattered that my employer took an interest in my work beyond its monetary value, no matter how unschooled he seemed to me. But at the time I was more annoyed than appreciative, and more in the mood to sculpt than teach. "Look," I said. "Sculpting isn't like some other forms of art, like writing a novel, where you spin the whole thing out of nothing. For me, it's just the opposite—I usually begin with the assumption that the product I desire is buried within the rock, so to speak, and that my task is just to remove the packing material."

"So my little girl is trapped inside that block of stone, then."

"I hope. Now, what I'll do, more or less, is carve a series of increasingly accurate approximations, until we get—"

"—the perfect one."

"—the best possible one. Now this," I said, warming a little now, "is what we call the pitcher. You drive it in with this heavy hammer, and it doesn't cut the stone so much as break huge chunks of it off altogether. After you knock off the angles, you move to this—the heavy point—then to this—the fine point—and by then you'll be close to the final surface of the thing. Then you use all kinds of special tools for the detail work—"

"Are these the inventions of monkeys?" Prospero said, frowning. "Chipping and breaking, instead of doing what you want. I don't see"—he ran his fingers over the surface of the immense piece of granite—"why you don't just treat the thing as if it's wooden. As if it's soft. Why don't you carve it and shape it. Treat the stone like the writer treats a blank page, not the other way around."

What he said seemed asinine to me at the time, but I was later to learn under Prospero's tutelage that it wasn't. Later I found that Prospero had, shall we say, novel ideas concerning form and function.

Nonetheless, I tried to humor him. "You can't treat stone as if it's wood, because it has a different molecular structure," I said. "You must respect the nature of the material when you work. What you're talking about is seventeenth-century stuff, when master artisans tried to pass themselves off as makers of miracles, making flames out of stones and three dimensions out of two. But twentieth-century art's a different animal, no longer Michelangelesque. We have learned to take things for what they are. We cherish canvas for its flatness and stone for its density—"

"I want you to take the rest of the day off," Prospero said, cutting me off. "I don't believe you're thinking about this properly." He pulled out his wallet, extracted a few bills from it, and pressed them into my hand. "Go somewhere and have dinner, and sleep, and come back fresh tomorrow. Today you are making me angry."

Utterly confused, I replaced the chisel that I'd been gesturing with as I spoke back on its cart and prepared to storm dramatically out of the studio, as is an artist's prerogative, but then Prospero laid a hand gently on my shoulder.

"Don't let your ignorance frustrate you," he said. "Ignorance gets the best of all of us sometimes, even me. Rest, and return tomorrow. Tonight I will invent something to fulfill your secret heart's desire."

It might have made me angry, but with his money in my pocket, I did what he told me. When I showed up at the Tower the next morning, Prospero was already in my workshop waiting for me, wearing a gleeful smile. In his hand he held some kind of jerry-rigged electrical device that looked unsafe to touch.

I had barely gotten through the door before he pressed the thing into my hand. "Try it on the granite," he said, nodding his head. "Try it!"

The thing he handed to me consisted of a heavy handle, wrapped in rough leather, with a single thick, gently curved wire leading out of it that looked as if it were clipped out of a coat hanger. The handle of the device was unexpectedly heavy, and had an electric switch embedded in it, set to OFF (Prospero had labeled the switch by hand, with tiny letters that seemed as if they were printed by a little girl).

"Turn it on," Prospero said.

I flicked the switch with my thumb, and as the tart smell of ozone filled the air, the wire sticking out of the handle began to glow: first yellow, then red, then white, then blue. The handle became warm in my hand, then hot.

"I haven't yet fixed the heatsink problem," Prospero said. "Try it. Before it gets too hot to hold. Cut the granite with it."

Having no other idea of what else to do, I approached the enormous granite block that had undergone only a few changes since the mechanical men had brought it into the studio. Then, lightly, I ran the end of the curved wire across the stone's surface.

The wire smoked and cut through the granite. But it didn't just break the stone, or chip off small pebbles or shards of it. It *peeled* it, like a whittling knife cutting through pine. Little curled granite shavings began to collect on the floor.

"I built this last night," Prospero said. "Just spun it out of some parts lying around the shop." He tapped his forehead. "I used my imagination."

I haven't had a single good night's sleep in the past year. And when I startled awake night after night to find that my bedsheets were wet and stinking with my sweat, or that I'd been biting down on my tongue in my sleep hard enough to make it bleed, I wondered if, had Prospero not spoken his next words, I would have come to do the terrible things I did to his daughter, Miranda.

But he did. Looking down on the blue-hot line of light in my hand that threatened to burn me, he said, "Yesterday you said some unwise things to me, about the need to respect the shapes of things. But we are men, not animals, and our thoughts are stronger than whatever forces hold the molecules of stones in line. Because we are men, we do not submit to such forces. We take it as our challenge to overcome them, and we bend them to suit our wishes.

"The girl is imprisoned within this stone, you say. But with the hammers that you have brought with you to set her free you are just as likely to split her head open. So use the new tools that I will bring you instead. This granite is not sacrosanct. You have the talent, and I have the machines: we'll break its will together."

He invented more devices for me to work with, which I won't describe to you, as you seem as if you're in a hurry. But let it suffice to say that a work that I expected to take ten months was completed in five. It was a sculpture of Miranda Taligent, in a linen dress, one-to-one scale. I worked the surface of the dress last, for it took Prospero a month, working each night, to build the machine I requested for the task. Any machine I asked for, I got, whether it existed in reality or dream, and on that first sculpture of Miranda, made of granite, her simple dress was nearer to linen than I thought granite could ever possibly be: if you looked at it through a magnifying glass, you could see the dress's individual fibers, and if you touched it blindfolded, the only thing that gave it away was that you couldn't gather the impossibly cold fabric in your hand.

It was my best work, and I wouldn't have been able to accomplish it without Prospero's help. In spite of my fears, he'd done what I wanted and nothing more: he just built the machines for me and left me alone.

He was the first one to see the piece when it was completed. The two of us were in the studio alone, silent for several minutes as Prospero paced around the sculpture, looking at it up close and far away, frowning in thought, then smiling in that gentle way he sometimes used to, before he lost his mind.

Finally, he said, "This is beautiful."

"Thank you, sir," I said. "I couldn't have done it without your help."

"And you'll get your money." His eyebrows knitted, and he pursed his lips, gazing at the statue.

"Sir?"

"I mean—what I am thinking is, that I asked for an exact representation of my daughter, and this isn't it."

What does he want? I thought, restraining myself from screaming at him. *Does he want it to get up and walk?*

"See," he said, "this looks exactly like Miranda, when she was five years old." He sighed and ran a long-fingered hand through his hair. "But now time has gone by. Now she's five and a half. Now she's nearly *six*."

He looked away from the statue to me and hesitantly smiled. "No two ways about it," he said. "You'll have to do another."

So that was how I got the job as the Taligent family's permanent artist-in-residence, moving out of my one-room downtown studio and into a suite on the 125th floor of the Taligent Tower. The hundred-fifty sculptures I was to make over the next seventeen years were all to have the same subject, but I had no right to complain. She kept changing, her legs and arms and fingers stretching out, her breasts and hips appearing. Every time she sat before me she was someone new.

There was another reason I couldn't feel justified in bemoaning what might seem to others to be the monotony of my life: the job security. Frankly, I was having more and more trouble placing pieces in galleries, and the kind of art that was being shown and sold in those days was becoming increasingly distant from my own. A certain insincerity had crept into it. By the time I did the terrible thing to Miranda, the artists in the outside world who got the most notice, who received the write-ups in magazines with glossy pages and a cover price fifty times that of the local paper, were the ones who pulled stunts devoid of what I still thought as craft: submerging counterfeit holy relics in urine; ripping tossed-off paintings of pinup girls out of magazines and enshrining them in gilded frames; exhibiting lumps of flyblown human dung in sealed glass boxes. Sometime during the twentieth century the elite's idea of beauty became tied to discomfort. Everything worth looking at for more than half a second had to turn your stomach, and if you found the simple things of the world beautiful, like sunrises and grins and starlight, well, then, there was something clearly wrong with you—you were common at best, moronic at worst. So remember this, that Prospero and I had the same ambition: we were both trying to bring back a dead kind of beauty, each in our own way. We were both after that lost idea of sincerity; we were both trying to breathe life back into the dead, sewed-together things of a damned, dead age. When you hear about what happened later, please remember that, and try to forgive me.

Miranda wasn't the only person who changed in the years she sat for me. Her father did, too: he got older, as I did, and he lost his mind, day by day, as the girl grew into a woman. It was in response to his begrudging request that I finally began to vary the materials I used to sculpt. He hated to say it: the idea of carving Miranda out of something besides the hardest of stones flew in the face of all his ideas about overcoming the natural forms of things. "But she keeps *changing*," he said, sitting on my studio floor with his fists balled and his legs crossed while I worked (yes, he was in my presence while I sculpted; I came to like him there and missed him when he was gone). "Always different from day to day. Sometimes I watch her sleep and I feel like I can *see* it, the bones of her face stretching behind her skin. Maybe . . . maybe you should use something else. Something more pliable, that could keep up with her."

With the help of Prospero Taligent's engineering I made about a hundred-fifty sculptures of Miranda between the ages of five and twenty-two, out of granite, and basalt, and marble, and clay, and wood, and ice, and wax. I'll admit that many of them were hack work to keep my patron happy, a matter of quantity over quality. If I had ever embraced Prospero's vaguely declared ideas of "exactness," I soon threw them out the window, and he never said a word. Anyone could have seen that what he wanted was not portraits of the girl turning into a woman as she sat for me year after year, but images of the mask that his imagination laid over her face whenever he looked at her. And he wanted to believe that those were "exact," that what he saw when he looked at her was what everyone else saw.

My sculptures of Miranda became more unlike her the older she grew, as if the doppelgängers I made of her had some other path for their lives that veered off into fantasy. Except for her hair, a stunning shade of red mixed with gold in an almost equal measure, I found her to be somewhat unpretty in her adolescent years, with a crooked and somewhat bulbous nose and thin shrewish lips. These things I fixed. While my fifteen-year-old Miranda had skin of finest porcelain, the real one sat before me in my studio, digging with her chewed fingernails at splotches of angry red acne that had erupted across her face, and would soon riddle both her cheeks with pockmarks.

This is never what showed up in the blurred photographs of the woman that you saw in the morning papers, her image smearing as its ink blackened your fingertips. This is what never appeared in the out-of-focus newsreels that you watched in the dark while you waited for the feature presentation. Because every time anyone makes an artistic image of anyone else, no matter what the medium, the subject is lent the mythic power of art, yes, but only at the price of making them so much less than what they truly are.

I'm trying to make my case in advance here. So that when I tell you what happened eight months ago, you won't think of it as a transgression upon someone's rights, or as the commission of a crime, but as an act of atonement, an attempt at redemption for the sins of my graven images.

I delayed the onset of puberty in my sculptures for as long as I reasonably could, over three years, but after a while it became ridiculous to pretend anymore. When the first Miranda with a woman's body came out of the kiln, the representation I made of her to mark her sixteenth birthday, Prospero was there, and he stared at it for a few moments, frowning and biting his lip.

"So you see it happening, too," he said finally. The heat from the oven made shimmers in the air around the clay Miranda, and it stung our faces. "I was hoping, faintly, that you might never notice. Silly, isn't it. Isn't that silly." He looked as if he wanted to cry. "I knew this would happen eventually, and you'd have to make her grow up all at once to catch up."

He sighed and shrugged his shoulders. "I suppose the secret's out."

On peaceful days, when the work was not so fast that it consumed me, but not so slow that I felt at a loss every time I picked up a tool, I liked to take my lunch seated on the sill of a large window inside the Tower that looked out onto a large, high-ceilinged hall with its floor three floors below me. On those days I was the angel of typewriter girls.

The hall beneath me was filled with row after row of heavy wooden desks, each of which held a cast-iron typewriter and two stacks of paper, one of clean white sheets, the other inked. At each desk sat a young woman, typing away, and a strange music filled the place as they made the information that kept the business running. The staccato striking of thousands of keys melded into a constant susurration, muffled by the glass of the window where I sat, punctuated by warning bells and the thuds of carriages slamming back to beginnings of lines.

I would look down on the women from my high window, watching them make the music of moving information. They were all beautiful, to a one. In the morning, before I laid eyes on them, they tumbled out of bed all curves and lumps and disarray, but by the time they arrived at work, they had transformed their bodies into the purest possible expressions of the simplest, most perfect colors and forms. Their legs, clad in nylons and shaven smooth. Their blouses, with pads that set their shoulders off at perfect right angles. The brassieres that gave their breasts the shapes of cones. Their perfect, true-red fingernails flying over the typewriter keys, and their deep red lips that sounded out the words, and the faces made over their other faces, carved out of marble.

Prospero Taligent is upset. "Damn," he, who almost never curses, says. "Damn it." It is the morning of Miranda's birthday, and as on all the birthdays before this, I am in my studio, expecting her to show up for her annual portrait, the work that I always try to take some extra effort with. But Prospero is here instead, and he is trembling. "Do you know what she did?" he says. "Do you?"

"No, sir."

"She *ran away from home.*"

"Again?"

"She's never thought to do such a thing before. What was there in the world for her to want? What thing could there be that I didn't give her myself?"

"Mr. Taligent, sir. I think you're confused. Miranda ran away from home three years ago. Remember: we cut her out of ice that year."

Prospero shakes his head as if he's just been sucker punched, and curls his upper lip, staring at nothing. "Really? No—yes. That's beside the point. Do you know what I found in her bedroom."

"No, sir, I don't."

He has picked up one of my smaller ball-peen hammers and is nervously thwacking its head into the open palm of his hand. "I found a nightgown. There was a nightgown and do you know what was *smeared all over it.*" He flings the hammer away from him, sending it skittering in quick circles across the floor.

"Sir, I don't really think that it's any of my—"

"Coal dust. It was covered in *coal dust.*"

He stands and waits for me to say something in reply, and I ask, quietly, "Mr. Taligent, will Miranda be coming to sit for me this morning?"

"No. I don't want you looking at her." He spins and strides out of the room, yelling as he leaves the studio, "I don't want *any of you* with your eyes on her."

The next morning he comes to me in the studio, all apologetic. He has something in his hand for me, an ovoid thing wrapped in newspaper. "I made this for you," he says.

I take the proffered package and unwrap it. It is a plaster cast of a woman's face: Miranda's. I can tell from the slightly uneven nose and the thin pursed lips.

"I want you to keep working," Prospero says. "I think it's important that you keep working. So last night I took a cast of Miranda's face. Now you'll have something to work from, and you can sculpt all the Mirandas you want."

"Sir," I say, "if I may—"

"Oh don't you worry, she's not *dead* or anything," he says, clasping his hands together, working the muscles in them. "I've just hidden her away for a while. She needs to not be seen for a time. That will make her better for all of us.

"I want you to work in a new way," he continues. "You should take more time with the new ones. I want you to solve the problem of making Miranda, even though she keeps changing. When you first started working for me, I asked for an exact copy of Miranda, and you *somewhat* understood what I was talking about, and many of the things you made were pretty, even though you seemed to be in a rush. But now I want something smarter, something you will make with care. Now you need to make sculptures of a higher *order* of exactitude."

"I don't understand what you mean," I say, more than a little put out by his dismissal of over a decade's work as "pretty."

"See," Prospero says, "the girl keeps changing. But I want you to make a sculpture that will always be exactly like Miranda, no matter *how much she changes*. Not what she was yesterday or will be tomorrow, but the thing she always is."

I am still confused. "Do you want something with moving parts, or—"

"No *no*! You are thinking: He is the crass bastard that builds the tin men; he thinks engines can solve everything. I just want a sculpture that—" (he sighs forcefully and places the palm of his hand to his head) "—that means *change*. Pretend she's a function and take the integral. That's what I want.

"Listen. The girl who sat before you years ago has become a woman who has learned the arts of deception and coquetry. She keeps fooling you into thinking that what you see of her is what she really is, and every time you finish a new work it's further from the mark. And she laughs at you for this, and she laughs at me. Not to my face, but a father knows his daughter—I know she shuts her door at night and laughs at me. Because the way we think of her has not been of a high enough order.

"So I don't want you to see her anymore. The perfect and correct Miranda isn't sitting behind the eyes of the girl that I've hidden away from you for your own good. She resides in our minds now—partly in yours, partly in mine. We only have to chisel her out of our minds, just as you released that first little girl from the block of granite that imprisoned her.

"We don't need the girl here to make her: she'll only trick us again. Tomorrow you will use the mask of her face and go to work.

"I think we are close now. We are very close."

It is late at night, and the clock's hands are in awkward places. Four years have passed since I received Prospero's permission to start on what I came to call the transformation series, and although he thought we were very close then, it soon became clear, at least to him, that we weren't close at all. I never leave the Tower anymore, and I have developed a strange internal clock: I sleep and work when I like, with little or no regard for whether the sun is above or beneath me.

But this building becomes more quiet when all the workers leave, so I have some idea that, when I visit the gallery of Mirandas with my eyelids pinned back by insomnia, I ought to be sleeping. But Prospero is here, too, wandering among the sculptures, as if he expects me.

This has been happening more and more often: the two of us come upon each other by accident in the early hours of the morning and take solace in each others' company, weathering out the peril of being awake at this time of night, when thoughts that are neatly ordered or justly murdered during the day come loose from their moorings and out of their graves, to tie themselves to each other in new and dangerous ways. Mostly I tell Prospero stories, and he listens, despite the fact that after all these years he must have heard them several times. They are from the time before I came to work here, when the events of my life gave rise to genuine narratives, tales with beginnings and endings. Since I have come to the Tower, every day has been more or less the same to me, and except for the accumulation of false Mirandas in her gallery while the real one goes unseen, the only means I have to remind myself that clocks have moving hands and calendars shed their pages is the telling of stories.

We have a special kind of friendship now, the rare kind that happens when the necessary, continual talker meets the impossibly patient listener. He understands that I need this shriving at this time of night, and he never asks the same of me. So I tell him stories I'd never consider telling anyone else, not even you, to whom I am telling the last tale I ever will. I tell him of all the little events that duplicate themselves in all our lives that we nonetheless think are singularly important, that we think would make excellent material for novels but aren't really worth a damn to anyone but yourself in the end. I tell him of my hesitant first kiss, and the fumbling loss of my virginity. I play puppeteer with the skeletons that stuff my family's closet. I list the names of people I'd once considered killing.

We are seated on the carpeted floor of the gallery, surrounded by phony Mirandas. I have removed my shoes. These days I rarely think of the fact that I haven't seen or heard from the real Miranda for four years, that all I've had to work from when I sculpt is a death mask. Occasionally Prospero will refer to his daughter in idle conversation, and that is enough to keep her alive for me. Thoughts sometimes cross my mind: *The man who stands before me is keeping his nearly thirty-year-old daughter captive somewhere in this building. Perhaps she is bound hand and foot. Perhaps she wears ill-fitting doll's clothes. Perhaps she lives off water and week-old bread.* But such concerns disappear after a moment. In spite of what you might think, no cops or shamuses from

the outside world are poking their noses around. Like ninety-nine percent of celebrity figures, she has simply dropped out of the public consciousness to be replaced by some other unidentified favorite little rich
girl, newer and fresher, her pupils virgins to the penetrating flash of
camera light. Miranda's aged images in newspapers are soiled with the
grease of fish and chips. The strips of celluloid that preserved her child's
face in black and white have seized in their projectors and burned beneath the heat of their lights.

"There was this girl," I say. "Her name was Alexa Graham. She was a
cheerleader for the Xeroville High School Fighting Automata. And her
nickname—though she didn't know it as far as I knew—was Onion Butt.
Because if you got one good clear look at that girl's ass it would make you
weep for joy. Now one evening my friend Greg throws a party while his
parents are away on a trip. And he's found the key to the liquor cabinet
under the rug. And *everybody's* there at the party! And let me tell you Mr.
Taligent we were *wasted*, all right? And who comes up to me smiling and
drunk off her tits but—"

"Can you imagine me looking at a woman's ass?" Prospero says.

"Wha?"

"Me, staring at a woman's bottom. Can you imagine a journalist or the
like saying, to give an example, 'Prospero Taligent looked at the woman's
ass and nodded with tacit approval.' Can you imagine reading such a thing?

"Or how about this. Can you imagine me doing any of the things that
you have told me that you did when you were young? Taking first steps?
Holding a girl's hand? Learning to read? Can you think of me having a
first failed love affair that I still regret, or a broken marriage? Or of having brothers and sisters, or a mother and father?"

"No," I say. "I can't."

"You've told me many secrets," Prospero says, and smiles. "Now I
will tell you one. It's my darkest. Are you ready?

"It is this." He leans toward me and spreads his arms in mock sur-
render. "*I have no past.* You may think that I was once small and young
and unwise as you once were, but I have always been as you see me before you. Always an old magician in exile."

"Some things always stay the same, sir," I say.

"Yes. It's good, isn't it. Some things never change."

He comes to his feet, places his hands in the small of his back, and bends backward. Three of the bones in his spine click in series. "Perhaps I will make up a past to confess to you one of these nights," he says, leaving the gallery. "To keep you entertained."

On another of these sleepless evenings I tell him tales of transformation. This night we punish ourselves, making a bad thing worse by drinking coffee of a brand that Prospero imports from a tropical nation with a perpetually unstable government and a boundary that confounds cartographers. He bombards the beans with high-intensity Röntgen rays and brews them hot enough to scald the tongue. The result is a cup of coffee whose first sip will make you grind your teeth into a fine white powder. That's the stuff.

We are two old men, drunk on wakefulness, starting to look alike. Around us sit the sculptures of the transformation series. They are made from materials engineered by Prospero in his laboratory, invented substances with names made of nothing but rootless suffixes and prefixes, that designate long molecules that bite their own tails and wind around each other like the links of a chain. I have worked the death mask of Miranda and my memories of her body into other forms: a giant spider whose eight hairy legs each end in a delicate, neatly manicured human foot; a bird with a human head and Miranda's sullen face, crowned in bright red feathers; a tree with porcelain-pale bark whose branches are made from hundreds of wrong-fingered hands.

We are taking swigs of coffee from a single flask, of a peculiar construction invented by Prospero. He calls it a "vacuum flask." ("Keeps hot foods hot, *but*," he says, raising a teaching finger, "keeps *cold foods cold!*") His coffee is burning a smoking hole in the lining of my stomach. "Transformations," I say. "Arachne had the gall to weave a picture-perfect tapestry that documented the crimes of the gods in exacting detail. Io was so beautiful that she incited the lust of Jupiter, who later had to hide the maiden from his wife in plain sight. Jupiter raped Callisto by assuming the guise of Diana, but Callisto made the shame public by giving birth to a son. So Juno felt she had to take revenge. All of these women—Arachne, Io, Callisto—shifted their shapes, by choice or force."

"They were all turned into beasts."

"Many of them. Some were turned into trees, or plants."

"But they are always robbed of the power of speech," Prospero says. "So when the gods choose to punish women, they make their tongues dumb."

"No, not exactly . . . In Ovid's moral universe the gift of language is what makes us human, but it's not always a curse to have your speech stolen. Take Daphne, for instance—she was Apollo's first love, owing to the malicious shaft of one of Cupid's arrows. But at the same time Daphne's heart was pierced with an arrow of the opposite nature that caused her to reject all suitors, mortal and immortal. Apollo never gave up pursuing her because whenever he lay eyes on her the arrowhead worked its magic and he saw not what she was, but what he thought she had the potential to *be*—"

"—the most beautiful woman in the world."

"—a woman so beautiful that it would not have been possible for her to exist. The two of them were an irresistible force and an immovable object, never to meet, and finally Daphne begged her father to rid her of her human shape and transform her into a tree. Better that, she thought, than to remain a woman and collapse under the weight of an infinite series of images and dreams, placed on her shoulders by men, too heavy for any mortal to bear."

"—wait. I forgot about someone. Echo.

"It's not always true that transformation causes the loss of a voice. Take Echo. She has a gift with language that sets her apart from all the other characters in the *Metamorphoses*. When her fellow nymphs scattered off to make love with Jupiter, Echo would divert Juno's attention away with stories, long shaggy-dog tales with other tales nested within them, all of them withholding their resolutions, prolonging their climactic moments. . . . But the stories always ended, lasting just long enough for the nymphs to finish their business with Jupiter and flee.

"So Echo's first punishment came at Juno's hands. She took not the power of speech from her, but the power of storytelling. Juno was a busy woman with a continually philandering husband to keep an eye on, and no time to squander on stories. After her curse the best that Echo would do was to repeat random fragments of the speech of others, but she could not string together a narrative or express an original thought of her own.

"Later, she fell in love with Narcissus, a near mirror image of Daphne: while Daphne loved no one, Narcissus loved only himself. It is possible that, had Echo still possessed her original unparalleled gifts, she could have woven a spell with language strong enough to tear him away from his endless contemplation of himself. But when she revealed herself to him at last after months of watching him, concealing herself behind trees and following in his footsteps, the only thing she could do was throw her arms around him and spit disconnected splinters of his own thoughts back at him. And of course he scorned her. And of course it broke her heart.

"And now came Echo's second punishment. Unable to express the inexpressible, she retreated to a cave, and while the world forgot about her, she starved herself. Time stripped all the flesh off her bones and turned them to stone, making her a sculpture of the living woman she used to be. Then the stone crumbled, and nothing was left of her but her voice."

"You have sculpted Miranda in the forms of all these transformed women," Prospero said. "Daphne, and Io, and Callisto, and Arachne. But not Echo. Why?"

"Because it can't be done. It's easy to make representations of spiders, or trees, or bears. And it's easy enough to tell the story of Echo. But how do you sculpt the shape of a voice?"

And now we come to the time when I did the terrible thing to Miranda.

The thought of doing something awful to the woman hadn't crossed my mind when I awoke on the morning that everything began in earnest. I pulled on my clothes, made myself presentable, left my rooms and took an elevator down seventy-seven floors to the company cafeteria where, as usual, I sat alone at a table in a corner with enough chairs for ten, listening to the jargon-riddled conversations of entry-level employees and making a breakfast out of a Danish and a couple of cups of coffee. After that, it was back up to the 101st floor, where I had planned to spend a few hours frittering around the studio and cleaning things up, since I was between projects and stuck for ideas.

But when I opened the door to the studio, I saw that everything was changed. It had been turned, overnight, into an operating theater.

The walls were the first thing I noticed. They were completely covered, every square inch, with sheets of paper: pages ripped out of centuries-old anatomy texts, illustrated with woodcuts of flayed-open corpses with slender arrows pointing into their guts; more pages ripped out of cheap paperback copies of Shakespeare plays; blueprints for phonographs and automobiles and mechanical men; hundreds of cryptic drawings in pen and ink of men and women and animals and strange machines, some of which were topological impossibilities.

In the center of the room was a gurney with a nude woman strapped to it, bound across the waist and at the wrists and ankles. All of the hair was shaved off her body. Her mouth hung open slackly and her eyes were wide-open, her pupils fully blown despite the surgical lamp that hung over her, shining right into her face. Without her eyebrows, her face seemed to be the most naked part of her.

Two carts sat next to the gurney, one holding a variety of surgical instruments, the other my sculpting tools.

There were a few doctors, dressed in red close-fitting skullcaps and facemasks and robes, and they stood to attention when I entered, lining up like soldiers on parade. Prospero Taligent was there too, in the same red robes, and he approached me when I entered, smiling.

It wasn't easy to take this all in, and I had trouble making sense of it. If the woman's head hadn't been shaved clean, I might have figured it out immediately. As she was, though, it took me a moment to place where I'd seen her thin lips and acne-scarred cheeks and slightly crooked nose.

"Miranda," I said, and the woman on the table said nothing in response, but all the same, I knew.

"This is going to be a great day for both of us," Prospero said. "We've finally figured it out. The thing we've wanted to do for all this time."

"I don't understand this, sir," I said, but even then I could feel myself lying to myself, because I *did* understand. And because Prospero knew that I understood beneath my false profession of doubt and my pretense of morality, the ensuing conversation had the language of an argument but the easy rhythms of a catechism, one that both of us had recited in our heads in silence for years, waiting for that special day when we would at last have the chance and the reason to speak it aloud.

"You don't understand," Prospero said. "Then I'll lead you to an explanation. Tell me your profession."

"I am your portraitmaker, and have been for more than twenty years."

"And what has been your single subject?"

"The woman strapped to the table over there."

"No. Answer again."

"But for over twenty years I have made sculptures of Miranda Taligent."

"Yes. And what have been their materials?"

"Stones: marble, basalt, granite, limestone. Wood. Wax. Ice. Clay. Then, toward the end, the substances you engineered for the transformation series, with names I can't pronounce."

"Yes. All of those were your work, but can you see how you and I have been working together in concert from that first Miranda chiseled out of granite? Your talent and my invention?"

"Yes. You brought me new substances, and new tools to carve them."

"And each sculpture you made was more beautiful than the one before. I never told you this, but it was true."

"But every one was a failure. I never got the one you wanted."

"And I failed, because I could never describe it to you. The exact perfect Miranda, the one that was always like her, no matter how this child changed that's now strapped to the table. But now I know what to do. I've known for some time, but now the time has come to put thought into action.

"Listen," he said. "You and I are going to make one last sculpture of Miranda. Once we finish this one, you won't have to make another, because I am certain that this one will be perfect. We are going to use a new material, one we haven't tried before, and one that I would never have been able to engineer myself."

Then he gestured at the woman tied to the table, who continued to stare at the ceiling wide-eyed and emotionless.

———

"It wasn't age that ruined the girl, but noise," said Prospero. "She would have stayed perfect if she'd come of age in silence.

"Do you understand that I've loved Miranda ever since I first laid eyes on her? And that because of this I wanted her to spend her life being everything that I'm not? I have no past, portraitmaker. I can never remember being a child. I look back on all my long years and I can never remember a time when my head has not been full of noises and filth. But if I had managed to keep the girl in silence then she would have stayed *pure*.

"Because a subtle shift in the balance of the hormones that saturated your brain was necessary but not sufficient to change you into an adult. It was the noise that the world shoveled into your head that finally made you into a man, wasn't it? Isn't it the sounds out of people's mouths that make us feel we've aged months in minutes? *Her tits look great*: you hear that for the first time and it ages you. *The cancer has spread to the lung*: you hear that and it ages you. *I think you should sit down for this*: you hear that and it ages you. The rattle of the tax collector's clearing throat ages you. The curse of the climaxing woman pinned beneath you ages you. The snap of the chicken's neck as it's prepared for the cooking pot ages you. It is not the bending of your bones but the noises of the world that make you grow old, and turn your heart to a block of granite in your chest, and make everyone's head like mine is. Filled with noise and filth.

"So I tried to keep the girl in a soundproof place, to make her perfect. Because if I could control the sounds she heard then I could control how she aged, and ensure that she would stay beautiful and not turn ugly like all the rest of us. But I couldn't stop her from *hearing things. . . .*"

Prospero went on rambling like this for several minutes, coming in and out of coherence, clearly more than half-mad, returning time and again to the same profound perversities—that children were somehow better creatures than adults; that ignorance was a worthy price to pay for innocence; that adults were inherently corrupt, and that given the chance they would speak the words of dark magic that would corrupt all those who were not already like themselves. And it slowly became apparent to me what he believed—that the perfect little girl that he'd adopted as a baby, the one who had never existed anywhere but in his own head when he looked at Miranda, was locked up inside the body of the woman strapped to the table in front of us. And that if we could some-how use our tools and our imaginations to somehow chisel that little girl out of the woman's body and set her free, just as I'd chiseled that first sculpture of Miranda Taligent out of a block of granite nearly twenty-five years ago, then everything would be set right again. Then everything would be perfect.

At this point in my tale, I wish I could take the liberties of a fiction-maker. Because then I'd have the ability to manufacture some compelling cause that forced me to act against my will, in spite of my essentially honest heart. Suddenly a cadre of soldiers poured into the studio and held great big bayonets with gleaming blades to our heads and Prospero said menacingly, "Perform the operation or die." Or: Prospero reached behind his back and produced a heavy suitcase stuffed to bursting with thousand-dollar bills and said, "I know about your gambling debts. How your wife and seven daughters are starving in a garret, living off thin gruel and week-old bread. Perform the operation and you get this suit-case, and four more just like it."

But if this is to be a confessional, then it must be free of lies and con-jecture, and the facts are these: I was an old man, and I had given most of my life to making Miranda and come up short time after time. And when Prospero held out the possibility of making the Miranda of our minds a real physical thing, no matter how impossible that might seem to you, I jumped on it. Because I was just a little bit mad myself by then. I might have been salivating when I accepted his offer. I wanted to cut the woman until she was perfect.

This is what you have to understand about Miranda: you might think of her as a damsel in distress, in dire need of rescue, but she was strong—strong enough to inspire you to dream of her, but weak enough to allow you to map that perfect dream of her onto her living face. I did the terrible things I did because I was in love with Miranda: not the one you might think of as real, but the one that her father and I had dreamed of together, who was Miranda in a way that the real one would never be

without our help. I ask you: how could I responsibly pass up the opportunity to bring such a beautiful being into the world?

The surgical operations that we executed upon Miranda Taligent took
almost eight months, working seven days a week, fourteen hours a day.
You'll have to forgive me if I don't go into the details of the whole thing.
I don't really understand much of the technical aspects of what we did,
despite the fact that I was one of the directors of the project. I made
vague suggestions, and the surgeons ran with them. The most I can
really say is that over the course of the surgery, I developed a studied in-
difference to Miranda's body. I lost my sense of its sanctity, its sacredness
as a repository for the soul that all of us but doctors believe in. The doctors are forced to see the flesh for what it is, and for all their talk of
miracles, they know, even if they deny it to themselves and cover up
their sentiments with noble talk, that they are dealing with machines.

Of course, on the first day of surgery I had to run from the room to
vomit. The surgeons all got a laugh out of that one. After I returned to the
studio, my mouth still tasting of bile, one of the doctors pounded me
heartily on the back with his open hand and said, "Listen. My third year
of medical school we were taking a class on musculoskeletal systems.
And one day the subject of discussion is an actual hand and lower arm,
hacked off a cadaver at the elbow. First the prof holds it up, you know, so
we can see it; then we have to pass it around from person to person like
show-and-tell at grammar school while he mutters and makes notes on
the board. We were skittish at first, scared shitless, but after a while we
got a little cold about it all, you know? Because we were becoming initiates to *secrets*. And by the end of the class we're actually *throwing* the
hand around the room, like we're practicing for some kind of sports
event, and the prof is *letting this happen*, because he knows that this is
something we have to go through, that this process of becoming cold is
one of many initiations. And we are *laughing*. Now you think of all the
things that hand might've done, and maybe you think it's sacred. Maybe
it slid a wedding band onto some other hand; maybe it jerked off; maybe
it clutched the rail of a swaying steamship; maybe it spanked a son's
bare bottom; maybe it played the viola part of a symphony with no sur-

viving copies. Then you think: screw it. It's just *meat*. So buck up, little camper!"

When we could, we worked in shifts. I led the team that worked in the morning up until the late afternoon; after a short break, Prospero's team came in and worked on Miranda until as late as midnight. For all Prospero's talk about the two of us sharing a single image of the perfect Miranda, we were oftentimes at cross-purposes, and we would spend days repeatedly undoing each other's procedures in the service of our own creative visions. This antagonism went unaddressed and lasted between us for the entire duration of the operation. At times he would lock me out of my own studio, and I'd stand quietly outside the door and listen to him bawl out his team of surgeons until he lost his voice: "If you're so damned concerned about the few pounds of flesh that holds the information matrix—what! You come to me *now* with talk of *ethics*? A little late for *that*, I think. Now you'll do what I say. You cut her *there*, and you cut her to the *bone*, and you cut her in C-sharp, with a *blueness*."

When we were almost done with that last magnificent sculpture, one or maybe several of the wonder drugs we shot Miranda up with to keep her pacified gave rise to a tumor in her stomach that grew at an astonishing rate, so that within a week the woman looked ten months pregnant. We decided that we had no choice but to remove the tumor if we wanted the woman to survive.

What the doctors lifted out of her when they split her stomach open was the size of a Christmas turkey and weighed twenty-six pounds. It was a mass of featureless, shining gray flesh, threaded through with a network of thousands of hair-thin, purple veins. The doctors huddled over it at a table and went at it with gleaming carving knives, expecting it to yield up some profound medical secret, and what they found embedded in it when they cut it open were the dead parts of all of us, their growth gone haywire: long, curling fingernails; single, small pointed teeth; knotted clumps of red-gold hair.

Then they put the tumor in a glass box on a countertop, all cut up, and left it there while they went back to work on the woman. Later, after everyone had finished the day's work and cleared out of the studio, I took the box with me and carried it down to the museum of false Mirandas and placed it on a pedestal with the rest of the sculptures. It stayed there, in a place of honor, until it had to be disposed of. It was, after all, Miranda's self-portrait.

TEN

"And suddenly one day we were done," the portraitmaker said. "We didn't even know the day before that the next day, Miranda would be perfect. But on the evening of that last day, Prospero called me into my studio, and the two of us stood there alone and looked down on the woman sleeping, and we knew. The two of us knew that we'd somehow performed a miracle, even as we'd worked against each other, even though what we did was shameful. And we also knew that, if that miracle was to persist in the world, it could not be looked upon by eyes other than our own.

"Because do you know what someone like yourself would do if you were to lay eyes on her? You'd be speechless for a few moments, yes, but then you'd do the thing that I myself am wise enough not to do—you'd start to string together killing words to *describe* her. You will say what she is, and each word will chip a little bit of that miracle away. Then, when you've assembled enough words, she'll become commonplace and understandable, and she'll die. In order to keep her alive and perfect, she must reside in the sky. In the realm of the imaginary.

"And so, though it breaks his heart to leave this world, in a matter of minutes Prospero Taligent will join his daughter aboard a specially constructed high-altitude zeppelin, the largest ever made. It will circle the earth forever, never touching the ground. And everyone will look to the sky when the ship passes overhead, and they will imagine the woman inside. They'll know that their dreams have been given shape, even if they cannot remember their dreams upon waking and cannot conceive of their shape. She'll exist in all the minds of men set free from language. Which is how she should be.

"The rest of the story you know. We've made the perfect woman, and I was left behind to burn all the rest."

The coldness of the frosted chamber had crept into my knees and elbows, and they briefly flared with pain as I rose to my feet. I was running out of time, I thought—the policeman that I'd run across in the Tower's lobby had indicated that the zeppelin was due to lift off in three hours, and though I wasn't wearing a wristwatch, it seemed to me that Ferdinand's tale had taken about a half hour of that time, and the portraitmaker's had eaten at least a whole hour. What if each of the labeled doors on the 101st floor of the Tower had a storyteller lying in wait behind it, ready to demand my attention, leading me on with the promise of a hint that would lead me to the woman? Not only would I never find Miranda before the ship lifted off, but I might end up wandering these halls until doomsday.

"For the moment, let's put aside the fact that it seems as if you've taken advantage of my patience and wasted my time," I said to the portraitmaker. "This doesn't make sense to me. You sound as if you believe you've done something wonderful for Miranda, but the reason I'm here is because she sent me a note this morning, by private courier, asking me to save her."

"Oh, I'm reasonably certain that she's not *happy*, not a whit. And what do I care for her happiness? It was my *duty* not to care for her happiness. I'm not happy to have to destroy the contents of this museum, either. But some things have to be done in the service of the greater good. What do the rights or the goodwill of a single woman matter in such a situation? They don't."

"But I'm here, and as long as I feel that I can save her, I'm going to try—"

"Another thing about which I'm reasonably certain," the portraitmaker spat at me, "is that she's no longer in need of saving." He began to fiddle with his flamethrower, and I got the impression that he was itching to get back to his business. What a waste of time this little man had been. I turned to leave the chamber without saying another word, but as I placed my hand on the door's handle, he stopped me with a word: "Wait."

I waited, not turning back to look at him.

"If you're going back into the halls, there are many, many doors with cryptic words on them. But doors with signs you do not understand are not for you."

I closed my eyes for a moment and attempted to contain my frustration. Then, when it seemed as if he weren't going to say anything further, I pushed the chamber's door open and moved into the darkness of the museum.

"Wait," the portraitmaker called again.

I waited.

He paused in silence, as if he couldn't make up his mind whether to go on. Then he said, "But there's one door here, with no sign on it at all. It's where I think he keeps his most secret projects. I don't know how you'll get in—my keys won't let me in there. But if she is anywhere in this building, she's there."

When he finished speaking I bolted from the gallery, but as I dodged between the pedestals and jumped over the broken bodies, I heard the portraitmaker call behind me once more: "Wait!"

I turned to face him this time, still walking backward. He had opened the ice chamber's door just wide enough to poke his head out.

"I wish you the best of luck, if you think you need to do this. But I really do believe that, should you find her in the end, you'll discover she's not in need of rescue."

Then he turned away from me and shut the chamber's door behind him. A moment later the chamber lit up like a lantern, full of yellow flame. I imagined the icewoman's face melting, twisting out of shape.

ELEVEN

It took another half hour of running through hallways before I found the nameless door that the portraitmaker thought might have Miranda behind it, near the end of a corridor and between two doors that were labeled NICKNAME and PRODIGY. I felt through my pockets for the identification card, fished it out, and jammed it into the slot next to the unmarked door, wondering if the key would work at all: not only had it been damaged by the last door I'd entered, but by its nature this door seemed as if it would require more security clearance than the others on this floor.

The slot took the card, holding it while the light beneath it blinked on and off; then the receptacle emitted a high-pitched whine and spat the card out, shredded into pieces that fluttered to the floor.

The whine grew louder, then a thin tendril of smoke drifted out of the card slot as I caught a whiff of ozone in the air. The door suddenly sprang open six inches, just wide enough for me to quickly get a foot and hand in the crack and wedge the rest of my body in after them, tearing a button off my jacket in the process. The door shut and locked itself behind me the instant I got through it.

TWELVE

Later, aboard the zeppelin *Chrysalis*, I'd have ample opportunity to reflect on the frantic hours I spent searching the 101st floor of the Taligent Tower, looking for the woman but only finding men. The first two men I met, the master of the boiler room and the portraitmaker, had both lost their minds, each in his own peculiar way, but I wouldn't have gone so far as to call either of them monsters. But the third man I met on the 101st floor was a beast. From the brief time I spent with him I got the clear impression that he was one of the most intelligent human beings that I had ever met in my life, possibly more so than the genius Prospero Taligent himself. But he was all the more a beast for that.

The room behind the unmarked door had another, smaller room contained within it, with a heavy steel door that contained a single window. The door was padlocked shut with a lock that was almost the size of my fist. A key that seemed to match the padlock hung by a loop of twine on a hook next to the door.

As I looked through the door's window, I saw that inside this smaller room was a cage of stout iron bars, suspended from the ceiling by a chain. The inside wall of this smaller room was lined with neat arrays of rubber tubes, each with a tag on its end. Though the tubes were neatly gathered into bundles on the inside of the wall, they became tangled into rat's nests as they punched through the wall of the inner room to cover the floor of the larger room in which I stood, leading into what looked to me like thousands of randomly arranged holes in the floor and the walls and the ceiling.

From my vantage point just inside the larger room, I couldn't see what was inside the cage (and what seemed to require such extreme security methods to keep it restrained). As I moved closer to the steel door, brushing aside some of the rubber tubes that snaked into the ceiling, I heard from within the cage the sharp snapping sound of a typewriter's typebar striking its platen—after all the years I'd spent writing in one form or another, there was no mistaking it.

"Hello?" I said loudly, coming closer to the small room, almost at the steel door. "Can you hear me? I'm looking for a woman. Her name is Miranda Taligent."

Then I reached the steel door and looked through the window, and saw the monster.

THIRTEEN

He had skin like a patchwork quilt, all different colors sewn together with keloidal scars. It was as if all the parts of his body were borrowed from other men: an arm from one person, a foot from another, a nose from another, a cheek from another, an eye from another. One of his lips was thick; the other was thin. One of his eyes was brown; the other was blue.

He was naked, and his body was featureless in strange ways that weren't immediately apparent. Then I realized that he had no hair—he was not only bald, but he had no eyebrows and no pubic hair. He had no nipples, and no genitalia. He seemed as if he had been poorly fed: each rib of his torso was clearly delineated beneath the surface of his patched-together, multicolored skin.

He looked as if he would be five feet tall if standing. He sat in a corner of the cage with his spindly legs folded beneath him, and in his lap he cradled a heavy, cast-iron typewriter. The typewriter had a small, metal box welded to the back of it, and out of this box led a cable as thick as my wrist. The cable looped over the monster's shoulder and plugged directly into the back of his skull, where it was surrounded by a circular metal plate studded with rivets.

I might have screamed when I saw him and I could make sense of what I saw, but I don't remember. I do remember him staring at me through the window, not even blinking, cradling his typewriter, tilting his head and smirking with his odd little mouth. Then he extended a patchwork hand and curled his mismatched index finger toward himself: *Come closer. Come inside.*

FOURTEEN

I took the key off its hook and unlocked the padlock that held the door shut, figuring that the monster was still locked in a cage within the smaller room itself, and that even if he managed to escape from the cage through guile and attack me, then his typewriter would prove too unwieldy for him. For some reason I didn't dare to enter the room completely, preferring instead to stand within the arch of its steel door. I saw that a padlock similar to the one that held the steel door shut was attached to the door of the cage, and guessed that the key I held in my hand would open that lock as well. I didn't believe that this creature had left its cage for years, though—his muscles had atrophied so much that it was a wonder that he was capable of standing.

The monster clambered across the floor of the cage toward me in an odd sort of shuffle, pushing the typewriter ahead of him, sending the cage swinging gently back and forth on the chain from which it was suspended. When he reached the other side of the cage, he sat down again with his legs folded beneath him, holding the typewriter in his lap. From here I could see that the typewriter's keys were decorated not with letters, but symbols: a stylized sun, with eight rays pointing away from a circle; a bell; a clock's unnumbered dial; a rictus; a half-lidded eye.

The monster poised his fingers above the keys and poked at one, then another. Then he spoke, in a raspy, scratchy bass too large for his small body, a voice that made him seem as if he smoked four packs of cigarettes a day. "My name is Caliban," he said. "I'm Miranda's brother. And I know you," he continued, tapping on the keys as he spoke. "You're the greeting-card writer. That we've all heard so *much* about."

"Miranda never told me that she had a brother," I said.

Tap-ta-tap-tap-ta went Caliban's fingers on the keys of his typewriter, and then: "They never tell you about the other men in their lives, do they?"

He sniffed the air theatrically with a nose far too large to suit his face, then pressed a few more keys on the typewriter. "I smell whiskey on you. On your clothes. Pathetic. Did you bring any?"

"I drank it all," I said, feeling sheepish about it.

Tap-ta-ta-tap-ta. "You shouldn't have dulled your senses on an evening like this. I've been following your progress through the Tower from this listening post." Caliban gestured at the arrays of tubes that lined the walls of the room in which he was caged. Then: *tap-tap-ta-tappeta-tap.* "You're doing well, but not well enough. Not a hero; not even a normal person who finds he has some kind of capacity for heroism that's been left untried until a crucial moment. Father is going through a good deal of effort to walk you through all of this."

"Prospero Taligent is your father?"

Tap-ta. "He made me," Caliban said, and would say no more.

I stood staring at him for a few moments longer, and he looked back, unblinking. What was the function of the typewriter that was so crudely attached to his head? Why did he have to press a few keys on it before he spoke? At first I thought that I misunderstood the creature I saw in front of me, and that its intelligence and ability to reason was somehow within the typewriter instead of the brain that the creature's body housed. But that didn't make sense—that seemed beyond the reasonable reach of Prospero's talents.

Tap-ta-tap-tap. "She's not here anymore. She's already been loaded aboard the ship, moored on the roof of the building. Do you still want to rescue her?" Caliban paused for a moment, then jammed his thumb down on the key of the typewriter that was labeled with a grinning mouth. "Ah-ha-ha! Ah-*ha*! Ha-*heh-ha*! Heh. Whew."

"If you can't help me," I said, "I'll have to leave."

He started at this, then scanned the typewriter's keyboard intently, his eyes darting back and forth in his head. After a few seconds he pressed the proper keys to get him to speak: "Wait. I'll lead you to the roof of the building. But you have to do something for me."

He took the typewriter out of his lap, and with that odd shuffling crawl, he moved himself over to another corner of the cage, where a stack of stained and rumpled notebooks with faded covers sat in a disordered pile. He grabbed up one of the notebooks in his hand and brandished it at me. Then he put it back in the pile, tapped out a few keys, and said, "These notebooks represent the complete treasury of my thought. Should you succeed in killing my father, you *must* get these papers published at a *reputable academic press*."

"Wait a moment," I said. "Wait just a—"

Tap-tap-tappeta-tap-ta-tap. "Oh yes—that's the other thing. You'll have to kill my father. How else do you expect to finish this? Perhaps the liquor will give you the nerve, if you managed to get more down your throat than you spilled over yourself. Pathetic."

FIFTEEN

Tap-ta-ta-tap-tap. "I've been listening to the noises of this entire building for my whole life—though I've been imprisoned in this cage, I know the design of this place like my own hand. Most of the elevator shafts here stop before the building's top floor. But there's a service elevator accessible from this floor that opens onto the roof of the building—it's the same one that Father has been using to transport the parts for the zeppelin. You'll never find it without my help. You have a half hour left, maybe less—it's certainly not enough time to climb fifty flights of stairs."

Caliban fidgeted, wiggling his fingers nervously over the keyboard.

Then he jabbed a key and barked at me, "Don't pause! Decide!" That startled me into action, and I unlocked the door to his cage, thinking that it would be best not to think about it. He pushed the pile of notebooks over to the door of the cage, and I gathered them into my arms, about twenty of them. Then with a surprising nimbleness he hopped out of the cage, gathering the cast-iron typewriter after him. He waddled out into the larger room with its tangle of tubes that led into the walls and presumably to almost every room of the Taligent Tower, placed his typewriter on the floor, sat down in front of it, pecked on a few keys, and said, "I won't be able to speak again until we reach the service elevator—this typewriter is too heavy for me to carry with one hand while typing with the other." *Tap-tappeta.* "So follow me carefully, and don't get lost. I see that you have no reason to trust me, but you'll have to trust me all the same. Once we reach the elevator, I'll explain to you why I hate my father so much that it will be a pleasure for me to watch you kill him."

He picked up the typewriter and nodded at me, huddling over it as if he were a new mother and the typewriter were a baby that he needed to protect from the elements. I yanked open the last door that divided Caliban's prison from the rest of the Tower, and we were off, down the endless corridors of doors with secret signs.

SIXTEEN

Ten minutes of jogging through twisting hallways brought Caliban and me to the enormous sliding gate of the Tower's service elevator. I pushed the button to summon the elevator's car, but it took a solid five minutes to descend from the roof to the 101st floor. Eventually the gate of the elevator slid open, and the two of us ran inside, me with Caliban's notebooks, Caliban with his typewriter. The car's floor had a thin covering of snow that was already half-melted, and Caliban brushed some of it out of the way with his hand as he sat down, placed the typewriter on his lap, and held his hands over the keys (and each of his fingers was a different color, shape, and length, with a scar circling its lower knuckle).

I ran my fingers over the elevator's panel, pressed the button labeled R, and the gate (slowly, very slowly) creaked shut and the car (slowly, very slowly, perhaps not fast enough) began to rise. Caliban began to speak then, in his rasping bass so ill-suited to his scrawny, frail body, typing out the arcane symbols as he told me the story of his life and the elevator car climbed (slowly) to the roof.

SEVENTEEN

"Look at how beautiful I am," Caliban said, inviting me to gaze on his scars. "Look at how beautiful my Father made me. You have always thought of Prospero Taligent as the inventor of the mechanical man. But what most people don't realize is that the initial stages of his research that led to the development of the mechanical man involved human cadavers, obtained from morgues by mostly legal means, though he wasn't above taking delivery on a surreptitiously stolen corpse when he found it necessary. Duplicating the human body in a mechanical form has always been his true ambition, even if it meant forgoing the construction of machines more elaborate and more capable than mere imitators of humans could ever be. In order to accomplish this, he needed to have original models to work from, at his leisure.

"He had next to no trouble developing mechanical equivalents for human hands, and eyes, and hearts. But a mechanical brain with the complexity and the volume of the human brain has always been beyond his reach. This is in part because the size of the smallest meaningful working part of the brain is much less than the smallest meaningful working part of an arm, for instance. A few cleverly attached rods can go a long way toward mimicking the actions of a human arm, but the same number of gears won't come near duplicating the actions of the brain. I myself have suggested to Father that he might design a means of controlling electrical impulses in order to replicate the simple abilities of a mechanical calculator, as a beginning step toward miniaturizing the mechanical components that stuff the heads of his mechanical men, but controlling electricity in such a meticulous fashion seems to be either beyond his means or his ability to imagine. For all his genius, he has his blind sides and his shortsightedness. So the heads of his tin men are still crammed with the same devices that lie behind the face of a wristwatch, and even though their bodies have improved significantly with each successive design, their minds are still relatively basic, and will remain so into the foreseeable future.

"But Father's incapability to understand the potential of electricity to store and transfer information did not prevent him from attempting to make maps of the mind. It became possible for him to make these rudimentary maps when he deduced that, by delivering controlled electrical impulses directly into various parts of the brain, he could trigger simple emotional reactions in living subjects, such as the feeling of despair, or the perception of humor.

"This gave him the idea of creating an optimally designed human being, not from mechanical parts, as he would later, but from the parts of cadavers. Each component would be the best possible specimen of its kind. It took him four years to secretly cull the parts from all the corpses. Look at how beautiful I am! One of my eyes is from a champion archer; the other is from a professional sharpshooter. My heart is from a marathon runner, as is one of my legs. My larynx is taken from the body of a world-class opera singer. One half of my brain is from a poet laureate; the other half is from a chess grandmaster. I can tell that you think me hideous, but pound for pound I have the most beautiful body in the world, if you forget about all the scars.

"Father's genius shows itself, however, in the addition of this typewriter, attached directly to my brain through this cable. Each one of the keys of this typewriter sends an electrical impulse directly to a corresponding area of my brain. I cannot speak or think without first pressing keys on this typewriter, but the trade-off for this is that I have complete control over the functioning of my own mind. Let me give you an example. You don't really have a clear idea of exactly what it is in life that makes you laugh. One person could tell you a joke and have you doubled over in stitches, but another could tell the exact same joke with a different delivery and leave you mirthless. But if I press this key on my typewriter, the one with the picture of a grin, then I will instantly find you funny, and anything you say, whether you intend it to be humorous or not, and the décor of this elevator car, and this typewriter, and my own appearance. And if I press this key, I will become sexually aroused, even though I have no means of gratifying that arousal. This one, and I burst into tears. This one, and I get an urge to kill. This one, and I fall asleep. This one, and Jesus brings me the good news.

"I spent the first few days of my existence repeatedly pressing this particular button here, whose symbol is worn off. It stimulates my pleasure center, and it turned me into a worthless beast. I stopped eating and sleeping, just so that I could press this key, thousands of times an hour, hour after hour. I came near an ecstatic death, but Father pointed out to me that there were higher pleasures than the simple ones, pleasures of the intellect that are granted to humans alone.

"So I found that by pressing a series of keys in rapid succession, I could elicit more elaborate responses from my mind than those associated with the simplest emotions. I experimented with various combinations, and quickly left behind my obsession with base pleasures—I'd go so far as to say that I developed a strong distaste for them. My first major discovery came when I found a series of seven keys that, when pressed, would give me an inspirational stroke of genius. You, who have no real control over your own thinking, have to twiddle your thumbs and *wait* for what you call 'inspiration,' for some fictional muse or a series of fortunate accidents to give you one of your rare original ideas. But with these seven keys I can summon hunches at will that always work out, and intuitive leaps that would confound someone like yourself.

"It was this discovery, of the thing inside our minds that causes genius, that made it possible for me to embark on my career as an intellectual. I pressed the genius keys almost as often as I pressed the pleasure button in the days after my inception. I filled the notebooks you have there with my ideas, which would take a person such as yourself, who has no ability to actively steer his mind in new directions of thinking, centuries to fathom.

"Eventually, as it must to all enlightened people, it occurred to me to ask myself a question. If I could not think without pressing keys on this typewriter, then how did I have the initial thought that gave me a sense of self? How did I know such a simple thing as when the spatial boundary of my body ended and the rest of the world began? What was the thought that gave me the feeling of a presence of mind? If there was a single key on this typewriter that would cause me to be happy, and a short sequence of keys that allowed me to be a genius, then was there an even longer sequence of keys that would have encoded in it my own unique sense of identity? And if this was true, what would happen if I were to press those keys—would I not truly know myself, to an extent that no man had known himself before?

"I asked Father about this during one of his visits to my cage, and he told me that after he constructed me, he gave me an electrical shock that gave my body life; then he typed a series of seventy-two keys on this typewriter that awoke my mind. Encrypted within those seventy-two keys was all that I was, he said; however, he refused to tell me what those keys were.

"Of course, I immediately set out to discover them for myself, for I knew that they must contain the secret of my soul, that all enlightened men search for. And my resentment that my creator could possess this secret and have the cruelty to withhold it from me could not be measured.

"Even with my ability to invoke strokes of genius at will, it took me a long time to solve that last great mystery. Along the way I made dozens of lesser discoveries in which I had little or no interest, but which I'm sure would have amazed someone like yourself: a series of twelve keys that allowed me to name the year in which an unidentified wine was bottled after tasting a sample; a series of eighteen keys that taught me how to tell the time without the help of a clock; a sequence of twenty-four keys that granted me perfect pitch; a sequence of thirty-six keys that gave me a limited low-level telepathy, so that I could sense the concealed emotions of nearby women, even if I could not read their thoughts. But that last discovery continued to elude me for months.

"At last, after nearly exhausting my talents in what almost seemed to be a futile task, I deduced the series of seventy-two keys that symbolized my true name. And here is why I want you to kill my father: because after a day of meditation during which I cleared my mind of all other thoughts, when I finally typed that cursed series of symbols, I knew myself to the depths of my soul, and I lost all hope. Were I not such a weak man, I would have strangled my own throat before all the color and life burned out of me, so that I could have died still thinking that I was a brilliant mystery. But I wasn't strong enough, and now instead of a beautiful creature, I look at myself and see only my scars.

"Once I ceased to be a mystery to myself I became a thing of darkness. As long as you do not fully comprehend your own nature, you can pretend that you have a soul, and believe it, and believe yourself a miracle. But I have seen my soul for the simple thing that it is, and I tell you that there is nothing worse than knowing, truly knowing, that through and through you are nothing more than a machine.

"This is why you have to kill my father, then: because he invented the mechanical man. I ask you to kill my father for the crime of bringing me into existence."

A tiny, high-pitched bell rang softly then, and the service elevator's gate slid open, revealing open air, and bitter cold, and flakes of flying snow, and the zeppelin *Chrysalis*.

EIGHTEEN

The zeppelin was moored to the roof of the tower, about two hundred yards from me. Standing in the elevator, I handed Caliban his notebooks and quickly ran both hands over all the floor call buttons. Then the two of us stepped outside, with Caliban waddling behind me with his typewriter in his arms and his notebooks stacked on top of it, pinned there with his chin. The elevator shut and began to descend, one floor at a time.

Spotlights were mounted everywhere, shining through snow flurries and panning back and forth across the surfaces of the zeppelin, lighting up the Tower's roof like morning. The zeppelin's gasbag, an immense, cigar-shaped white balloon emblazoned with the Taligent Industries logo, was nearly full, and in the high winds of this height it strained against the dozens of steel cables that kept it lashed to the Tower, filling the air with a continuous rhythmic creak. Several thick black hoses were attached to the underside of the gasbag, each one leading to a huge gas tank decorated with the single letter H. The zeppelin's gondola was slung snugly beneath the gasbag's belly, its main door open, with a flight of movable stairs leading down from it to the roof of the Tower. Several mechanical men moved back and forth in lanky strides across the roof, carrying boxes of supplies onto the zeppelin. Consoles with monitors and banks of lights and crazily spinning dials were scattered over the roof, and bundles of multicolored wires led out of them, coiled on the roof in huge heavy loops, and snaked into various apertures of the zeppelin's gondola.

Huddled over one of the consoles with his back to me, intently examining its readouts, was someone who I thought might be familiar.

But it took me a few moments to realize that, yes, this was him. The last time I had seen Prospero Taligent in person, I had been ten years old, and I remembered him as towering over me. After that I'd grown up with his images in newspapers, and I'd heard his voice on the radio, and I'd heard the tales, distorted by repetition, that others told about him. Most of these depictions disagreed violently about the makeup of his character, but there wasn't a single one that didn't make him seem larger than life.

So I was surprised to see him in person, after all these intervening years, even a hundred yards away from me where I couldn't make out his features, and see how *small* he was, the ordinary human size of him. It seemed to me that if I'd grown in stature during these past twenty years, then he should have as well. I should still have had to look up to see him.

I didn't think that it would take much longer for the gang of false mechanical men presumably led by Artegall to make its way to the roof—they'd had to climb the Tower's stairs, but if they'd paced themselves so that they didn't tire out, they'd be here any minute. Now that I was up against it, with the enormous zeppelin hanging over me which I had only seen from a distance earlier this evening, and with what I suppose was my nemesis standing just in front of me, I no longer felt the sense of youthful immortality that I had when I'd charged into the lobby of the Taligent Tower a few hours before. The booze I'd downed earlier had lost its effect, leaving me with nothing but the beginning of a headache and a numb metallic aftertaste in my mouth. I felt old, and ordinary. I felt glad that the next day was a holiday, because at the rate things were going, I would never be able to rescue Miranda and show up on time at the greeting-card works the following morning. Not to mention that Caliban (who was edging away from me, slowly, moving across the roof in a long arc that would lead him to the zeppelin's gondola) seemed to expect me to murder Prospero in some sort of righteous rage, as if you can just call up strangers fresh off the street and ask them to commit patricide for you.

In short, I was uncertain how this was all going to turn out. I wasn't expecting anything nearly as dramatic as my own death—here alone on the roof with Prospero, Caliban, and a few mechanical men, my life didn't seem to be at all in danger. I thought that the most likely outcome would be that I'd approach Prospero, and not remembering that I'd been his guest in this place twenty years before, he'd accuse me of being the crackpot that I arguably was and have me forcibly escorted out after I'd said my piece.

At any rate, I was sure that once the gang of vigilantes made its way to the roof, things would get more complicated, and it would be best to get this all over with before much longer. If I talked to Prospero and explained to him that his daughter had sent me what seemed like a rather desperate message summoning me here—well, that would have to be enough for me to be able to say to myself that I'd fulfilled my obligation to Miranda, even if nothing came of it.

So I made my way across the roof, the high cold wind stinging my cheeks. During the occasional heavy gust, the whole sky would tilt slightly out of true as the entire building bent like a half-mile-high reed.

Beneath the zeppelin, the mechanical men continued to ferry their supplies, taking no notice of me as they worked. As for Prospero, he was so distracted by whatever information he was receiving from the console's display that he didn't hear me approach, even though I made no attempt to disguise my footsteps. I actually had to tap him on the shoulder to get his attention.

NINETEEN

He turned away from the console and squinted up at me, shielding his eyes with his hand. He was immaculately dressed: a black pinstriped suit with a black silk shirt and tie; black wingtip shoes; a black woolen overcoat; a smart black fedora with a black silk hatband and a collection of snowflakes sitting on its brim. His narrow, deep brown eyes peered at me, cradled in a nest of wrinkles that spread across his entire face. He pursed his bloodless lips in confusion, then his thin, nearly nonexistent eyebrows lifted in sudden recognition.

"Little Harry Winslow!" he said. "I was wondering if you were going to make it." Then, oddly, he smiled and began to go through the pockets of his overcoat, as if he were checking to make sure that his wallet wasn't lost.

"It certainly took you long enough," he said, inverting the lint-dotted lining of one pocket, then another. "Here's a question: on your way into the Tower, did you happen to see a young little urchin child, running around and banging a pair of cymbals together?"

"Yes," I said. "He was banging them together and screaming. Yah, yah, yah. Like that."

"Good," said Prospero. "Then everything's going according to plan. Oh, *here* they are." From one of the inside pockets of his suit jacket he removed a small stack of index cards.

He took a pair of rimless spectacles from another pocket of his suit jacket, unfolded them, and placed them on the tip of his long, narrow nose. He peered at the cards, squinted up at me from beneath the brim of his hat, then looked at the cards again. Then he looked at me again.

"At last we meet!" he crowed.

Then he took the top index card and placed it on the bottom of the stack and read the next one.

"If you want Miranda for yourself. Shaking finger. Then you'll—oh, wait, I've stuffed it up." He pointed his finger in my face and started to shake it vigorously. "If you want Miranda for yourself then you'll have to kill me first!"

Then he stood there, smiling up at me, as if he were waiting for me to do something.

"Well, then?" he said, after a moment.

By this point, I was somewhat confused.

"I'd prefer that you shoot me in the stomach," Prospero said. "It's a long, slow death, but the damaged organs will be much easier to replace, I think. I suppose we can work with just about anything, as long as you don't stave in my skull or anything like that."

I looked behind me at Caliban. He was hopping back and forth in the snow from one bare foot to another, holding the typewriter and the notebooks, a feral expression of glee on his face.

I looked back at Prospero, whose gaze was now fixed on Caliban. "You let him out. I suppose that's good. Poor Caliban. I only grafted the typewriter to his head to try to give him self-esteem."

Prospero sighed, then, in growing impatience. "I don't think we have much time left. Besides, if we don't get this over with soon, I'm going to lose my nerve. It'd be far easier for me to board the zeppelin myself, you know—

"Wait a moment. You came all the way up here without a *gun*, didn't you?"

"I had a bottle of whiskey," I said, "but now it's gone."

"You have no *respect* for me," Prospero said, flinging his hands in the air in frustration. "You're a child come to his exam day without his pencil—that's what you are. Well, I have a pencil for you." Holding the stack of index cards in one hand, he began to go through the pockets of his coats again. This time he came out with a gleaming revolver with its barrel sawed off, which he presented to me, handle first.

I took the pistol from him and held it in my open palm. "There we go," said Prospero. "Now where were we?" He started to shuffle through his index cards again, but we were caught then in another heavy, sky-tilting gust of wind which blew the cards out of his hands. They scattered across the roof, turning end over end, caught in spinning vortices of air.

Prospero cursed and tried to chase after the cards and gather them up, following after them with a strange waddling hunched walk that was not too dissimilar from Caliban's gait, but that proved fruitless as some of the cards had already blown right off the roof and were on their way to the ground, a hundred and fifty floors below. He gave up that endeavor, then, and returned to face me.

"Now everything's stuffed up," he said, and rubbed the tip of his nose with a hand clad in a black lambskin glove.

"Mr. Taligent," I said, "I have no idea what in the hell is going on here."

Prospero closed his eyes and placed the tips of his fingers to a throbbing temple. He breathed once, then again. "This is what comes of trying to make people happy." Then he opened his eyes and looked up at me. "Listen. This is how things were supposed to turn out. This morning you received a message by private courier, addressed from Miranda Taligent, begging you to rescue her from my dastardly clutches, correct?"

"Yes, but how did you—"

"Of *course* I knew, because Miranda didn't send that message. I did."

"What—"

"*Listen.* Some way or other, I figured that that message would eventually bring you here, to the roof of this tower. Here, after various trials and tribulations, the archvillain—myself—awaits. We struggle; you get the upper hand; you murder me with the gun that any person who had taken the time to *think ahead*, anyone with any *respect*, would have thought to bring with him; as my last request as I'm dying ever so dramatically, I ask you to inter me in an absolute-zero chamber that I've installed aboard this zeppelin. That part was risky, because I would have to be dependent on your goodwill, or the probability that you'd be ridden with guilt after your impulsive act. But I think I know you. I think I know you well enough to be certain that you'd come here, and that you would have heroically charged aboard the *Chrysalis* with my body in your arms, thinking the worst was over with the archvillain dead, ready to rescue Miranda and carry her to safety. But what you wouldn't have known is that the *Chrysalis* is designed to launch *automatically* once you're aboard, so that roughly two minutes after you enter the gondola, the zeppelin, piloted by my most advanced mechanical men, will lift off with you trapped inside. And then, like all the other ninety-nine boys and girls at that birthday party twenty years ago, you will finally have your heart's desire."

"My *what*?"

"The zeppelin." Prospero gestured with a wave of his arm at the fantastic flying machine that loomed above the two of us, straining against its bonds. "I'm giving it to you. It's yours. Merry Christmas."

TWENTY

While Prospero told me this, I saw, over his shoulder, Caliban sneaking aboard the zeppelin, carrying his stack of notebooks.

"The zeppelin *Chrysalis*," Prospero said. "It's yours. I give it to you, the storyteller, the luckiest boy. And with it comes the best of all stories for you to tell—of you, and me, and most of all, my darling daughter, Miranda.

"The zeppelin is not mounted with death rays, however. It really *does* have a perpetual motion machine, but I'm afraid the death rays are just a bunch of science-fiction folderol. They didn't believe that, did they? The—what do you call them—the populace?"

"They do," I said.

Prospero smiled, then laughed. "They *do* think the world is some kind of science-fiction novel, then. Do you realize how fervently most people will believe in the promises of technology, even when those promises fly in the face of common sense? Take Caliban, for instance—"

"He's boarded the zeppelin, by the way," I said.

"Oh, he's just stowing away his precious notebooks. His only reason left for living is to see me dead. Once you kill me, he will probably dispense with himself as well. He thinks that the contents of his notebooks will somehow serve to make him immortal. But living one's life out as a bunch of marks on a page isn't very exciting, if you ask me." Prospero winked, and an array of spidery wrinkles bloomed across his face and vanished. "But I have a plan worth two of his. Which I'll explain in a moment."

Prospero sat down on a nearby wooden crate and patted the space next to him with his hand. I sat down there, and he looked up at me and smiled again. "When you're writing all this down, you should make it clear that this, what I'm saying now, is the archvillain's last supremely villainous monologue, before he's eliminated. Just like the way things go in the cinema serials. Even though I'm not making much of a villain so far—losing my script full of appropriately menacing lines, handing out lavish gifts, things like that. Not doing too well, so far.

"So then. I assume that Caliban told you a tale, about the misery of his life, and something about a name with seventy-two letters, and how he knows himself to the depths of his soul and all that."

"Something like that," I said.

"Well, parts of that story are true. It's true, for example, that I assembled Caliban's body from parts of cadavers. In some instances I harvested parts from people who were, if you wanted to put a fine point on it, still technically alive. It was something I did early on in my career as a researcher. I do regret it, if it makes you feel any better, and somehow an apology doesn't seem to suffice—I don't know who to apologize to, at any rate, to make things right. All I can say is that no scientist with the kind of renown that I have gets to where he is in the world without engaging in just a little bit of vivisection, sometime in his early days.

"Anyway. When I finished putting Caliban together, I saw how hideous he was, in spite of what I'd envisioned, and I knew two things: that I could never reveal him to the world or I'd be tarred and feathered and ridden out of town on a rail, and that if I wanted him to have any hope of happiness in the solitude to which he was doomed, he had to somehow believe that he was the most beautiful, wonderful human being that ever existed. That he was not too ugly, but too beautiful for the eyes of lesser men.

"So I found a broken typewriter, and I rubbed out all the letters of the keys and drew appropriately cryptic symbols in their places. Then I attached it by a cable to the back of his head. I shocked him to life and taught him language; then, when I thought he was ready, I told him what was basically a cock-and-bull story about how he was the culmination of my research, mapping the human mind.

"Harry, make no mistake: I've cut up a few brains here and there, but I haven't mapped the mind. I look at it and see a complete mystery locked up in flesh. Caliban's typewriter is perfectly ordinary—its type-bars still have their original English letters. But he *believes* in it, and so for him its technology is so advanced that it may as well be magic. I could never have guessed that the fiction I'd constructed for him would have made him so unhappy. But telling him the truth after all of this would have made things worse.

"I stuffed it all up in the end, Harry. It's no wonder that he wants to see me dead."

Now Caliban was coming out of the zeppelin's gondola, carrying just his typewriter in his arms. He walked away from the ship and stood a fair distance off from us, staring as us seated on the supply crate, and he waited.

"Did he tell you all about his magical powers and such?" said Prospero. "He goes on about them sometimes. I never disabused him: if it makes him feel better to believe it, then fine. The monster has magical powers."

"He told me that the contents of his notebooks are works of incomparable genius," I said.

"Well, some of them are admittedly fairly interesting," Prospero said, "in the way that the writings of insane people sometimes seem singularly profound. There's a lot of self-important ranting and raving. But what he calls the 'heart of his argument' is really nothing but a series of randomly chosen words, strung together and punctuated, with no meaning to be found in them.

"Trust me. No one knows better than me how hard it is to tell the difference between madness and genius, between profoundly difficult truths and pure nonsense. There are no miracles to be found in Caliban's books. There is nothing at all between their covers but words."

TWENTY-ONE

Another heavy gust of wind blew, and Prospero pulled the lapels of his overcoat more tightly around himself. The sky tilted ever so slightly, and tilted back.

"You can't see the building bending from the ground, or in the lobby, or even if you're inside a room in one of the upper floors, looking through a window," he said. "It's a fraction of a degree, and the architects of this Tower planned for it to bend just a little bit, so that it would be able to take the stress from high winds without sustaining structural damage. But up here, at the outer part of the arc, that infinitesimal bending sometimes makes it seem as if you are aboard a ship at sea, with a tempest on the way."

Prospero shivered, and his voice began to sometimes falter. "Have you ever been happy? You are too young to have the lines on your face that you do, and they tell a tale of an unhappy man. But there was one moment—and I *know* what it was, so don't you lie to me. Tell me the happiest moment of your life.

"No—I can't wait. I'll tell *you* what it was. It wasn't when you slept with Miranda, or when you kissed her ten years before. It was when you *rescued* her. When you chased after the windup beasts that menaced her in her playroom, waving around your little tin sword, that was just a dress rehearsal, but in that moment when you were with her in the abandoned warehouse, just after you reached out to put your hand over her mouth to stop her from screaming, but just before you touched her: *that* was the happiest moment of your life. Because it had *possibilities*. In that moment, the future, the moment just after the one in which your hand was outstretched over her sleeping and vulnerable form—it could have been *anything*. That woman could have been perfect, and she could have fallen into your arms, and you could have slung mud at her and she still would have shone like new. But once you touched her all those infinite futures collapsed into one, and all of those possibilities vanished. And then she was just the thing that she was; just a woman.

"But wouldn't it have been wonderful if you could have taken that moment, and photographed it, and found some way to live in that photograph forever? Because an imperfect grace is never what we seek when we fantasize about our futures, when we dream of a long life with someone we claim to love or we build the machines that we read about in science fiction. We want all possible things made actual, the perpetual possibility of perfection, the best of all futures all at once. But whatever we accomplish in the end never measures up. We always fail. We always fall short. Because when we see the perfect thing before us we feel we have to *touch* it. And then it vanishes or bruises or turns to show its hidden flaws or turns to dust.

"But once you board the zeppelin, you'll have your heart's desire. The happiest second of your life will be frozen there, stretched out forever. You'll hear Miranda and you'll know she's there, but you won't be able to find her or touch her. You will always be about to rescue the damsel in distress, but you will never succeed. And as long as that moment exists, your world will be full of nothing but possibilities."

"But that's not what I want," I said. "I came all the way here to save Miranda. I'm certain."

"Oh, I promised you your heart's desire all those years ago," Prospero said. "I didn't say I'd give you what you *wanted*."

TWENTY-TWO

"How did you know?" I asked.

"Know what?"

"In the warehouse. I put my hand over her mouth to stop her from screaming when she woke up. How did you know?"

"I staged it all," Prospero said. "The two men—they chose to call themselves Talus and Artegall—they were actors. Their real names were Gideon and Martin—they'd been in my employ for years. They were making noises behind a door when you rescued her, screaming and banging pipes against shelves. But the door had a peephole in it that Gideon could see through.

"I had Gideon tell that story over and over to me until he wore it out. Do you know what he said? He said that when you were bent over her while she slept, you hesitated. Not for a few seconds, but for fully five minutes. Stretching that perfect second out until you couldn't anymore. You didn't even notice that both Gideon and Martin had gone quiet while they watched you watch the girl in silence. When he told me this I knew that my certainty about you was correct. And that out of all the hundred boys and girls that came to Miranda's birthday party I had to save your gift for last. And that it would be the best."

TWENTY-THREE

"There's something I don't understand," I said. "This afternoon I saw a man who I believed was Martin, rounding up a mob of men to stage an assault on this building. I saw more men like him when I entered the lobby this evening. They all had the same funnels strapped to their heads, and the same silver paint on their faces. Are they actors? Did you hire them, too?"

"No," Prospero said, "I didn't. I don't know what happened to the two of them after they finished their work for me—I have thousands of employees and can't keep track of them all. But Martin—I remember that he seemed a bit more serious about the role I wrote for him than Gideon did. When I told them all that business about the Virgin and the Dynamo, which really was just something I'd gotten out of an old book and embellished a little with some appropriately fantastic details, Gideon just smiled and took it all in, but Martin—his eyes lit up like he believed it was gospel truth. If what you say is true, he is taking this all a bit more serious than I'd like.

"Justice, I suppose. The inventor of the mechanical man is turned upon by his own invention. Nice."

TWENTY-FOUR

The clouds began to clear as Prospero and I talked, and the snowfall slowed, then stopped. In the east, the sky began to brighten as the sun rose, lighting the underside of the zeppelin's gigantic white balloon in shades of rose and gold. The mechanical men had finished loading the ship's supplies, and now they climbed the stairs to the zeppelin's gondola, the line of them marching step by step in synchrony.

"I'm not boarding the ship," I said. "I won't do it. I don't know what you have in mind here, but it's too much. I can't just leave my life—"

"What life?" said Prospero. "I know about your life. A loveless life like yours is no life at all. You can be replaced at your job, by someone else willing to whore himself out writing doggerel—I'm sure there's someone. You spend your evenings in solitude with your fingers in your ears to shut out all the sounds. You can vanish and you won't be missed. I think you know this.

"And here? Here in this world of so much noise? Do you trust yourself to even form a tenuous friendship with a stranger, much less fall in love? Do you trust yourself to always have faith that the person you're hearing speaks the constant truth to you, or that you haven't heard the curse she whispered at you under her breath because the noise from an engine of a passing automobile drowned it out? Do you trust yourself enough to be sure whether she speaks to you with sincerity or sarcasm? Will you ever be able to be certain that the meanings of her words haven't changed between the time they leave her lips and the time they reach your ears? I know you, and I don't think you do—if you're not faithless, you're nearly so. I think you know that if you do not board that ship, you will die a lonely, bitter man."

"But I'll die alone if I board the ship as well."

"You'll have Miranda."

"But you said I'll never be able to touch her," I said.

"And this is how you know you want it to be," he said, "even though you won't admit it aloud.

"Listen," said Prospero. "I know you. I know you are a storyteller, and therefore a maker of lies as well as tales. I think that even right now you're constructing a new and pleasing story out of the facts that lie before you. I think that even if I tell you straight out that if you were able to locate Miranda aboard the *Chrysalis* and take her away from her hiding place, then she would die within minutes: even if I say that, you will find a story to tell yourself that will give you a reason to board that ship. Because even now you are thinking to yourself that the space inside that zeppelin's gondola is the only place left on earth where it is safe for a man as broken as you are to fall in love."

TWENTY-FIVE

"Kill him!" Caliban shrieked from the other side of the roof. He wasn't even bothering now to peck the keys on his typewriter before he spoke. "You have to kill him!"

"You don't have much time to think this over," Prospero said. "This is all going to work out for everyone. Listen: the ship is a masterpiece of engineering. The noises of all the machines on board are dampened to inaudibility. The only sounds you'll hear about the ship will be those you make, and the voices of you and Miranda. Just the two of you speaking to each other, in clear untroubled transmissions. And while the machine-riddled world beneath you goes deaf and loses its mind, while everyone speaks in screams, while babies are delivered from their wombs with burst eardrums and missing tongues, you will refine your private language until you converse with the confidence of people long in love, certain beyond a doubt that you will always be understood. And together, in that soundproof place, you will preserve the beauty of language against the machines."

TWENTY-SIX

"Why do you want me to kill you?" I asked.

"Oh, yes," Prospero said. "Look: I don't want you to think of this as murder, in the conventional sense. I have a feeling that the society of this age is about to go through a painful adolescence, and although I'm partly responsible for its present state, I'm secretly convinced that we are about to embark upon one of the most miserable periods of human history. And though it's selfish, I want to sit this dance out.

"After you shoot me, you're going to place me in a chamber aboard the zeppelin, as quickly as you can. Close the chamber's door and pull a lever on its side, and the temperature within the chamber will drop to within a few degrees of absolute zero. This will place my body in a state of *cryogenic suspension*, where it will remain for a century, perhaps two, until earthbound scientists work out the last secrets of the human body. At that point I will be retrieved from the chamber, the organs damaged by the bullet will be replaced, and I will be brought back to life.

"Think of it. Going to sleep and waking up later in a science fiction future. It'll be fantastic. The shock and the wonder of it."

TWENTY-SEVEN

On the other side of the roof, about a hundred and fifty yards from the zeppelin, was a small hutlike structure with a tin corrugated roof and a door labeled STAIRS, and on the other side of this door, a hammering began.

"I believe we're running out of time for second thoughts," Prospero said. "It's time for you to make some rather important decisions."

He sidled closer to me and slipped his arms around me, resting his head in the crook of my neck. His hat fell off.

He reached down between us, then, to the pistol between us. He turned the gun in my hand and pulled it toward him, pressing its barrel into his stomach.

Dents began to appear in the door to the stairway as it began to come off its hinges.

Standing at the edge of the roof, Caliban was screaming himself hoarse. "*Kill him.*"

I looked up at the zeppelin hanging in the air above me, and tried to imagine the woman that waited for me inside—what she might look like, what she might say to me when she first saw me. But all I could think of were certain recurring dreams: of the woman twirling at the tower's edge and falling off. Of young Miranda giggling at me as she stood behind a tree in her playroom: *Silly boy. You were trying to rescue the monster.*

The head of a double-bladed axe burst through the door to the stairs, sending splinters flying: it was almost down. I heard a concerted chant coming from its other side. Heave. *Ho.* Heave. *Ho.*

Then I made a decision, not out of any heretofore untapped reserve of courage or heroism as I'd like to pretend it was, but of the weakness of will that is, I'm sorry to say, the defining element of my nature.

"I'll do it," I said, attempting to speak in the tones of blunt surety that I thought a hero would use.

"Kill him," Caliban screamed.

"You do realize," Prospero said, digging the tips of his fingers into the small of my back, getting ready to take the bullet, "that I couldn't make it easy for you. That would have been unfair to you, and her, and *me.* You do understand that?"

"Of course," I said.

The stairway's door collapsed, and false mechanical men with painted silver faces came pouring out of the doorway like circus clowns out of a tiny little car, wielding axes and clubs and rifles and revolvers.

"Wish me luck," whispered Prospero Taligent.

"Good luck," I said, and pulled the trigger.

TWENTY-EIGHT

The pistol resounded between us with an unholy crack, and I dropped it immediately as if my hand had been stung by thorns. Prospero's arms immediately clenched around me.

"Oh me," he said, thick liquid in his voice. "Oh my."

He lifted himself off me, steadying himself with his hands on my shoulders, and looked me in the eye.

"Get this fixed up, maybe," he croaked. "Hm."

He looked over at the crowd of false tin men on the roof who looked back at us, then at grinning Caliban, then at me again.

"Question," he said.

"Yes?"

"Do you think we made a mistake?" he asked, and collapsed.

TWENTY-NINE

I came to my feet then, knelt, and scooped up Prospero's impossibly light body in my arms. How much time did I have if this was going to work? Not too long.

Then I looked over at Caliban, near the edge of the roof.

He was cackling hysterically, with his typewriter placed on the roof beneath him and his twisted body bent over it, held there because of the shortness of the cable that attached the typewriter to the back of his head. In his awkward position, dancing from foot to foot, he seemed as if he was vomiting up his laughter.

Then he picked up his typewriter and cradled it in his arms. "We've won!" he shouted across the roof to me. "We tricked him, you and I!"

One of the mob of false mechanical men pointed at Caliban, his mouth open. "One of you guys has gotta tell me what the hell *that* thing is," he said.

"Listen!" said Caliban. "Take his body and throw it off the roof. Then everything will work out for everyone. You'll be proclaimed a hero. You and I will take the Tower and the corporation for ourselves."

"It's a *monster* is what that thing is," said another of the false mechanical men.

"I know *secrets*," said Caliban. "I'll tell you the secret of human genius. I know about laundered bank accounts and hidden passageways. I'll tell you everything—"

"My God that thing is *hideous*—"

"My *thought*!" cried Caliban. "I'll walk you through all my theories step by step. I promise that I'll be as patient with you as I can. You'll be enlightened like none other. You'll be able to hold your own at the cocktail parties of the most—

"Now wait.

"You're going with *her*, aren't you?"

The crowd of false tin men on the roof began to drift, slowly, toward Caliban, their weapons at the ready.

Caliban began to perform his strange, hysterical dance again, hopping from foot to foot, coming dangerously close to the edge of the roof. "Are you honestly shunning the lifelong companionship of one of the greatest minds of the twentieth century for that *tart*? What kind of man *are you*? . . . Are you not *human*? Are you nothing more than an *animal*?"

The mob began to move faster, breaking into a run.

Caliban looked at the crowd, then at me, pure desperation on his scarred and patched-together face.

Then he suddenly spun in a circle, three times, holding his arms out, and flung his typewriter off the roof.

It flew outward into thin air for a short time; then it plunged. Caliban had turned halfway around again, and so he was looking straight at me, his gaze full of blame, when the cable attached to the typewriter jerked his head backward, snapping his neck with a crack. Then he was gone.

THIRTY

That left the false tin men, and me.

They stared at me, and I stared back at them, and none of us moved, and none of us said anything.

Blood ran out of Prospero's wound, covering my hands and my pants and my shoes, leaving a trail of red on the roof beneath me.

In my arms he was breathing shallowly, his eyes closed, and smiling.

We stood there, all of us silently, for another minute.

Then I turned my back on all of them, and boarded the good ship *Chrysalis*.

EPILOGUE

aboard the good ship *chrysalis*

When I entered the *Chrysalis*'s observation room this morning, I saw that the mask of frost that had once covered Prospero Taligent's face had melted, and that a hairline crack had appeared in the pane of glass set in the door of the chamber in which he is interred. It's not surprising, really: many of the machines in this zeppelin have begun to operate in a less than optimal fashion in the months that I spent writing this manuscript, and what was once a soundproof place is now becoming plagued with rhythmic hums and rattles, reminders of the world I left behind.

Still, though, I wonder if perhaps it's not best for Prospero that the absolute-zero chamber stopped working. In the moment when he died at my hand he had his own heart's desire—not the actual future, but a hope for the best possible future, one that he could not himself imagine. And, just as he said of me, the thing that his heart desired was not the thing that he professed to want. Had his plan succeeded, and had some doctors in a future century boarded this zeppelin, retrieved his corpse from it, and managed to bring it back to life, I'm sure that when he saw what had resulted from all the time he'd skipped past, he would have been disappointed. Nothing would have been good enough; no sight would have been amazing enough. *Is this all there is?* he would have said. *I'm sure I could have done better than this, if only I'd had the time that you had. Take back the life you gave me; put me back in the chamber; wake me up in another hundred years.*

So today I am finally grieving, for the first time. Now I know how it feels and now I know what it means. I am grieving the death of the Author of my life, and in the wake of that grief come other grievings, long delayed. My father and my sister. Dearest Astrid.

I know how it feels now. I'm a wreck. It's wonderful.

And Miranda? She is silent this morning. She is waiting.

Most of the rest of the story you know, from the moment I entered the zeppelin to now: as soon as I boarded the ship, it broke free from its moorings and lifted off with its crew of mechanical men, all automatically. It hasn't touched the ground since. And aboard the ship were the few amenities with which the practical Prospero had thought to provide me—food and drink, and his recordings and Caliban's notebooks, and in a single room, reams and reams of paper and dozens of pencils and pens and hundreds of bottles of ink, more than enough to write everything down. And it was then that I began my willful imprisonment.

I'm near the end now, and as I look through the stack of pages that sit here, it seems I've done a decent job of working my life into the shape of a story. The now dead Author who managed my life and bent its path to suit his wishes did so well enough, and even if I resent this and always will, at least I have this to say: that everything in the tale of my life is tidy and ordered, and all of the loose ends are gathered up.

Except for one.

Where is Miranda? Where has her never-ending voice been coming from, all this time?

———

The truth is: I don't know. Or, more accurately, I do know—I'm nearly certain of it. But knowing does me little good, and I'm afraid to say much more.

Once again I have the blueprints for the zeppelin spread out in front of me on the observation room's obsidian desk, and the sheets are covered with drawings and notations and plans and diagrams of electrical circuits, all in Prospero Taligent's neat and microscopic script. Little of it makes sense to me, but this doesn't matter. When looking at most of the blueprints I need a magnifying glass to read the long, strange names of all the machines that toil away behind the gondola's walls, but there is one area which has almost no writing, and little else but empty space: the giant cigar shape of the zeppelin's hydrogen-filled balloon.

Drawn inside the balloon, at its very center, is a simple shape, a circle with eight rays projecting from it in the eight compass directions. Inside this circle are printed three words, and it is here that I believe Miranda resides, here that her father placed her after the months of operations that he and the portraitmaker performed upon her.

I believe that Miranda Taligent is the perpetual motion machine.

I could say more—I have ideas of what she might look like, or guesses at the least. I can speculate on what it must be like to breathe hydrogen, or to see the colors of sunrise muted each morning as they shine on her through the canvas of the zeppelin's balloon, and as she readies whatever thing serves as her mouth to speak into the microphone that carries her voice throughout the ship to me, no matter where I am.

But describing words are killing words, and so I'll choose not to describe her—there's been killing enough. If the reader who comes across this manuscript in an unforeseeable future believes my tale to be true, then he will understand and forgive my reluctance to speak; if he believes this to be an idle fantasy, then he will tear up these pages and curse my final failure of imagination. So be it.

Let it be enough to say that, in the end, after a life of brilliant inventions, Prospero Taligent managed a single miracle, his first and his last. His love for his daughter was twisted, but that does not mean that it was not true. What he did to her with the help of the portraitmaker was undoubtedly terrible, but he did it because he loved her, and because it is terrible it is no less a miracle for that. He sculpted the shape of a voice; he built a virgin dynamo. That is enough.

Not that, in the final balance, I am the most credible person when it comes to speaking of matters of the heart. I look back through these pages and I see, not the tale of heroism and true love that I must confess I'd hoped to write when I began, but the tale of how I became a loveless man who could barely summon enough empathy within himself to write a decent greeting card. A man who was weak and inconstant; a man without the strength to act, but who allowed himself to be acted upon by others without protest.

And it would be nice to draw some sort of overarching moral from all of this, wouldn't it. It would be nice to point a finger at some omnipresent moral force that made me what I am; to blame Society, or Dynamos, or Women, or all those men who are lesser than myself, or everything but my own failure to listen to the music of the world instead of its noise.

But I think that I have had enough of blame. I think that it's time to begin.

I've had enough of stories and lies; enough of silent scribbling. Enough of gears and engines. Enough of daydreams and false futures. Enough of virgins and dynamos.

One word from you is all I want, she said. *Just speak one word, and we'll begin.*

Enough of wasting time.

It is time to put down the pen; time to clear the throat. Speaking is a different thing altogether from writing. The spoken word has different properties, and different powers. If I have learned anything from writing down my own tale, it is this.

The machines of this place are failing, and the woman and I are here all alone. The perpetual motion engine, as brilliant and beautiful as it is, is running down—nothing lasts forever. But before this little world falls out of the sky there might still be time enough for redemption. There is still time for me to say the words that I should have had the courage to say at the beginning.

There is still time, perhaps, for one more miracle.

Hello, Miranda.

ACKNOWLEDGMENTS

Michael Wood and Adam Gussow made useful comments on early drafts of the opening pages of this novel that ended up determining its final direction.

Elements of the look and feel of the setting were inspired by discussions with Daniel Novak, Nicholas Brooke, and Robert Bowen.

Daniel Robinson, Keef Owens, Robert Bowen, and Drew Purves were kind enough to read an earlier version of this novel in its entirety.

Jeffery Renard Allen gave me helpful advice when the time came to stop writing (and rewriting) the novel and start attempting to publish it.

My literary agent, Susan Golomb, provided an invaluable critique of the manuscript and worked hard to find this novel a good home. In addition, I'd like to thank Rich Green, Casey Panell, Jon Mozes, Corey Ferguson, and Terra Chalberg.

Thanks to all the people at St. Martin's Press who helped to transform these strings of ink marks into an actual book. In particular, my editor, Michael Homler, has been all I could have wished for and more.

Finally, thanks to my family, for a list of reasons that would run as long as the book itself.

—Dexter Palmer
March 13, 1996
May 4, 2009
Princeton, New Jersey/Tampa, Florida